Advance Praise for

THE F...

"Ferguson's trademark wit ... exuberant, entertaining, and unconventional novel."

SHARI LAPENA, *New York Times* bestselling
author of *Someone We Know*

"So much fun. Filled with memorable characters and exotic locations, Will Ferguson's new book should be enjoyed by thriller fans, travel aficionados, and those who like a story where you have no idea where it's going to take you. It's an interesting and rewarding universe that Ferguson's mind occupies. I want a cottage there."

DREW HAYDEN TAYLOR, author of *Chasing Painted Horses*

Praise for

THE SHOE ON THE ROOF

INSTANT NATIONAL BESTSELLER
A *GLOBE AND MAIL* BOOK OF THE YEAR

"Ferguson is a skillful and original writer, and overall, the novel is full of life. . . . *The Shoe on the Roof*'s lasting strength is in such sly jabs at the 'alternative facts' and deep divisions we're now reckoning with, making it a tale for the times."

The Globe and Mail

"Often laugh-out-loud funny despite its serious and tragic underpinnings. But it's also thought-provoking, occasionally violent, and will likely stay with readers long after the last page is read."

Calgary Herald

"Absurdly funny."

Quill & Quire

"Another gem from this Giller Prize–winning author."

Canadian Living

Praise for

WILL FERGUSON

WINNER OF THE SCOTIABANK GILLER PRIZE

"He bears comparison with North America's leading satirists. But where Joseph Heller is heavy, Tom Wolfe is dark, and Carl Hiaasen is strident, Ferguson is light, bright, and very funny."

Daily Mail

"Frequently and savagely ironic, he is also not afraid to declare his feelings—which means you trust both his humour and his insights."

The Guardian

"A very gifted writer."

BILL BRYSON, bestselling author

"Sometimes touching, sometimes amusing, and always true."

Boston Globe

"Sharp-eyed and irreverent."

Washington Post

Praise for

419

"Ferguson, who swings so deftly from humor to thriller, is a writer who can genuinely surprise."

Toronto Star

"A deeply ironic, thoroughly engaged politico-philosophical thriller from a comic writer best known for winning a trio of Leacock Awards. . . . You won't sleep until you finish, and then rest won't come easily. Riveting. Provocative."

The Globe and Mail

"Ferguson is a keen observer of landscapes and cityscapes, and has a brilliant ear for dialogue and accent. . . . You will never see those creative 419 emails in your inbox in quite the same way."

The Gazette (Montreal)

"Tautly paced and vividly drawn, *419* captures the reader in a net of desire and deceit drawn tight by the interconnections of humanity in the twenty-first century."

VINCENT LAM, Scotiabank Giller Prize–winning author of *Bloodletting and Miraculous Cures*

"A powerful read. . . . Ferguson is a heavy-weight now."

Now (Toronto)

THE
FINDER

WILL FERGUSON

PUBLISHED BY SIMON & SCHUSTER

NEW YORK   LONDON   TORONTO   SYDNEY   NEW DELHI

Simon & Schuster Canada
A Division of Simon & Schuster, Inc.
166 King Street East, Suite 300
Toronto, Ontario M5A 1J3

This Simon & Schuster Canada edition September 2020

SIMON & SCHUSTER CANADA and colophon are
trademarks of Simon & Schuster, Inc.

For information about special discounts for bulk purchases, please contact
Simon & Schuster Special Sales at 1-800-268-3216 or
CustomerService@simonandschuster.ca.

Manufactured in the United States of America

1   3   5   7   9   10   8   6   4   2

Library and Archives Canada Cataloguing in Publication

Title: The finder / Will Ferguson.
Names: Ferguson, Will, author.
Description: Simon & Schuster Canada edition.
Identifiers: Canadiana 20200162365 | ISBN 9781982139698 (softcover)
Classification: LCC PS8561.E7593 F56 2020 | DDC C813/.54—dc23

ISBN 978-1-9821-3969-8
ISBN 978-1-9821-3970-4 (ebook)

It is only in fairy tales that coins glint
clearly enough to be found.
—Heinrich Böll, *The Clown*

IN THE LAND OF THE BLIND, the one-eyed man is not king, he is dangerous and possibly mad, and needs to be contained. Case in point:

On February 2, 1959, a small four-seater airplane crashed into a cornfield in Iowa in the middle of a snowstorm. On board were three legends of rock and roll: Buddy Holly, Ritchie Valens, and the Big Bopper. They'd been touring the Midwest in a bus with a broken heater. Shivering, tired, and miserable, Buddy Holly and the Big Bopper decided to hire a plane and fly to the next town, with Valens winning a coin toss for the last seat. It would go down in history as the day the music died.

Items retrieved from the crash site were tagged and stored as evidence. Among these were the Big Bopper's wristwatch, smashed at the exact time of the plane crash; a set of dice they had used to kill time on the road; and Buddy Holly's iconic horn-rimmed glasses. After the inquest, these same items were filed and forgotten.

In March 1994, fumigators sealed off the Mason City Courthouse and bombed the interior with pesticides. Soon after, coincidentally it would seem, Buddy Holly's glasses appeared at an auction house, still tagged as evidence. They might have gone missing at any time during the previous forty years, perhaps retrieved by a grieving relative or a courthouse employee. Whatever tortuous route they took, when the glasses re-emerged, they sold for $670,000 and now sit in the Rock and Roll Hall of Fame in Cleveland, Ohio. And that's where the story ends, we're told.

One person was not convinced, however.

Gaddy Rhodes, a senior investigator with Interpol's International Crimes Agency, the ICA as it is known, had recently flagged this forgotten news story, noting the name of the company that had performed the fumigation: TLT Pest Control. When she checked up on this, Gaddy discovered that TLT had long since vanished. That in itself was not suspicious; companies come and go all the time. But this one had appeared and disappeared on a single breath of air, it seemed, incorporating and dissolving all within a week. As far as she could tell, TLT had only ever performed that single on-site fumigation. The contract workers the company had hired remembered a small man in a mask and protective coveralls entering the building amid the fumes, but it was so long ago, who could say who the man was or whether he was even there? Memory so easily turns into myth.

A security cam image, dated two weeks earlier, now lay on the desk in front of her: a blur, barely there. Less a man than a shadow, a silhouette captured in front of a Japanese tomb. She was convinced, without any direct evidence, that this was the same person who had walked into the poisonous fumes of the Mason City Courthouse. Was Gaddy Rhodes deluded? Deceived? A one-eyed figure in the Land of the Blind? These were questions not easily answered.

She closed her laptop under the dim light of a swaying lamp. Considered whether she should leave a letter behind. Probably. But she couldn't think of anyone to write to, so instead left only a brief note and inventory for her supervising officer in lieu of any final goodbye message:

To the attention of Lieutenant Addario, ICA:

Dear Andrea, if anything happens to me, anything at all, please ensure that the following items, recently recovered, are returned to their rightful owners: one (1) terracotta Buddha's head, three (3) shards of funeral pottery, one (1) Icelandic chess piece (walrus tusk ivory, circa. 12th century).

Yours,
Agent G. Rhodes

The Buddha's head, no bigger than her fist, along with the shards of funeral pottery, were sealed in plastic like pieces of a puzzle that didn't quite fit together. Wearing cotton gloves to protect the patina, Gaddy held up the chess piece, examined it closely. A scowling bishop, crudely carved with bone tools, rescued from a forgotten drawer in Reykjavík, it was one of the missing pieces of the medieval Lewis chessmen, worth thousands on its own. The complete set? Tens of thousands. Millions, even. But without this missing bishop, the complete chessmen would never be assembled. She smiled. Looked to the photograph of the security-cam silhouette that was lying on her desk. *Want it? Come and get it. I dare you.*

She imagined a vast and infinite chessboard stretching out in front of her, invisible lines of attack radiating down endless avenues, an ever-expanding horizon of possibilities, and somewhere out there, the opponent she conjured into existence quietly waiting, silent and faceless, perhaps planning a countermove of his own. They strike at an angle, bishops. They come at you from the side. You might manage to catch sight of them from the corner of your eye, but by then it was too late. Was Rhodes the bishop or the pawn? That, too, was a difficult question to answer.

The floor lifted beneath her, hung in midair, then dropped down on a stomach soar of vertigo. A rap on the door, sharp and metallic. Rounded corners and rivets. Battleship gray. A voice on the other side: "Agent Rhodes? *Onegai shimasu.*"

Another swell, another sudden drop. Her cabin began to list.

The voice on the other side: "We are waiting. Everyone is waiting."

She put the scowling bishop away, carefully peeled off the cotton gloves, tucked her handwritten note under the corner of the chessboard, and then stepped outside onto the deck of a *Tsugaru*-class patrol vessel, into the clear blue of the Okinawan seas.

A Japanese naval officer led her across to where the midrange search-and-rescue helicopter was tethered and waiting. Gaddy Rhodes, hair as insubstantial as corn silk, blowing every which way. Gaddy Rhodes, empty and awake.

Slowly, the blades began to turn.

PART ONE
HERE BE DRAGONS: THE LONG BICYCLE RIDE OF OFFICER SHIMADA

A STEM FROM THE TEA LEAVES was floating in his cup, standing perfectly on end like a small omen.

"That's good luck," he said, leaning across the cluttered kitchen table to show his wife. She didn't bother looking up from her magazine. She knew what a stem looked like.

"Mm," she said.

He fished it out, gently, the way one might with an eyelash, flicked it to one side, drank down the rest of his morning *ocha* in a single, decisive swallow.

A tea stem, suspended like that? It foretold an auspicious day.

Police Inspector Atsushi Shimada, senior officer, Hateruma Island Substation, Okinawa Division, Japanese National Police Force, pushed himself up from the kitchen table with renewed purpose. "Well," he said. "I suppose I had better go check on that foreigner."

He spoke with resolve, as becoming his status. He was, after all, representing the entire precinct. Decorum was in order. As the sole officer assigned to a small island—a village, really, perched on a jagged bit of coral at the farthest reach of Japan—Officer Shimada *was* the Hateruma Police Department.

"Your shirt," his wife said. "It's not tucked in properly."

Shimada's wife, as portly as he was thin, didn't bother looking up from her magazine for this, either. She didn't need to; his shirt was always loose around the hips. As surely as her police officer husband was dressed in *his* uniform, she was dressed in hers: the standard-issue

7

apron and headscarf of the Japanese Housewife. If she could keep her uniform in order, why couldn't he? Mrs. Shimada unwrapped a *sembei* rice cracker on a crinkle of plastic, studied the glossy celebrity photospread in front of her. "Can't believe she's wearing that."

Shimada shoved in his shirt, tightened his belt.

"Arrived yesterday," he said. "Came in on the last ferry. A foreigner." He wasn't sure why he was using the formal *gaikokujin* instead of the more usual *gaijin*.

Tamura-san from the ferry port had stopped by earlier that morning, had stood at the front desk waiting patiently for Police Inspector Shimada, senior officer, Hateruma Island Substation, Okinawa Division, to appear.

Officer Shimada's cement-walled home was attached to this police station by a single sliding door. Shimada stepped through and up to the counter, Tamura-san smiling his apology for having interrupted Shimada's breakfast.

The two men exchanged nods.

"A foreigner, you say?"

"That's right. On the last ferry."

Foreigners came to Hateruma Island now and then, it wasn't unheard of, and for much the same reason as Japanese: for the quiet beaches and flying fish and white sand, but mainly to stand, fist on hips, looking into the wind above the coral cliffs at Cape Takana so they could say, with a satisfied frown, "This is me at the end of Japan." After that, there was nothing much to do but turn around and begin the long plod homeward, island-hopping by boat, ferry, and plane back to Naha City, back to the mainland of Japan, away. What made this foreigner any different?

"He was strange."

"Foreigners are always strange."

"Not strange. Agitated. Was alone, all by himself, not part of any tour group."

"So . . . a backpacker. How is that strange?"

"Wasn't a backpacker. Was lugging this really heavy, awkward duffel bag, wouldn't let anyone carry it for him. Came all the way from Ishigaki Island, but had nowhere to stay when he got here, hadn't called ahead or anything. We were tying up for the night when he approached us, all agitated-like. Kept saying 'Firefly, firefly.' "

"Firefly?"

"He was trying to say 'hotel.' Took us a while to figure that out. The way he said it, sounded like *ho-ta-ru*. Firefly."

"There are no fireflies on Hateruma. Not this time of year."

"He wasn't saying firefly, he was saying— Anyway. We pointed him to the guesthouse by the dock. You know the one, the widow's place."

How sad, thought Shimada. She was once a name, a wife, a person, was now was simply "the widow." There were other widows on the island, but none so young. When her husband was swept away from that boat, he took her name with him.

"No children," said Shimada, more to himself than to Tamura-san.

Shimada's own children had long slipped free of Hateruma, one to college in Naha, another to Nagasaki. The outer islands were shedding young people like fireflies.

Tamura-san nodded. No children. A tragedy. "Anyway. I just thought, you know, I should tell you in case you wanted to check in, make sure she's okay, the widow."

After Tamura-san left, Senior Police Inspector Shimada had gone back to the kitchen table to finish his breakfast: miso soup, now cold in the bowl; a papyrus square of nori; yesterday's rice. A cup of green tea with a single stem suspended. He made his decision.

"I'm going down to the dock."

Why didn't he say where he was really going, to the widow's house? Was it because the other wives didn't approve of her? Didn't approve of her taking in guests so soon after her husband's death? At night, people passing by had heard her singing to the radio, had spied her, framed by her kitchen window, dancing—swaying, really—not proper for someone in mourning. When Shimada heard these stories, he thought, *Not dancing, just sad*. Was that where his interest in this came from, not a foreigner alone and acting peculiar, but simply as pretext, an excuse to see the widow, to be asked inside? Or were there darker currents at play, ones that Shimada himself could barely articulate, a vague, ill-defined sense that this was a day heavy with portents, one that would end badly, perhaps; strangely, at the very least.

He cleared his throat. There was no reason to hide where he was really going. "Not the dock," he said. "The guesthouse."

"The widow?"

"That's right. Thought I'd check in, make sure everyone is safe. The foreigner, I mean. He might be lost. Could be stranded." Was he still speaking about the foreigner? Shimada stared at his wife, nested at their kitchen table, a plump daughter of the islands. Theirs had been an arranged marriage, and a happy one—or near enough. And yet, every year, he seemed to grow thinner and thinner. He could see it in the morning mirror, a gauntness that had perhaps always been there, waiting to come out.

Their kitchen, like the rest of the house, looked as though it had recently been stirred by a large wooden spoon. Lost objects were constantly emerging and then disappearing in the Shimada household. "Not lost," his wife would scold. "Misplaced."

Officer Shimada was a file in a folder in a cabinet in the corner of an office in a building half-forgotten. He knew that, had long come to accept his fate: to be overlooked. Police officers were regularly shuffled among posts, but Shimada had settled, or rather been abandoned, on Hateruma Island like an exile waiting for the war to end because no one had thought to call him home.

He sat at the kitchen table trying to remember who he was going to be.

Years ago, Police Inspector Shimada had been rotated out to Ishigaki, the unofficial "capital" of this particular cluster of islands, and he had reveled in the hubbub. Ishigaki had traffic lights and hotels and rhinestone pachinko parlors and black pearl beaches, but his wife missed her little isle, and he had dutifully applied for a return to exile. He'd felt partly relieved, partly resigned, partly defeated, like a prisoner returning from a day pass. He wondered if prisoners ever missed the prison.

And now this: Abrasive Tokyo accents, filling their messy home. Feigned laughter, cries of *"Uso!"* and *"Subarashiiii!"* One of NHK's morning talk shows, bright and relentlessly sunny, had taken over: bits of news and titterings of gossip with large dollops of banter in between.

"Shhh," his wife said. "My show."

The small TV in the kitchen, perched beside the rice cooker, next to the dish rack, in front of the toaster oven, on top of the oven mitts, was frantic with banter. He could set his watch by his wife's viewing habits: talk shows in the morning, variety programs in the afternoon, detective dramas after dark. Those last ones were particularly engrossing: dark tales of distant cities, of plucky female sleuths and world-weary pros, the complex machinations of housewives and hapless salarymen broiling in blackmail and infidelity, beamed in like distress signals from that semi-mythical realm known as "the rest of Japan." Staged laughter in the morning, staged dramas at night, followed monthly by feigned passions in the bedroom after the lights were doused. He could set his calendar by that as well.

Shimada picked up his police cap, tugged it snuggly into place, adjusted the brim and checked that his name was pinned properly. Short sleeves and no tie for the summer months (hardly distinguishable in the subtropics of southern Japan, but the nation ran on Tokyo time and Tokyo seasons, so a summer uniform it was).

"I'm off then."

Without taking her eyes from the TV, she said, "Don't forget your gun."

This irritated him immensely. He hadn't *forgotten* his gun; it was locked up, as per protocol, in the adjoining police station. It didn't seem proper to show up at the widow's home, armed, just to check on one of her guests. His wife was right, though: a sidearm was required while on patrol. She was always right. It was one of her more annoying habits.

"I didn't forget," he said, but she wasn't listening.

The morning show was now presenting a sneak peek of this evening's detective drama. "It wraps up tonight!" gushed one of the hosts, full of breath. Cut to: a scar-chinned villain in a sharkskin suit standing under a streetlamp while a housewife waited, furtive in the shadows, ready to turn the tables. The tables were always being turned in these dramas. It was the one thing you could count on: if there was a table, it would be turned. *"Kowai!"* squealed the same host when they cut back to the studio. Looks scary!

Hateruma's *kōban* police station, a "police box" as it was more commonly known, was little more than a cement-walled cylindrical kiosk attached to the house behind it. Officer Shimada's service revolver was in the gun rack along with the precinct's shotgun and riot shield, never used. (How a single officer would go about containing a riot was never properly explained to him.) He threaded the holster through his belt, tucked in his uniform (again), rummaged around in the drawer for an English-language phrasebook: *Nationality please? Japanese law requires that you present a valid passport upon request.* He wouldn't try to render the mashed-yam sounds of English himself, would just point to the questions as needed.

Being the only police officer on Hateruma Island and manning its only police desk mainly involved giving directions to visitors. That and overseeing a lost-and-found box: cell phones and wallets mainly, usually pebble-dashed with sand, along with forgotten trinkets and orphaned earrings and other oddments, even the occasional damp towel, which he would accept in as begrudging a manner as possible. "This is a police station," he would harrumph, "not a hotel customer service desk." But this only confused the matter, as there were no hotels on Hateruma Island, just a series of guesthouses and rented rooms. "A hotel? Really? Where?"

The only crimes, as such, were ones of disorderly conduct (drunkards and battling in-laws primarily), minor acts of vandalism (boys breaking bottles behind the bento shop), and the occasional petty theft (as often as not perpetrated by the same bottle-breaking boys). He had once been called in by an irate sugarcane farmer whose backhoe had been pushed onto its side. The farmer had blamed a neighbor with whom he'd been having an ongoing territorial spat, accusing said neighbor of encroaching on his property. A further escalation of the feud was averted when, upon examination of the crime scene, Police Inspector Shimada had determined that the farmer's backhoe had been parked at too steep an angle on too soft a soil and had toppled over on its own accord. No charges were laid. It was the biggest case he'd ever worked on, and he still had the letter of commendation from the main office on Ishigaki Island for having resolved the issue so punctually.

Shimada slipped the English phrasebook into his shirt pocket, turned the ON PATROL sign over, and stepped out into the shrill heat of midmorning. In the report prepared later by the Ishigaki main police station, investigators would ask why the sole officer on duty had not entered the requisite information into his daily log: where he was going, who he was planning to interview and why. But of course, by the time these questions were being asked, it no longer mattered.

The trill of cicadas. A heavy weight in the air. Shimada straightened his collar while grandmothers in cotton bonnets and billowing smocks bicycled past: a uniform as surely as the short pants and peaked caps of the elementary school students that flowed by twice a day—out in the morning, back in the afternoon: the ebb and flow of running feet and laughter. Fewer feet and less laughter every year.

In front of the Hateruma police box stood a weathered noticeboard displaying photographs of Japan's Most Wanted, a parade of mug shots more ceremonial than practical. Fugitives never fled to Hateruma. Why would they? It would be like sprinting down a long hallway with no exit, like leapfrogging across poorly spaced stepping-stones only to find yourself surrounded by open water and deep currents. When you reached Hateruma, you had run out of Japan to cross. From here, you could only turn around and retrace your steps back to the world, much like the tourists who came to stand facing the wind at Cape Takana.

Shimada considered taking the island's lone patrol car; it added a certain dignity—he could imagine the young widow being secretly impressed—but opted instead for the precinct's official bicycle. In a car, one could drive clean across Hateruma Island, end to end, in ten minutes. Pedaling took twenty-five. From the police station to the port, less than twelve. A short ride, yet also very long, depending on one's state of mind.

He unlocked the bicycle, checked the tires. A little soft, but not worth looking for the pump.

The southernmost police box in Japan was right beside the southernmost post office, which was just down the lane from the southernmost elementary school, tucked in behind shaggy fernlike stands of *sago* palm trees—the southernmost such trees in Japan. Tamura-san's wife ran an *izakaya* restaurant, which proclaimed itself "the southernmost *izakaya* in Japan!" Everything was the southernmost something down here. If you opened an umbrella stand it would be the southernmost umbrella stand in Japan. Which is to say, at that very moment, Senior Inspector Shimada, Hateruma Island Substation, was the southernmost police officer in all of Japan, with the entire Japanese nation balanced swordlike above him and no one at his side. He was on his own.

ISLANDS OF THE BLACK CURRENT

THE LANE WAS LEAFY WITH BAMBOO, the shadows playing along the wall of his home as Shimada leaned down to check the chain. Recent rains had left a patina of rust on the gears, but otherwise good. How had he ended up here?

How does anyone end up anywhere?

Officer Shimada was born and raised on a larger island, farther north, and as a child Hateruma had seemed so far away, it hardly existed. So when he found himself posted here—rather than, say, amid the neon glow of US military bases on Okinawa's main island—it was as though he had fallen off the map, had landed in an upside-down world, vaguely familiar, yet oddly distorted. Even its name was lonely. *Hate-no-Uruma*, "the last reef," an island of coral at the far end, a reminder that beyond this final outpost there was only open water, heavy seas, starry skies, and dragons.

Hateruma was the outer edge of the outer edge, the last island in the last cluster of what had once been a kingdom of the sea: the Kingdom of Ryukyu, with its own language and religion, its own trade routes and intrigues, its own treaties and alliances, legends and lore, death chants and court poetry, the darker olive complexions a reminder of older migrations, of Polynesian forebears and open-sea journeys in rudimentary canoes. *Crossing open ocean in a canoe*, thought Shimada. *Can you imagine such a feat?*

It was a kingdom based not on conquest but commerce, part of a mercantile network that reached as far as Java and Siam, Formosa and Shanghai, Malaysia and Macau. The cotton grown in Okinawa could be traced to the arid plains of Afghanistan, and the islands' feral ponies to the steppes of Mongolia, such was the extent of the Great Loo-Choo's trade routes, as the kingdom was known in the inner courts of China's Ming dynasty.

This was a point of pride among Okinawans, even now. Ryukyu seafarers were plying the Straits of Malacca when their Japanese cousins were still struggling with the swirling currents between China and Japan. Ryukyu scholars were being entertained in the Great Halls of the Ming, while their Japanese counterparts could only look on in sullen envy. Rice wine from Bangkok, pottery from Pusan, silks from China, spices from Indonesia. All gone. With the Japanese invasion and eventual subjugation, the kingdom became a colony, the colony a prefecture, and the prefecture a quiet backwater. Lost in the sea.

But here the history turned dark. With the advent of World War II, Japan rediscovered Okinawa—with a vengeance. Under military rule, Japan would turn these islands into an armed bastion, and the people of this in-between dominion would pay a heavy price. Were they even Japanese? When the soldiers of the Emperor waded ashore, bayonets raised, they found that the older islanders couldn't even speak the language of their conquerors. They were the colonized. A lower caste, less than human.

The kingdom was gone, and Hateruma remained mainly as an afterthought, a crumbling outpost, a vague memory, more an apparition than anything real. Officer Shimada knew this all too well: The past is a lost continent. It lingers in the undergrowth, half-hidden in family tombs and funeral rites, in dialectal turns of phrase, in the dance steps and hand gestures, in that strange parallel realm of folk creatures and ghosts, in the sharp taste of the *gōya* melon, a fruit so bitter it is almost inedible.

There were smatterings of outsiders on Hateruma Island, people who washed in and out like so much tidal flotsam: schoolteachers, doctors at the medical clinic, pilots before they closed the airport, and even—Shimada supposed—Shimada himself. Outsiders aside, on an island like Hateruma, everyone was someone's cousin. The surnames circulated, and nicknames lasted for generations. An island of sugar-cane farmers and small-scale fishers. And goats.

Lots of goats. They seemed to outnumber the human population at times. Shimada remembered the son of one sugarcane farmer, still young and plagued with ideas, who decided to import more pliant, fat-tailed sheep instead. They kept falling off cliffs. Sheep were not as sure-footed or as resourceful as your typical hardscrabble goat. *Goat Island*, Shimada thought, as he walked his bicycle down the alley be-side the station. *That's what they should have named it. An outpost of goats in the middle of the sea.* Whether tethered or running free, rip-ping up scrub grass from among the coral or chewing thoughtfully on sugarcane, Hateruma's goats were treated like communal pets as much as they were livestock—albeit pets that ended up in cooking pots. He'd never eaten so much goat stew. Goat stew and sugarcane sweets.

Like bamboo, sugarcane is rigid and jointed. But where bamboo is hollow, sugarcane is densely packed, thick, and wetly fibrous, with a pulpy interior. In Japan, every clan worthy of a name has its own family crest, a *mon*: whether a bird or a flower, a falcon's feather or a bent-cross swastika, the symbols were ancient and almost endless. Officer Shimada was descended from a lesser line—retainers to an adjutant to an adviser to the royal house of Okinawa—and as such, had a mon of his own: a bamboo stalk with leaves. Hollow, but alive. He had no doubt that if his wife's family had had a mon, it would have been sugarcane. Pulpy and rich. *Perhaps they should have called it Sugarcane Island*, he thought.

He was alongside his house, still he hadn't left. Why was he lin-gering with his bicycle, like an eavesdropper at a funeral?

Through the side window, he could hear the muffled laughter of his wife's TV. A twelve-minute bike ride to the dock—he had timed it one dull afternoon—and with a wobble and a shift of his holster he pushed off, down the lane and toward the sea, bell ringing as he went.

Shimada's wife was listening for the sound of his departure, and when she heard her husband pedal away, she flipped open her phone and texted her lover: *Not tonight, maybe tomorrow. We have guests.* (They didn't have guests; her detective drama was wrapping up and she wanted to know how the tables would be turned this time around.) Her lover would be distraught, and there was some satisfaction in that. On an island like Hateruma, infidelity was as much about boredom as desire, but her moping young schoolteacher from Naha, alone in his moldering apartment, had mistaken this for love in much the same manner that the tourists who straggled in mistook Hateruma for the end of Japan. It wasn't. There were other islands farther out— there are always other islands farther out—islands beyond Hateruma, but still in Japanese territory: half-moon atolls and semi-submerged reefs, sharp rocks shredding the surface; they just weren't inhabited. One could never reach the end of Japan, because the end of Japan was unreachable. Her young schoolteacher was clinging to one such rock. Or was it a buoy? A small light lost at sea.

She unwrapped another *sembei*.

That her husband, trained in the art of investigation and detection, had not a clue about this affair (or the others) only added to the frisson, such as it was. Why was she still volunteering at the school's parent-teacher society, long after their own children had gone? Why was there always a bustle of activity when a new crop of young teachers arrived? He had never bothered to ask, and she had never bothered to answer. Arrivals and departures. Lives, intersecting. And somewhere in the middle, the unexpected appearance of a foreigner arriving on the last ferry, agitated and alone, lugging a heavy duffel bag and asking about fireflies.

LION-DOGS AND TURTLEBACK TOMBS

ON OBJECTS THAT ARE HIDDEN JUST below the surface:

Once a year, at the lowest ebb tide of spring, on the tropical island Shimada grew up on, a massive coral reef emerges from the sea like Atlantis. His earliest memory was of crowds on the shore, plastic pails in hand, waiting for this reef to appear so they could wade out over shallow layers of salt water, hurrying to gather shellfish and loose chunks of premium coral before the reef sank back down again. It was an illusion, of course. As his father explained, the reef never moved, only the sea. The reef remained: always there, but out of sight.

The island of his childhood lay low along the water, so low it had been completely submerged during the reptilian age and was—a rarity in Okinawa—snake-free. Wild boars rooted through the melon groves, vexing farmers who stalked them with ancient hunting rifles. But no snakes. Never snakes.

Not so Hateruma.

This small island was rife with habu, a particularly lethal strain of pit viper that seemed to exist as much in the imagination as in the underbrush. They were ghostlike, these habu, rarely seen but very real. Irritable and aggressive, they lay in wait, two meters long at times and loosely coiled, ready to lash out. The Japanese had a saying: *These*

four things are the most terrifying: earthquake, thunder, fire, and father.
On Hateruma, they might add a fifth: *habu.* The habu of Hateruma
moved through the shadows with a sibilant ease, in and out of abandoned lots and grassy fields, through crumbling tombs and unkempt
yards. Night dwellers that fed on rodents, habu were notoriously
unimpressed by humans. Their venom worked quickly, on a cellular
level, breaking down the body from within, turning their victim's in-
nards into a pink slurry. It was a decidedly painful way to die.

The island's medical clinic had antitoxin on hand, as did the police
station, and on occasion a tourist who had stepped on a sharp stick
would rush in, shrieking for an antidote. But there was no antidote for
fear, and the habu's effects—like its presence—were more insidious
than real. Dragons of the mind.

The island Shimada grew up on took pride in its streetlights and
pedestrian malls, even a KFC and a MOS Burger. It was anchored in
the modern era. Hateruma belonged to another age entirely, a snake-
riddled realm, thick with older idioms. He'd noticed this when he first
moved here, how the locals, instead of saying "Take care!" on parting,
as was the norm in most of Japan, would say instead "Take care, and
watch out for habu." *Habu ni kiwotsukete.* It was something he had
never gotten used to, any more than he had gotten used to the bottles
of *awamori* liquor that were sold with pickled habu floating inside,
jaws agape and fangs bared, or the dried sea snakes that were peddled
as elixirs in dusty shops. He understood that this sort of bravado was
a way of facing one's fears, of confronting those things that lurked in
the shadowy undergrowth, but none of that made it any less queasy,
any less unsettling.

Shimada on his bicycle.

He rattled down narrow lanes, past jumble-stacked coral walls.

The wisteria was in bloom, faintly aromatic, and they hung over the walls, pink and blue and ripe, like grapes on the vine.

The walls of Hateruma, hand-piled over generations from rough-cut coral limestone, formed a loose labyrinth in the heart of the village. Like the leather-leafed *fukugi* trees that crowded the homes he bicycled past, these coral walls acted as windbreaks. They provided protection from monsoon rains and typhoon winds, just as the wide-hipped rooftops of the homes behind them, with their wraparound verandas, provided wellsprings of shade in the summer, pools of cooled air, a refuge from the punitive heat. The walls also kept the world back a step. For Shimada, these rugged blocks of coral, loosely piled yet immovable, were clotted with shadows and secrets.

Behind these walls, massive roofs rose up, heavy and propped above the modest homes below. And such roofs they were! Grand and lordly, with terra-cotta tiles and ceramic lion-dogs perched atop, demon chasers, rooftop protectors. These were the *shī-sā* who stood guard over hearth and home, gargoyle-like in their ferocity. The *shī-sā* lion-dogs kept evil from entering, but Shimada found them unnerving in their own right, especially when, bicycling past, he seemed to make eye contact with one.

A parallel village appeared, hidden in the groves, standing at the roadsides. A village of the dead.

Okinawa's ancestral tombs represented rites older than anything found in mainland Japan. Elsewhere, Japanese might cremate their familial remains, but not in Okinawa. Entire ancestral lines were interred in these tombs. Once constructed out of coral, now cement, round at the rear and flaring outward at the front, they'd been dubbed "turtlebacks," *kameko-baka*. But they were actually built to resemble wombs. Life, returning to its source. Visitors might stumble upon these tombs anywhere: beside a parking lot, behind a grocer's, next to a school, nestled in someone's backyard. In Okinawa, the dead inhabited the same space as the living.

The souls of these dead were a long time departing; it took thirty-three years to cross over. Rites and rituals helped them along on their journey. As Shimada pedaled past a clutch of such tombs, he wondered what it might have been like to hide inside one of them, among the bones and decaying flesh of one's kin. He couldn't imagine. But during the Battle of Okinawa, that's exactly what happened, both on the main island and elsewhere: entire families, terrified and starved, taking refuge from the American maelstrom outside in darkened tombs where habu and ghosts dwelled, a world of hungry ghosts and restless souls, and it occurred to Shimada as he pedaled on that perhaps the foreigner was one such restless ghost.

Perhaps the foreigner's descendants had fallen lax, neglected his grave, forgotten to offer the proper prayers or foods. Maybe this foreigner who had washed up on Shimada's shores was simply a soul untethered. It would certainly explain the agitation.

He was traversing boundaries, the spirit tracks that crisscrossed the island. Buddhism had barely made an imprint on Hateruma—there were no temples anywhere—but the older religions were still very much in evidence, one just needed to know where to look, and how. Hateruma was overlaid with invisible prayer routes and sacred areas, *utaki* as they were known, rarely marked but always there, much like the spectral paths of the habu or the wanderings of ancestral ghosts. Contact points with the Nirai Kanai, the Other World, the utaki were everywhere—and nowhere. Sometimes it felt like a fairy tale to Shimada, a child's story deserving of a small, indulgent smile. At other times, it felt as though the entire island were one extended utaki.

When Shimada had first arrived at his post, the retiring inspector before him advised Shimada not to trespass on these spots. "Best not to enter any area the islanders consider sacred," he said. "They take that sort of stuff seriously out here."

But the utaki could be anywhere, in a forested grove or a tramped-down clearing, beside a field, even hidden inside a coral cave. "How will I know?" he asked, to which the retiring inspector had laughed and said, "You'll know it when someone comes out and yells at you."

There were utaki that even the locals avoided except on certain equinoctial cycles. Older calendars, lunar arcs. It confounded his sense of order.

When he'd met and married his wife, Shimada had asked her how many utaki there were on Hateruma. "Three," she'd said.

"Just three?"

"Three main ones. Five secondary ones. And another that encompasses the sea."

"So"—he counted it on his fingers—"nine?"

"Oh no, more than that." There were any number of minor utaki as well. "And some of the minor ones are more important than the major ones," she explained with a cheerful lack of clarity. He felt dizzy trying to make sense of it.

"There is no sense to make," his wife said. "It just is."

As hard as it was for Shimada to believe, Hateruma Island was still under the sway of *noro* priestesses, women who acted as envoys to the Other Side, a human chain that stretched back into prehistory, older than Buddhism, older than Japan. Shimada had come across scorched earth in bamboo groves, blackened stones outside coastal caves, had wondered whether a nascent arsonist was in their midst only to be told, no, these were the work of the noro, drawing the gods out in order to placate and petition Hateruma's obstinately moody deities. They always needed praising and prodding, these island gods.

He'd seen one such ritual early on, at the sea's edge, a young woman in white robes falling into a trance and then wading out only to return, cleansed and cold, robes clinging to her, as drums kept a doleful beat on the shore. When stronger rites were needed, the noro would sacrifice goats, sending out the severed heads on a makeshift raft that was intentionally designed to sink beneath the surface.

Noro priestesses were no mere conjurers. When the spirits inhabited them, they didn't merely speak for the gods, they *were* gods. Temporary gods, but gods nonetheless. In Hateruma, their status remained, stubborn and impenetrable and ancient and absolutely maddening to outsiders like Shimada.

A team of researchers from a university in Osaka had come tromping through, not so long ago, looking for tales of the noro. They called themselves anthropologists, folklorists, but really, they were thieves. That was how his wife put it. Here to record for posterity what was already timeless. They had contacted his wife when they first arrived. But why? Why his wife, of all people? It was Shimada's first inkling of something moving below the surface. When was that, three years ago? Four? They'd brought in a woman from Australia as well, or maybe America, he couldn't recall. The Japanese interpreter, from Tokyo, a keen young woman fascinated by "island ways," was soon bogged down in frustration and ambiguity while trying to translate Okinawan terms for the foreigner. These were concepts that barely fit into Japanese, let alone English. The women sat around a table as Shimada hovered in the background, listening in, but it soon became clear that they not only spoke different languages, they also inhabited entirely different worlds: his wife, the foreign woman, the lady from the Japanese university. No stories changed hands that day, not as far as Shimada was aware.

"We don't like to talk about it," his wife said over sashimi and grated daikon, after the other women had left in a flurry of bows and overly polite thank yous. Japanese were always so much more formal than Okinawans.

Mrs. Shimada dipped a small slab of mahi-mahi into the vinegared sauce, dripped it across the table to her plate.

During the interview, she'd let slip that several of her childhood friends had been high priestesses, and now that the others had gone, Shimada asked, "Is that true?"

"Sure. You know Mrs. Kagawa?"

"The one who owns the sweets shop?"

"That's right. She was a top-notch priestess back in the day, when she was younger."

Shimada stopped, chopsticks poised midair, hovering over the loosely arranged plate of sashimi. "Mrs. Kagawa? The one who's always off-key at karaoke? The one who forgets to bring her futon in at night? Her?"

"She was the head noro. Her daughter has taken over now."

"Her daughter, the public nurse? The one with the wonky eye?"

"That's the one."

"But she's—she's medically trained. In science. Surely she's not some sort of magician as well."

His wife laughed. "People can live in more than one world." She delicately shoveled more slices of the fast-melting fish into her mouth, and at that moment he knew—knew without having to ask—that his wife had also been, perhaps still was, a noro of the under-realm herself. She smiled at her husband as she chewed.

THE DOOR TO NUMBER FOUR

HE COULD FEEL IT IN HIS thighs now, the gradual rise in elevation, had to lean forward to avoid changing gears (he only had the three to choose from), could hear his breath whistle in his chest as he approached the height of land—little more than a subtle swell in topography; but on an island as level as Hateruma, that was all that was needed. Beyond these heights, such as they were, the road began its long, graceful descent toward the harbor. His pedaling was done. Officer Shimada could now coast to whatever it was that was waiting for him at the end of this. He picked up speed, avoiding his brakes, arcing from one curve to the next, his tightly tugged police cap almost flying off at times.

Along the way, he passed the island's forlorn cement factory, where a chalky taste hung in the air, and, soon after, the sugarcane processing plant and the island's distillery, where Hateruma's version of awamori was aged in clay vats much the way bodies were stored in tombs. Sixty proof and highly flammable, spiced with cinnamon and honey on occasion to lessen the blow, but still lethal, awamori was the island's liquor of choice. Folk legends told of a drunkard who, having overimbibed, put a lit cigarette into his mouth the wrong way and set his insides on fire. Just a story, to be sure, but Shimada had never developed a taste for this witch's brew either way. He had only ever drunk it down, deeply and wholly, once, on the night of the dry wood. That was how he thought of the moment he discovered his wife's infidelities.

It was a sliding door that did it, the swollen wood having first expanded with humidity and then dried over time, a common problem on Hateruma, where doors often stuck, often didn't close properly. Officer Shimada was coming back from a night of beer at the izakaya, was walking down a lane past the junky backyards of the teachers' residences, two-floor row housing, lined up, in poor repair. The coral walls that surrounded Hateruma's homes did more than protect against typhoons, they also shielded inhabitants from their neighbors' gaze. Several of the walls out back of the teacherage had crumbled into piles of rubble, and as Shimada made his way down the lane, warmed by beer and good cheer, he saw, under the light of a partial moon, a sliver of brightness from one of the rooms. A back door hadn't slid closed all the way, leaving a noticeable gap, and Shimada, ever the policeman and concerned over possible burglars and (equally unlikely) wayward habu, decided to investigate.

As he approached the back door, he stopped. Could see a pair of plastic slippers in the rear entranceway. His wife's. Shimada recognized the broken strap and skewed daisies over the toeholds, even the way they had been kicked to one side—she never bothered to stop and line them up, as was considered proper protocol—and as he stood there, Shimada heard laughter coming from inside. A laughter that was very familiar. And he knew: His wife hadn't been at a sick friend's. She was administering to other needs.

When Shimada got back to the station, he grabbed hold of a bottle of awamori, given as a gift on some congratulatory milestone, never opened, and drove the island's sole patrol car down, and then onto, the beach. He threw it into park, stumbled to the water's edge, and drank the liquor straight from the bottle, burning all the way down.

That was the night he saw the sea turtle.

He was lying on his back, staring up unfocused at the Milky Way, feeling unsteady and unsure. He missed her already, the wife he thought she used to be, her loud laugh and daikon legs. That's the problem with marriage, even one astutely arranged through a matchmaker: love always gets tangled up, like seaweed in a net.

Shimada under the moon, listening to the sigh and slap of waves along the shore, the *shh-shh-shh* of slippers on tatami, and he knew that nothing would really change. That was perhaps the worst part.

He heard a splash, sat up, shirt crusted with sand. Another splash, softer than the first. Was it just the sea among the mangroves? Mangroves were strange creatures. Saltwater trees able to live in brackish waters, roots like legs—"walking trees," they were called—they had colonized the tropical coastlines of Okinawa. Here they formed an ominous-looking wall along the beach amid the ebb and swirl of murky waters. But it wasn't the mangroves and it wasn't tidal waters he was hearing. It was a sea turtle, pulling itself out of the ocean, wet and rare and greenish-blue in the night. It lifted its head, looked around. It was an old man's head squinting at the world with eyes at once wise and weary—and the wise are so often weary. It blinked, slowly, then slid back into the waters of the South China Sea, pushing itself into the foam, disappearing as cleanly as a dream. Shimada watched it go, could chart the turtle's path below the water, in the trail it left behind.

When he got home, his wife tutted, "Your bath. It's gone cold."

"How's your friend?" he asked, demanded.

"Better."

He waited for her to confess, but she didn't.

"Good," he said. *I'm sure he is. I'm sure he's much better.*

Officer Shimada had left his patrol car on the beach, had backed it up above the line of detritus that marked high tide and had made the long, drunken walk home alone.

"Nami—" he said, for that was her name. But she didn't let him finish.

"You can't take a bath now," she said. "It's too late and you're too drunk. I'll go drain the tub, heat up water for a shower instead." Every year, drunken husbands drowned in bathtubs across Japan, often suspiciously so.

Nami. It means "wave."

"I'm not drunk," he said. He was the opposite of drunk. He was awake.

But Nami had already left to drain the water, and he was now talking to himself. He stared down at the tabletop. "I saw a sea turtle," he said.

And now, here he is coasting into sunlight, down to the docks where the widow is waiting, standing outside her home, a pained smile on her plain face, hair parted and pulled back, streaks of early gray evident even from here, surprising in someone not yet old.

She was wearing the same apron as his wife; there were only two clothing stores on the island, so it was a coin toss when it came to shopping. The widow bowed as he rolled up, bobbing from the waist. "Good morning, Mr. Walkabout." It was an affectionate term for policemen in Japan, even when they arrived by bicycle. It suggested someone turning circles.

Shimada came to a stop, bowed in return, still straddling his bicycle.

"You knew I was coming?"

"Your wife phoned."

"Ah." It was Mrs. Shimada's way of saying, by way of cheery reminder, "I know where he is, you know that I know, and I want you to know that he knows that I know."

Shimada dismounted, pushed his bike onto the stone-covered gutter in front of the widow's door, kicked the stand down. Didn't bother with the lock.

The guesthouse was a squat cement-walled arrangement, a study in muddy colors much like Shimada's. On Hateruma you had two choices: wooden homes that breathed but tended to rot, or drab cement structures that did neither. The amenities offered at the widow's guesthouse were simple to the point of severe: four separate rooms out back, each with its own door opening onto the outside. Beds, not futons, and cement floors rather than tatami, which was just as well. Tatami would have gone soft with mildew in the wet air of Hateruma. Shimada found his own cement-walled home suffocating at times, missed the dank scent of wood and tatami that he'd grown up with. (Whenever he dropped by the older homes on Hateruma, he always made a point of taking a deep breath, inhaling the smell of it, the calm of it.) If nostalgia had a smell, it would smell like aged tatami.

Fortunately for the widow, her clientele wasn't overly concerned with aesthetics. Dockworkers and road crews mainly. The occasional government inspector who had missed the last boat back. The pier was a short downhill walk from there; hers was the last home in Hateruma, and as they stood in the glare outside, Shimada could hear the distant bellow of an incoming ferry, a low bassoon above the high cry of cicadas.

It was hot out. They agreed on that, and after further pleasantries and concerns about the weather and the asking after one's health—mandatory in such situations—Shimada-san cleared his throat. "So . . ." he said, letting the unasked question hang in the air.

The widow's smile grew more pained. "He arrived last night."

Shimada knew that smile. It was a smile of distress, a smile of

31

extreme discomfort, a smile that foreigners often mistook for friend-liness, an invitation to come closer when it was in fact a polite hand raised to keep you at a distance. He had seen that smile at the memorial, that smile of pain. A husband washed away, never to resurface. She'd had to bury an empty tomb. No children, and bones gone missing.

"American?"

"English. He wrote his passport in the guestbook. 'UK' means English, right?"

They'd built the guesthouse near the docks so that her husband could be close to his boat, the same boat that had returned empty, found floating off the coast, swamped with seawater. It was tied up at the pier even now, within sight of the guesthouse. Shimada took out his notepad, tried to clear his thoughts. Clicked his pen authorita-tively several times, but didn't write anything down. What was it like to see your husband's boat every morning when you stepped outside to shake the doormats or hang up the laundry? Was it a blessing? Or a curse?

"He was jumpy, looking around, like he was waiting for someone to show up."

"Afraid?"

"I think so. He kept saying '*Ichi-ban minami? Doko? Doko?*'" The most south? Where? Where?

"He could speak Japanese?" Perhaps Shimada wouldn't need the embarrassing ritual of the phrasebook after all.

"He did, yes."

"How?"

"Like all foreigners, badly."

Shimada nodded. "Age?"

"Hard to say, isn't it? They always look so much older than they are. Could have been forty. Could have been twenty-two. I'm not really sure. Red hair. Maybe yellow. Large nose. He was loud, but not angry, just, you know, *loud*." She was describing every foreigner that ever lived, the foreigner in the Mind of God. "He wasn't very tall, though. Not for a foreigner. He was—your size. Kind of petite."

That stung.

"May I?" he asked.

"Certainly."

She ushered him into her home, through the sliding doors, and he stepped up, out of his shoes and into a pair of guest slippers.

"He didn't come out for breakfast," she said by way of apology for not having cleared the plates before the officer arrived. "I thought it might be evidence of some sort. Best left undisturbed."

Shimada could see the rolled omelet and fried fish still at the table like offerings to an absent god, the way one might leave oranges and mochi at a family altar, more as a gesture than for any actual sustenance.

"I went to check on him," she said. He could hear the waver in her voice.

They walked through the dim interior of the kitchen to the back door, stepped out of the guest slippers and into outdoor ones—memories of his wife's errant footwear gnawing at the edge—then along a shaggy path behind the house, past a row of bicycles in a rusted rack, reserved for guests, he imagined. Four rooms. Four racks. Three bicycles.

Shimada would have asked about the missing bike, but the widow had pushed on, was calling to him over her shoulder.

"I don't know if he's out, or just not answering. Maybe foreigners are heavy sleepers." But she didn't sound convincing, even to herself.

"Perhaps," said Shimada. *Tabun.* That all-purpose Japanese phrase, evasive, polite, fraught with meaning. *Maybe.*

The guestrooms had doors that opened directly onto an overgrown and, it must be said, neglected backyard garden, a tanglement of weeds barely kept at bay. A breeding ground for habu, he was sure.

"I knocked and I knocked," she said. "But he wouldn't open the door."

The widow jangled her keys, trying to find the correct one. They were now standing directly outside the last door. A faded number 4 was painted on it. Unlucky, that, the number four. It meant "death." Strange she hadn't skipped it; most hotels and guest inns went directly from three to five.

She segregated the correct key, saw him looking at the number on the door. "I'm not superstitious," she said. "Never have been."

Perhaps you should be.

The wooden veneer on the door was rotting from the bottom up, black mold reaching partway toward the handle. She hesitated, voice dropping to a whisper. "I heard him when I came out at night to empty the wash pail. In his room, behind his door, arguing to himself, almost shouting."

"Alone?"

She nodded. "I wasn't sure if he was on his cell phone or just . . ." She twirled a finger around her temple. Crazy.

"Maybe."

Shimada straightened his shoulders, leaned forward, and hammered on the door in a virile and by no means petite manner, calling out as gruffly as he could—in English. *"Police! Please!"* The way he pronounced it, they sounded like the same word.

Nothing.

He nodded to the widow, who, with hands slightly trembling, slid the key into the lock and pulled down on the handle. The door swung open and Shimada stepped through, into the darkness on the other side.

FUMBLING FOR THE CORD ON THE overhead light, Shimada took a moment for his eyes to adjust as the florescent tubes flickered and buzzed into life.

The bed hadn't been slept in. That was the first strange thing. The cover was still pulled straight, sheets crisply turned down, no discernible indents on the pillow. Shimada caught his own reflection staring back at him, eyes hooded by the overhead glare. He was looking at the mirror above the washbasin. No bathroom—that was in the house, shared with the other guests—but each room did have a faucet and a hand towel and a small square of soap, still unwrapped. And a mirror to peer into.

In the mirror, Shimada could see a large, misshapen shadow sprawled on the floor next to the bed, and now his hand was on his holster and his chest was tight. He stepped wide, around the bed. Waiting for him on the other side was neither a slumbering demon nor an ambush brewing but only a large duffel bag, unzipped and gaping, empty.

Not quite.

The officer crouched down while the widow stayed back, watching from the doorway. Inside the duffel bag was some loose dirt, a fragment of what looked to be pottery, and—he opened the bag wider—a block of money, shrink-wrapped in plastic.

Shimada reached in, pulled out more blocks of money, and more. American currency, shrink-wrapped. He then examined the fragment of pottery. Held it up to the light. He recognized it. It was from a funeral urn, the type interred in turtleback tombs. This fragment had a partial pattern, raised like a welt on the surface, and he recognized that too. It was the family mon of the Kara clan, Okinawa's royal dynasty, the last kings of Ryukyu. Some family mons were famous, and this was one of them. The Taira family crest was a long-tailed butterfly. The Yamato, a cherry blossom. The Ishida, a crane. The Kara family? Their mon resembled a stylized cicada, but was in fact a *hotaru*. A firefly.

Shimada straightened up, knees stiff, and as he did so, his foot kicked something. It rolled across the floor. A red plastic tube. The officer retrieved this with his pen, wary of fingerprints. He recognized this item from his childhood boar-hunting days, running down grassy trails with his father and uncles. It was a shotgun shell.

Later, they would try to determine why their officer hadn't called the main police station on Ishigaki Island directly, rather than leaving it to a flustered widow. There was no clear answer. Perhaps the officer had thought a fraught call from a civilian would get quicker results, or perhaps he'd felt that time was of the essence and he needed to pick up the trail quickly, couldn't afford to waste time talking his way up the chain of command. Maybe. Or perhaps, addled and unsettled, he simply wasn't thinking at all.

Shimada turned to the widow. "Call the main police station on Ishigaki. Have them send backup, right away. Code— Code"—he couldn't remember the number—"Code Important."

The widow hurried off and Shimada stepped out into the shrill, cicada-infused heat. He knew the meaning of the missing bike at the guesthouse, and he knew exactly where the foreigner was—he just didn't know why.

Shimada did the calculations in his head. They would take a speedboat from Ishigaki Island. Forty minutes, at least. The airport at Hateruma had closed down, but the runway was still maintained for charter flights and emergencies. If they commandeered a small plane, they could do it in twenty-five. But it would take the Ishigaki police station at least half an hour to clear a flight, and even then, if they could get approval to scramble an aircraft it would take another twenty to get to the airport, board a plane, lift off. And they would still have to get from the abandoned airport on Hateruma into town. No. They would come by boat.

Forty minutes. That was the soonest they could arrive. If he bicycled back to his house, uphill for the most part, grabbed his car keys, and took the patrol vehicle, it would add another fifteen minutes. Or he could go to the dock, flag down one of the miniature trucks, have them run him across—if there was a truck, and if it was available—but at this stage it was quicker simply to bike it. He looked down at his feet. After he got rid of these slippers, of course.

HATERUMA BLUE

EVERY LABYRINTH HAS ITS DEAD ENDS. Hateruma was no exception.

Coral walls pressed in from either side, funneling traffic into narrow lanes and cul-de-sacs and unexpected turnarounds. Whenever that happened, when a path or a road came to a sudden T, ending on a wall or a front yard, special heavy stone markers had been rolled into place. These markers were inscribed with Chinese characters to turn back malevolent spirits. Evil travels in a straight line, you see, hates to tack right or left, hates to change course, and Hateruma's *ishi-gan-to* stones deflected the razor-like routes that evil followed. The island's spirit lines formed a network, blocked here, averted there, redirected this way, then that, eventually leading to the cliffs at the island's edge and then into the sea, in much the same way a wild boar might be corralled. A malicious presence would thus be directed away from the village, avoiding homes and businesses, and Officer Shimada wondered if perhaps the foreigner had wandered into this labyrinth and found himself unable to escape. Perhaps Shimada had done the same.

He rode awkwardly, holster joggling with each turn of the pedal, leaning into his own momentum to make up time. A toad hobbled across the road in front of him. The wind was growing restless, the sugarcane was swaying back and forth, grassy fields were alive with whorls and rippling waves. At times like this, it felt as though the entire island were in motion. He was now skirting the very edge of Hateruma on a tarmacked road with open ocean on one side, a tumult of wind on the other. Clouds were boiling up in the distance. He could see the end approaching.

All roads eventually led here, to the cliffs of Cape Takana, where the island sheared into the sea, jagged free falls of coral limestone, exposed to the full brunt of it, with the ocean swelling and dropping on every heave. A blue so deep it had its own name: *Hateruma-no-ao*.

Set back from the cliffs was the domed tower of the Hateruma Observatory, a research station whose colossal telescope prowled the skies at night, the only building out here, often mistaken for a lighthouse. Low latitudes and a lack of light made Cape Takana ideal; it was one of the few places in Japan where you could view the Southern

Cross, low along the horizon, the very constellation that featured so prominently on the Australian flag. Perhaps the foreigner was a scientist or an amateur astronomer. Perhaps it was a telescope he was toting in that bag, not a shotgun. Perhaps the foreigner was simply homesick, had come to view the Southern Cross from the other side, south by southeast. Except that the widow had said he was from England, not Australia. And, anyway, the observatory was closed for the season.

Shimada parked his bike next to the commemorative stone marker that heralded the southernmost point in Japan—a lie, as noted, but a much-photographed lie nonetheless. There were no tourists about on this blustery morning. No one at all, except . . .

Farther out, a bicycle lay on its side, its front wheel angling upward, rotating on the wind. As Shimada walked down to it, he knew before he got there that this was the missing bike from the widow's guesthouse; he recognized the rust and pale green paint. It looked as though it had been flung aside in a panic—but no. The kickstand was up. The bicycle must have fallen on its own accord, most likely tipped over by the wind; people fleeing for their lives would rarely have the presence of mind to put down the kickstand first.

A flapping noise, and he spotted a strap of some sort wedged in the coral nearby. When he pulled on it, a black fabric bag came loose. He recognized this as well: it was a padded shoulder case typically used to transport long-bore rifles. Shotguns, for example. But the weapon itself was gone.

What are you hunting, gaijin-san? Habu? Ghosts?

The officer looked out, into the wind of Cape Takana. He could see the curve of the earth in the ocean. Hateruma blue. *Where have you gone, gaijin-san? There is nowhere to run. Only the cliffs and the sea and the wind.* Coral convolutions. Jagged hillocks. Nowhere to run, perhaps, but a thousand places to hide. If Shimada was going to be ambushed, it was going to be now.

The officer picked his way across the sharpened coral and ragged ankle-rolls of rock, out to the very edge of Cape Takana. Carefully, carefully, he leaned over, peered at the waves below. Seabirds wheeled. Waves came in on cymbal crashes of foam. And, buffeted by a sudden shove of wind, Shimada stumbled forward, lurched to keep his cap on his head, just as quickly stumbled back on a surge of vertigo: fear and elation in equal measure. He could picture himself falling, end over end . . .

He picked his way back across the coral. If there was a body at the bottom of the cliffs, he hadn't glimpsed it, and even if there was, the undertow would have been battering it on broken rocks for a long while yet. It could be days, if ever, before the body was spat out again. He thought of the widow's husband, of the sea reaching up to pull him off his boat.

When Shimada got back to the side of the road, his bicycle was rocking on its stand, ready to topple as well, and he would have ridden back to his police box to await the arrival of the other officers had he not noticed something odd. The observatory, on its sweep of hill. The front door was open. He could see the square of black even from here. But the observatory didn't operate during the summer; the current team of astronomers had returned to Tokyo and Osaka, wouldn't be back for at least a month. They didn't mingle much with the locals, these scientists, though his wife had always taken an interest in them. "Such fascinating young men! To think that they spend their lives searching the heavens. They must get lonely."

Leaving his bike to rock on the wind, Officer Shimada made his way uphill to the observatory. He was in no rush, because he knew.

He knew exactly where the foreigner had gone. *He's inside, my lost gaijin. He's waiting for me. He doesn't know it, but he is.*

In a tuft of grass, something thin was caught: a snake skin, turned perfectly inside out like a dried windsock of scales, unraveling like a discarded party favor.

The door had been pried open. Shimada could see the splintered wood on the frame. He unlatched the clasp on the holster of the gun that he had never fired, had never had cause to fire, and for the second time that morning, he stepped across a threshold, not knowing what was waiting for him on the other side.

HE NEVER THOUGHT TO DRAW HIS weapon. Unlatching the holster was as far as he got.

"Gomen kudasai!" He still wasn't sure why he was speaking so politely.

He stood in the doorway, the light outside fanning inward, catching arbitrary angles and sharp corners. It looked like a classroom, and in a way it was. The first floor of the observatory was open to the public, and display cases and educational panels were arranged accordingly. Momentarily blinded by the darkness, eyes adjusting to an empty room, he entered.

"Gomen kudasai!" But his voice was swallowed by the silence.

It was faint at first, a hesitant rustling, almost rhythmic, like a broken wing trying to take flight, feathered bones moving in vain, back and forth. Or a moth trapped in a jar. The wind was searching the room, had found something apparently, and Shimada traced the sound to a far corner, where a secondary hallway branched off.

He looked down and there it was. Exhibit A. Not a bird's wing, but a book. A journal of some sort, lying open on the floor with the pages flipping back and forth in the cross breeze as though turned by an impatient hand. Shimada crouched down, didn't want to disturb it, noted the scribbled writing and something that looked like a smear of rust, but wasn't.

Just past the discarded journal, jutting out from behind the corner, was the polished wooden stock of a shotgun. A piece of coral had been wedged into the trigger, and although the end of the barrel was out of view, he could smell it. Scorched powder, burned flesh, like a matchstick that was still trailing smoke.

With a steadying breath, Shimada stepped around the corner. A body was sprawled backward into the hall, legs splayed. Cheap running shoes. Baggy cargo shorts. A pastel polo shirt, belly exposed. Arms akimbo. Face missing. No features, only a charred absence. A pool of sticky syrup was coagulating beneath the back of the head. A congregation of flies. Exclamation points of blood radiating outward.

His first corpse, in situ. Shimada leaned in, studied the open wound, the absence in front of him. It was as though the man's face had been yanked inward. Embedded in the sunken wound were glimmers of dull ivory. Those would be teeth. A glimpse of pewter. Those would be fillings. No eyes, no nose, no lips. And Shimada wondered, Why would you kill yourself by firing a shotgun *into* your face? Wouldn't it be simpler to hold the barrel in your mouth, blow out the back of your head instead? And if the goal was suicide all along, why not take a long step off one of the many conveniently located cliffs outside, let the sea do the work for you? The body, the rifle, the journal: it almost seemed staged, a tableau arranged as though for public viewing.

He pulled his own notepad from his pocket, opened it to a new page, wrote DEAD FOREIGNER across the top in large kanji characters, then, "Discovered at . . ." He checked the time on his watch. But that was as far as he got, as far as he was allowed to get, because before Shimada could jot down the hour or minute or even the day, he felt a low thrum in the air. Then he heard it: a *whomp-whomp-whomp* outside the observatory.

When he stepped into the sun, shielding his eyes, Shimada saw it coming in, low across the water, fighting updrafts all the way, blades thumping, pushing a wave of noise in front of it, and for a moment he thought, *They sent a helicopter?* But as it swept over the coral cliffs and circled the observatory, he could see the insignia on the side, not that of the regional Okinawa prefectural police, but the Coast Guard's SST unit, part of Japan's National Security Agency. The helicopter hovered a moment like a dragonfly in midflight then tilted away, toward the landing strip at the abandoned airport. Through the open sides, rolled back and ready, Shimada could see a cohort of dark-garbed officers, flak jackets and opaque helmets, and in their midst, a flurry of blond hair blowing every which way and a thin face staring back at him. Their eyes met for a moment—and then she was gone, pulled away as if by a rip cord.

And with that, the investigation was no longer his. Police Inspector Shimada, senior officer, Hateruma Island Substation, wheeled his bicycle onto the tarmac, climbed astride with a wobbled lack of grace, and pedaled back to his village to await further instructions, back to a life of lost and found, of sugarcane wives and messy kitchens, of bamboo and bitter melons, where widows smile through their pain and the tables are never turned.

PART TWO
THE LAST TESTAMENT
OF BILLY MOORE

FOR AS LONG AS I CAN REMEMBER, I've had a knack for finding things.

It began in childhood, as most things do, amidst the threadbare and doily-laden flat I shared with my mum, surrounded by knick-knacks and keepsakes and the stifling presence of a semi-mythical father, long gone. The entire place, I realize now, was little more than a museum of the mundane, a diorama of sadness—Belfast sadness, a peculiar breed all its own. Clocks that needed winding, mantels that needed dusting, ceramic figurines with rictus grins, holiday snapshots in ill-fitting frames. *This is Blackpool. That was Portrush.*

And yet, as narrow as that flat was, my mother still managed to mislay things, was constantly walking in and out of rooms like a character in a play who has forgotten her lines, endlessly baffled by the turns her life has taken. *"Now, where on earth did I . . . ?"* and quietly, consistently, I would find it for her: reading glasses (atop the refrigerator), her pocketbook (behind the sofa), memories (sinking fitfully into photo albums).

There were tricks involved. Memories could be nudged into place with soft-spoken queries. "Mum, who is this again?" "Oh, that's your uncle Bertie." "And when?" "The war." "Which war?" "Does it really matter?" "Yes. Yes, it does. Which war? Think, Mum. Think." Sometimes all that was required was a shift in gaze, looking *up* instead of across, for example. Most of us slumber-walk through life at eye level; a simple tilt of the head can divulge entire kingdoms. This

47

was how her glasses revealed themselves atop the Frigidaire. At other times, one had to back-walk through events, reeling in one's movements until you came to the crux of where you and the object had parted company, like running a film in reverse. A lost reel, respooled. Sometimes locating lost objects involved entering a trancelike state, allowing one's gaze to go ever-so-slightly out of focus, reducing the jumbled details to a mottled glow against which the lost object might pop out, into the foreground. One looks for incongruities. Such was the Case of the Missing Pocketbook, wedged deep between faded cushions, where a thin gap created a subtle but distinct break in the floral pattern of the sofa's fabric. The pocketbook was also florally arrayed; it was the blackness of that gap which had revealed its presence.

My mother always said it was no fun hiding jelly beans for me on Easter morning, because instead of charging about pell-mell as other children were wont to do, I would move through thoughtfully, methodically, removing each candy one by one. What she didn't understand was that the color of the jelly beans was so at odds with their surroundings that very little searching was required, although a few times I did indeed pretend to be fooled, if only to make her feel better; she was so much more excited about Easter than I was. "Ooo, you didn't think to look inside the teapot, did you!" In fact, the teapot was one of the first places I spotted; it had clearly been moved—I could see at a glance that it was sitting slightly off-center on its doily, all but screaming, "In here!" That teapot, by the way, purchased in advance of a would-be Royal Visit (canceled when the bombs began to go off across Belfast), was the most valuable thing in our flat, worth quite a bit today, I imagine, if it hadn't been thrown out with everything else after my mother died and the landlord foreclosed. I was in Indonesia by then and heard about the funeral too late and too far away to make a difference. I wonder if my da showed up. Not that it mattered. That hideous teapot with Princess Anne's toothy grin stretched across it most likely ended up in a landfill somewhere, buried under other discarded items along with the jelly beans my mum stored in it after I was too big for Easter. Or maybe it wasn't discarded. Perhaps that teapot sits in a secondhand emporium, collecting dust, waiting to be rediscovered, the petrified jelly beans still tucked within. Wait long enough and everything becomes a relic.

When her memory started to go, my mother would joke that one of the advantages of this slow erasure was that she was now able to hide her own Easter eggs. Only much later did I realize that Easter was meant to be a celebration of life restored, not a crass treasure hunt. I'd always thought it was a holiday of the lost and found.

I grew up on Shankill Road, which, I imagine, means nothing to you—or everything, depending on your degree of familiarity with the niceties of Northern Ireland. The flat I was raised in is still there, but the missing house, farther down, must surely have been replaced by now. It's been so long since I've been home, I really can't say. Named for a king, so I was. William the Third on his snow-white horse, a drawn sword pointing ever forward. *No surrender!*

The missing house—it should probably be rendered in capital letters, the Missing House, such was its import—was haunted, or so it was whispered. But it wasn't really haunted and it wasn't really missing. It was in disarray. The working-class ruins of a family bungalow, it stood swaybacked and forsaken at the far end of the Shankill, on the dreariest stretch of the dreariest street in the dreariest part of Belfast—and that's saying a lot.

The Missing House had been destroyed, not in a spasm of sectarian violence, but over a perceived slight to one of the Loyalist paramilitary groups that prowled the Protestant reaches of Belfast in those days, and still do for all I know. A bullet-like bottle with burning rag attached had exploded through one of the windows, had turned the house into a hollowed husk, a burnt-out shell on the edge of an empty lot. The roof had partially collapsed, whether from smoke damage or water wasn't clear, and the burnt wood lay amid slabs of plaster, with sodden mounds of drywall heaped in peaks along the floor. Charred furniture. Light fixtures dangling like eyes without a socket. It was beautiful, in its way.

The day everything changed I couldn't have been much more than eight or nine. It was threatening rain—it was always threatening rain; Belfast is a city held captive by the weather—and I was walking home in the worst kind of darkness, the darkness that comes from broken streetlamps. Whistling an elaborately brave tune, trying to stir up some courage, I hurried past the gawping maw of that missing home under the light of the only streetlamp left. My mum had sent me for chips and mushy peas, a treat of some sort, though I can't remember the occasion, and I was clutching the newspapered package to my chest, whistling, whistling. It's funny. Even now, the smell of damp newsprint will hurtle me back to that moment, to that ruined house, to the warm embrace of mushy peas and a single streetlamp, flickering.

It was that lone streetlamp what did it.

Among the ruins of the missing house, I spotted . . . something. A glint of . . . *something*. Probably just a shard of glass or a bit of broken metal, but—*what if?* That's where stories begin, isn't it, with the question: What if? What if the world is secretly filled with wonders? What if the miraculous lies hidden among the everyday quiddities of life? And what if that gleam wasn't glass, but a diamond ring? A jewel, a pearl, a polished gem? It could be anything. Ruined buildings are a trove for treasure hunters. I stopped, and with that I overcame my fears—forever, as it turned out. I crept into the cavern of that fallen house and from the debris I extracted my reward: a single, one-pound coin. I can still feel the weight of it in my palm.

The sky was heavy, I remember that. Pushing its darkness down on the city. And when I ran back to that pool of light on the sidewalk, coin in fist, newspapered dinner now tucked tightly under my arm, I felt something shift, like a vein under the skin. All down the street, squares of yellow light glowed through drawn curtains, the homes resembling an Advent calendar from which the chocolates had already been gouged. Row housing: two floors stacked atop each other, a single bare bulb above the entrance to ours. My mother had left a light on, would be waiting, fretfully, for the sound of my key in the latch, would be watching the door, wondering if I was too young for such errands.

Beyond these row houses, at the end of our street, another light glowed liquid in the night. The local newsagent, and that is where I hurried. I purchased a one-pound National Lottery Lucky 7 scratch card and then ran home to deliver my gift. "It's for me mum," I had told the shopkeeper. "She's feeling lucky." He shouldn't have sold it to me, but he did, and with a kindly smile as well, one that might easily have been mistaken for pity.

My mother's careworn face, trying to smile. She had set the table, just the two of us; I remember that as well, how heartbreaking it was to eat mushy peas and chips on a linen tablecloth with folded napkins and complete place settings. She was always doing things like that, cleaning the house for hypothetical visitors or setting a full table for takeout, sending me on errands in my best blazer, hair spritzed and combed, trying through some sort of magical gesture to keep despair from gaining a handhold. Yet she never thought to dust. I think maybe her eyesight was going by that point. Our house smelled of mice, though I only ever recall dead ones, behind a dresser, in the back of the closet, and so on.

A one-pound coin? That was milk for our tea. That was a sticky bun to share or a can of tinned spaghetti, a newspaper with want ads to pore over. It was any one of those. What it wasn't was a game of chance purchased on a whim. I could see a flash, not of anger, or even displeasure, but what I can only call *anticipatory pain*. Those who expect the worst of life are rarely disappointed, and any ire my mother may have harbored quickly subsided, and with a soft voice—she was from Ballymena, my mum, and carried the Scots-Irish lilt even then—"Let's have a look then, see how close we came."

She scratched out 100 pounds on that one-pound ticket.

That wasn't milk for our tea, that was a new floral scarf for her, a school satchel for me. That was dinner for two at the Europa Hotel, where we ordered dessert even though we were full and she laughed and her eyes brimmed and I made her laugh and we toasted with cranberry juice, for luck and a steady eye and a coin among the ruins. I had seen my mother smile before; I had never seen her beam, and for that one evening we could pretend that this was the life we were meant to have, a life misplaced along the way, one of chandeliers and proper silverware, not a rictus home that smelled of mice where the doilies hid the age of the fabric.

At times I wonder, had that scratch card revealed not 100 pounds but TRY AGAIN, how differently my life might have turned out. I might never have left Belfast, might still be ensconced on Shankill Road under pewter skies. Perhaps it was the Devil who placed that coin in the ruined home. If not the Devil, a trickster god of some sort.

You ask how I came to find myself on Hateruma Island? It started in Belfast. I was carried forth on tidal currents, on dark oceans.

My mother died, as they do, and I drifted to Southeast Asia, as you might. Bangkok. Malaysia. Bali. Seoul and Shanghai, eventually washing up here on the shores of Okinawa, where I quickly set myself up in that liminal world, somewhere between night and day, heart and loin, pandering to the appetites of American servicemen. I specialized in finding girls who looked younger than they actually were, presenting them in dimly lit rooms as though they were children, which I suppose they were, though not in the legal sense. Amphetamine-numbed encounters. Blackmail follow-ups. I take no pride in any of this. It is simply a statement of fact. I was wounded, and in my pain sought to wound others, if only to have someone to share the burden. I could see the shabby future that awaited me and self-medicated myself back into the present, into a holding pattern above a closed runway as the fuel ran low.

Okinawa City is a giant claw game with gears exposed. The clang and clangor, the ricochet and tilt-a-whirl lights. I was spiraling downward and I knew it, was sampling the very wares I was meant to be peddling, both chemical and physical, was finding it harder and harder to look those young girls in the eye—most of them with the smell of the earth and the sea still clinging to their cotton kimonos; they came from whatever the Okinawan equivalent of the Shankill was, these girls, as I paid them their pittance and pocketed the rest. There were yakuza to be bought off, supplies to be purchased, my own jangled nerves to be assuaged, even as the spiral sucked me deeper, drew me downward.

What rescued me from the whirlpool was not a sudden conversion, no Saul-to-Paul epiphany, but a chance encounter on a deserted beach with a man who came from nowhere in particular. A prophet of sorts. He spun me the tale of Lazarus, of lives restored, of dead men rising.

"I have a proposition," he said. "A proposal, and a modest one at that."

What happened now seems preordained, as befits my Presbyterian roots. Perhaps I am a Calvinist at heart, after all. The man on the beach unwrapped a strange narrative of parallel worlds, of baubles hanging in plain sight.

He told me that I would make a lot of money, and that I would disappear. Those were his very words: "I present to you the opportunity to earn a great deal of money, and to then disappear."

Part of a nefarious international organization, or so he said. Shadowy contacts. Vague assurances. An offer of lucre and a new life. This was the seduction he trapped me with over sugarcane drinks in a bamboo bar. *You will make a lot of money. And you will disappear.* It was the possibility of reinvention more than the money itself which proved irresistible. Perhaps it *was* the Devil I was hearing, true and good now, whispering in my ear, my own desires echoing back at me.

I would once again be searching for lost things. That was how I justified it, ranging from one end of Japan to the other, liberating an ancient calligraphy set from a Kyoto monastery, retrieving a samurai scroll from Sado Island or a Gutenberg Bible from Nagasaki, a relic of Japan's doomed Jesuit incursion wrapped in silk and stored in a temple until it became forgotten. My job was to un-forget such things, to extract them from life's tendrils. I wasn't stealing, I was restoring. Bringing things back to the light.

There is a rich market for objects thought lost, now found. But there is a richer market for thieves, and only too late did I realize that

I was not as invisible as I fancied. Somewhere along the way, I had triggered a trip wire of some sort and I found my regular avenues and corridors of escape blocked. It began with a police raid, sidestepped only when I caught the silent throb of approaching lights in a shopwindow. They had sent four patrol cars to catch me, had failed—but only just. There is no shame in admitting I was unsettled by what was happening. Contacts who failed to show. Cars with tinted windows that were parked across from whatever low-end inn I was currently habituating. I slipped through side doors, took overnight buses, avoided airports, even considered back-alley plastic surgery at one point—but my face has never been memorable, and I knew it was not *me* per se, but the trail I left behind that had tipped off—who exactly? Interpol? Perhaps. More likely the International Crimes Agency, an anagram of CIA, appropriately enough, though not, as far as I know, associated with espionage of any kind. The ICA is the strong arm of Interpol. It shares data and pools its resources with other agencies, whether it be Scotland Yard or the FBI or XYZ. I never took the ICA seriously, assumed they were just another bureaucratic make-work project in the endless alphabet soup of organizations that were doing their best not to catch me.

I hadn't counted on a certain agent, however. A tenacious and wholly unlikable person I came to hate with a passion worthy of a better cause. Let's call her Agent Rhodes, because that's her name. Gladys Rhodes, to be precise, and honestly, who names their daughter Gladys these days? (Though I understand she goes by "Gaddy," hardly an improvement.) I know her name because she showed it to me—inadvertently, mind you; but still, it doesn't say much for her powers of subterfuge, does it? I spied the name when she pushed herself past me, rather rudely, I must say, flashing her badge at a luckless hotel night clerk. She was asking about me, or rather, the name I was then currently traveling under. Here I was, her prey, standing right beside her, and she never knew! Heightened observational abilities would not appear to be her forte, either. One wonders how she was ever accepted into the ranks of the ICA in the first place. Fortunately, that hostel-like inn was a frequent habitué of dissolute gaijin such as myself, and the night clerk didn't recognize me—we do all look alike—or chose not to, anyway, discretion being the better part of valor. And so I slipped away while she was waiting for the clerk to slowly pull out the guestbook and laboriously flip through the pages to locate my room and presumably a key.

She is a thoroughly unattractive person, our Ms. Rhodes. Thin-featured, pinch-faced, I would say, were I less charitable. Tall, true, but brittle as a bag of pigeon bones. Some may claim to find the anemic look attractive; I do not. I imagine she smells of Vicks VapoRub and loneliness. It's an unattractive nature, more existential than physical. Beauty may be skin deep, but true ugliness comes from the core. A holiday would do her wonders, I am sure.

At first I found it almost comical, then merely tiresome, the way she was constantly circling the playground like a feckless beagle, sniffing the trail, trying in her clumsy way to flush me out. Comical, then annoying. Then worrisome. Then aggravating. I caught glimpses of Gaddy Rhodes and her flyaway hair across many a crowded floor. (And really, could a six-foot skeletal blond call more attention to herself in a country like Japan? Here's a tip: wear a wig.) Over time, her constant presence began to frazzle my admittedly frail frame of mind. She became, not my nemesis exactly, but my banshee, wings folded, voice screeching its relentless wail, a death foretold. In Ireland, banshees are considered folkloric harbingers of fate. But I assure you, they are quite real. They come in the guise of thin-faced women brandishing badges.

Under the gaze of her banshee eyes, my carefully constructed network began to collapse. I was harried, harassed, hounded at every turn. As one deal after another fell through and former confederates began to turn, I realized I was trapped—not just in Japan, but in Okinawa. That's the problem with islands; you are always surrounded. I could feel my banshee drawing nearer, and in desperation I sent her an offer, a proposed truce, shall we say, left in a locker in Naha City. She had the staff break through the padlock with metal cutters, expecting a terra-cotta bodhisattva saint inside; instead, only a letter containing a gentlemanly proposal: *I wish to come in from the cold. If you provide me with immunity, I will provide you with names.* Her reply, posted in an online want ad, as arranged, was simple and to the point. OFFER DECLINED. What she wanted was not concessions but complete capitulation, unconditional surrender, as the Yanks had after they'd obliterated Hiroshima and Nagasaki, reducing the populace to shadows stenciled onto city walls. That's who I was up against. A pale crusader who would not let me rest. A heart like Hiroshima.

Cornered in Okinawa City, bank accounts frozen, with no access to a means of escape, I went all in for a final payday: a royal tomb, rumors of riches, a willing buyer. I had been reduced to the role of common grave robber. All for naught. There was no treasure. Only femurs and broken clay. Such is life. Problem was, I had already accepted initial payment, the rest due on delivery. But there would be no delivery. Dragging a rucksack filled with money and hunger—and a gun, let's not forget the gun; easily purchased in the alleyways of ill repute that fan outward from the US Army base—I was crossing a street that was palpitating with American servicemen, palpitating and salivating both. I was trying to fight my way into the First Chance, Last Chance Saloon, something of an institution in Okinawa City, even if it has been inflicted by the scourge of country music. I was going there to return the money, try to buy some time, when what did I see, floating like a halo above the mutton-headed mob? That damnable pale hair, those sour features, my would-be banshee.

I had no intention of getting caught, least of all by someone as preposterous as her. So I ran. First to Ishigaki Island on an overnight ferry—was there ever such a sleepless night?—and then on to Taiwan, slipping free of Japanese jurisdiction. Or at least, that was the plan: to island-hop along secondary routes until I could melt into the liberating confusion that is Taipei. But the Ishigaki airport was being watched, and my banshee was drawing ever nearer. I could feel the noose tightening, my throat constricting, was having trouble swallowing.

A final ferry, one last island, and I find myself here on this godforsaken outpost at the end of Japan. There is nowhere left to turn and, as I scribble down these words, I remember a hollowed-out home on Shankill Road, a scratch card win and the false hopes it engendered, like riches lost in a swamp, and I wonder if I should ever have left Belfast to begin with. When I look ahead, I see only darkness. I can find no way forward, no way back, and with the dying of the light, I find myself—

THAT WAS THE POINT THEY REALIZED they were no longer reading a confession, but a suicide note.

A young US military clerk with pit-pony eyes, a corporal by the insignia on his shoulder, quietly lay the clicker to one side.

Projected onto the screen in front of him was the final entry in the diary of Billy Moore, esq., (deceased). A fan rattled in the corner, more audible assurance than actual temperature modification. Even with the blinds closed, meeting room 2-B at Kadena Air Base, Okinawa City, US Armed Forces, was basting in its own heat. A narrow table ran the length of the room, and in the middle of the table, like a holy relic or a lost manuscript, was the journal itself, sealed in a plastic evidence bag, its blood-bespeckled pages blurry but visible within. A jug of water, sweaty with condensation. Ice cubes melting into nubs. Rings of wetness along the tabletop. Notebooks and pens, and aligned on either side of the clerk, radiating outward like a scene from the Last Supper, a dozen figures sat, partially silhouetted, facing the screen, printed transcripts in front of them, but all eyes on the screen, on the original diary itself, its spidery handwriting slanting down to the edge of the page: *I can find no way forward. . . .*

SHARDS OF BONE

IN 2-B, AN ASSEMBLAGE OF UNIFORMS had gathered, Japanese and American, military and prefectural police, dress whites and navy blues, caps parked on the table in front of them like cars in a lot. Among these uniforms were the loosened ties and disheveled presence of civilians as well: members of the British consulate, their attendance more pro forma than anything. The dead was one of theirs, after all, even if it was the Americans who had cornered him and the

Japanese who had pounced. The layers of paperwork and flurries of requisitions required to set up this trinational briefing represented a bureaucratic feat—or nightmare, depending on one's point of view. And all of it to catch one poor soul from the streets of Belfast.

"Would someone mind turning on the AC? If it's not a bother."

"It *is* on."

Can build a stealth bomber, but can't figure out how to cool down a room. The damp-faced Brits shifted in their seats, smiled in that uniquely ingratiating way of theirs, waited for the corporal clerk with pit-pony eyes to move on to the next slide.

The silence grew, became heavier. They were waiting for something to happen, but weren't quite sure what.

Within this Last Supper arrangement, a dark-haired woman, face drawn in broad strokes, sat in the Judas position, steadfast and stoic. No uniform, none was needed; she carried her authority in her deportment and unblinking gaze. Her name was Andrea Addario, an alliterative arrangement which often gave rise to jabs about Alcoholics Anonymous or, considering how rarely she drank, Assholes Anonymous, though not to her face. Never to her face. Lieutenant Addario was the highest-ranking member of Interpol's ICA division in the room, and this—ultimately—was their investigation.

Standing behind her, and the only person not seated, tall and thin and angry, was the banshee herself, arms crossed at having weathered a barrage of insults from a dead man. Pale hair. Skin so thin as to be translucent. Eyes a startling blue. As lead investigator, she should have been triumphant, at the very least satisfied, but Agent Rhodes was neither. If anything, her frown was more deeply etched than ever, thin lips bracketed by angry parentheses. Everyone in the room was aware of her presence. Painfully aware.

Farther down were Officers Gushiken and Kawaishi, whose work was now complete. Officer Gushiken was dying for a cigarette, almost literally. (The cancerous sac in his left lung would not make its presence known for several months.) Officer Kawaishi, younger and more attuned to international sensibilities, had had his name rendered in English on the business cards he presented at the start of the meeting: "River Stone," he said. "My name means River Stone," which had annoyed Officer Gushiken, because his name didn't translate as readily.

Gushiken was older, with softer angles and a rheumy gaze—and isn't it odd how life wears down the edges like pebbles polished in the tumbler of a tidal pool. They could have been before and after photos, Kawaishi and Gushiken: Before the Years Piled Up, and After. They were there to answer any questions that might arise about the Japanese side of the operation, but there were no questions that needed answering. Gushiken and Kawaishi had executed their manhunt admirably, with a poised precision that reflected well on their department. A language interpreter sat beside Officer Gushiken whispering words, which Gushiken ignored, as a point of pride primarily.

At the far end of the table was the person hosting this confab: Colonel Andrew J. McNair, flight commander, Second Wing, Kadena Air Base. Eyes too small for his face. The type of man who looked on life as a series of tactical maneuvers. The lowly corporal overseeing the slideshow was afraid of the colonel, even though the colonel himself went out of his way to present a portrait of patience and good manners. A false portrait, to be sure, but one he came by naturally; a touch of the Deep South hung about the colonel the way mist might cling to a landscape. Not quite a drawl, but the memory of. He turned with a slight tilt of the head. "Son?" he said.

"Yes, sir. Sorry, sir."

The clerk jumped to the next slide. The last pages of a man's life.

—peering over the edge of a precipice, into a greater emptiness. I have been chased to ground by an unrelenting agent of iniquity. The banshees of Ulster are small creatures; mine is a towering figure capable of straddling oceans. (With my earthly departure, I can only hope she will find solace in what is surely a loveless and lonely existence.) But I delay the inevitable. It is time for me to exit, stage left.

With sins unforgiven, I face the darkness alone, a single shell in the chamber. All those countless things I shall remember: the moribund plans and pre-emptive surrenders, the scotched schemes of lesser men, this torn and tortured world. A reliquary of broken dreams. A bone drawer of mistakes.

The past haunts us all, I suppose, with its usual regrets and small defeats, the might-have-beens and should-have-saids, the lovers we let slip from our embrace. And Agent Rhodes, what haunts you, late at night when the darkness comes?

The past fades like skywriting, dissolving into air: my mother at the Europa Hotel, laughing in the half light, a single sad moment of happiness in a life that was hardly worth the living. May God have mercy.

A MOMENT OF SILENCE, AND THEN—

"Fuck this."

It was Agent Rhodes.

She squeezed around the table, not caring who she jostled,

snatched up the plastic-encased journal with a lack of respect that caused the clerk to gasp. "This?" said Rhodes, holding up Exhibit A. "Pure unmitigated bullshit." She threw it back down onto the table with palpable disdain. It landed like a slap. "Fuck this and fuck him."

Lieutenant Addario, sharply: "Agent Rhodes—"

"It's not him."

"We have the body."

"You have *a* body."

"We recovered the artifacts."

"You recovered those artifacts he wanted you to find."

Lieutenant Addario took a steadying breath, brought her temper into check. "We have his journal, don't forget."

Suicide is always a form of confession. Agent Rhodes knew this, but she stood her ground nonetheless, stubborn, defiant, unreasonable. She gestured to the plastic-encased relic before them. "This? This isn't a confession. It's an elaborate prank arranged for his amusement. He's laughing at us."

"He's dead."

"No. He's not." She referred again to the journal. "That's a transcript, a spoken record. You can *hear* it. A narration. This was dictated."

"By whom? He was alone."

"And the wound?" Rhodes asked. "A shotgun—to the face? Really?"

"Not unheard of," Addario replied. "Unusual, but not unheard of. And again—if he didn't pull the trigger, who did?"

Rhodes ignored this, turned to the British representatives in the room instead, who were befuddled by what was going on. This was supposed to be a simple briefing, a formality, not a sparring session, certainly not a cross-examination. They'd been told the investigation was complete; they hadn't expected to walk into an internecine firing range.

"Sidewalks," said Rhodes. "In the UK you would say 'pavements,' am I right?"

"Well yes, but—"

"I take this text, run it through analytics, I fucking guarantee more anomalies will jump out. It'll be riddled with them."

Addario sighed. "He spent much of his time in the company of Americans."

"That's true," said one of the Brits. "A certain amount of vulgarisms are bound to have rubbed off. I know, I sometimes catch myself saying 'gas' instead of petrol." He started to laugh but no one joined in.

Agent Rhodes referred again to the Last Testament of Billy Moore wrapped in plastic in front of them.

"He refers to 'sins unforgiven.' No self-respecting Presbyterian would talk like that. They believe in predestination; one is born damned or saved, sin hardly enters into it. Those are Catholic sentiments."

Addario again, losing patience: "But he *isn't* self-respecting. That's the point. You're asking for theological consistency in a suicide document?"

"It's not a suicide document. This—this so-called confession tells us absolutely nothing. Except maybe what he *isn't*. The only thing we can say for sure is that he *isn't* from Belfast, he *isn't* Irish, he *didn't* grow up on Shankill Road, has probably never been to Belfast, wasn't raised in poverty by a sad-eyed single mother, poor baby. He no doubt had a doting father, lots of siblings, never found a one-pound coin in a ruined home, never met a mysterious figure in a tropical tavern. And I'd wager my badge that he can't whistle a tune to save his fucking life."

"So," said one of the Brits with a slight smirk. "We're looking for a non-Irish, non-poor, nameless, faceless someone who can't whistle." He'd meant it sarcastically, but Americans are always so inept at reading irony.

"Exactly," said Rhodes. "We have to flip this entire thing on end. Start with the assumption that everything he wrote was designed to mislead us, to send us off the scent. We went one way, he went another. Why on earth would anybody try to escape by fleeing to Hateruma? There are easier ways to get to Taiwan."

"He explained why," said Addario, not bothering to hide the weariness in her voice. "Weren't you paying attention? He made it very clear."

"A tiny speck at the very end? Hateruma Island? Really? He knew he would get caught, *wanted* to get caught. He wanted us to find that body, wanted us to find this journal. It was the only way to get us to call off the hunt. I was closing in, that part is true. I almost had him, I could taste it, the fear and finality, his arrogance dissolving. Panic setting in. So, what does he do? He leads us as far away from him as possible and then slips free. It was a feint, that's all it was. An act of misdirection."

The Japanese were confused. "Feint?" asked Officer Gushiken.

"Like in a magic show," said Rhodes. "You know, when they draw your attention to one hand, while they're palming a coin in the other."

The interpreter whispered in Officer Gushiken's ear, but this only confused the matter more. "He was—magician?"

"Not actually, no, of course not. What I'm saying—"

Lieutenant Addario interjected. "What Agent Rhodes is saying is that she does not accept the authenticity of this document. Agent Rhodes worked many years in our forgery investigation department. However"—she glared at her unruly protégé—"Agent Rhodes was dealing with art and archeological artifacts, not written documents, certainly not diaries."

"I can still smell a fake. Can smell it from here. It reeks of artifice." She turned to the clerk. "Go back," she said. "The previous page." The clerk complied, and Rhodes pointed to the screen. "Here, and here. And here. He repeatedly insults me. Why?"

What followed was a pause so pregnant one was tempted to boil water and gather up bedsheets. The Americans didn't want to say anything. The Brits looked everywhere except at her. The Japanese were conciliatory.

"Please, Miss Rhodes-san," said Officer Gushiken. "Do not feel sadly. He is very impolite, what he says about your appearance. I can assure you, on behalf of my colleagues, that we find you very—"

"Oh, for chrissake. It's not that my feelings were hurt. I don't give a shit *what* he says, I want to know why. Look, if you were writing your final confession, would you go out of your way to poke someone in the eye like that? It was a message. To me. He's mocking us, he's mocking me—not from beyond the grave, but from whatever beach he's currently lounging on, no doubt raising a toast to the linear predictability of law enforcement officials. We're investigators; we live and die by Occam's Razor. *The simplest solution is the preferred solution.* That's our greatest strength, and our greatest weakness. He's using that against us, presenting us with a perfectly packaged explanation, wrapped up with a bow—and we're using Occam's Razor to cut the ribbon. He's laughing at us!" She delivered that last line more sharply than she intended.

"I see," said Officer Gushiken, but of course he didn't. *These for-eigners, always flying off the handle. It must be exhausting to be a gaijin.* The interpreter whispered, "She's saying something about a razor."

Lieutenant Addario, voice curdling. "Ms. Rhodes has spent a great deal of time and energy on this case. She may be having trouble let-ting go. It happens sometimes." Addario was trying to get her agent to sit down through sheer will.

Rhodes chose not to notice. Instead, she stood in front of the pro-jector with the words from Billy Moore's journal tattooed across her stomach, facing her Last Supper as though it were a jury of her peers, hands knotted in front of her. She was fiddling with her empty ring finger, rubbing it, twisting back and forth as though turning a ring, a nervous habit that she was hardly aware of anymore. "He's not dead."

Lieutenant Addario, to the room. "Shall we move on?"

But Gaddy Rhodes wouldn't let it go, couldn't let it go. "If I'm wrong," she asked the room, "*if*—then why the second grave? An-swer me that."

No one could, because they didn't understand the question.

"Um, a second grave?" one of the Brits hazarded. (They were more or less interchangeable, these men from the consular office.)

Rhodes, twisting the missing ring on her finger more urgently now: "O-jina. The Island of the Dead." She turned to the clerk. "Bring up the map of Okinawa, the main island. The Motobu Penin-sula north of Naha."

When the contours appeared on the screen, Rhodes moved closer, pointed out a small drop of land offshore. "Here. Where the peninsula turns back. A small island, an islet really. Just a stepping-stone be-tween Yagaii-jima, here, and the main island of Okinawa, over here.

No one lives on O-jina, though its population numbers in the tens of thousands. It's a burial island."

"Dying to get in, I imagine," said one of the Brits brightly. But nobody appreciated the joke, and his smile fizzled. *Fuckin' Yanks.*

"O-jina used to be off-limits," Rhodes explained. "Almost taboo. A spooky place accessible only by small boat. But a few years ago, the prefectural government built a pair of bridges at either end, pinning O-jina in place, connecting it to the rest of the main island. Traffic now rumbles across the islet unimpeded. This has shortened driving times considerably, but it's also stirred up sleeping ghosts. At least, that's what the locals objected to—and were blithely ignored." She turned to the clerk. "Bring up image file O-JINA."

A photograph taken on the island was now flung onto the screen. A crowded venue, O-jina, replete with tombs and stone pillars, burial sites stacked this way and that, practically on top of each other at times. A village without people.

"Among the dead that live on this island are members of royal lineage. The main Kara Family tombs were located in the south, at Shuri Castle. These were destroyed by the American bombardment during the war, but the lesser outlying family graves escaped relatively unscathed, were left undisturbed. Until now. The pottery we recovered in Hateruma came from—"

She looked to the corporal, who was struggling to keep up. An expansive turtleback tomb, larger than those around it, appeared on the screen. The front had been split open.

"—this tomb. He went in here"—she pointed—"with no attempt to cover it up. The break-in was quickly discovered by the caretaker the next morning."

"Agent Rhodes, we're all familiar with the facts of the case."

"Whoever entered—"

"We know who entered."

"—was surpassingly slipshod in their approach. Pulled down some burial urns, threw a couple of them into a duffel bag, overturned a few more, and then left. It looks staged because it is."

Lieutenant Addario sighed. "He was misinformed, that's all. He was searching for a hidden cache that wasn't there. He says as much in his journal."

"He also crows about how methodical he is, how carefully he operates. Remember his poor Irish mother trying to hide the jelly beans? Such a sorrowful tale. This?" She gestured to the crime scene. "This is not the work of a methodical mind."

Rhodes nodded impatiently to the clerk, and the cave-like interior of the tomb now came up: broken pottery, shards of bone, a dirt floor with the stone walls illuminated by the flattening effects of a flashbulb. It smelled musty even from here.

"Certainly appears well looted, doesn't it?" said Rhodes. "But is it? Look. Here—and here. Several of the urns haven't even been opened. An Easter egg hunt would have been better executed. No. This wasn't someone plundering a royal grave, this was a ploy, nothing more. A shell game, except instead of shells, he used turtleback tombs. And the phone? What about the phone?"

"What phone?"

"His cell phone."

"He didn't have a cell phone," Addario said.

"That's my point. What happened to it?"

"The owner of the guesthouse said she heard him talking to

himself late at night and assumed he was on a call, but no one saw a cell phone. He may very well have been having a mental collapse at that point. Or perhaps he did have a phone, and he threw it off a cliff."

"Or maybe," said Rhodes, "someone took it."

The colonel gave Rhodes a faint approximation of a smile. "Is that Boston I hear?"

"Salem," she said. "I grew up just outside the city."

He nodded, satisfied, as though it confirmed some pet theory of his. "Salem," he said. "That's where they burned the witches, isn't it?"

"We didn't burn any witches in Salem," she said. "That's a myth."

He was genuinely surprised. "Is it?"

"We didn't burn them, we hanged them." She turned to the clerk. "Go to the next map."

A bird's-eye image of the Island of the Dead appeared.

Rhodes pointed to a spot on the other side of the island. "A second grave was looted over here. It's the burial site of a minor Okinawan family. No obvious royal connections. We might never have known about it, because, unlike the break-in at the first grave, there was some effort made to disguise this one."

The heavy stone that had covered the entrance of the second grave had been rolled back into place. Any footprints seem to have been swept clean.

"This break-in at the second grave was discovered only by chance, and several days after the fact, when the same grounds-keeper noticed that the vegetation out front had been disturbed. Even then, he wouldn't have thought anything of it except, with the royal Kara tomb desecrated earlier, he figured he'd better err on the side of caution and call someone. The prefectural police arrived and, sure enough, someone had been inside this tomb as well. No damage, but one of the urns had clearly been moved."

"Treasure?" asked the Brits hopefully. So far there was a decided lack of treasure in what had purportedly been a treasure hunt.

Officer Gushiken answered for Rhodes. "No treasure. Is very rare to have valuables buried in such a place. Is just bones. And sometimes—What is the word in English?" He leaned in to the interpreter, who whispered, "Mementos."

"Mementos," Officer Gushiken repeated. "Not valuable. Just mementos."

Lieutenant Addario tried to steer the conversation back on track. "We don't know that there is any connection between the two graves, and even if there is, Mr. Moore may simply have targeted the wrong tomb at the outset, recognized his error, and then moved on. As should we."

"But royal tombs are very distinct," said Rhodes. "You can't miss them. They're much grander in size. The royal one that was broken into had this image of a stylized insect above the entrance. Easily spotted."

"A firefly," said Officer Gushiken. "The insect. It is the Kara family mon—like a symbol. Very famous."

"Exactly. I can't imagine any self-respecting grave robber mistaking the tomb of a minor military family for that of Okinawa's royal line."

Lieutenant Addario said, "There's that word again. He *wasn't* self-respecting. He *wasn't* coolheaded. He was frantic. Perhaps this other grave was from an earlier scouting foray. Perhaps he was testing security, checking to see if it was doable."

The air-conditioning had finally kicked in. Their sweat had chilled like frost on the skin. Damp hair grew cold.

Addario sighed. "I think we're done here. Colonel?"

Protocol would dictate that he close the meeting. It was his base, after all. But the colonel looked at Rhodes, tilted his head as though trying to bring her into focus.

"You said 'military.' What did you mean by that?"

"Pardon?" said Rhodes.

"The second grave," the colonel replied. "You said it was the burial ground of a minor military family. How military? How minor?"

"That was, ah, actually it was Officer Gushiken and . . ." She stumbled over the other name, which pleased Officer Gushiken to no end.

"River Stone," Kawaishi offered helpfully. "My name means River Stone."

"They were the ones who looked into this."

River Stone flipped through his notes, happy to have something to contribute. "Yes. The second grave. It is listed in cemetery records as belonging to the Matsuda family. They were traditionally merchants. But a separate family line—the Ono-Isu—are also in this grave. Their bones, I mean. The Ono-Isu were a samurai family. A clan, I think you'd say? Retainers to the Kara. The Ono-Isu have a long tradition of military service. The current head of the family is an officer with the National Defense Force, stationed in Sapporo, I believe." He looked to his superior for confirmation even though he knew this was correct. Gushiken nodded his assent.

"You've contacted the family?" asked the colonel.

"Yes. But as far as we know, no items were removed from this tomb. We are still waiting for confirmation on that."

"And," Officer Gushiken said, "any items inside would not be of value."

"Oh. Right," said the colonel. "You mentioned that. Just mementos. What kind exactly? Are y'all talking about family photos and such? Medals maybe?"

The two police officers exchanged looks. Several members of the Ono-Isu had been tried as war criminals after the Japanese surrendered in 1945.

"Maybe," said River Stone.

But Officer Gushiken was firm. He was from Okinawa, after all. "No," he said. "No medals in this grave. Not valuable like that. Just"—he checked the word again—"mementos."

"From the war?" asked the colonel.

"Maybe."

Colonel McNair leaned back, smiled a crooked smile. It was almost a grin. "Now, isn't that something? Never would'a thought'a such a thing. Never would've entered my brain."

They assumed the colonel was charmed by Okinawan rituals. And he was—though not quite in the way they imagined. If the room had stopped breathing, if they had killed the AC and listened carefully to the underlying silence, they might have caught the faint voice of a dead man reaching out to them. The colonel's smile widened, and now it really was a grin. The dead are more alive than we realize.

Lieutenant Addario closed the file in front of her. "If it's all right with everyone, I would move that we adjourn."

The colonel nodded absentmindedly, waved his hand in a vague motion of agreement. But Rhodes stopped them.

"I'm not done."

Lieutenant Addario leveled a steady gaze at her agent. "Yes. You are."

People had begun gathering up papers, realigning caps and collars, cricking necks and suppressing yawns that were yearning to be released.

"Wait!" Gaddy Rhodes turned, wild-eyed, on Addario. "What about the egg?"

The egg?

"The Fabergé egg. Seventeen million dollars."

"Oh, for god's sake." Addario rolled her eyes, almost audibly. "Agent Rhodes, this is neither the time nor the—"

But Rhodes had outflanked her. The colonel lowered his haunches back onto his seat, gestured for her to continue. She slid a memory stick across the table to the clerk. "Can you bring up the main file? The one marked FINDER."

THE BIRTH OF ROCK AND ROLL

IS WELL PAST TEN WHEN BILLY calls, texts it really, five days gone and only this, a terse reply, not like Billy at all, what with him so garrulous and full of boisterous proclamation like the bog Irish mick he is, and only three words and a measly question mark for his old pal peachy:

Who is this?

> Ya feckin' wanker, who do you think, its peachy innit,
> wondering if youse are back and full of riches like
> you promised or have you forgotten yer old friend now
> that yer a rich twat sittin arse friendly on a bag of
> cash somewhere and are ye not back in oc yet?

OC?

> Okinawa city you twat. What the feck is up with you,
> has all that loot you was promised gone to your huge
> irish head, and when are ya goan t'hoist a pint and
> spin me the tales of billys adventures and how many
> armenian hookers and bags of blow can we get for
> what the wee man paid you? Rough estimate like.

A long pause, splintered with ice.

Let's meet.

> Of course you wanker, lets meet, that's the hole entire
> point innit, to meet and toast billys luck and peachys
> good fortune at knowing youse, which never thought
> id say, you being a layabout and wastrel of the first
> order as most of you belfast boys are. When?

Tonight.

> There ye go! Was that so hard billy boy, usual place
> then, same table if we can get it by the window,

where last I saw you in thet rockabilly place past
the night market out by ginjos pachinko, and you
are buyin you feckin wanker, you are buyin.

I will be waiting.

THE BALLAD OF BILLY AND PEACHY began at the Peace Love Rock Festival in Naha City—or was it the Peaceful Love Festival? The posters didn't always agree. A pair of hardscrabble Ulstermen crossing paths on a tropical isle? A wonderful confluence of fortune, the two of them pooling their acumen and pimping their wares together like that. It had the feeling of something preordained.

Up in Okinawa City, with its US bases and yakuza feuds, it was the Wild West. So said Billy, who had never been to the American West, who had never been to America, but who understood appetites and the festering desires they whetted, all those itches that needed scratching, and that, my friend, was universal.

Billy and Peachy talked themselves into an alternate world as they soaked their bodies in the salubrious Japanese waters and egg-odored baths. Serpent gods and seahorses. The nonchalant nihilism of Buddhist teachings. And Billy always deep in books, as though there were a lost piece of him somewhere in those pages. "It's the wheel of karma, y'see." And oh his eyes would shine.

Okinawa was a giant pachinko board, silver balls cascading into a din of light, and here was Billy and Peachy in a state of exultation, their euphoria fueled as much by a future they could see taking shape in front of them as by any methamphetamine in their bloodstream, dreams wheeling out of control. Burner phones. Midnight rendezvouses. Untraceable calls. Conversations garnished with fabled confidences and whispered asides. And now, wouldn't you know it but Billy had hit the jackpot. He had whispered in Peachy's ear, scarce heard above the tub-thumping rockabilly tunes, "I'm not t'say a thing, but tha' wee man over there, in the corner? *Don't look!* I just said, Don't look. Didn't I just say? Anyways. Has a proposition for me, so he does." *And you can trust him?* "Aye. An Ulsterman, same as us. Lost his accent some-where along the way, but still of proper Nord Iron stock." *Not some Falls Road Fenian feck, surely?* "Nah. Kicks the football with the cor-rect boot, so he does."

Peachy only ever saw the wee man that one time. It was dark and noisy in the rockabilly joint near the market by the corner past Ginjo's pachinko, but even then, even as fleeting as that encounter had been, Peachy knew he was in the presence of something. Probably greatness.

A man of his word, that's what he tells Billy, and Billy believes him. "Will come back rich," Billy assures Peachy. "It's a done deal like." So off he fecks to Shangri-La, our Billy. "Not a word of con-tact till I am back, Peachy. Not a word. Y'unnerstand? Not a word." Opaque intentions enshrouded in guile, and Peachy promising on his mother's future grave (god forbid) that he wouldn't say to any'n. But Peachy was Peachy and he couldn't help himself. Easily excitable and lacking in grace. There was a restlessness in him, born of Sandy Row bonfires and kings on white horses. Exiles in our own home, us Prods. Shit upon from all sides and now, here it was, the future they'd dreamed for so long, suddenly within grasp. And now, Billy's back and it's time to celebrate.

Peachy tugged on his jean jacket, stepped out . . . and was swal-lowed by the night.

• • •

THE PACHINKO PINBALL OF OKINAWA CITY was firing wilder than ever. A ricochet of lights, streets thick with sounds, swimming with humidity. The ripple and wave of neon billboards, the traffic lights like an orchestral conductor. The cars stop and go, stop and go. Girls on long legs, like young deer. Throaty-voiced office ladies pealing by in cascades of laughter. Cries of *"Mensore!"* shouted in the noodle shops as customers entered, punching their way through the hanging half curtains.

Alleyways radiating outward, haphazardly at times, with the narrow lanes circling back as though they'd forgotten something. Chinese characters, red and orange like spatters of paint. The darker corners of a watery world. Hooded doorways littered with louche young men of dubious intent who watched Peachy thread his way through, gave haughty nods as he passed. Here, clearly, was a man on the cadge. A tight-permed thug sucked on a cigarette, grinned at Peachy as he passed, let the smoke leak through his teeth.

Peachy was among his own now, the tattered and the torn, the slipshod and the shoddy, and by the time he reached the end of the alley, he had acquired a tout of his own, a doughy bow-tied man who clung to Peachy like a barnacle on a prow. "Piss show," he hissed. Touts, unmovable, and women procurable. Peachy wrestled himself free. *"Dah-meh,"* he said. Leave me alone.

"You like girl? You like boy?" whispered another tout as he passed. "Filipina, very pretty."

"Dah-meh, all of youse."

Peachy could hear the distant thrum of taiko drums. A festival was mustering somewhere in the city. There was always a festival mustering. Summer in Okinawa was one long dance.

Past a *yakiniku* restaurant, its street-front grates rolled back to let air through, slabs of beef bleeding pink, US personnel boisterous and unbridled, guffaw and counterguffaw, muscular boys calling out for beer like they were summoning a medic. "Biiru, *koo-da-sigh!*" Bottles of Orion arriving as if on a treadmill, and Peachy spotting some of his customers in among the throng as he pushed past. "More *biiru!*"

The street widened and Peachy waded into a sea of food stalls. The sound of the festival grew louder, and pork knuckles were simmering in hot pots. Pig ears with vinegar and sliced cucumber. Vendors calling out. Purple sweet potatoes, roasted hot, served split and steaming. Fermented tofu steeped in awamori liquor, as thickly rendered as cheese. Paper lanterns that bobbed and bowed on the night wind.

The twang of Okinawan banjos, the slow building thunder of taiko drums, the *hachimaki* headbands twisted over brows, dancers turning, two steps forward, one step back, voices shrill and relentless. He could see Ginjo's Silver Castle pachinko lit up in diva dressing room light bulbs, but his route was blocked by the festival that was now unraveling like a banner down the main streets. Rows of women, sorted by age, moved past in a procession of yellow and blues, Okinawa kimonos, so much more vibrant than the subdued colors one sees on the Japanese mainland. These were the last days of Obon, the Festival of the Dead, and the *eisa* dancers were out in full force. It reminded Peachy of the Glorious Twelfth, of flutes and Lambeg drums beating out their lonely defiance. They, too, honored the dead.

Obon was a lively event, all things considered, and the spirits of the departing ancestors were being sent off with a raucous farewell. *And how to separate the dancer from the dance?* Billy had asked Peachy that once in a drug-fevered haze, and Peachy had laughed it off—he was always too deep for his own good, our Billy—but now Peachy could almost see it, what Billy was referring to, the shadow world behind the forms.

Then came the dragons.

There were four of them, slumbering in the street. Dragons green and dragons black, dragons red and gilded with gold. Shaggy bodies, chests heaving in fitful dreams, eyes rolled back and closed. Sleeping dragons must first be roused, and female dancers prodded them with tinny cymbals and yelping shouts. They woke with angry snaps, came to life, charged the crowds, stomped, shook their manes to and fro, rose and dropped to the beat of their tormentors.

Dragons, once woken, are hard to contain. On older maps of uncharted seas, sailors would warn each other on the edge of the page: *Here be dragons*. Perhaps it was Okinawa that the sailors were warning about. So thought Peachy as he walked with strange monsters down the street. He veered left. Narrow steps, leading to a basement jazz club. Cutting through a bedlam backbeat, smoke saturated, bodies swaying, loose limbed and dreamlike in the isolation that only loud music allows. *The birth of the cool.* Figures moved, became detached, and someone was following him and he spun around, but there were only silhouettes and the music of Miles Davis. He was getting jumpy.

Out the back, up the stairs and into an alley. Oily puddles and naked light bulbs, and again that feeling of being followed, and again he turned, and again no one was there. Peachy hurried on, panic rising.

Over a rusting pedestrian bridge, clattering down the stairs and then into the rockabilly club where Billy would be waiting for him, except that he wasn't, and Peachy worming his way through the crowd, surveying the room as the Japanese DJ played Murasaki's "Double Dealing Woman." This was where Japanese rock and roll was born, in this city, in these streets, a fusion of island rhythms and American conventions, of Okinawan dialects and African echoes. Next on the turntable was Condition Green, "Life of Change." They were playing the oldies tonight, and Peachy waved for a beer, but was too anxious to drink. *Mixed up. Life of Change. And where the feck is Billy?*

Peachy tried to wait, patient like, but his leg was restless and it bounced around nervously and his mind couldn't sit still either. Something was wrong. Seriously wrong. *Have t'get outta here.*

Back on the street, not sure what to do.

Into the mayhem of a night market, bingata cloth and lacquerware with mother-of-pearl inlays. An American collector was holding up a piece for his wife to admire. "Okinawan lacquer, honey! Finest in the world. And it only grows more valuable with age."

Like wine, thought Peachy. Like rock and roll. Like friendship.

Beyond the lacquer, an oilier market, sheaved with fish, their gaping mouths caught in a permanent surprise. No one ever expects the hook or the net. Rubber-aproned matrons, hosing down the pavement. Parrot fish and scarlet octopi. Fat-bellied tuna. Medusa-like squid, tentacles slopping over the sides of their trays, looking alive even in death. And in the next alley, a fish-fed cat and a chained-down dog squared off in competing tails: the curled Akita question mark of the dog, the raised tail and puckered anus exclamation point of the cat. A hiss, a single bronchial woof—and the cat bolts.

And again Peachy spins around, and again there is no one there. Not Billy, not anyone.

Where did'ja go, y'fecker?

Was that Shankill Road idjit confused, did he go to the saloon instead? Peachy tried to check his texts, but now his phone was gone. *Jaysus feck.* He looked around in case he'd dropped it, but it could have been anywhere. A cheap pay-as-you go burner, but still. *Feckin' hell.*

There was nothing to do now but trudge all the way to the First Chance, Last Chance Saloon, so named because it was at the head of Gate 2 Street, practically at the doorstep of the US military base. This saloon was where American servicemen first stopped when they headed out for a night on the town, and the last place they visited on their way back. Which is to say, the First Chance, Last Chance featured only two levels of inebriation: fresh faced and full blown. The sober and the wrecked. There were no in-betweens in the First Chance, Last Chance Saloon. *Like life, my friend, like life*, Billy had said. *Go all in, or feck off.*

As Peachy walked up Gate 2 Street, the Kadena Air Base grew closer; he could see the searchlights pointed heavenward as though searching for Luftwaffe formations. Some of the bars along the way had signs posted on the door, in English: NO FOREIGNERS ALLOWED. Meaning no US personnel, meaning servicemen, meaning Peachy's main clientele. But America is everywhere. In the scrum of soldiers bullying their way down the street, in the loud voice of Japanese Yankee boys, hair slicked back, in the aggressive revving of Harley Davidsons slow-crawling down the street, perpetually on the lurk.

He angled his way into the saloon, pummeled by voices and braying laughter, the sudden shiv of profanity. "Peachy!" shouts an American male. "Long time!" "Have y'seen Billy?" he shouts back. "Who? Your buddy? No. Come have a drink." But Peachy pushes past.

A Japanese band is playing hurtin' songs. *We feature both kinds of music*, the barkeep joked: *country* and *western*. Songs of love and love's departure. Peachy waits, but no point to it. That fecker Billy is somewhere else, not here, and Peachy, feeling the walls closing in, escapes, heads back outside, into cooler air and the open arena of the street.

Kimonos are coming home, faces flushed and smiling. Parents are herding their children down the street. Kids in their summer clothes. Drummers lugging suddenly heavy taiko. The elation that comes with the end of any festival. Dragons, placated. Ancestral ghosts, entertained and sent off. Peachy crosses the street against a surging and indifferent tide, and now, coming toward him—a face both familiar and forgettable. Where has he seen that face before? This is what he thinks as they pass, and their eyes meet, and there it is: recognition, and a sting in Peachy's thigh. Peachy turns, angrily, is about to say something, when he sees the wee man look back at him, dissolves into the crowd, and Peachy, confused and in pain, can feel the lights change, the sidewalk begin to tilt.

He almost makes it to the other side before he collapses.

THE CATALOG OF LOST THINGS

HERE, THEN, WAS THE INFORMATION Agent Rhodes presented, her dissertation in a sense, ten years in the making, a PowerPoint parade of objects, once lost, now found, complete with timelines cross-referenced by date and location and mad leaps in conjecture.

It began with an image of polished perfection: an alabaster sphere, decorated to look like a miniature royal carriage pulled by an intricately rendered angel, a bejeweled egg that had opened up to reveal the finely crafted bronze filigree of an ornamental clock, hiding inside.

CASE #1: THE LOST FABERGÉ EGGS

"Easter, 1885: Russia's imperial family, the Romanovs, commission a series of decorative eggs from the House of Fabergé to be given as gifts, one-of-a-kind creations, each with a surprise inside waiting to be found. It might be a ruby pendant or a diamond-encased manicure set, a miniature tiara or a clockwork hen. Breathtaking creations. Elaborate. Opulent to the point of garish. Playful and intimate and magnificent, all at the same time. These annual Imperial Easter eggs symbolized the very best and the very worst of royal affluence. It was the final glory of a dying star. In 1918, the Romanov family, unceremoniously deposed, were lined up in a basement and shot by their Communist captors. The Fabergé eggs were confiscated. Some were sold off by the Bolsheviks' cash-strapped regime, others were put on display at the Kremlin as examples of bourgeois decadence, others still were filched and smuggled out of the country. Of the fifty eggs that Fabergé created for the czar and his family, forty-two are accounted for. Eight are missing. Those missing eggs have a combined value of more than $140 million. None has ever been recovered. Until now. Two years ago, this very egg—the one you're looking at, Cherub and Chariot—surfaced in Ukraine. Long thought lost, Cherub and Chariot was discovered inside a strongbox in the manor of a recently ousted oligarch. The egg was then flown under armed guard to Saint Petersburg, where it was verified as authentic, and now sits in a place of pride in the Hermitage museum. How it came to be in the oligarch's possession is less clear. The egg's provenance, its chain of ownership, is murky at best."

"Why not just ask him?" said one of the Brits. "The oligarch who owned it."

"Because, unfortunately, said oligarch is currently lying in a radioactive grave. He fell ill during the trial, you see. A bad case of Putin-was-pissed. We have since learned that the deceased man had surreptitiously purchased Cherub and Chariot years before, through a brokerage firm in Amsterdam. He paid $17 million for it. Today, it is worth almost double that amount. You would think tracking a large lump-sum payment such as that would be easy—after all, we have the name of the brokerage firm, TLT Limited. But our investigation quickly turned into a maze of mirrors. The firm was a shell—inside a shell, inside another shell. The financial equivalent of a Russian nesting doll. The original payment had long since disappeared into an offshore account in Panama, and TLT had likewise disappeared into a puff of air."

"But—where is the crime in that?"

"We believe that whoever sold this Fabergé egg to our now-deceased oligarch used that money to fund his later activities. We believe everything that follows came from this initial windfall."

"Not we," said Addario. *"You."*

Agent Rhodes advanced to the next slide.

CASE #2: MUHAMMAD ALI'S GOLD MEDAL

"Louisville, 1960: A young Olympian by the name of Cassius Clay returns to his hometown, jubilant. He has just won a gold medal in boxing at the Rome Games, for his country, has been feted and celebrated abroad and is now back in the US of A. But nothing has changed. The bigotry hasn't abated—if anything, it's gotten worse—and after being refused service at a restaurant, he flings his gold medal into the Ohio River in disgust and walks away. Four years later, Cassius Clay would become heavyweight champion of the world and would change his name to Ali. His gold medal would sit in the muck at the bottom of the Ohio River for more than forty years. Enter TLT Shipping and Dredging. Through a series of what turned out to be dubious contracts and forged permits, TLT begins dredging the river, ostensibly as an aid for increased traffic along the Ohio. Soon after, coincidentally, I'm sure, Muhammad Ali's gold medal appears at an elite auction house. You see, Ali had never flung his gold medal into the Ohio River. He'd lost it during his early years bouncing from place to place and had been too embarrassed to admit it, so he concocted a story of righteous anger. The medal itself had turned up in an attic of unclaimed goods, its fortuitous discovery confirmed by witnesses and fully notarized. No one thought to wonder whether the medal hadn't already been discovered and then simply planted there in order to be found. *Storage Wars* on steroids."

"Why go through all that trouble? If they rescued it from the river, why not admit it?"

"Because the city would've had dibs on it. That medal sold for $1.7 million at open auction. A Vegas casino owner, I believe. Remember, too, that the city of Louisville had covered the cost of dredging as an economic incentive. If they realized they'd been duped into footing the bill for what was, in essence, a private salvage operation, there would have been lawsuits flying in every direction. As it was, wouldn't you know it, but TLT Shipping and Dredging shut down just before the medal reappeared. The rusted hulk of their dredging operation is still standing knee deep in the Ohio River, even now."

The black-and-white image of an African drum appeared, dark-sheened wood, a taut cowhide skin.

CASE #3: THE KALINGA DRUM

"You are looking at the dynastic symbol of Tutsi royalty in Rwanda. An emblem of authority, the Kalinga drum served in much the same role as"—she turned to the Japanese officers—"the imperial jewel, sword, and mirror of the Emperor, or"—to the Brits now—"the way that the throne of Westminster represents Britain's royal line, or"— to Colonel McNair—"the way the Declaration of Independence represents American sovereignty. The Kalinga drum had been handed down for four hundred years. It was traditionally adorned with the testicles of the king's defeated enemies."

The Brits snorted at this, because of course they did.

"When the last Tutsi king of Rwanda was toppled by the Hutu majority in 1959, the Kalinga drum was locked away, deep in the presidential vaults. Most people assumed the drum had been destroyed, in much the same way the Romanov family was wiped out—to erase the past. But even the most vocal of Rwanda's anti-Tutsi hardliners lacked the courage to destroy an object imbued with such power."

Another image came forward. It was a snapshot from a nightmare: human skulls. Thousands upon thousands of human skulls, stacked in rows, stretching back into infinity.

"The Rwanda genocide. In 1994, this small central African nation collapsed into bloodshed and madness. Under the ethnically obsessed ideology of Hutu Power, the ruling regime unleashed a second apocalypse aimed at wiping out the nation's Tutsi population once and for all. One million people died in the span of one hundred days, the most efficient genocide in human history; even the Nazis didn't reach a killing rate such as they did in Rwanda. And it was an intimate genocide as well. The victims were murdered by their neighbors and in-laws, friends and coworkers, chopped down with machetes, chased into swamps, burnt out of the fields they'd been hiding in. When Rwanda's Hutu Power regime was finally pushed out by an army of Tutsi rebels, the genocidaires fled across the border into eastern Congo, where they set up a murderous government-in-exile. They brought with them Rwanda's entire national reserve of gold and all its foreign currency. They'd looted the treasury, leaving their country in ruins as they departed. They also brought with them the royal drum."

Another image: a mud-splattered refugee camp, drooping with blue tarps and small fires, packed with people ragged and shell-shocked.

"The refugee camps in eastern Congo soon disintegrated into anarchy and mob rule, as UN workers and Oxfam volunteers tried to sort the genocidaires from the real refugees. In the middle of this suppurating wound, a small international NGO set up camp, ostensibly to distribute water and blankets: TLT Ministries. By the time they left, a dozen people had been killed and the Kalinga drum had been recovered. It was an operation that spun out of control. TLT mercenaries attacked, the Presidential Guard returned fire, and the civilians were caught in the crossfire, as civilians always are. But what are a dozen lives against a million? The drum was spirited away and was later sold back to the current Tutsi-led government of Rwanda for an undisclosed amount. Make no mistake," said Rhodes, "there is a body count associated with these objects. A record dealer in Memphis tried to get cute with an early recording of 'Hound Dog.' He ended up floating facedown in a hotel pool. A stamp collector in Madrid was turned inside out over a forged One-Cent Magenta. An antiquities dealer we spoke with in Vatican City later had his tongue cut out. This isn't a treasure hunt. This is a dark river. Massive criminal interests are involved, millions of undeclared dollars are moving across international borders with impunity. It's not fun and games, it's not hide-and-seek, it's not cat and mouse. This is a hyena loose among the wildebeest."

Colonel McNair leaned forward. "You're saying a single person was responsible for—all of this?"

"I am. We almost had him, too, in Vatican City, but he . . . Well, he vanished. We got a lucky break in the Congo, though. This was back when I first started out, a junior officer, still in training. I wasn't directly involved in that operation, but I can tell you, during the bloodshed in Rwanda and Congo, our Africa bureau received its first, and so far only, physical description of the person in question. It came to us from a doctor with Oxfam who'd set up her clinic right next to TLT. She only ever saw him in the dark, and she understandably had other things on her mind, but she described the small man as quiet, unassuming, well mannered, Caucasian, vaguely unspecific accent, nondescript features."

"So . . . not a description," said one of the Brits. "More a lack of description."

"Yes, but using that we can eliminate who he isn't." It was like a round of Guess Who? the board game where you jettison suspects until you narrow it down to a single face. "Not female, not black, nor Asian, not old, nor physically imposing. That is who was in the Congo. That is who we are hunting. A white male, diminutive stature, uncertain nationality."

The Brits were unconvinced. "We can certainly see the seriousness of this. Murder, perhaps. Theft, certainly. But these still seem more like local matters."

Rhodes advanced to the next slide: a violin, deeply adored. One could see the patina of care, the generations of love involved. It glowed with it.

"A Stradivarius," said Rhodes. "Protected under the World Heritage Act. Would that be a local matter?"

CASE #4: THE STOLEN STRADIVARIUS

"Italian violin maker Antonio Stradivari, born 1644, died 1737, left behind a legacy that is unsurpassed. He crafted the most prized musical instruments the world has ever known, famed for their lush sounds and pitch-perfect notes, coveted for their artistry, their history, their enduring and deserved fame. When they disappear, they disappear forever."

Officer Gushiken frowned his approval. "Very famous," he said. Even he, who had no interest in classical music—he preferred Okinawan rock and roll—knew of Stradivarius.

Rhodes brought up another slide of another violin.

"In 1995, thieves broke into the home of ninety-one-year-old violinist Erika Morini as she lay dying alone in her Paris flat and stole the Stradivarius she had owned since her youth. Made in 1727, it was valued at $3 million. Never recovered." Rhodes brought up a list of others:

The Karpilowsky Stradivarius (1712): stolen 1953

The Arnes Stradivarius (1734): stolen 1981

The Colossus Stradivarius (1714): stolen 1998

The King Maximilian Stradivarius (1709): stolen 1999

The Le Maurien Stradivarius (1714): stolen 2002

"Combined value: in excess of $18 million. None has ever been recovered."

One of the Brits tried to laugh it off. "So? Someone is collecting Stradivariuses. Surely you're not suggesting our man Billy from Belfast has been stealing priceless violins for more than fifty years. Tricky that, considering he wasn't even born in 1953."

"That's not what I'm saying. Not at all." She pointed to the screen. "None of these violins ever resurfaced. They were taken as objects of art, and no doubt sit in lonely vaults, are played late at night when no one is listening. You can't resell any of these, they're too renowned, too well known. You can't put a $2 million stolen Stradivarius up for auction. Interpol would be all over you."

"So why are we——?"

"Last summer, violinist Min-Jin Kym stopped for a sandwich at a London train station. In the moment it took for her to put her case down to take out her wallet, her violin was lifted. A 1696 Stradivarius valued at $1.8 million—*gone*. The pair of thieves who took it clearly had no idea of what they had on their hands, because they first tried to sell it on the black market for $167. They were caught and convicted, but the violin had vanished. Two months later, an East End Cockney moneyman took a nasty stumble and fell out of a six-floor window. Tragic accident. He was, coincidentally, I'm sure, a known associate of certain petty thieves who haunted the rail stations of London, but any connection to the stolen violin is only conjecture, I'm afraid. They had to scrape him off the pavements with a spatula. Soon after, the violin reappeared. A nameless person contacted the London Met, gave them the good news: he had Min-Jin's lost violin. All he was asking for was a finder's fee of $2.5 million. It wasn't a ransom, you see, it was a reward—albeit one he set himself. When they balked, he replied, sympathetically, 'I understand. If it is hard to come up with such a large amount all at once, why don't I sell it back to you piece by piece?' " Agent Rhodes paused for full effect. "They paid."

"Billy Moore was a bottom feeder. I don't see how—"

"Exactly my point. Recovering that violin took resources. It took discipline, it took finesse, and it took skill. Qualities in which poor, faceless Billy was sorely lacking. Ah, but this time, when the Met paid its 'finder's fee'—a ransom, by any other name—we were waiting. I knew how he worked, had already zeroed in on an innocuous accounting firm called, yes, TLT Holdings. The $2.5 million was deposited into a time-release account and the stolen Stradivarius was returned, but just as the money was about to be transferred, we made our move, froze the account, recovered the ransom."

Even the Brits were impressed—and Brits are impressed by very little. "So, you got back the violin *and* the money?"

"We did, but TLT was scrubbed off the face of the earth, for good this time. Must have realized we were tracking him. He wasn't quite as invisible as he imagined himself to be. He must have panicked, gone dark. The entire network of companies he'd been using vanished overnight. But I wasn't fooled, not for a moment. I sat, and I waited—and not for long. When news of a Gutenberg Bible from Nagasaki surfaced, I knew it was him. He was now operating in Asia, probably somewhere more lawless and less surveilled than Japan, at first anyway. Macao or Taipei perhaps. We recovered the Nagasaki Bible, retrieved the terra-cotta Buddha. Came within a heartbeat of catching him, as well. We were closing in."

"Did you ever figure out what TLT stands for?" Brits were suckers for a good puzzle.

"Oh, that? Yes, I think so." She skipped ahead a few images. A Chinese carving of a jade toad appeared. Elegantly ugly, a squat creature, sitting on its haunches, peering up at the world, looking like the sort of thing one found in thrift-store bargain bins and tacky aunt's apartments.

"Not all of his finds are million-dollar deals," said Rhodes. "The item you're looking at was valued at $128,000. In this case, though, he appears to have changed his mind. This one, he kept for himself."

"He kept it? Why?"

"Honestly? I think he just liked it. I think it spoke to him. He'd been hired by a realtor in Hong Kong to retrieve a family heirloom gone missing in British Columbia a hundred years before. Pure jade, carved by a master artisan. The realtor's great-great-uncle had taken it with him when he went to seek his fortune in the New World. Ended up as a coolie on the railroad, dangling over granite cliffs, setting gunpowder charges as they blasted a line through the Rocky Mountains. Sold it at some point, probably for pennies. Died in a cave-in soon after, a common fate of Chinese workers in the 1880s, unfortunately. We believe this jade carving was recovered from a curio shop in Revelstoke, a small town in the interior that was on the original rail line. No description of the person who purchased it, but whoever it was paid five dollars for it."

"We don't know that this buyer is the same person," Addario said. "Again, this is just conjecture on Agent Rhodes's part."

"So, what're we lookin' at?" asked Colonel McNair, peering with his small eyes at the image on the screen. "A frog of some sort?"

"A mythical creature. The elusive three-legged toad. Highly sought after, never found. In Chinese cosmology, it's a symbol of the unattainable." A fleshy tripod carved in jade.

The Japanese counted the legs. She was correct. There were only three.

The room was puzzled. Gaddy elaborated. "Don't you see? It's what he does. He obtains the unattainable. I think maybe it's his emblem. I think that's what the TLT stands for. *Three-Legged Toads.*"

"TLT could be anything," Addario said, cutting in. "Random letters, obscure family initials. It could stand for Totally Legitimate Transactions. This is all conjecture, remember."

Agent Rhodes might yet have swayed them—it was improbable, but fascinating, this idea that Billy Moore was just a shadow cast by a shadow. Who doesn't love a good mystery? But when Rhodes brought up The Map, that was the end. She didn't often show The Map to other people; it was a work in progress, after all, but she was so close to sealing the deal that she pushed on recklessly. This was a miscalculation, and at some level she sensed it, began speaking more and more rapidly, words tumbling into each other, almost out of breath, trying to tie everything together while Lieutenant Addario sat back, let her run with it. When your opponent is defeating themselves, don't get in their way. It was one of the first laws of Sun Tzu, or perhaps General Patton.

"Occam's Razor—the principle that the simplest solution is the correct one—would suggest that these are unrelated items and that Billy Moore died alone on a small island by his own hand, but if we look carefully, we can see patterns. Patterns connecting these various sites where the objects were uncovered, together with the probable locations of where they were lost and the financial conduits used to sell them."

The Map was a mess. A cat's cradle of such far-flung locales as Nagasaki and North Dakota, Mason City and the Congo. Lines everywhere, from Zanzibar to Zurich, Cancun to Istanbul, Helsinki to Hateruma. Several cities had been circled; others had been crossed out vigorously. Dotted lines represented possible flight paths; dashed lines represented bank transactions; wavy lines, ground transportation routes. None of it made much sense.

"Now, I know—I know what you're thinking, you're thinking most conspiracies aren't true, but this isn't a *conspiracy*, this is a parallel world, and this map, this map is just a glimpse inside, a peek behind the curtain. We can be one-eyed kings in the Land of the Blind, if we just open our eye—our other eye—the one that isn't blind, and see everything, because it's all here in front of us, most of it anyway, the key parts. We just have to *look*, it's like—it's like one of those 3-D pictures that only becomes visible when you squint."

She took a breath, looked around her. The Last Supper stared back with impatience, bemusement, concern. She'd lost them, and she knew it. The Americans were impatient, the Brits bemused, the Japanese clearly worried for her mental health. A collective realization had occurred; the entire room was suddenly aware that they were in the presence of a crazy person.

A long silence.

"Agent Rhodes? A word, if I may. Outside."

IT WAS LIKE BEING SUMMONED INTO the hallway by the school principal. Rhodes could feel her anger swell like a blister, filling with blood. "You're sabotaging me. Every step of the way."

"You're sabotaging yourself," said Addario. "You don't need any help from me."

"What about the Buddha's head, or the chess piece, or the shards of pottery or—or any of the other items we recovered?"

"Those will be returned to their rightful owners."

"But we can use those, lure him in, set a trap."

"Gaddy, this has to stop."

She waved a contemptuous hand toward the meeting room door. "Don't tell me you believe that BS. An open journal lying beside a staged suicide, a sob story about a gullible dupe seduced by the agents of a nefarious international organization. 'A nefarious organization.' Give me a break."

"We're Interpol. We deal with nefarious international organizations all the time. It's kind of what we do."

"There is no organization. *He* is the organization."

"*He* is dead. We know his name, we know who he was, we even have his passport, for Christ's sake. The British consul has confirmed his identity: William Moore, formerly of Belfast. Shankill Road. Single mother. It all lines up. DNA confirms it. As for those other fanciful thefts, the Nagasaki Bible and the Buddha's head, we can't find any connection between those and Mr. Moore whatsoever. You launched a trilateral raid, and for what? To recover a few pieces of broken pottery? Some shrink-wrapped blocks of US currency? There was no criminal network involved. Just a desperate man lugging a heavy bag."

"And where do you think that money came from? There was nothing in those tombs to justify the amount of cash we recovered. You know that."

"The only thing I know is that Mr. Moore is dead, the file is closed, and I have some serious explaining to do. Agent Rhodes, all you may have succeeded in doing is hounding a man to death."

"I chased him into a corner. I wasn't the one who pulled the trigger."

"No one will miss Billy Moore. That much is true. He wasn't exactly a paragon of virtue. There was a warrant out for his arrest in Bangkok, did you know that, Agent Rhodes? Procuring under-aged girls, meth, some penny-ante attempts at extortion. He was a low-level pimp and a small-time dealer. Hardly a criminal master-mind."

"And yet," said Rhodes, "he never mentioned any of that in his journal—Thailand, I mean. Odd, don't you think? If it really was a confession, wouldn't he want to come clean on everything, including the fact that he was a fugitive? So why didn't he? I'll tell you why. Because the person who wrote that journal *didn't know*. He didn't know, because Billy didn't tell him. Billy was probably worried that being on a watch list would hurt his chance at whatever scheme he was being groomed for. Poor fucker. He thought it was a job interview, didn't realize he was a sacrificial lamb. Further proof that the journal is a fraud."

Lieutenant Addario sighed. "The British consul contacted one of Billy's aunts in Ballymena. She provided a letter that Moore sent her a few years ago asking for money. It matches. That absolutely is Billy Moore's handwriting."

"Ha! Written under duress—or for money. You can buy a lot of diary entries for the kind of cash we found."

"And the killer didn't take Billy's money, because . . . ?"

"It had to look credible."

She could feel a headache coming on. "You said yourself that the journal contained incongruities. Personal insults aimed specifically at you."

"It was dictated. Billy just wrote it down. Make no mistake, that's our man, speaking through the corpse of Billy Moore."

"You're shoehorning evidence, Gaddy. You're forcing the pieces to fit, looking for patterns that aren't there. Evidence should suggest a theory. Not the other way around. You can't concoct an outlandish scenario and then go looking for evidence to support it. We don't even know this other man's name, or whether he even exists."

Rhodes was becoming frustrated at repeating herself. "He isn't in Japan anymore. I said that. He's probably not even on the same continent, or even in the same hemisphere. You weren't listening."

"Billy Moore arrived on that island, alone. He bicycled to the cape, alone. He placed the barrel of that shotgun to his face, alone. It might as well have been a locked room. If there *was* a phantom-like companion with him, how did he get there?"

"An island like that? Easy to land a boat. I identified several possible sites. Satellite images can provide confirmation. We need to look for an unregistered vessel docking at one of the smaller coves on the night Billy Moore arrived."

"You think I'm requisitioning a satellite review? I'm not requisitioning a satellite review."

"It's called due diligence, Ms. Addario." They were friends; the use of "Ms." was an intentional twist of the blade.

"It's called operational overreach. This is confirmation bias run amok. And I would suggest you dial back the attitude, *Ms.* Rhodes."

But Rhodes was no longer listening. "Confirmation bias. Of course! That's what he was counting on. He *did* tell us something, after all. Not in that stupid journal with its fabrications and red herrings, but in his choice of patsy. He was looking for someone his size, a small man, petite even. But why? In case he'd already been spotted or had been caught on camera. The dead body had to resemble him, even after he erased the other man's face, so that any accidental witnesses would confirm what they *thought* they saw." Her eyes were bright now, as though lit from within. Addario knew that look. Rhodes was capable of remarkable alacrity, lightning strikes of insight that could leave you breathless. She was also capable of leaping headlong into folly. That, too, could leave you breathless. "Why?" asked Rhodes, beaming.

"Why what?"

"Why pick a man who was a mirror of himself? Because he knew he might very well have been captured on camera. Captured, but where? In a crowd? Who cares! That would prove nothing. No, it would have to be on or near the scene of the crime. Andrea, don't you get it? He was on O-jina Island!"

"I don't follow what you're . . ." her voice trailed off. The migraine was getting worse.

"Billy Moore sacked the royal grave; that much is true. But our man sacked the other one. That was his real target all along!"

"There was nothing taken from the second grave."

"Nothing that we know of. But if someone *had* seen him, a caretaker or a security cam, he would've been able to pass for Billy Moore. Don't you see? I bet they were even dressed the same. See?"

But of course she didn't. "Talking to you is like talking to a kangaroo with ADD. It's exhausting."

Didn't matter. Gaddy Rhodes was already pursuing this latest notion down fresh corridors of the mind. "Here's what we do: we obtain access to the security cameras leading in and out of O-Jina Island, see if we can prove that Billy Moore had to have been in two places at the same time."

At which point the door to the meeting room opened and the young sad-eyed corporal stuck his head out. "Ma'am? The colonel was wondering if we're done in here."

"Oh, we're done," said Lieutenant Addario. *We're done.*

Three days later, Agent Rhodes was removed from active duty and transferred to an administrative position stateside. Their friendship did not survive this.

THE BOY IN THE TREE

COLONEL MCNAIR HAD TAKEN THE HIGH ground. He did this out of habit more than anything, one acquired over the course of thirty-some years of military service, where one learned to see the world primarily as terrain, as a series of contour maps offering various degrees of advantage. Not that there were any ambushes waiting for him—although, he had to admit, that was the nature of ambushes: you didn't see them coming.

He wiped sweat from his eyes. His small eyes. Waited. *If you see it coming, it's not an ambush.* The colonel was now off duty, but even in a Hawaiian shirt and Cardinals baseball cap, he carried the gravitas of his rank with him. Even when he wasn't in uniform, he was in uniform. A nimbus of power surrounded the colonel; it was like his own personal brand of cologne. (His wife always said he was the only man she knew who could strut sitting down.)

A shrill summer. Cicadas singing themselves in and out of existence. The lackluster flutter of trees on humid winds. The *kii*-cry of hawks tracing circles in the sky. Sea and sun and jungle, all distant, all oppressively near at hand.

Any trace of morning mist had burned away and a haze of heat was slowly removing the horizon; it had become little more than a blur between planes. Colonel McNair stood, legs apart, arms at ease behind his back, at a point where the path narrowed, giving the colonel a clear view of the stone-cut stairs that ran up the escarpment toward him. The very stairs he had just climbed. Frond-like leaves moved on the permanent updraft at Cape Kyan. Somewhere, out at sea, a typhoon was brewing; weather stations were tracking its landfall. But up here, there was only the stultifying heat of a barometer rising. The storm was still days away.

Blocks of stone, netted with vines. A jumble they called Gushikawa Castle, ruins by any other name. Twelfth-century ruins, *so at least this one they couldn't blame on us. It was already broken when we got here.*

It was at Cape Kyan that the US bombardment of Okinawa had finally ended, if only because they'd run out of island to bomb. A rolling barrage had pushed the Japanese Imperial Army to the very edge, and with them a population of the dispossessed. Families. Children. Seniors. Students. All fleeing in terror to the cliffs at Cape Kyan. Stories of the war referred to Cape Kyan as the "point of no return." The castle itself had fallen centuries before. The Americans were shelling debris at that point.

Colonel McNair took off his cap, ran a palm across his head. Bristle-cut hair, crisscrossed with trails of sweat. He could see a small figure below, coming up the steps toward him in a slow but deliberate gait. A slight man, but not unimposing. When he reached the viewing platform, he smiled at the colonel.

"Brave day," he said.

The colonel nodded, not entirely sure what that meant.

There was a faintly feline cast to the other man's face, the way a fox seems more catlike than canine. Other than that, the small man remained nondescript, memorable only in his lack of memorability. Even the suit he was wearing, trim and well tailored, was tasteful to the point of being utterly forgettable. If someone had asked the colonel about it later, he would have been unable to swear for certain what color the suit was, or even what type. Not so much a man as the outline of a man. There was an absence there, inhaling all the light.

The colonel picked up the briefcase on the ground next to him. "Shall we?" he said, stepping aside to let the other man pass.

But the outline didn't move. It carefully retrieved its handkerchief from its inside jacket pocket, folded the cloth neatly, dabbed perspiration from its brow. Every move was deliberate, precise, gave evidence of energy held in reserve, the way a spring might. Or a bullet. Or a ballet.

The small man smiled at the colonel, but not with his eyes. "After you," he said. "I insist."

Colonel McNair didn't like it, having this man behind him. True, he would still have the high ground, but the other fellow now had the advantage. They walked up and up and up, single file, until they reached a clearing at the top. A panorama of cliffs and hazy seas greeted them. Almond trees and hibiscus. A wealth of flowers, growing wild on the heights.

"There are snakes in those bushes," the colonel cautioned. Then, with a half smile, "They never bite officers, so I'm told. Professional courtesy, ah suppose."

Colonel Andrew McNair, flight commander, Kadena Air Base, US Third Wing, carefully placed his briefcase on the ground and then turned his back in a calculated act of trust. He walked over, admired the view. "Fortress Britain," he said. "That's what they called it. It's how the English defended their isle: at the very gates, drawbridge raised. Same way they built their castles. Thick walls meant to withhold a frontal assault. Y'all can see the same principles at play in the Battle of Britain. 'We will fight on the shores and on the streets, we will never surrender.' Their fortress island held—barely, but it held. Turned back the assault. Might well have been a medieval battle, the way they fought it. Japanese castles? Those are very different. The magnificence of a Japanese castle lies in its *outer* defenses; the central keep itself is really just decorative, made of wood—tends to burn. It's the outer walls, designed to hold attackers back as far as possible, that is the key to Japanese defensive thinking. Works fine, too. Up to a point. Problem is, once those walls are breached, it all collapses. Okinawa was Japan's outer wall. Was meant to hold back the barbarian hordes, keep 'em at bay. But after the outer walls fell, Japan lay naked and exposed. The line that stretches from Pearl Harbor to Hiroshima runs directly through Okinawa." He pointed to the next headland, jutting out, a slab of rock plunging into the ocean below. "Those cliffs, over there? That's where they would'a jumped. Hundreds of 'em, thousands even. Leapt in pairs and groups, holding hands or alone. Entire families. Starving and frightened. Women and children, mothers holding babies, elderly ladies and elderly men." He turned back around. "Even today, they call those the Suicide Rocks."

His briefcase was still there.

"You're not going to count it?" the colonel asked.

"Is there a reason I should?"

"No, I suppose not." He looked inland now, past the small man to the coral landscape beyond, hills pocked with crevices and caves. "A

Typhoon of Steel, that's what we unleashed upon them." By "we," he meant Americans. The colonel wasn't there, of course, hadn't even been born when the Battle for Okinawa was underway; ancient history—but not quite. "Civilians hunkered down inside their turtleback tombs, took refuge among the dead as our artillery lay waste to their land. Then the Japanese soldiers came, forced them back out, into the open, took over their hiding places. It was a battle of the graves in many ways. At Tomari Port was an international cemetery. During the battle for Naha, American troops took cover under heavy fire, crouching behind the headstones of US sailors who'd been buried in Okinawa a hundred years earlier. The Sixth Marines fought their way through that graveyard, tomb by tomb. Hard to imagine."

The small man reached inside his jacket, quietly withdrew a manila envelope, but the colonel wasn't ready, not yet. He pointed out a hacksaw ridge of mountains running across the island. "My father," he said.

The other man nodded. "A bad drop."

"Yes, sir. A bad drop indeed. The paratroopers were coming in from—let's see, over there, other side of that ridge. A gust of wind shoved three of 'em over, onto this side. That's all it took. Just a single gust of wind. Funny isn't it, how things can turn on something so trivial? They were captured and they were tortured—for what I am still not sure. They were GIs, didn't have access to any military plans. I suppose their tormentors just wanted to vent their anger on someone. The Japanese tied up the first two—none of 'em over nineteen, you understand, just boys—used them for bayonet practice. And my father, well, they saved him for special treatment. From Kentucky, you see."

The air was growing heavy. Clouds were boiling over.

"You've heard of him, the Kentucky Kid." It wasn't a question, not really. "Came from samurai stock. The Ono-Isu. As a young man, he had trained in the US, at West Point. Part'a some sort of Japanese-American military exchange. Was later stationed in Kentucky. Wasn't treated very well during his stay, apparently. Nursed a grudge, it would seem. Honor and such. Or maybe he was just a garden-variety sociopath. Psycho or not, doesn't really matter, ah suppose. He returned to Japan just before the war began, volunteered his services as an interpreter. That was his official designation, though 'chief interrogator' would be more accurate. I do believe it was the technicality of him being an interpreter following orders that allowed him to slip free of the war crimes tribunals that ensued. During the conflict, when the Japanese Imperial Army was steamrolling over the rest of Southeast Asia, he liked to visit the POW camps, would ask in a warm southern drawl, 'Anyone here from Kentucky?' Sure enough, a few youthful hands would go up, and they would be separated for singular consideration. By the time he got done with my dad, well, my dad was no longer there. Nineteen died somewhere in the process."

The colonel walked himself into the shade and the small man followed with the briefcase. If he'd wanted to slip away with both the briefcase and the envelope, Colonel McNair would scarcely have noticed, or cared.

As they walked, the colonel spoke—to whom, it wasn't clear. "He never really left Okinawa, my dad. The Kentucky Kid went on to have an illustrious career. My father? Not so much. But that's okay. I understood. With every fall of the belt, I understood. I knew, *He's not hitting me, he's hitting the Kentucky Kid*. Never held it against my dad. How could I? My father was a war hero." The path narrowed and they followed it around. "That was a singular bit of genius, by the way, going through the cemetery records like that. Never would'a thought of it, and even if I had, wouldn't have known where to start. Would've assumed it had all been destroyed in the Typhoon of Steel. Didn't realize there could be more than one family buried in an Okinawan tomb."

A long path, overgrown. Crumbling walls. Not a castle, but the memory of. Not a fortress, but the echo of. "Y'hear that occasional crunch?" asked the colonel. "Those are pottery shards from China, a thousand years old."

The wind was picking up. The weather was turning. Not a typhoon, but the precursor of.

"There's these cone-like seashells you find on certain beaches down here. Delicate and beautiful, with intricate patterns on the surface. Makes for a terrific souvenir, except that these shells host a nasty creature: a certain type of snail with a poisonous barb on one end, like a harpoon. Injects a powerful venom. Highly toxic. Blinds its victims. Paralysis follows. Intense pain. Can't talk, tongue swells. Y'start to drool. No known antidote. Wife of one of our servicemen, she brought a cone shell home with her as a memento of her time in Okinawa. The snail inside had curled back. She thought the shell was empty. But it wasn't. Two weeks later, she's holding it up, showing her book club and—well, you know how the story ends."

"It's how all stories end."

"That's the gospel truth, it surely is. My father in his grave these many years and Mr. Ono-Isu too. His son is doing well, though."

They had reached the end of the path. Coral cliffs tumbling into the sea. The colonel turned, looked at the other man. "So, what's next for you?"

"There's a unicorn horn on Kume Island I need to inspect."

"Unicorn? Really?"

"Narwhal. A tusk that was handed down from a royal prince four hundred years ago."

The colonel nodded. *He's testing me. If police swarm Kume Island, he'll know I can't be trusted, he'll know I talked, and he will be back.* The colonel dry-chuckled, assuming a nonchalance he didn't feel. "Well, if you're gonna go huntin' unicorns, I wish you good luck and Godspeed. You certainly played Billy Moore for a fool, didn't you? Harpooned him well and true." The colonel said this with a certain admiration, but the response he got was sharp.

A red flash of anger. "I never lied to Mr. Moore. I do not traffic in falsehoods. I honored my side of the bargain. I always do. Mr. Moore was promised a great deal of money and the chance to disappear— forever. To become rich and then vanish, in that order." He stepped closer, an underlying rage barely contained, his voice hitting every word like a blow: "I. Keep. My. Promises."

The colonel felt his throat go dry. *Disappeared, all right. With a shotgun to the face.*

Then, softer, the small man asked, "And Agent Rhodes, how is she?"

"The skinny blond? Oh, she's done, finished. Removed from active duty. Was transferred to the New York office, ah believe. Administrative."

"A demotion, then?"

"Would appear so."

"That's a shame. She was a good agent, very good. She got closer than anyone else ever has. Did she— Did she take it personally?"

"How else could she? It was pretty bad at the end," said the colonel. "She was having a nervous breakdown of some sort. Was talking about one-eyed kings and shadow worlds."

"Erasmus," said the small man. "She was quoting Erasmus. 'In the Land of the Blind, the one-eyed man is king.' Alas, that isn't true. In the Land of the Blind, no one listens to the one-eyed man." He held out the envelope. "This is what you came for."

But the colonel didn't take it. He turned his face to the sea instead. That dark horizon.

What he wanted to ask was: *Were you really in the Congo, did the mercenaries you hired storm the Presidential Guards, capture the Kalinga drum? Did you track down a stolen Stradivarius, throw a Cockney yob from a window? Did you find Muhammad Ali's missing gold medal?* But the colonel knew he was only one or two questions away from certain death himself and so elected to say nothing.

Two tours of Afghanistan, under heavy fire in Iraq, staring down North Korean incursions in the East China Sea, but still he was unnerved by this small, unassuming man with the forgettable face.

Incoming waves.

The swell and sudden drop of the ocean. A sea without color, not even gray. Colonel McNair finally accepted the envelope, with a lack of enthusiasm that surprised even him. He slid it open, tilted the contents into his palm: a pair of rusted tin tabs, stamped with Japanese characters. These would be the dog tags of Lieutenant Musashi of the Ono-Isu family, Okinawan Forty-Second Army.

"You saw his bones?"

"I saw his bones."

"So, he really is dead."

"Has been for some time."

The colonel held the tags in his hand as though weighing them. They were so light they were barely there. He could feel the small man watching him.

"What will you do?" the small man asked. "Now that you have them."

"Y'know, I imagined this moment. Thought about it for a long time. Figured, first I would piss on them, then melt 'em down, then mold them into the tip of a bullet, fire it into the heart of his son. Now? Now I'm not so sure."

The cicadas had stopped and the circling birds had taken shelter. A stronger wind was shaking the trees.

"I will tell you a story," said the colonel. "It is the story of two bodies: a little girl under a castle and a boy in a tree. During the Battle for Okinawa, the American bombardment cleared away layers of history, exposed old secrets. And after the war was over, when they were excavating one of those fallen castles—not far from here, in fact—they unearthed the skeleton of a young girl buried under the foundations. Fourteenth century. From her position, it was clear she had been sacrificed, placed there as an offering. If it hadn't been for our bombardment, she would never have been found, would never have been laid to rest or given the burial she deserved. Okinawa is full of restless ghosts."

"And the boy in the tree?"

"Oh, that's one of ours. Not the boy, but the handiwork. In the Battle of Mabuni, north of here, the villagers were trapped, caught between retreating Japanese troops and advancing American forces, between the hammer and the anvil. Hundreds of children died. The entire village was razed. Whole entire landscape was systematically pulverized. Some forty years later, a banyan tree brought up a young boy's shoe embedded in its roots. There were shards of human bone inside. Youth is always sacrificed, isn't it? In castles or in trees. We think the past is buried, but it always pushes through."

The colonel held out his arm, as far as he could, let the dog tags slip from his fingers, watched them tumble as they fell, end over end, until they disappeared. There was no way to know if they ever hit the water. Might very well have been blown inward, gotten tangled on a branch or caught on an outcrop. It didn't matter anymore.

When the colonel turned around, the small man was gone. Later, the colonel would look up the phrase "brave day" online. It was British in origin, a greeting common to certain areas of Scotland, Wales— and Northern Ireland.

DAYS: BRAVE AND OTHERWISE

The Okinawan archipelago of southern Japan runs along the outer edge of the East China Sea. Drowned mountains, coral reefs, a dragon ascending. An arc of outcrops and outposts, a jagged curve of vertebrae: these are islands of the Black Current. The Kuroshio is a river in the sea, one hundred kilometers wide, that flows up from the Philippines, drawing warm waters and turbulent weather with it as it goes, until it comes at last into conflict with colder, northern currents. The monsoons of spring, the typhoons of fall: it all begins here. Hateruma Island, at the southern tip of the spine, is where the Black Current first touches Japanese territory.

—T. Rafferty, "Okinawa: A Land of

Contrasts," *Island Views*, Jan/Feb 2004

Gaddy Rhodes dog-eared the article, put the glossy travel magazine into a creased folder marked HATERUMA. Years out of date and nothing worth noting, but she saved it anyway. There was so little written about that small island at the end of nowhere, and what there was, was paltry: references to sandy beaches, sunny skies, an academic essay on traditional beliefs and priestesses. Magical trails and spirit lines. Gaddy wasn't interested in any of that.

"Knock knock!"

God how she hated that, how her fellow cubicle-bound colleagues at Interpol's New York office insisted on pretending they all had doors. *Knock knock.* Just come in, for chrissake.

It was the curly-haired pup from two cubicles over. Patrick, was that his name? She wasn't sure. Big smile, electric teeth.

"Cathy's card," he singsonged. "Don't forget."

Card? What card?

"It's with Sue, at reception. Supposed to be a surprise, so don't say anything!"

"Retiring?"

His smile faltered. "Birthday. Why would she be retiring? She's, like, thirtysomething." Then, looking at the image on her computer. "In the market for a new urinal, are you?"

The image was labeled PARIS 1917.

"What? No. That's—that's an iconic work of art. Modern art."

"Looks like a urinal."

"It *is* a urinal." At the 1917 Paris Exhibition, a disgruntled artist named Marcel Duchamp signed a urinal with the name 'R. Mutt' and then hanged it alongside other, more traditional pieces in the gallery. It was an audacious act: part protest, part manifesto. For many, this autographed urinal marked the birth of modern art. But how to explain this to Patrick of the Curly Hair? "The original is lost," she said. "Probably forever. But the artist signed sixteen other identical urinals. Over the last ten years, someone has been quietly buying up these replicas—and destroying them, one by one, so that in the end there will only be one left."

"Why?"

"Well, when there's only one left, its value will soar."

His attention shifted to the jar of murky liquor on her desk shelf. "Nice," he said, so flatly it could be taken only as sarcasm.

While other cubicle denizens had photographs of children and spouses, or crayon art and World's Greatest Dad mugs, Gaddy's desk sported a large bottle of awamori with a habu coiled inside, jaw distended, fangs bared. Dragon liquor. Leaning against this formaldehyde curiosity was a folder stuffed with loose papers, marked FINDER.

"The snake. A friend of yours?"

"A souvenir. It's from Okinawa, my last field assignment—" but he didn't care.

"Just make sure you stop by reception later. Don't forget, okay? Coffee and cake in the common room to follow."

She said. "I don't like coffee. I drink tea."

Exasperated. "That's just an expression. I'm sure there will be—Whatever. Just sign the card, okay?"

So she trudged down to see Sue, the swivel chair sentry, who was manning the desk across from the elevators on their third-floor hide-out. "Something about a card?" said Gaddy.

Brightly. "Right!" She produced a comically large cartoon of a card. *Lordy, lordy, look who's forty!*

Behind reception, a piece of sky. Buildings were lined up like mismatched books on a shelf. Among them, an undistinguishable block noticeable only because of the gridwork crane that was now perched atop it. A grit of smoke was rising up.

"The hotel," she said.

Swivel Chair Sue, pirouetting. "That? Tearing it down, I think."

Of course they were tearing it down. Anyone could see that; the top floor was already gone. Why didn't they just implode the damn thing, get it over with? Why this slow, methodical erasure?

Gaddy walked over to the window, stared through her own reflection at the modest chunk of skyline beyond. She knew that hotel, knew it well. An uninspired arrangement of brick and beams, five floors, no balconies, the Commonwealth Inn had stood vacant for years, had been turned into a women's shelter at one point, then a used furniture depot (ground floor only), then a "dream center" (whatever that was) and now? It was finally going down, for good this time. She twisted her empty ring finger. GR + ML 4 VR.

Intoxicated and alive, they'd promised each other they would come back on their 10th anniversary, and their 20th and their 30th, would book the same room, stay in the same bed. But of course, they never made it to ten, let alone twenty. Gaddy was forced to pass that hotel every day during her long sullen commute into the city, but now that it was being dismantled, she wasn't sure how to feel. Relieved, she supposed. Sad, too.

It seemed so long ago.

Tremulous desires. The tentative touch and bold-shy confidence of new lovers, awkward almost by definition, captive to their hunger, curling into each other like smoke, mesmerized by their own reflections looking back at them in each other's eyes. Young, both of them, and unforgivably so. Her, in art history, and him in drama, and the two of them able to afford only their initials. *They charge by the letter, so we have to be careful!* He was going to be hailed as an actor and she was going to stride through the rarefied corridors of the Louvre as though she owned it, at least that was the plan, though last she checked— eleven hours, twenty-four minutes ago—he was still teaching drama at a community college in Lakeside. His Facebook family looked very happy, though, as did he, although you can never be sure with actors, even failed ones—especially, perhaps, the failed ones. She never did take possession of the Louvre.

They married young, too young. Everyone does. Gaddy had been prepared for the tedium of wedlock, it was hardly a secret (was there ever a more appropriate word than "wedlock"?); what she hadn't been prepared for was how hypnotic that tedium would become—or how quickly. Graduations (plural), a mortgage (singular), the first fumbling attempts at a career, recycling on Wednesday, the Visa bill is due tomorrow, don't forget. The same tired recursive arguments, endlessly repeated, never resolved. All those petty and predictable conflicts. (And what is marriage but accumulated resentment? A running tally of debts owed, a ledger book where the entries never quite reconcile even as the sums cancel each other out.) It was less a marriage, she realized now, than a hostage-taking. A mutual case of Stockholm syndrome. A slow asphyxiation. They were drowning in the shallow end, in the gaps between words.

Under ancient Common Law, when the accused refused to enter a plea, they were subjected to a method of interrogation known as *peine forte et dure*, "hard and forceful punishment." Defendants who "stood mute"—that is, who would not take part in their own destruction—were tied down as heavier and heavier stones were placed on their chest, until a plea was either given or the defendant died. Marriage is not a marriage, she thought, it is an ongoing round of *peine forte et dure*.

From the window of the third floor, peering out from the glass cube that was the Interpol Admin Office, the Commonwealth Inn seemed to be growing larger even as the building itself was being stripped away. It was like a parable given form. But what type of parable? One that doesn't have a moral at the end. *Sometimes, when things are lost, they are lost forever.* Love, youth, balloons into a summer sky, and wedding rings: they were all of them of the same category.

Maybe that was when it went wrong, right at the start, at the Commonwealth Inn, with a ring disappearing down a drain. *Our room faced the bridge, I remember that.* Gaddy had mismeasured her ring finger, or perhaps the discount jeweler at that Salem shopping mall had made a mistake, or maybe, nerves jangled in the weeks leading up to the Big Day, she'd simply lost too much weight—a habit she fought even now: forgetting to eat when things became tense—but whatever the reason, while Gaddy, our young bride, was running shampoo through her hair, the ring had slipped free, had disappeared like a vanishing act in a magician's repertoire.

They had counted out the initials carefully; the engravers at Northshore Mall charged by the letter, so Gaddy and her beau had been forced to pare their eternal devotion down to a set of initials and a simple cypher. GR + ML 4 VR. Love on a budget. But the ring had seemed to leap off her finger of its own accord.

She'd told her office-appointed therapist about this, a silently flatulent man named Syd Something-or-Other, how it had seemed to leap away from her, but Syd had just nodded professionally and said, "Perhaps that is why you are so obsessed with finding things." "Not *finding*," she'd snapped. "Retrieving." But he couldn't see the difference and she couldn't be bothered to explain.

"Hellooo? The card?"

Gaddy turned from the window. "The what?"

"The birthday card."

It never ends. Keurig pods and coffee cup chitchat, the feigned smile and too-loud laughter, the conversational eddies, the birthday cards that always needed signing. Gaddy Rhodes avoided her coworkers—for all the good it did her—and, as a result, had garnered a well-deserved reputation for being standoffish, which was absolutely fine with her. The amount of fucks she didn't give bordered on the infinite.

"You sign it," she said. "Something nice."

And with that, she left, wading back into her cubicle sea.

Gaddy knew full well that she had been relegated to the fringe ranks of conspiratorial nuts and free-range cranks, to a minor post, aggressively ignored, but with this came a certain amount of freedom: the freedom of diminished expectations. No one was keeping track of her anymore; as long as she met her deadlines and submitted the proper follow-up reports in the correct order, she could have placed a mop with a wig in her stead and no one would have been the wiser. It was a defeat, certainly. But beyond defeat lay a certain courage, a certain defiant lack of hope. It was the courage of lost causes.

She stuffed the folder marked HATERUMA into the larger one labelled FINDER, bulging now with false leads and paper trails, scrolled through another article that had popped up. She was searching for lost objects that had recently resurfaced. *Where are you?* He probably wasn't even in the same hemisphere, let alone continent; she herself had said as much. *Where are you?* And beneath that, another question: *Who are you, and how are you able to move so smoothly across international borders, in and out of shadows as though made of liquid?*

It occurred to Agent Rhodes that perhaps the real question wasn't "Who are you?" but "*What* are you?" What do you *do?* What sort of employment would provide the proper cover, would allow you to hopscotch across the map, alibi intact, from Okinawa to Rwanda and back again? Art curator? Maybe. Archeology? Too specialized. Military? Too visible. Import-export ventures would be too dangerous, too tightly monitored. And it occurred to her as well that instead of tracking *objects*, she should have been tracking people. It was a crucial insight, but one that came too late. She was lost now—lost behind a wall of folders as surely as Fortunato in his tomb. The might-have-beens and should-have-saids, the things we meant to do, the people we planned to become, the lovers we let slip from our embrace. We are all of us drowning in the shallow end, she supposed. But still the question remained: *Who are you?*

What Gaddy Rhodes didn't realize—couldn't have realized—was that the key to the conundrum was already in her possession, was in the very travel article she had, moments before, stuffed into a folder, a folder for a case now closed, one marked HATERUMA. It wasn't the name of the island, or the destination that was germane, not even the article itself. It was the byline of the writer who had penned it: *T. Rafferty.*

PART THREE
SOUTHERN CROSS

THOMAS RAFFERTY WAS ON HIS THIRD gin and cider when the shaking began, something he initially attributed to a long flight and a lack of sleep: *jet lag plus gin equals palsy*. A simple formula, really. But it wasn't the DTs and he wasn't shaking, the building was.

The table suddenly lurched, as though pulled violently to one side, his drink skidding off, shattering. The array of upside-down glasses hanging above the barroom counter began clacking wildly. Reminded him of castanets.

He felt the ground heave beneath him, as though trying to buck him off.

"Jesus H. Fucking Christ." He was drunk on fear and vaguely aware that these might very well be his last words, spoken to no one, a final plea to be buried with him. *Here lies Tom Rafferty. Jesus H. Fucking Christ.*

Would that count as a dying prayer?

He stumbled for the door the way one does on a train, leaning one way, then the other, coming outside onto the street just in time to see the cathedral fall.

It was February 22, 2011, and Christchurch, New Zealand, was collapsing in on itself.

A LAND OF CONTRASTS

EIGHTEEN HOURS EARLIER, and Andy the Englishman is holding forth, center stage, as per usual, with an exhausted eloquence and ever-expansive arm gestures. Andy wrote for the Guardian, freelanced for Condé Nast, was currently on assignment—or "commission," as he called it—with Granta. Something arch and irreverent, no doubt. That's what Andy the Englishman specialized in: arch irreverence. It was kind of his beat.

Rafferty pulled up a chair next to him.

You know you've been traveling for too long when every place reminds you of someplace else. They had arrived in clusters and clumps throughout the day, making their way down to the bottom of the world, dragging battered luggage tattooed with decals through various airport holding pens, collecting their next poker hand of boarding passes, trooping on to their next connecting flight, and their next, with the strained perma-smile of their Travel New Zealand host already starting to slip from her suntanned and unconscionably healthy face.

These were travel writers on a press junket, and every place reminded them of someplace else. Auckland had reminded them of Sydney, and Sydney had reminded them of Vancouver, which reminded them of Seattle, which reminded them of Auckland. They had descended—quite literally from thin air—onto Christchurch in the South Island, amid the vast and pastoral Canterbury Plains, the Avon River wending through, the very names an echo of Olde Country longings. To be colonial is to be born into exile, and New Zealand, it seemed to Rafferty, was as much a cargo cult as a country.

Theirs was a disheveled invasion. Bedouins of the minibar, they had gathered now at the hotel's pub, hotel pubs being the natural habitat of travel writers everywhere, in front of a window where the name read, in reverse, BUSBY & HOBSON'S. An Irish pub, allegedly. Rafferty was the last to arrive, as was his habit—not fashionably so, just slow to unpack. His lower back was acting up again and he'd had to swallow a handful of ibuprofen and muscle relaxants before he could face his colleague's company. "I have a love-hate relationship with my fellow writers," is how he liked to put it, "but without the love part."

More importantly, he had slipped away during the morning's champagne reception, had hopped a streetcar to the art gallery, to no avail. She was gone. And so, he had returned, back to this dissolute den of wordsmiths. This pox of pundits. This veritable—

He spotted Freebie Frank across from him, already well into his cups. With his Bob Ross hair and carious grin, Freebie Frank worked almost exclusively for corporate newsletters and in-house journals, notoriously low paying, yet somehow managing to turn a profit on these press trips, all without ever actually writing anything of note. Every now and then, Freebie would convince a specialty magazine to sponsor one of his wildly improbable mash-ups—he'd been to Papua New Guinea for Modern Bride, Botswana for Poodle Smart Monthly—but generally he stuck to newsletters and their ilk, always returning with more money in his pocket than when he left. How Freebie managed to do this remained something of a mystery. *Need to ask him about it*, thought Rafferty. *At some point, I really should try to earn a living at this.* So entrenched was Freebie Frank's reputation that when people shortened his name, they dropped the Frank instead.

"Freebie," said Rafferty with a nod.

"Raff!" cried Freebie, greeting him like a long-lost brother returned from the war with a winning lottery ticket in his pocket. He was already several sheets to whatever wind was blowing.

Down from Freebie was a trio of rather grim-faced, semi-autonomous guidebook authors piggybacking on the press trip. They disappeared during the day, swept back at night. Germans, by inclination, if not nationality. Efficient. Meticulous. The Sour Krauts, as they'd been dubbed. Their attitude was understandable. You needed laser-like focus and a touch of OCD to write guidebooks. *What time does the museum open, what time does the museum close, and on which days, and what about holidays? What are the fees? Any discounts? The nearest train station? Bus stop? Taxi stand? Cockfight? Which bus do you take from the station to get to the museum and where is the nearest laundromat? Nearest bank? Money changer? And which one offers the best rates? Nearest post office? Schnitzel house? Tattoo parlor? And when do these venues open/close/offer discounts/tattoos, and how much and for whom?*

Rafferty was nowhere near organized or disciplined enough for this type of travel, as he'd discovered several years ago when he'd been hired to update a budget guide to Japan. At one point, he had sent his readers into the ocean. A letter from a backpacker explained: "Dude, on pg. 84, you advised us to turn left when we get off the ferry and continue 400 meters to the hostel on Sado Island. That actually sends you into the Sea of Japan." One wonders how far they waded into the water before catching the error. The guidebook trio that had landed in Christchurch were listening to Andy the Englishman with the same grim dedication they brought to their task. Guidebooks: travel writing, with the fun removed.

Other writers had already landed. Luciano from São Paulo, with Go'Where magazine, Javier from Madrid, here with ABC (the

Spanish-language journal, not the American network), and the always adorable Anya with the Moscow edition of Barti's Travel Tips. Rafferty recognized a features editor from Gourmet magazine, treating herself to a free trip on the pretext of researching an upcoming feature. How was the food so far? "Well, it's New Zealand," she said, "so if you don't like lamb . . ." The rest of the faces in the bar were less familiar.

By now, Andy the Englishman was in full flight.

"—I says to myself, self I says, 'If I am in Peking, I am bloody well going to have Peking Duck.' So, I flip through my Chinese-English dictionary, piece together a request, and, wouldn't you know it, something gets lost in translation—always does. I was merely asking for directions and he joins us! At the table! Our rickshaw driver! Sits down, enjoys all forty-seven courses with us. They eat the entire bird, you see, the way a Red Indian might eat a buffalo.'"

"Beijing," said Rafferty. "The name of the city. It's Beijing. Hasn't been called Peking in years. And it's Native American, not Red Indian."

"Yes, but the story isn't as funny if it's Beijing."

"I don't think it's Native anymore either," said Freebie. "I think the correct term is Aboriginal."

"That's only Australia," someone else said. "It's Indigenous now."

"Well," said Rafferty. "Whatever it is, it sure as fuck isn't Red Indian."

Andy smiled at Rafferty. "You look like hell, Tom. A surfeit of alcohol and a paucity of sleep, I imagine. One is tempted to ask after your health, if one were to care. Nice to see you joining us lesser mortals on a lowly press trip junket. Peddling our usual emetic prose, are we?"

Rafferty waved the waiter over. Ordered a scotch, no ice. Cricked his neck. (Later, he would look up the word "emetic" and think, *Should've punched that Limey fuck in the head*.) "Beijing," he said, just to piss Andy off one last time.

"Ah, yes. Tom Rafferty. Once a prick, always a prick."

Rafferty lifted his glass. A half-hearted salute in Andy's general direction.

That was when the rest of the table realized. *Rafferty*. The younger writers at the table—and they were mostly younger now—exchanged glances, eyes flitting back and forth, the visual equivalent of a murmur. It was the "rhubarb, rhubarb" of background players in a dinner theater, for they knew that they were in the presence of royalty, or the closest thing to it in the rapidly crumbling genre in which they wrote. *Oh my god, that's Thomas Rafferty. He looks so, so . . . old.* They'd barely noticed him on the flight down; he'd been silent, almost catatonic: a middle-aged slab of a man, frayed at the edges, skin creased in a palimpsest of sunburns past, face like poorly thrown pottery.

Rafferty swirled his glass as though panning for some lost thing. Took a hard swallow. The burned-wood taste of single-malt scotch. He could feel the rest of the table watching him.

"Is it, is it true . . . ?" one of them started.

"Yeah." He nodded. Whatever they were going to say probably was, and even if it wasn't, what did it matter?

But before this first writer could broach the subject, another had cut in. "You wrote *Casablanca to Timbuktu*." A journey around the bulge of Africa on overcrowded ferries and long-haul buses. Diarrhea and malarone-induced hallucinations mainly.

"That was a long time ago," he said. He'd only ever written one travel memoir of note. It was considered a cult classic, meaning "out of print." Meaning, rarely read.

"And *The Great Railway Bazaar*. Loved it!"

"That was Paul," he said. When they blinked, he added, "Theroux."

"You know Paul Theroux?"

"Bastard owes me forty bucks on a Hanoi handshake." He finished his scotch. "Long story," he said, but didn't elaborate. There was no such thing as a Hanoi handshake. He was just messing with them, wanted to see if anyone would admit to not knowing what a Hanoi handshake was. No one did.

"And Sara Wheeler? You know her?"

"Met her when she was en route to Antarctica, in transit—can't remember where."

"And Pico Iyer?"

"In Japan, I think. Some sort'a temple or shrine in Kyoto. Can't recall the details." *What a paltry collection of anecdotes I've amassed.*

"And is it true?" asked the first writer, circling back, a woman with a distinct Aussie twang. "You were there, right? In Rwanda, during the—the killings?"

"I was."

"News?"

"Travel. One of my first overseas assignments, actually. Sunday Times. A puff piece on nature tourism. 'Gorillas in Our Midst,' I think they called it. When I went up the mountain, the country was at peace. When I came back down, it was at war. Wrong place at the wrong time."

They had similar stories of escape, embellished and burnished over time, of civil wars narrowly avoided and bomb blasts averted. It was a common enough ritual for travel writers to swap what they, somewhat grandiosely, called their "war stories." But Rwanda? Rwanda was of a different order.

"You've heard of the luck of the Irish?" said Andy. "Well, Rafferty here has whatever the opposite of that is."

Rafferty waved for another scotch. "Not that I'm Irish," he said. "Not that I'm anything."

"With a name like Rafferty, there's an Irishman somewhere in the woodpile."

"You're with Lonely Planet," said the Aussie, proud by proxy. A homegrown imprint, that.

"Was. Past tense." They owed him his last two royalty checks; he owed them a manuscript. In the world of publishing, this was considered a draw.

"And New Zealand?" asked a skinny kid with an overactive Adam's apple, tittering in anticipation of his own incoming jape. "How would you . . . hee . . . describe New Zealand, Mr. Rafferty? Would you . . . heh-heh . . . would you say it was"—he let it drop with all the subtlety of a wet bag of cement—"a Land of Contrasts?"

Everyone laughed. A few applauded.

In the world of travel writing, Thomas Rafferty held the current unofficial world record for describing travel destinations as "lands of contrast," an unbroken streak going back 147 articles and counting, and not a single editor had cottoned on to what he was doing. *Sweden: Land of Contrasts! The Mexican Riviera: A Land of Contrasts! The Vatican: City of Contrasts!* If his editors changed the headline, he would sneak it in somewhere else, in a sidebar or a photo caption if need be. In one particularly inspired move, he had written it out in seashells on a beach for a full-color spread in Zoomer magazine, or was it Island Views? *Okinawa: A Land of Contrasts!* His ongoing campaign was legendary among other writers, every bit as celebrated as having survived an African genocide.

"A toast!" cried Andy the Englishman. "A toast to these never-ending lands of contrast that keep us employed—"

"Quasi-employed," someone corrected.

"And to Tom for elucidating us!"

"Hear! Hear!"

Rafferty raised his glass again, could see it in their eyes, the young 'uns rehearsing their version of events for later. *Had a drink with Thomas Rafferty. Looked like he got dressed by crawling through a clothes hamper.* They seemed disappointed he wasn't drinking more. Undaunted, they told tales, tall and otherwise, about him, rumors and apocrypha mainly, as though they were speaking about someone else, someone far distant, and maybe they were. It was like eavesdropping on your own eulogy. "President of Panama tried to have him deported!" "He's still persona non grata in Iceland." The stories were always much bigger than he was.

Rafferty slipped away soon after, moved over to the bar, switched to gin. He wanted to drink his misery down to the dregs. She wasn't here. Not in Christchurch, not on the South Island—maybe not in New Zealand at all. He'd already been to the art gallery, but she was gone. Long gone. It was like she knew he was coming, but how? "She has something of mine," he'd explained, but they wouldn't give any details on where she went. "Perhaps you could leave a message?" they'd said. But there was no message to leave except one, and she'd already heard it many times by now.

Some things are lost, some are mislaid, some are stolen. Rafferty asked for a wedge of lemon, got a slice instead, twisted it into his drink, thought about leaving. The bar, this assignment, the world. His ruined-cake face stared back at him in the mirror behind the bar.

"So," said the bartender with a nod to the loose affiliation of riffraff at the table behind them, who were now whooping and laug-ing like prisoners on a day pass. "You're travel writers? The lot of you?"

"Allegedly."

"And you?"

"Me? I'm barely a traveler. Hardly a writer."

A women's voice elbowed in: "Modesty is not your forte, Mr. Rafferty." To the bartender: "Mr. Rafferty is very accomplished, both as an author and a traveler." It wasn't true, but he'd take it. She sidled up next to him, threw another glance at the bartender. "Give us a minute, will you?"

Their barkeep relinquished the floor with a shrug, moved down the line to the next customer, a tie-loosened businessman who had been waiting patiently, as Rafferty studied his new companion in the mirror. She was younger than he was, but who wasn't at this point? He remembered her from the airport, the flight down, the shuttle to the hotel. Thick red lips, kissable in the way that wax fruit is ed-ible—only in error. He nodded to her reflection; her reflection nod-ded back. An interesting collage, her outfit. Looked like something the sea had washed up: layers of ragged-hemmed cloth resembling pastel burlap, lots of bracelets and dangling bits, all quite fashion-able, to go by the compliments she'd been receiving. She was very young and very sure of herself, steeped in certainties and brimming with unearned grievances. Had he been that insufferable when he was her age? Probably.

"Mr. Rafferty," she said. "I'm what you'd call a fan." But the tone of her voice suggested anything but.

Couldn't have been more than twenty-two, twenty-three. The age he was when he was about to embark for Rwanda, and he wondered,

130

Had we met back then, would she have given me the time of day? Probably not. Success, such as it is, breeds interest.

"A fan, you say?" This called for more gin. "Flattery will get you everywhere," and he waved the barkeep over. Maybe the night wouldn't be so empty after all. She was clearly a mistake waiting to happen, a poorly packed forklift poised to topple, but Rafferty didn't care; he'd always been drawn to incipient disaster. It was a carefully nurtured flaw of his. "Let me buy you a drink," he said.

She brushed the offer aside. "I'm on a cleanse." To the bartender: "Do you have any carrot juice?" But of course they didn't have any fucking carrot juice.

"I can do a nice cranberry cocktail?"

She waved that away as well, impatient. It was carrot juice or nothing.

"A fan . . . with reservations," she said, pivoting on her stool, forcing him to turn and face her directly rather than via the mirror. Here was the big reveal. "I'm Erin from TravelWrite Now." She said this as though it should mean something. It didn't, so she elaborated. "I provide multimedia travel content. Erin and Ewan's travel tips?" Still nothing. She leaned closer, touched his leg lightly, a slyly ambiguous gesture. "We have more than one million unique visitors a month. If there is anything close to an influencer in this industry, it's us."

"Well . . . good for you." He raised a toast with his empty glass. He'd downed his gin in the time it took her to not order. He didn't know much, but he knew that a million of anything was impressive.

"We did a feature on you, Mr. Rafferty. On the outdated modes of male privilege you embody."

"Good on you," he said. "I'm sure I deserved whatever it was you lobbed my way." He'd been called worse things by better people.

Rafferty had met Erin—had met her many, many times. He knew exactly how this conversation would unfold, could chart it with a predictable precision: Her increasingly polemic comments would ratchet up, outrage by rote; pull the string and out came the same slogans: capitalist colonial patriarchal privilege, shriller and shriller until only dogs and other thin-lipped sloganeers could hear her. Who needs nuance when you have ready-cut slogans?

Rafferty sighed. "Erin, is it? Look, I know you think I'm part of some sort'a evil cabal, a secret Masonic illuminati power structure, but the sad truth is, I'm just trying to get through the day like everyone else, pay the bills, make it to the finish line without blowing a knee. So, if I agree—right now, right at the start—that I'm a dinosaur and an oppressor and that you are a better person and more virtuous and morally superior to me in every conceivable way, can we end this rhetorical foreplay and just go upstairs and fuck?"

She looked for a drink to throw in his face, but of course had none. "You're a pig," she said.

"But an honest one." He didn't know much, but he knew that "patriarchal oppressor" was the modern equivalent of "Oooh, you're a bad boy aren't you?"—something to be cooed into the ear under cover of darkness.

She straightened her shoulders, all business now. "If you'd like to respond to our piece, you are welcome to."

"Nah, it's true, all of it, whatever you wrote. Hardly a scoop, though. Would'a been more of a scandal if you'd written, 'Thomas Rafferty, not as big an asshole as we thought.' Now *that* would'a been controversial!" He was starting to slur his words, if not his sentiments.

She stared into his pale eyes as though examining a strange bit of flora long thought extinct. "You really don't get it, do you? Times have changed. Your world is over."

"And?"

She didn't know what to say. It was the power of Not Caring.

"You aren't on social media, are you, Mr. Rafferty?"

"Nope." He sucked on the slice of lemon, wondered how her lipstick tasted. Waxy and red, no doubt, a hint of cinnamon? Devil's heart, isn't that what they called those spiced candies of his youth? She probably tasted of devil's heart. It was the gin working its way through his body, untying knots, loosening what was left of his libido.

"At TravelWrite Now, we believe in cultural inclusivity, we believe that travel can be an agent of social change. We do things differently."

"And yet, here you are on a press junket like the rest of us."

"The difference, Mr. Rafferty, is that I try to *engage* with the world."

He shrugged. "Go ahead, engage away. No one's stopping you." He was calling for another drink when a lumberjack loomed large in the mirror behind them. This would presumably be the other half of Erin and Ewan.

"Is, ah, something going on?" asked the lumberjack, trying, and mostly failing, to be intimidating.

"Pull up a seat," said Rafferty. "Your better half was extolling my merits."

She shot a glance at Ewan in the mirror, a flash of anger that told Ewan everything.

"Upset about our piece, I see." The boyfriend sat down on the other side, bookending Rafferty between the two of them, surely some level of Dante's hell, caught between Virtue and the Virtuous.

"What're you drinking?" asked Rafferty.

"I don't drink."

Of course you don't.

Not a lumberjack, Rafferty realized. Just someone hiding behind a beard. Buttoned-down short-sleeved shirt. Hair more sculpted than styled. Superfluous suspenders. And, of course, one of those thick full beards that were all the rage these days.

When the drink arrived, Rafferty asked the bartender, "Y'ever noticed how, as men's testicles get smaller, their beards get bigger? Y'ever wondered why that is? I'll tell you why. It's because growing a full thick beard is just about the only thing left where a man can at least claim the trappings of masculinity. It's why the young women who've declawed them love those beards so much, find them so compelling." He turned to the lumberjack. "When y'look in the mirror it must reassure you daily, no matter how self-emasculating you've become, that you can still grow a manly beard. They can't take that away from you, buddy boy! Congratulations."

Ewan's face grew splotchy and red. Rafferty waited, but nothing happened. Instead, Erin got up and left. Ewan followed. They would no doubt vent their anger online. At best, he would live on as an anecdote, the lowest form of immortality. *Thomas Rafferty? We met him once. A real asshole.*

The night spun on in a reverse Dance of the Seven Veils, each drink adding another layer of blurred reality, until Rafferty found himself trapped in a corner, he wasn't sure how, with the Adam's apple from earlier. He was saying something about Winterset.

"That's where you're from, right? Winterset?"

Rafferty nodded. "Pride of Iowa. Birthplace of John Wayne and George Washington Carver. Only pretty thing about it is its name."

That wasn't entirely true. Winterset had its charm—a drowsy charm, to be sure, but a charm nonetheless. What it didn't have was a reason for him to go back, not anymore. He'd buried Carol and Jim years before. His last remaining tether.

"I should probably confess," said the kid, Adam's apple bobbling, voice dropping to conspiratorial levels, "you're the reason I became a writer."

"Oh, um . . . mea culpa, I guess. Not too late to change your mind. I mean, you're still young."

"No, no, it's a good thing. I read your piece in *Zen and the Art of Travel Writing*." It was an anthology that Rafferty vaguely remembered contributing to. "I still practice what you preached," said the kid, slightly embarrassed; it was like admitting to a high school crush. "Whenever I arrive at a new destination, I always set aside a block of time to just sit and . . . watch. A café or a park bench or a bus stop. I sit, clear my mind, and just *observe*."

"I said that? Oh. Well, that's—that's good advice then."

"Best I ever had." His eyes were shining. Everyone is looking for a savior. "I heard you speak at NATJA as well."

"Nad'ja?"

"The North American Travel Journalists Association."

"Oh right, in Dallas."

"Denver."

"Right."

The boy knew his acronyms.

On it went. Rafferty was dimly aware that this stuff mattered, that he should be paying more attention to a landscape that was shifting beneath his feet, but when the kid started going on about "search engine optimization," he was gone. People talk about their eyes glazing over; for Rafferty it was always his ears that went first. The young man's voice got fainter and fainter until all Rafferty could hear was a distant murmur, like Charlie Brown's teacher, like the sea in a conch.

The other writers were now dissecting the finer points of the Kiwi accent and the speed thereof. "For people who don't have a lot to say, they're certainly in a hurry to say it."

"Except with vowels, did you notice that? They slow way down for those. They don't just stretch their vowels, they torture 'em."

"Dude, you're from Oklahoma."

"We soften our vowels, we don't torture them. Here. Say 'yeast.'"

"Yeast."

"Now drop the t."

"*Yees.*"

"There you go, Lesson One. How to say 'yes' like a Kiwi. It's a weird accent. There's something sneaky about it, right? They're not a sneaky people, but there's something sneaky about their accent."

When Ewan of the Mighty Beard strode past, ignoring Rafferty loudly, Rafferty used this as an excuse to extradite himself. "Just a sec," he told the others. "I'll be right back."

He followed the lumberjack into the men's room.

"Wanted to apologize," Rafferty said, taking up the urinal beside him. "I was out'a line. Y'should'a punched me. Should'a punched me in the face. I had it coming."

The young man behind the beard, eyes tersely forward, replied, "I don't believe in violence."

"Well," said Rafferty, giving it a shake. "*You* may not believe in violence, but the world sure as hell does."

When Rafferty got back to the table, studiously sidestepping the suction-like gravity well of Adam's apple and his acronyms, Freebie

Frank was in the middle of a heated debate with Andy the Englishman, this one about whether company catalogs, brochures, and hotel chain lobby fodder counted as "true" travel writing.

"Don't knock travel brochures!" Freebie roared. "Word for word, with the amount you write and what you get paid, they are the second-most-lucrative type of writing there is." The most lucrative? "Ransom notes."

"Libations!" cried Andy, moving on. He flipped the drinks menu open, recited the liturgy of cocktails within. "Manhattan. Grasshopper. Screwdriver. Wall banger. What else? A B-52, to get properly bombed. Sex on the Beach, what say you? A wholly unsatisfying proposition, that last one, what with the scouring effect of sand in regions best left lubricated and grit-free."

On he went, with all the grace of a Bavarian oompah-pah band. Andy was a man who spoke solely in superlatives, a P. T. Barnum in search of a circus. Everything was the best! *or worst.* Biggest! *or smallest.* Fastest! *or slowest.* There was no fair to middling in the world that Andy the Englishman inhabited, only winners! *and losers.* Anecdotes presented as adventure, and adventures presented as allegories; it seemed at times that Andy's only goal in life was to present an impressive obituary. Rafferty couldn't have known—couldn't possibly have known—that when the darkness came calling, it was Andy the Englishman who would invite the Devil in for a drink.

Hubris and hyperbole. Elliptical arguments only ever tangentially related to the topic at hand. Loud voices, overtalking, and slowly the room began to tilt like a ship settling on a sandbar. Rafferty left the bar, veering down a hallway and then up the back stairs of the hotel, thirty-nine steps, he'd counted them, thirty-nine steps to his room on the third floor, had to swipe the keycard three times before it would let him in.

As always, his hotel room was criminally underlit with coyly arranged lamps that needed to be felt up before you could locate the chain, and even then, he went through the entire dimmer cycle twice before he got it to what was ironically called "maximum." *Fuckin' hotels.*

Rafferty rolled the swivel chair over, sat at the desk with its improbably large blotter—hotel decorators presumably felt that most of their guests still penned correspondence with ink and quill—powered up his laptop, began to peck at the keyboard: "New Zealand is where bungee jumping began, and even today it remains a hotbed of adventure travel! You may want to try a bungee jump yourself, but there are many more extreme adventures you can undertake along the way." He ran the word count up to 750, thought a moment, said, "What the hell," and added a title: "New Zealand: Land of Contrasts!" hit SEND. He was in the bathroom chewing on his toothbrush when the laptop dinged.

It was his editor, stateside: WTF is this??? Rafferty peered at the screen as the words came slowly into focus.

It's a family feature, you nitwit. NOT adventure travel. FAMILY TRAVEL. The entire Sunday insert is about FAMILY. We've already sold the ads! Re-write and re-send, asap. We have the typeset standing by.

Rafferty replied: ASAP means 'as slowly as possible,' correct?

Fuck you.

With a sigh, Rafferty brought up the article he'd just sent, went through it line by line, making the necessary changes: "New Zealand is where bungee jumping began, ~~and even~~ but today it remains a hotbed of ~~adventure~~ family travel! You may <u>not</u> want to try a bungee jump yourself, but there are many more ~~extreme~~ family adventures you can undertake along the way." He did a final search and replace, "family" for "extreme," hit SAVE.

He had to rewrite the sidebar from scratch, though. It had originally been "Inside Tips on Adventure Travel in New Zealand!" as cribbed from one of the pamphlets in his press kits. There was no time to rummage through it again, and instead he typed: "New Zealand is a Family-Friendly Destination!" Everywhere on earth was a family-friendly destination, if that was the assignment. Baghdad was a family-friendly destination if that's what was called for. No writer was going to go all the way to, say, Bermuda, to write a family travel feature only to file an article reading, "Sorry, but when it comes to family travel, Bermuda sucks."

Under the new heading "Family Travel in NZ," he typed, "Here's a handy tip!" then sat back, tried to come up with some handy tips. After a moment he wrote: "Remember to pack lots of wet naps for those long drives through New Zealand's scenic countryside!" There wasn't a nation on earth that didn't boast scenic countryside. (That's what travel destinations did, they "boasted." They boasted more three-star Michelin restaurants than any other city in the tristate area; they boasted some of the best shopping in eastern Europe; they boasted scenic countryside.) Rafferty checked the word count, scratched his crotch, thought some more, added: "And don't forget to top up your 'petrol,' as the locals refer to it, before you hit the road, because if you're that fucking stupid, you deserve to run out of gas and starve to death in a muddy sheep paddock with the rest of your braying snot-nosed brood." He thought about this, deleted that last bit, hit SEND.

The reply came back quickly: About fuckin time.

Rafferty had been cutting his deadlines closer and closer in ever-decreasing increments, an apparent Zeno's paradox, seeing how near he could get to infinity before he missed one. So far, he never had. He was a professional, after all. Took pride in his work.

A few moments later his laptop dinged again:

You owe us three more, jackass. It's a series, don't forget. Next one is for our Valentine's Day insert. "New Zealand is for Lovers." That kind of thing. We've already sold the ads: cruise lines, package deals, etc. so don't SCREW IT UP.

Hadn't Rafferty read something about nude bungee jumping being invented in New Zealand as well? He opened a new document, titled it "New Zealand is for Lovers!" and began to type: "Spice up your love life with his-and-hers bungee jumping—in the buff!" *Mental note: check that that's really a thing.* Rafferty couldn't imagine anything less appealing than naked flesh flappity-flapping on the boingy end of a bungee cord, but any time you could mention nudity in an article, it was a wise move. Almost axiomatic in the trade.

He would have run up the word count even more, maybe added another sidebar—a "secret getaway" or an exclusive "off the beaten track" insider's tip—if it hadn't been for a sound so incongruous, he almost didn't recognize it, not at first. It echoed across the years, from somewhere in the farthermost hallways of his childhood: the rise-and-fall peal of church bells. This late at night? He lugged back the hotel curtains, apparently made of the same lead used by old-time X-ray technicians—it was one of his many peeves, the fact that the average hotel curtain could stop a bullet, yet still couldn't keep light from bleeding in—and he saw the square lit up below, cobblestones pebbled with rain as people made their way into the cathedral, its graceful arches and open doors. A midnight mass of some sort.

Christchurch never seemed entirely real to him; he'd been here before, maybe ten, twelve years ago, and nothing had really changed. It reminded him of one of those miniature landscapes you see in model railways, lovingly mimicking a larger world, yet somehow tidier, tinier, more dreamlike and surreal. This most English of English cities, out here on the outer reaches of the world, beyond Tahiti, beyond Pitcairn.

A city of the plains, a collection of gardens, of roses and costly mosses, of staid Edwardian architecture and ornate Victorian shoppes. (As a travel writer, Rafferty knew that Edwardian architecture was always "staid," Victorian was always "ornate.") Christchurch even had its own miniature railway, chugging tourists around on an endless loop. In Christchurch, it was always four in the afternoon. Even when it rained, it was sunny.

A soft rain was falling now. Framed by the hotel window, the city's namesake cathedral, a Gothic re-imagining without plague carts and scurvy boils, bell tolling, was calling out to its wayward flock—and at some level all of New Zealand was a wayward flock, a lost kingdom set adrift in a southern sea, and Rafferty watching from the window.

What the hell, I must have some sins worth confessing. The priest can tell me whether they're original or not. He pulled on his jacket, was galumphing down the back stairwell when he ran into Erin-of-the-Blog coming up the other way. They stopped, awkwardly, Rafferty unsteadily above, Erin craning up at him from below. "You," she said.

Might as well settle this tab, too. "Erin, is it? Just want you to know I feel bad about, y'know, the way I was acting. It was the gin talking."

"I'll take that as an apology."

"And Paul Bunyan? Where is he, this fine night?"

"Ewan? He's back in our room, not feeling well. Travel doesn't really agree with him."

Asleep, then. No doubt dreaming his blue ox dreams.

She held his eyes, just a beat too long. *Tipped your hand, Erin. Gotta watch that.* She hesitated—and in that hesitation entire continents appeared. Continents of possibility, of turn and counterturn, of small gasps and low moaning sighs deep into the night. *Pleasure pumping pleasure into hips.*

"I, ah . . . I should be going," he said.

He squeezed past her, face to face, was three steps down when she called back to him. "The offer still stands, by the way."

He turned, looked up. Their positional advantages had shifted. She held the high terrain, was now calling in artillery.

"The offer?" he said. "What offer?"

"To tell your side of the story. The hit-piece we did on you. If you'd like to respond, we can do it tonight, we can do it right now, in fact."

He smiled. "As long as you used the phrase 'devastatingly handsome' somewhere in there, I'm good."

She laughed, for the first time since they'd met. "Ah, but we didn't," she said. "An oversight on our part."

He could see the night branching out in two directions: regret versus loneliness. He chose loneliness; were he younger, he would have chosen regret. "I appreciate the gesture," he said with a wobbly nod of the head. "I truly do. But I'm afraid I would only disappoint," and he left her there in the stairwell to watch his retreating shoulders with a mix of pity and puzzlement. It was a look Rafferty often left in his wake.

•   •   •

AN ANGLICAN CATHEDRAL, AS IT TURNED out, so no priests, no confessional sins-be-gone phone booths, no wine into blood, no papal decrees.

Not that it mattered. By the time Rafferty got past the hotel bar, the one dubbed Busby & Hobson's (he'd veered in for a bit of Dutch courage before crossing the cobblestones to face his conscience), the church service was already over. People were filing out, the organ was playing a dirgelike hymn—and hymns were always dirgelike, even the happy ones. He looked around, returning to a hometown he hadn't been to in years. Everything was both familiar and strange at the same time.

Above the altar, an empty cross. In an alcove, a crucifix, arms held out somewhere between surrender and embrace. These etiolated images of Christ, so far removed from the rough-knuckled carpenter with his booming presence and healthy appetites whose voice could command a thousand in a Sermon on the Mount. When did that change? When did *we* change? When did we begin to want our gods so weak?

Inside churches, all voices become whispers. Rafferty walked through the cathedral, and it opened up an emptiness he didn't know was there. The smell of candle wax, more a presence that a smell. Accumulated layers of prayers and sins, and sadness unburdened. The rose window at the cathedral's end. Works of mercy in the mosaics below. Mary, mother of God, draped in blue, and now he was crying and lighting a candle and he didn't know why or for whom, and maybe this was what we are all searching for, those fleeting glimpses past the world and into yourself, like looking through your own reflection in a train window to the landscape beyond, and maybe it was here, in a temple in Nara, in a mosque in Kuala Lumpur, amid the stone circles of Battleford, or a sleepless night on Lough Derg, a medieval island oratory in Donegal, said to be an entranceway to the underworld, an antechamber of lost souls caught between departure and arrival, maybe it was here, in the blessings and confessions, in the Stations of the Cross, everyone searching for a state of grace. The beggars at Tibetan monasteries. Prayer wheels in Nepal. Candles in Christchurch. *You know you've been traveling too long when every place reminds you of someplace else.*

Rafferty searched his pockets for coins, for some sort of offering, but had none to give, bowed instead, clapping his hands, once, twice, as he'd seen in Japanese Shinto shrines, where petitioners roused sleepy gods with the rattling of an empty husk.

Outside, on a night that was wet with rain, Rafferty turned, looked up at the spire of Christchurch Cathedral one last time. It was the same steeple he would see fall twelve hours later.

CHRISTCHURCH: 12:51 P.M.

TWENTY-EIGHT SECONDS. THAT'S HOW MUCH WARNING the city had: twenty-eight seconds.

A clap of thunder, but from below, a rending sound like fabric ripping. The cobblestone streets began to judder, then jounce, then bounce—a phenomenon known as "trampolining," layers of the earth separating along strata. The looser upper levels lifted above the slower swell of bedrock below, then dropped down, as one wave pushed the next farther up. On February 22, Christchurch was caught on the trampoline, unable to escape, as wave after wave rolled in. On the edge of the city, boulders crashed through affluent homes like bowling balls, a tumble of rock that stopped just short of a public school, sparing the students who were huddled inside, terrified, crying.

A gray tide followed.

Across the city, the tremors had transformed the soil into a liquid state, earth and water separating to create a sludge that bubbled up like a blocked drain. Hundred-year-old oak trees began to topple; their roots, suddenly standing in the liquefied soil, couldn't hold. The Avon River ran gray. (This same silt would later dry and be blown into the air, cloaking the city. But by then, Rafferty would be gone. So would the small man who had arrived, well dressed and unannounced, in the aftermath of the destruction.)

Rafferty was alone at the bar and deep in his third gin-and-cider when the shaking began, rattling the upside-down glasses. *They sound like castanets.* A bone crack of rafters, and the bartender ducked behind the counter, as the entire building seemed to expand and then contract. Rafferty stumbled out onto the cobblestones of Cathedral Square, watched the spire fall, sending its weather vane and cross onto the steps below. The sound of them hitting was like a physical blow, a shove of air that struck Rafferty full force in the chest. Instant darkness and a mouth filled with grit; he would feel it on his teeth for days. Eyes gummy, lungs choking, and when the dust lifted, the rose window was twisted in agony. Sirens and car alarms, and beneath it all, a terrible silence.

Across Christchurch, heritage buildings were falling. Windows were imploding, brick walls were collapsing into cubist avalanches, falling outward onto passing traffic. There was an arbitrariness at play: some of the oldest structures rode out the rise and fall, others unraveled in an instant. One hotel, twenty-six floors high, had fallen at a dangerous angle, was propped up only by the office building beside it. Wrenched free of its moorings, a fire escape dangled in midair, barely attached, like a child's loose tooth.

The cloud of dust pushed Rafferty back, into the bar where bottles had shattered, wet on the floor and sickly aromatic, but the hotel itself, four floors tall, was still standing. He picked his way through broken glass, grateful not to find the bartender lying dead behind the counter. Small mercies. Soaked a bar towel in water, tied it around his nose and mouth, headed back onto a street populated with silhouettes.

The noon sun had been transformed into a blood orange, bloated in the sky, swollen and ripe. Disembodied voices. Trapped pleas. A mother, crying frantically. A child, answering. Rafferty climbed onto the first pile he came upon, began pulling aside the rubble. He was still there at nightfall, amid the ruins, searching for survivors under the glare of rescue floodlights, was still there when Tamsin arrived on scene.

Emergency crews set up triage stations as best they could to help the shell-shocked and the walking wounded. Tourniquets and the fast twist of cloth bandages. Facial wounds with bones exposed. Businessmen, ties tossed over shoulders, carrying stretchers, shop clerks joining in. The blood of it all formed a red paste in the settled dust, and a soft rain began to fall. First as mist, then a steady sheeting fog. The paste became a slurry, and the slurry ran between the cobblestones.

Nine major aftershocks followed, a rolling barrage that tore away further masonry, toppled landmarks. Damaged buildings would suddenly move, sending rescue teams scrambling to get clear.

Rafferty hardly noticed. Knuckles bloodied and face beaded with rain, he was wrestling a slab of drywall free from the beam that had impaled it when someone tossed him a pair of gardening gloves. He pulled them on, and the slab slid free. The rebar below was twisted like a mass of pipe cleaners, and wedged in, deeper down and caked in clay, was a face. Rafferty squirmed through, stretching to pull out—a mannequin's head. In the sixteen hours he spent in the rubble, returning to the hotel for water, but then right back, he never saved anyone. An apt epitaph, he realized, one to be chiseled onto his own gravestone when the time came: *Here lies Thomas Rafferty. He never saved anyone.*

The New Zealand defense forces arrived, helicopters airlifting rescue teams in and casualties out. Firefighters, paramedics, and army engineers: they poured in. Within hours, international teams began arriving as well. Military transport planes landed, carrying supplies and personnel. The first to appear were the Aussies. They brought a fully equipped field hospital with seventy-five beds. The Japanese arrived soon after. No strangers to urban disaster, they sent in their own teams with search dogs, as did Taiwan and Singapore and the UK. The Americans arrived with forty tons of supplies and equipment, and the county of Los Angeles, which had experienced similar catastrophes, sent a team of its own.

With the rescuers came members of the media, though the line between the two occasionally blurred. A TV crew from Channel Nine in Sydney was reporting on the disaster when their cameraman picked up a faint noise. He waved for his crew to stop talking. They listened. It was a woman's voice, buried deep in a building. Alerted by the TV crew, a band of rescuers rushed in to dig out what would be the last living survivor. After that, only bodies were retrieved.

Through contacts in the US Defense Department, Tamsin Greene had hitched a ride on one of the transport planes. Long acclimated to the presence of marines, she found the search-and-rescue teams more subdued, but still with that same muscular swagger about them, especially the women. Tamsin, meanwhile, looked like someone they had bullied in high school. Round-shouldered and short, stocky even, not unlike a compressed spring, a slinky, say, after it had reached the bottom of the stairs. She'd worn thick glasses throughout her school years, until corrective surgery had given her near-perfect vision. Near, because the operation had also left a strange afterglow, a halo effect in her peripheral sight, one that slipped away whenever she tried to look at it. And perhaps that was her strength as a photographer, the fact that the world around her was always slightly askew; she was capturing images that weren't entirely there.

Eschewing offers of manly help (from the women, as well), Tamsin lugged her camera gear onto the tarmac. Sweaty. Alive. Almond eyes and warm skin tones, "vaguely Asian" as she called it, Tamsin had Filipina, Welsh, Ecuadorian, and—if family lore is anything to go by; and it usually isn't—a bit of Cherokee as well, though that last one was more rumored than real. Her own family was firmly ensconced in the bland mire that is Wisconsin. "The only exotic thing about me is my name," she liked to say. "I'm just a cheese head with a camera." A camera—and a scar running down the left side of her face, thin as a razor, visible only in a certain light, a souvenir of war zones past and the endless rounds of plastic surgery that followed. (Which configuration of ethnicities had reared up the "Greene" surname was never clear, though, even to her.)

A jeep brought her into the heart of the matter and, from there, she hiked in, ducking under the danger tape that now lassoed the city center, a no-go zone deemed unstable. It was Iraq after Saddam. It was Beirut after the bombs.

A dark night. A fallen city. Floodlit beams streaked with rain. One precarious slab of wall stood, improbably upright amid the ruins like a new landmark. And there, in the middle: a lone rescuer, framed heroically against the glare. Tamsin adjusted her settings, focused through the rain, low res for a nice grainy texture, kicked up the f-stop half a notch, a low depth of field to really make it pop, and . . . "Son of a bitch," she said. *That's Tom Rafferty. Fucker owes me fifty bucks on a Hanoi handshake.*

Tamsin hadn't recognized him, not at first. So, she came closer— she always came closer; it was her job to come closer. Changed lenses. Zoomed in to confirm. Sure enough, there he was: Tom Rafferty, looking lost and wet amid the wreckage, hopelessly, haplessly, trying to find someone—anyone—to rescue. It brought back memories of other wreckage, other wars.

The image she captured would later be picked up by Reuters, would run in newspapers worldwide, in print and online, would earn Tamsin her seventh APA nomination: *Thomas Rafferty (uncredited) standing in silhouette. Christchurch, 2011, after the earthquake.*

She began picking her way across the various mounds of debris that separated them. "Raff!"

ROZENSTRAAT

THE TAXI CAME OVER THE BRIDGE, and Gaddy Rhodes leaned forward, peering out at what was both inevitable and unexpected: the hotel was . . . gone. Fenced off and rumbling with activity, a construction site now marked the spot. New York in motion, a city that was constantly erasing and reimagining itself. The Commonwealth Inn, removed. The edifice that had loomed so large at the heart of who she was, gone, gone, gone. Heavy machinery was taking great bloodless bites out of what remained, emptying wreckage-filled mouthfuls into waiting trucks, stirring up dust and ash and memories—asbestos, too. The orange-vested wrecking crew wore masks, looked like bandits from afar. From the back seat, Gaddy Rhodes watched as the rapidly disappearing hotel drew nearer.

The morning traffic that caterpillared across the bridge slowed to a halt. Heat and horns and anger on a slow simmer. The stop and go, the nausea and sweaty shouted abuse, a wedding ring falling down a drain.

Only the elevator shaft remained, stubbornly upright, refusing to fall. They'd have to detonate that later, she imagined. Mechanical buckets dumped rubble into large holding pens, the crews sifting through, the industrial mesh trays shaking the debris into pans below. And somewhere in this rubble, the remnants of a wooden bedframe. A bedframe with a hidden message carved into the underside: GR + ML 4 VR.

This brittle city. The daily ordeals and obstacles that sap your will, that numb your heart like Novocain in a slow-drip. And the Commonwealth Inn disappearing into its own dust.

It seemed so long ago.

Memories emerge, brutal and banal. A greeting card left for her on the kitchen counter on the morning after another argument. An argument about nothing, their specialty. Inside the card was an inspirational thought (not his; he was an actor, an interpreter of other people's lines, not his own): *Love is a garden, and every garden needs tending.* She'd had to stop herself from physically gagging. *We're a Hallmark couple now? Is that what we've become?* If he'd thought this was the gesture that would turn things around, he was sadly mistaken.

A garden? She had metaphors of her own. What was marriage? It was a quicksand picnic; struggling only pulled you deeper. It was a Pompeii of the soul: petrified postures, mummified figures, positions that have turned to stone. It was many things, but a garden it was not.

The interchangeable breakfasts and daily quarrels, the sad desultory marital bed, and Gaddy off to Europe (again), as he stayed behind, hamster-wheeling through endless rounds of auditions, the two of them meeting on designated cease-fires (anniversaries, Valentine's), opposing armies in a no-man's-land coming out at Christmas to play a muddy round of football before returning to previously entrenched positions. A garden? No. Not a garden.

Gaddy hadn't been unfaithful—not physically anyway, and for all she knew neither had he. But there are worse things than infidelity. The slow death of affection, for one. She'd taken an extended leave in Amsterdam, a two-week seminar on the latest in forgery techniques, and he had retreated upstate to a community college—just a temporary measure, you understand—to teach others to be as successful as he was.

The end of her marriage arrived postage due. He'd done the paperwork for her—she appreciated this; he was always considerate that way—and so, on a small table in a small room overlooking the Rozenstraat, Gaddy Rhodes had signed off on six years of her life.

What followed was predictable: lots of sex, very little love. These weren't even affairs, but escapades—escapades of the heart, and not even the heart, the flesh. She tried girls, but they annoyed her. Tried boys, but they bored her. Tried abstinence, but that just made her skin jitter. Stepped off the ledge again and again, flung herself at love—and missed. Again and again. Land mines everywhere. But even as she picked out the shrapnel of yet another affair, yet another escapade of the flesh, her thoughts turned ever homeward, to that tousled drama student, so full of promise, so short on talent, the boy who had surrendered so easily, who had settled for less: her husband, now ex, and the lost ring at the Commonwealth Inn.

The traffic came to a halt, throwing her forward, then pulling her back. Oh, the stop-and-go joys of a New York commute.

From the back seat, Gaddy stared above the machinery that was erasing the last remnants of her honeymoon, tried to imagine where in midair their third-floor "suite" would have been. *Our room faced the bridge, I remember that.* And her brand-new husband under the bed with a penknife, singing "Honeymoon Hotel" off-key, in homage to Elvis, socked feet sticking out like a marriage mechanic, and she was never sure if he knew those weren't the right lyrics, or was just being playful. He had carved those initials, underneath and out of view, to make her feel better, and it almost worked.

Disappearing down the bathtub drain, the rattle of a ring, and her in tears and him saying, *Never mind, we will buy a new one,* but of course they never did, and the hotel handyman shaking his head and explaining how it was gone for good because the pipes fell three floors into a holding tank and more tears and her sobbing apologies to her young husband and young husband saying it was just a ring and what did it matter we are in love, but were they really? And maybe it was a sign, a small omen. The ring had leapt off her finger so easily, as though trying to escape. "It was a mistake," she said. "A mistake, a mistake." And it wasn't clear, even then, if she was still talking about the wedding ring.

GR + ML 4 VR. It was the same message Marc had carved under the bed. (That was his name: Marc. She looked him up now and then on IMDb, was both secretly pleased and secretly sad when she saw no record of any roles beyond a short film he did in college. His best reviews were on Rate My Prof.)

It seems so long ago.

And yet . . . *Even now*, she tells her therapist, Syd Something-or-Other, *even now, after all these years, I still believe.*

In God?

In love. It was embarrassing to admit; it felt as though she were confessing to something foolish and disreputable, like being a charter member of the Flat Earth Society or a practitioner of naturopathic medicine. And perhaps she was right to be embarrassed. Gaddy would have explained more, would have told Syd about the initials on the ring and the message under the bed, but her time was up and she never went back.

The taxi crawled past the architectural vanishing act on the corner.

Even with the quicksand and the chasm gaps and the Pompeii postures and slow suffocation, she missed him—the idea of him. She missed being in love. She missed the person she used to be. Gaddy, the mooncalf. That silly girl, young and overflowing with possibilities and potentialities. Someone who believed in Art and Truth and Beauty, who felt (wrongly, as it turned out) that all three were interchangeable.

She twisted her empty ring finger as the missing hotel came up alongside the taxi window. She'd told Syd about the wedding ring, but not the childlike inscription inside: GR + ML 4 VR. Why? She wasn't sure except, maybe, like any secret worth keeping, it was too small to reveal, too important to share.

The taxi lurched. She could feel her stomach slosh. Leaned up, banged on the glass. "I'll get out here." She could see the blue cube that was her office. Two blocks. Three intersections. It would probably be faster to walk anyway. "But—now is picking up," the cabbie protested, referring to the traffic. She shouted again for him to let her out. Now.

Gaddy walrused herself from the back seat, pushed her way past the Commonwealth deconstruction site, where the work crews in the pit below had come up against the bedrock of the hotel's foundations, once hidden in the earth, now exposed.

Horses clattered by, hooves in disagreement, tourists in carriages trying hard to have fun. A bus stopped to decant passengers, lowering itself on a pneumatic hiss. Gaddy crossed the street, moving upstream against the flow of pedestrians, past a schoolyard surging with shrieks. The blame-shifting protestations of children. Alpha girls flouncing past, head high. The shy ones chewing on their hair. Boys in huddles. Pokémon sects. Older kids, louder shouts—on some hidden cue they will disappear as surely as a magician's flourish, into hallways, into classrooms. No children. They'd agreed on that, but now up pops his Instagram daughters and his Instagram wife, the four of them looking like a Sears studio portrait.

Rhodes spotted a sodden Pokémon card plastered on the sidewalk, had to resist the urge to lean over, scoop it up as she passed. *Some of these cards can be worth thousands of dollars.* Treasures, treasures, everywhere.

The glass cube was getting closer.

Here is what Gaddy Rhodes *didn't* do on this particular morning: she didn't enter the office lobby, didn't beep her card, didn't ride the elevator to her cubicle Knossos. Instead, she kept walking, past her building, could see her reflection swimming alongside her in the glass. And then it too was gone. Crossed one street, and the next, headed down an alleyway past an autobody shop muscular with mechanics and a pawnbroker with barred windows, its treasures under lock and key. It would take twenty-two minutes for her to walk it, if Google Maps was to be trusted—and it usually wasn't. And now her pace was picking up.

The usual tatty stores, permanently going out of business. Self-anointed "emporiums" with brummagem abundances, shelves stacked with designer goods of unlikely provenance. Knockoffs *of* knockoffs—and oh, for a decent Chinese reproduction rather than these shoddy Serbian versions thereof. Maybe even a three-legged toad or two.

None of this—none of it—was on official company business. Gaddy would be logged as late, if anyone bothered to check, which they didn't. True, she did have her Interpol ID on her, and she may have given the *impression* to the person she had contacted that this was, possibly, perhaps, an Interpol assignment, but those were assumptions on their part, not assertions on hers. An online forum, a query thrown into the ether, and Gaddy Rhodes had jumped at it. *I will be there first thing tomorrow morning. Please have it ready.*

Another street, another neighborhood. She was cutting across social strata. Older buildings. Colonnades, crumbling, but still regal, with angels and other architectural flourishes tangled up in a stone-work of garlands, of gargoyles. Pupil-less eyes. And brownstones lined up like leather-bound volumes on a bookshelf. She counted down the numbers, buzzed the correct door.

"Hi. Come on up."

Stairs that creaked underneath the carpets. Walls, freshly painted.

The entire place smelled of latex and linseed oil. A fretful woman, a fretful man. Newlyweds with expensive secondhand furniture. Living beyond their means; she could smell that too.

"It's, ah, it's over here." This was the husband. "Wasn't sure whether we should move it, might get damaged, so we sort of left it how it was."

A loose bolt of cloth on the dining room table.

The wife, eyes wide, watching Rhodes. "Do you think . . . maybe?"

Rhodes smiled tightly, said nothing, took a pair of cotton gloves from her pocket, unfolded the first large flap of the canvas. The surface was covered in a riot of hues, dribbled lines of color and wildly exuberant splatters of paint, this way and that, unbridled and overlain as though in a frenzy.

She folded the cloth back, peeled off her gloves.

The young couple, hearts wringing, waited for her to say something.

"I like your ring," said Agent Rhodes. "Elegant."

She was referring to the matching wedding bands they wore.

"Thank you. A friend of ours did them. And the—the painting?"

"It's not a Pollock."

"It's not? Are you sure?"

"It's a drop cloth, left behind by the painters." She flapped the cloth open again, not bothering with gloves this time. "You see the spatters of blue, here, on top of the orange? That's the same blue on your sideboards."

A pained look. "Worth nothing?"

"Nothing."

An alternate future, one attended by manservants and maids and droll British butlers, had melted away. Too many episodes of *Antiques*

Roadshow. Tales of dusty fortunes tucked into wardrobes, stuffed under mattresses. Treasures everywhere, true, but the fact remained that there would always be more drop cloths than lost Pollocks.

The husband smiled—more of a grimace really, the type of expression one sees on someone who has been shot in the stomach but is still trying to put up a brave front. With the wife, a look of someone perplexed to discover that reality is, yet again, at odds with her *idea* of reality. Rhodes knew that look. Knew that feeling. Still, they comported themselves well, all things considered.

The wife, voice barely audible. "Are you sure?"

Agent Rhodes nodded, handed her a business card. "If anyone else shows up asking about this canvas, call me. Right away."

"Who?"

"A smaller man, well mannered. He may have seen your post as well, may try to contact you. My office is just a few streets over. I can be here in fifteen minutes."

They took her card, nodded softly. But the small man never showed up and they never called.

Gaddy Rhodes returned to her glass corner cubicle, went about her work, waiting for a hushed phone call that never came. *"He's here now, in my shop! In my gallery! In my house!"* She waited for the kettle in the staff room to boil, dunked her tea bags. Waited, as the days slipped away, one after the other. It seemed so tepid, all of it: the tea, her work, the morning commute and the taxis and the Commonwealth Inn disappearing into its own dust. Eventually a birthday card arrived with her name on it. It was from Andrea Addario and was signed "Belated wishes."

So it went. Gaddy Rhodes added her name to get-well-soons! for people she hardly knew, submitted reports to administrative assistants she'd never met, waited again for the past to resurface. Eventually, the Commonwealth Inn itself would be paved over and sealed under a layer of asphalt, just another vacant lot awaiting investors who never materialized. The Okinawan snake on her desk, suspended in a cloudy liquor, slowly disappeared behind a wall of file folders and three-ring binders.

Personnel manuals and mission statements. Leaning towers of paper. Quarterly assessments are due Friday! And in the middle, sinking slowly: Gaddy Rhodes, formerly on active duty, now crossing items off a to-do list. Lost behind a wall of her own, murky and depleted.

She could feel the pilot light inside her flicker and go out.

Could feel her world being stripped away, layer by layer, until only that gnawing question remained: *Who are you?* She was still there, lost among the cubicles, when news first began to crawl along the bottom of her screen of an earthquake in Christchurch.

INTERESTING TIMES

As a well-known Chinese curse has it: "May you live in interesting times." A modern update might be, "May you find yourself in a news cycle." CNN, all frowny faced. BBC likewise. NHK too. Christchurch was trending.

The territorial army had cordoned off the city's central business district, and the entire region "within the four avenues" was now off-limits. Teams of engineers swept through, assessing degrees of damage, moving people away from the drop zones—those areas where taller buildings might still yet fall. Compromised architecture, poised to topple. Red zones, drop zones, no-gos: whatever the designation, it amounted to the same thing. Christchurch was being emptied out.

A slow-moving exodus was underway, biblical in scope, as thousands left the city in a haze, stumble-walking away from homes that had been left uninhabitable even as the helicopters continued to chirr overhead, releasing bucket-falls of water onto still-smoldering ruins. In Leicester Square, where the diaspora had gathered, someone began to sing "Amazing Grace," and one by one other voices picked it up, carried it forward. *"I once was lost, but now am found."* On the park's wrought iron gate, someone had draped a hand-painted banner: RISE UP, CHRISTCHURCH.

Rafferty's fellow typists had been on a sponsored jaunt to a local gallery to see a display of Maori artifacts "reimagined" in a modern context. (That's what conceptual art does; it doesn't imagine, it *reimagines*.) They were there when the earthquake hit, as light fixtures swung crazily and Maori war clubs jumped in the display cases. The Christchurch earthquake would kick-start several careers as this dissolute array of travel writers was suddenly thrust into the thick of it, elevated to the role of eyewitness reporters, on the ground at the very epicenter. Christchurch had found itself in interesting times, indeed.

And all the while, across town and past the cathedral, Thomas Rafferty kept digging.

He worked his way in, slab by slab, had acquired a safety vest from one of the crews at some point, took a break only when his back forced him to. His spine was killing him, and he eventually limped across to his hotel in search of water and ibuprofen, past the fallen cathedral. Heritage ruins. Culturally significant rubble. In an instant, the cobblestone heart of Christchurch had gone from city square, lousy with tourists, to an abandoned amphitheater, something you might see in ancient Rome or modern Sarajevo.

The dust that had plumed upward had not entirely settled, and a figure moved through this purgatorial dimness. A small man, impeccably dressed. The sort of man who seemed to be wearing a bowler even when he wasn't. He was carrying a large fold of paper under one arm, blueprints of some sort, with two heavyset construction workers accompanying him in hard hats and reflective vests.

Must be a civic administrator, Rafferty thought, or perhaps an engineer or an architect. He seemed familiar. *I know him. I've seen him somewhere.* A forgettable face, but still. *Where do I know him from?* It wasn't the face, Rafferty realized. It was the destruction, the pall. They passed each other in the rain, exchanging nods, and Rafferty couldn't shake that sense of unease, murky and ill defined. Travel long enough, and everyone reminds you of someone else.

A plastic CAUTION notice was posted at the entrance to the bar, with yellow police tape stretched across. Rafferty ducked under— EMERGENCY POLICE EMERGENCY POLICE EMERGENCY—walked through the abandoned movie set of the bar. Broken glass and bottles. Down the hallway and up the back stairs, thirty-nine steps to the third floor. *Cautioned*, he reminded himself. Not condemned. Cautioned.

The building was leaning like an ocean liner poorly moored, the floor creaking underfoot as he made his way, fun house style, down the skewed perspective of the now torqued corridors to his room. The power was out, but the hotel's backup generator had kicked in and the emergency lights cast wan pools along the way. His door had been wrenched open, was hanging on one hinge, and he entered to find his laptop covered in grit, but still glowing. He pulled a bottle of water from the dying minifridge, swallowed a fistful of muscle relaxants and anti-inflammatories. Sighed. Checked his inbox.

Messages had been cascading in, and he scrolled to the bottom, read through the ascending tones of panic, worry, excitement, impatience. "Are you alright??" "Is everything okay?" "Are you still alive?" "Where are you?" "Are you still in CC? Tell me you are still in CC!" "Front row seat, baby! Forget travel assignment. Our news editor wants an exclusive. Two thousand words, plus pics, if you can—camera phone images are fine—with follow-up, magazine rates, plus 50% on reprint. Couldn't believe it when I told her we had someone on the ground!"

Rafferty replied: Here is the article you asked for.

He attached a file, "New Zealand is for Lovers," hit SEND.

The response was immediate: What the fuck is this?? Are you trying to be funny? We want 2K words on the fucking earthquake, not nude bungee jumping! Write that up for us, pronto.

Pronto? Who the fuck says "pronto"? Rafferty re-sent the same article as before.

Quit messing around. If you can't write what we asked, you will never write for us again.

Rafferty: Promises, promises.

Fuck you.

He left his beseeching laptop, walked back down the leaning stairs of Christchurch and out again, onto the shrouded streets, oddly monochromatic in their pallor. Rafferty moved to the next collapsed building, began tossing aside the roof tiles and sodden drywall. He was still there, under the floodlights, in the rain, when Tamsin Greene arrived.

"Raff!"

He turned, wiped his face, watched as she made her way toward him, watched as though he'd been expecting her all along.

"I'll want royalties on that," he said, gesturing to the camera now slung over her shoulder under a protective rain sheath.

"I don't pay royalties to shadows. Jesus, Raff. You look like shit."

"Having a city fall on top of you will do that." Floodlights and needles of rain. Jumbled ruins in the dark. He looked at her. "Shouldn't you be in Libya?"

It was the Arab Spring, but they hadn't started killing each other wholesale—not yet. Her editor was keeping an eye on Syria, as well. *Could be trouble*, he'd texted (hopefully). *Protests have begun. Might be the start of something more.* In the meantime, she'd been pulled off rotation, sent here.

"So," he said, as though they'd run into each other at a farmer's market or in line at the bank. "What brings you to Christchurch?"

She could never tell when he was fucking with her. "Really?" she said. "You're asking me why I'm here? I'll give you three guesses."

"This isn't a war zone."

She looked around her. "Sure as hell is. Buildings start falling, I'm there."

He wiped his face again, using his forearm, considered this nemesis-friend standing in front of him. "Are you still with the CIA?"

She laughed, but the laughter was lost in the rain. This was a running joke of theirs, one that had been going on for seventeen years, had been going on since they first met. At least, she thought it was a joke; with Rafferty you could never be entirely sure. "I'm not with the CIA," she said.

"You're with someone."

"I'm not with anyone, you dick. Not at the moment, anyway." Her way of letting him know she was single again. Subtlety was never her strong suit. "And you?" she shouted. "Still writing magazine filler and birdcage liner?"

"Proudly so."

"Shouldn't you be reporting on this mess instead of, I dunno, crawling around in the muck like a subterranean mole?" She opened an umbrella, stepped up to him. He ignored the offer.

"Moles are subterranean by nature," he said. "That's a redundancy. If you'd paid more attention in school, you'd know that."

"Y'know, Raff, the fact that you haven't been throttled in your sleep remains a mystery for the ages. Seriously. This is a pretty big story. Why aren't you out interviewing survivors, capturing the moment, running up your bylines? We could link up. I'll provide the images, you do that typety-type thing you do."

"I'm not a journalist. I'm a travel writer." The spasms in his back were getting worse. It always got worse when he stood still. Rafferty returned to the task at hand. "Well, it was nice seeing you again, Sally McGhoul. Still have a lot more shit to move."

"You really think there's anyone under there?"

"Won't know till I look."

"Leave it for the professionals, Raff."

He turned to face her. "I am a professional. Remember? I've been here before. We both have." Rivulets of water running down his face. Salt water and rain.

"True enough," she said.

They had first met in a refugee camp in eastern Congo, Rafferty stunned and struck with fear, not sure which way to turn. Tamsin spotting him in the mass of humanity, pulling him free. And here he was, lost again in the rain. Rafferty, among the ruins. "Déjà vu all over again, eh Raff?" They had danced around it, but never faced it: what they'd been through. Allusions and sidelong glances, but never sobbing confessions in the dark. Rwanda and the Congo.

The rain was becoming insistent. "C'mon," she shouted. "Let's call it a night. You've done more than enough. We need to get you out of those wet clothes."

"I'm not walking away from this."

"No one said you were. But look around you, Raff. You're the only one out here. There's no one else."

That wasn't entirely true.

Across from them in the distance, in an open pit, heads barely visible, rain angling through the floodlights, the pair of workers he'd seen earlier were flinging wet debris out of the hole. The small man stood at the edge of the pit under an umbrella, perfectly still, backlit and barely there. That single slab of wall, masonry knuckled with rock, marked the spot as surely as a headstone.

"I know that guy," said Rafferty.

"You know everyone. C'mon, let's go."

"No, really. I've seen him somewhere."

But Tamsin was already making her way back across the obstacle course that was Christchurch after the quake. Rafferty caught up and they walked through it together, streets eerily still. Rain falling in sheets, listless, letting gravity do all the work. Territorial officers in rain gear were patrolling the drop zone; they waved them through.

Tamsin had her press credentials, but there was no need. Rafferty's hazard vest and work gloves were like an all-access pass. Puddles had become ponds, ponds had become lakes.

A broken avenue. Windows like empty eye sockets. "My hotel," said Rafferty.

"Still standing," said Tamsin.

The pub on the ground floor, Busby & Hobson's, was still intact as well, more or less. And as they approached, an inebriated voice called out to them. "Rafferty, you prick! You're alive!" It was almost an accusation, the way he said it. Andy the Englishman was standing in the open doorway, bellowing like Lear. "To hell with the weather, come have a drink! Bar's open! On me!"

A drink? "Trust Andy the Englishman to find the one bar that's still open," Raff shouted as he and Tamsin walked over.

"And trust Tom Rafferty to walk into a war zone and come out the other side with a girl on his arm!" Andy gave Tamsin a courteous, semi-satirical bow, then hustled them into the hotel bar. "We have coalesced, my friend! We have gathered in conclave!"

Inside was a remarkable sight. The hotel generator was keeping the exit signs illuminated, throwing doilies of illumination across the tables. Candles cast competing circles, overlapping in Venn diagrams. Shadowy figures were sitting, numb in the silence, waiting for the booze to kick in. A more subdued crowd than earlier, Rafferty noted. Faces flickering in the shadows. A scorched smell, like spent gunpowder. All of the rain in the world couldn't rid them of that.

"Is it safe?" said Andy, answering a question they hadn't asked. "Of course it is! Didn't you see the notice posted out front? Cautioned, but not condemned! That's us, Rafferty, in a nutshell. *Cautioned, but not condemned*. Freebie found loads of bottles packed in the back in cardboard cartons, still gloriously intact."

"You're looting the bar?"

"Certainly not! I'm not some common cutpurse. We're stuffing money into a jar to cover our tab, a pay-what-you-can sort of thing."

Tamsin turned to Rafferty. "I think you got the last round," she said. "Back in Malta. This one's on me. Gin?"

"If they have it. Anything else if they don't." She made her way to the bar—someone had pushed a broom through the broken glass, clearing a path—and Rafferty asked Andy, "There was this guy, small, well dressed. Had a pair of hired workers with him. He seemed familiar. I think he was carrying a set of blueprints. Know who he is?"

"I do not."

"But you did see him, in among the ruins?"

"I did. An engineer, I presume. Certainly seemed to be in charge. Addison, you prat!" And off he went, maître d' to the apocalypse.

Rafferty pulled up a chair next to Freebie, whose face was hovering above the candles like a campfire ghost story. "Raff! You're alive! We were taking wagers."

"You don't take wagers, you place them."

"And a happy fuck you to you, too."

The journalists were comparing notes: "Liverpool Street, completely gone." "Territorials doing a sweep." "I interviewed the mayor, he said the entire city is 'munted.' Anyone here have any idea what the fuck that means?" "The ground *billowed*, up and down like a blanket. Never seen anything like it."

On the other side of the room, under an EXIT sign that was urging her to leave, sat Erin of the rose madder lips. She was covered in dust, and in the strange glow of the sign, she looked as though she'd been painted in phosphorous. Raff shuffled over to see how she was doing. A bottle of wine and a pair of work gloves were laid out on the table in front of her. She must have had the good sense to come in before it rained. How long had she been sitting there?

"You okay?"

She nodded.

"And Ewan?"

"He left." The dust on her face was streaked with mascara-like smears. Tears, Rafferty realized. Tears, long dried. "He didn't stay to help," she said. "Didn't even try. Just left."

"Damn. A boy that big, could've lifted some major wreckage."

"That's what *I* thought." Then, with a hollow-chested half laugh. "You know the old adage, 'You never really know someone till you see how they behave in an earthquake.'"

"Wise words."

She tried to finish her wine, couldn't. "They had to amputate legs to get people out," she said. "An office building. Corner of Madras and Cashel. It folded in on itself like a house of cards, each floor falling into the next. There were students inside. A language school. International students. The roof collapsed onto a classroom. A steel beam had pinned three students across their legs. Japanese, I think. Couldn't speak English very well, only knew a few words. We could hear them crying, 'Dangerous. Dangerous.' Rescue workers cut their way through, crawled in. Couldn't move the beam, and anyway their legs were crushed. Medical teams were called in. Three amputations. We pulled twenty people out of that building, maybe more, and every time someone was rescued a cheer went up, like we were winning. Then the building caught fire." She looked at Rafferty. "There were people still inside."

He wanted to hold her, he wanted to rock her back and forth, wanted to make the pain go away. But he couldn't. *Here lies Thomas Rafferty, he never saved anyone.*

Her eyes were wet in the EXIT light. "One building fell on top of a bus. The entire storefront fell away. It looked like a doll's house that'd been opened up. You could see inside the rooms. A bus that was passing by was crushed. A bunch of us climbed up, tried to move chunks of the wall, but it was too heavy. I held one woman's hand as she died. You could feel it slip away, everything she was. The Number 3 bus. I remember that, the number on the crumpled front. Imagine, you get on the Number 3 bus, thinking ahead to the errands you have to run or the people you have to meet, and your world just . . . falls apart. How does that happen?"

How does anything happen? He wanted to say: *Maybe the world is supposed to break your heart. Maybe that's the whole entire point of it.* But he didn't. He sat quietly with her, instead. Paul Bunyan had fled the scene, and the better half of Erin and Ewan was now on her own. It was Erin, alone. Years later, Ewan would be watching a report on an insurgency in Yemen, would see Erin in a flak jacket squinting into the sun, trying desperately to give a sense of scale to the humanitarian crisis that was unfolding, and he would tell himself, "It took an earthquake to break us apart, that's how strong our love was." He would then go back to his online world of Twitter wars and hashtag activism, and with every telling of the story his actions in Christchurch on that fateful day would grow larger, grander, more beard-like.

"Raff! Get yer flabby ass over here." It was Tamsin, holding up a tumbler of gin like a beacon for the weary. "You still owe me on that Hanoi handshake!"

Erin asked, "A friend of yours?"

"I wouldn't say friend. More like a piece of gum that got stuck on the bottom of my shoe, years ago, that I can't get rid of. Everywhere I go, she turns up." Stage whisper: *"Madly in love with me, you see."*

Erin laughed, was grateful for a reason to. She would wander away soon after, into a ruined city on the far side of the world, trying to make sense of it and mostly failing, but still trying.

Back at the main table, Tamsin was braying over something Freebie had said. She had the most annoying laugh. Not like Erin's, not at all.

He shoved his way into the conversation. "What the hell is a Hanoi handshake anyway?" he asked.

Tamsin spit-laughed her drink. "You really don't remember?" She smeared a hand across her mouth, stevedore style. Might as well have belched, too. "If y'don't know, I ain't sayin'. You came up with it in the first place, don't you remember?"

"I did?" So that's why the phrase sounded so familiar.

Tamsin raised a glass. *"Chin chin,"* she cried. And then: "You know what '*chin chin*' means in Japanese? Penis."

"Penis!" said Andy, always delighted to learn something scatological. The rest of the table joined in. "Penis penis!" and, because it sort of rhymed, "Happiness and penis!"

Tamsin slung her camera, with telephoto lens still attached, onto the table the way a soldier might hoist a gun, finished her brandy with a flourish.

Freebie leaned over, asked her, "How does this stack up? Disasterwise."

"I've seen worse. East Timor. South Sudan. Sarajevo. Christchurch? Decent amount of devastation, but not too bad. They're saying maybe one hundred, one hundred eighty dead."

"Only that?" said Freebie. He sounded disappointed. "A miracle there weren't more, I suppose." But it didn't feel like a miracle. When legs are being amputated, it was hard to see divine intervention at play.

That figure in the rain was niggling away at Rafferty. This wasn't simply a vague feeling of familiarity. There was more to it than that, even if he couldn't quite articulate what that was. He turned to Freebie for help. "There was this guy, out in the ruins, had some hired help with him. Looked like an architect, maybe an engineer. You know him?"

"Little fellah? Kind'a dapper?"

"That's him."

"No idea. Heard he arrived on a private plane, though. Must have been with an aid agency or something. That would be my guess. Why?"

Good question. "I don't know. He just—he seems familiar."

"Perhaps he's the friend you never had," said Tamsin.

Rafferty swished his gin, stared into the glass. It was the closest he ever came to meditation, even after a dreary month spent at a Zen monastery in Shikoku for Vice magazine. *Zen Buddhism: A Study in Contrasts!*

Rafferty, moody and morose. Tamsin, sighing. It was a wonder he ever got laid, this guy. "Tell me," she said. "What is Thomas Rafferty doing on a prepackaged press trip? Since when do you sign up for tourist department junkets and sponsored content?"

"Times are hard all over."

"A commission?"

"A *commission*? You sound like Andy the Englishman. My *assignment* is to write a series of promo pieces on New Zealand, Land of Whatsit."

"What the hell happened, Raff? You used to write for National

Geographic, were a contributing editor at Travel and Leisure. Why are you squandering what little talent you have at newspaper rates, the worst rates in the world? A church newsletter pays more. What is it, a whopping twenty-five cents a word at newspapers now?"

"Twenty-six. I talked them up."

"Even with the cost of your trip covered by Tourism New Zealand, you'll be lucky to break even."

"Appearances to the contrary, I'm not an idiot. A press junket may have gotten me down here, but after that, I'm on my own. We can't all wait around for people to die like you do. I'm thinking I may head north, up to the main island. There's a Maori festival coming up. I might write something on spec, *Maori Mornings*, something like that, see if my former colleagues at Travel and Leisure bite, maybe try Zoomer if they're still talking to me. Maybe pen a side article about bungee jumping. It was invented here, they even have a nude version. Could pitch that to Men's Health or Outdoor Adventure or Nudists Monthly."

"There's a Nudists Monthly?"

"Probably. Why not? There's a Dog Fancier and a Cigar Aficionado and a Cuckoo Clock Enthusiast—I did a piece for them on Switzerland. If there are cuckoo clock periodicals, I'm sure there's a nudist magazine out there somewhere."

"I don't know, Raff. Might seem insensitive, pitching stories like that, what with the bodies still warm and all." But they both knew that with the typical six-month lead time for glossy magazines, the earthquake would have been long pushed off the front pages by then. "And anyway," said Tamsin. "Since when do you care about Maori culture?"

"Since when do I care about anything?" It was the first rule of travel writing: you care about what you're paid to care about. "It's the nature of the biz. They want Maori, I'll give 'em Maori. If I nab an assignment about the latest developments in sheepshearing technology, by gum, I will care about that, too, and deeply so."

"Freelance writer and dime-store hooker. Can you spot the difference? Not exactly a saint, are you Raff?"

"Never claimed to be."

"Oh, how the mighty have fallen."

"You didn't get the memo? My world is over. And anyway," he said, "I sold my soul long ago. You know that."

"Ah," she said, "but that was predicated on you *having* a soul in the first place. Any evidence of that is circumstantial at best."

"I'm not the one whose bread and butter is pictures of dead babies."

A cruel smile surfaced. "Ah, Rafferty. What an interesting man you could have been."

At which point, they were both so irritated with each other that there was nothing left to do but go upstairs and screw. It was a lesson hard learned: affection might fuel passion, resentment more so.

He finished his drink, got up. "C'mon," he snarled.

She snarled right back at him. "Fine."

It was the nearest they ever came to courtship.

PLASTER FROM THE CELLING HAD FALLEN across the bed, and the window had been blown outward, into the street, though a margarita crust of powdered glass still lined the sill. A standing lamp had timbered over, sending delicate shards across the carpet. A dresser had toppled as well, and the Christchurch spire, once perfectly framed by the window, was gone. The glow from Rafferty's laptop had died as well, its battery having finally dwindled into nothingness.

"Like what you've done with the place," Tamsin said as she swept the duvet aside, taking most of the debris with it, pulled back the sheets, gave them a shake.

Rafferty stumbled into her arms, groping for something: salvation perhaps; breasts, more likely. She shoved him back. "You're taking a shower." It wasn't a question. He pushed in again, the way men do, penises like a divining rod. *"Now,"* she said.

"Won't be any water," he protested, but Tamsin knew better. The water pressure at older hotels was gravity fed, and although the roof-top holding tank had sloshed about mightily during the quake, it had held. The heat was draining from the water, though, and Rafferty stood under a tepid shower, eyes closed. Spent some extra time soaping his balls, as an act of chivalry, y'see, but, really, he was trying to wash it from his body, all of it: the smoke, the ash, the acrid scent. But no matter how long he stood under the shower, the earthquake was still there. He could taste it on the back of his tongue.

She was waiting for him, under the sheets, clothes folded next to her camera case, head back, smoking a cigarette. "If we're going to go, Raff, we might as well go in style," she said. *And what is sex anyway, but just a series of squishy noises in the dark?* She knew that wasn't true, though, even as he plodded over to her, sidestepping shards of glass like a clumsy matador. You could try as much as you liked, but a kiss always gives you away. As she saw it, there were only two categories of kiss: sincere and insincere, and Rafferty was always lost somewhere between the two. A line from a Tom Phillips hurtin' song surfaced in her memory: *"He kissed me like he meant it every time."* It was the "like" in that lyric that made it so tragic.

She held him, calmed his horror. He held her and calmed her loneliness. Or was it the other way around? Horror and the lonely,

173

it reminded Rafferty of ships gone missing in the Arctic. What were they called, the two that had sailed first to Antarctica, then to the north, only to be lost forever? *Terror* and the *Erebus*. He whispered this in her ear. *That's us.*

The slow combat of lovers in a bed. The bold shyness, the shy confidence, the surrender that isn't really a surrender, but a ploy. The advance that is secretly a retreat, falling back only to surround, engulf, contain, defeat. To win, to win. They touched like burn victims, wary, tender, nerves raw, and when an aftershock shook the bed, she had to stop herself from laughing. *Did the earth move for you as well?* The building might collapse on them at any point, but neither of them could work up the energy to care. She had been under fire in Kosovo, been pinned down in East Timor, had climbed over dead bodies in the Congo. A tremor in Christchurch? That hardly got the heart rate up.

Waltz with the devil long enough and the danse macabre eventually becomes a two-step. But this was not a two-step; this was a tango. He flipped her over—rather, she flipped herself over; it was a tango, after all, and that takes two—but when another aftershock rippled through, stronger this time, Tamsin twisted free, pulled Rafferty around, on top of her instead, face-to-face. "If they retrieve our bodies, I don't want them to find you humping me from behind. And anyway, if the roof falls on us, I want you on top of me to provide extra padding."

"Shhh."

Making a woman peak suddenly—so suddenly, she has to catch her breath—was a trick Rafferty had learned years before in Bangkok. It usually worked only the one time, though; he had only that one magic trick, hence the series of opening-night performances and premature departures that had marked his life. Tamsin was one of the few who fell for it every time: start soft, end strong; start strong, end soft, with her inner thigh trembling like a tuning fork, in an aftershock of its own. He flopped onto his back, fumbled for one of her cigarettes.

Tamsin exhaled, and he got out of bed, pulling a tide of blankets with him. At first he tried to wrap them over his shoulders, but gave up, threw them to one side, instead. Slipped into his shoes—in case he didn't look ridiculous enough naked already—tread carefully across the glass to the window.

The rain had stopped, and the small man in the tailored suit was gone. Rafferty could still see that one shard of wall, though, the one knuckled with rock, balancing like an obelisk.

Tamsin, asprawl on the bed, lighting a cigarette of her own, letting the ashes drop onto the covers. What did it matter? They probably weren't going to get their deposit back on the room anyway. In a certain light, Rafferty's skin had a faintly yellowish hue, the malarial inheritance of some ill-advised journey she was sure, an Amazonian trek or an East Hastings bender. Jaundiced, she thought, in every sense.

He flicked his cigarette out of the window, into the wet streets below. "I need a drink." With Rafferty it was more a state of being than an actual thirst.

Tamsin, one hand behind her head, considered her misshapen lover. "Y'ever notice," she said, "how a flaccid dick only looks good right after sex? That's the only time." She leaned across, ground out her cigarette on the bedside table. "Y'know what I think? I don't think they added fig leaves to Michelangelo for moral reasons. I think it was purely aesthetic." She shifted, propped herself up, considered this sad specimen of masculinity standing before her now in profile at the window. "Jesus, Raff. You've really let yourself go."

"I'm trying for a certain ugly chic."

"Well, you've got the ugly part down, I'll give you that. You are one ugly son of a bitch." Appeals to pity never worked on Tamsin. "You had a six-pack when I first met you, Raff. Now, what is that, a keg?"

"There's muscles in there somewhere," he assured her.

"Yeah, right. Covered by a protective layer of suet, no doubt."

Fuck you. "You're no spring chicken yourself."

"Hey! I've kept my shape."

"Sure. Convex is a shape."

She threw herself back into the pillows with a great harrumph. "Times like this, I really wish I was a lesbian."

"You think they'd have you?"

"What are you implying?"

"I'm just saying, it's a bit presumptuous, no? We barely put up with you, what makes you think they would?"

She considered hurling something at him, a cushion, or brick maybe, but couldn't be bothered. Lit another cigarette, instead, lay back, smoke trailing from her lungs. A dragon, sated. "It's cold," she said. "Come back to bed, warm me up." But he stayed at the window, standing vigil, staring like a sniper at the broken streets below, looking for a man who wasn't there.

Tamsin peered down at her lopsided breasts, which were even more relaxed than she was. "I have these weird blue veins around my nipples lately. You have any weird blue veins?"

"My entire body is a weird blue vein."

That slab of wall below, balanced upright in the ruined city, looked more and more like a headstone the longer he stared at it, a marker of some sort.

"Raff, come back to bed."

He left the window, but didn't climb in beside her. Sat instead, paunch out, on the edge of the mattress. Took a drag from her latest cigarette, handed it back.

"It's good to see you, Raff."

Lives crossing like contrails.

He was facing away from her, but she could see his shoulders relax, just a little. "You as well, Tammy." He was one of the few people allowed to use her childhood nickname. "Always a pleasant surprise," he said, "when the stars align like that. Usually, when I'm scrambling to get out, you're rushing to get in."

She studied his broad back, oddly scarless considering the line of work he was in. "Funny, isn't it?" she said. "And a little sad, I suppose. We think of ourselves as a breed apart, swashbuckling buccaneers of the air, but really we're just travelers caught between destinations."

"Don't go getting all sappy on me now," he said. He thought of the cathedral and the candles, the arms outstretched, and perhaps she was right, perhaps purgatory was simply a departure gate at night, a flight delayed, forever.

"You ever think about it?" she asked. "The other you. The one you would have been or could have been."

"What, like a normal life?"

She nodded. "A normal life."

"Who wants normal?"

She sighed, postcoital wistful. "I do," she said. "Sometimes. Fleetingly."

"Well," he said, "I haven't given up yet, kiddo. I'm still workin' toward my lifelong dream."

177

"Which is?"

"To be a child prodigy."

She laughed, felt the wistful lift. Maybe this is why she fucked him, not for the sex but for the moments afterward.

He turned. "Why were you there? In the Congo, in Rwanda."

"I told you, I was on assignment."

"Would be the perfect cover."

"I suppose . . ." Then, with another snorting laugh, "I'm not with the CIA."

"You're with someone."

"I'm with you. God knows why."

Rwanda dissolved into the air between them like a secret they forgot to share—and a secret's not a secret till it's shared. They never spoke about the Congo or Rwanda, danced around it, never faced it. Why now? she wondered. And as quickly as she asked herself, it hit her: The chaos, the smoke, the screams. It must have brought it all back to him. The troops, the helicopters, the field hospitals.

It was how they had met, after all, how their unlikely, seventeen-year romantic friendship had begun, amid the flies, in the sweltering heat of central Africa, and then later in Hanoi, Lombok, Seoul, Western Samoa, the riots in Lyon, in happenstance and foresight both: sometimes luck, sometimes in scheduled stopovers and highway hotel rendezvouses.

And here he was, still shattered.

"Why are you here, Raff?"

"Me? I heard you were easy."

"Not this room. This country. This press trip. What's really going on? You've done New Zealand, Raff, more than once. It's not like you to retrace your steps. Have you finally run out of places to go?"

"Not even close."

"So, when did you become so keen to return to the Land of Mutton and Orcs?"

"When I got the assignment."

"Got? Or pitched?"

"Does it matter?" He put out their shared cigarette. "Let's go down-stairs, grab one last drink before this entire place lands on top of us."

Rafferty at the art gallery, the day before. Rafferty asking, cajoling, badgering the staff: "We don't have a number for her," they said, and he knew they were lying. "And anyway. She's gone. Left last week." Where to? "I'm not sure. The North Island, maybe? If you leave your number, we could pass it on to her—if she calls."

"C'mon, Tammy," he said. "Let's get dressed, go to the bar. Catch last call."

"Maori Morning." Tamsin snorted. "Since when do you give a shit about—"and that was when the penny dropped, with a rattle and a clink. "Oh, my god. She's here, isn't she? It's her."

"Her who?"

"What's-her-name. Fuck face. That archeology floozy you used to—"

"Ethnology."

"Whatever. Maori myths and legends, that's right up her wheel-house. Oh, for god's sake. She's here, isn't she? I never cared for her, Raff, *never*. She looks weird. She has a weird face."

"No, she doesn't."

"Her features all scrunched up in the middle like that, like a human wart. Never smiled. All the vitality of a fallen soufflé. Yippy little voice. Don't tell me you came all the way to the other side of the world just to mope after Rebecca the Human Wart?"

"She has something of mine."

"Like what, your balls?"

"Oh, I lost those years ago, remember? Pawned them for a night with you, as I recall. Never got 'em back."

"Your heart, then?" Tamsin fell into the bed, laughed at the ceiling. "Thomas P. Rafferty, still carrying a torch for the girl next door. Tom-Tom the incurable romantic, flouncing about like a love-besotted swain. I love it!'"

"Not my heart either."

"Right." She leaned up on her elbows. "How would she find it? It's probably all shriveled up by now. Must be the size of a raisin."

"God, you're annoying."

She ran her callused hand up his shoulder, and the room buckled and creaked. They held their breath, but it was only timbers, adjusting. A sense of imminent doom was as exciting as any foreplay, though, and she reached around, between his legs, fondled him as though there were some secret combination that might work. "Hey there, slugger," she said, in what she thought was a sexy purr. More asthmatic alley cat than kitten, but no matter, the intent was clear. "How about another go?"

He moved her hand away as gently as he could; she had a fair grip. "You're mistaking me for a much younger man," he said.

Another creak in the joinery. Another sift of the dust. Another omen calling softly, softly.

"Gather your stuff," he said. "We can only tempt fate so long."

FREEZE FRAME

IN THE BAR BELOW, THE CANDLES had died, the darkness had grown. Shivering aftershocks had thinned the gathering of journalists and travel writers; it was less a conclave now than a coven, an Algonquin roundtable of cutout figures backlit by the emergency exits, crowding around a single table. The jar on the bar was stuffed with various currencies and the front door was propped open, their one concession to safety, with each person ready to bolt on drunken legs at the first sign of collapse. They could outrun gravity, apparently.

Tamsin and Rafferty joined them, Tamsin with her camera, Raff with his laptop: tools of their trade.

"You're alive!" Freebie repeated woozily when he saw Raff, forgetting they'd already had this conversation. "We were takin' bets." An empty bottle of schnapps, looking not unlike a drained IV, lay on its side on the table in front of him. When Freebie spotted Tamsin, he added, "The war photographer! You grace us with your presence."

There were hardcore journalists among them now. No namby-pamby travel writers, these. They were disaster zone veterans in their own right, and they knew Tamsin, threw nods and perfunctory greetings her way.

"Still with Getty Images?" they asked.

"New York Times Magazine. A photo-essay."

This was followed by barely concealed glares of envy. Tamsin always got the plum assignments, and there was nothing plumier than a photo-essay.

She had entered the roundtable in mid-dialogue. "They call

themselves the Farmy Army," one of the coven was saying. "They trundled in from the countryside on tractors and front-end loaders, cleared the roads of debris."

"There was a student army as well," said another. "Eight hundred strong. All volunteers pushing wheelbarrows and toting shovels, immediately began cleaning up. I've never seen anything like it."

"I'll tell you one thing," said Freebie, hoisting a fresh bottle. "Kiwis are fuckin' amazing."

"Hear, hear." More toasts: to courage and kindness, and to the quiet understated competence of New Zealanders, perched down here like bats, upside down on the other side of the globe.

"I'm thinking of moving here after this is over. I really am."

"Me too!"

Everyone is always thinking about moving to New Zealand. It's one of the most hypothetical nations on earth, second only to Ireland.

Andy the Englishman reappeared—Rafferty hadn't noticed he was gone—bursting through the open door as though awaiting applause, and maybe he was. "Gentlemen! Like Eisenhower, I have returned!" This was met with a roar of indifference.

"MacArthur," said Rafferty. "It wasn't Eisenhower, it was MacArthur."

"Is that Rafferty, I hear? Still a prick, I see. Gentlemen!" he shouted. "I bring a guest. I found him wandering, lonely as a cloud among the ruins of the city." Behind Andy, a silhouette hesitated in the doorway. Andy misinterpreted this as nervousness. "Cautioned!" he exclaimed. "Not condemned, *cautioned*. Enter, enter! A soiree at the end of days! With the unerring instincts of the scribbler class, we have liberated a cache of hooch that had gone undamaged—until now! Such is the aleatory aspect of travel. One must always be prepared for

Plan B, to say nothing of C through Z." He pronounced it "zed," in the British fashion. "*Entrez, entrez.*"

But the shadow in the doorway didn't move. Andy, theatrically: "Gentlemen, I give you . . . What did you say your name was? Doesn't matter. We've been taking turns paying. Your round!" Andy said this with unalloyed chutzpah. Invite a fellow in and immediately get him to buy; it was the Englishman in Andy's equation, shining forth.

A voice, quietly. "I should be going."

"Don't be silly. Hide awhile with us."

The small man looked over his shoulder. "Maybe just till the patrol has passed."

"Exactly," Andy cried. "When the streets are clear, you can make your escape. Now—come, come. Join us! It's your round. You can't run off now. And here, I thought it was the Scots who were cheap!"

Rafferty saw the silhouette stiffen at Andy's comment. "Why do you say that?" the silhouette asked.

"Well, that is *Ireland* I hear, yes? Just a trace, very faint, but there like an echo. Faith and begorra, you've held onto a bit of that haven't you!" Whether it was a matter of congratulations or commiseration on retaining one's Irish identity wasn't clear. "I'm a student of dialect, you see. Ulster, am I right?"

Another hesitation, more revealing than the last. "Not Ireland, no. New England, I'm afraid."

Someone at the table yelled, "As long as it's not ruddy Old England! This table can't handle another Limey fuck."

"Gentlemen!" Andy admonished. "I expect sobriety and propriety. We have a guest." He turned to the silhouette. "Ruffians and reprobates, the lot of 'em. Pay no heed."

They waved Andy and his guest over, pulled up a chair for them.

The small man in the trim suit sat directly across from Rafferty, perfectly outlined. Rafferty stared at him. *I know you. From where?* The man carried a stiff self-consciousness with him, like someone on the wrong end of a job interview. A bottle of something and a glass of the same were passed down the table.

Before the small man could pour, Andy snatched it up, examined the label in the dim light. "Santa Rosa? Ah, yes, the plebian preferences of the great unwashed. It matters not! Rich or poor, gentry or prole, chambermaids and chamberlains alike, I am a man of the people! Gentlemen"—a belated nod to Tamsin—"and lady, drink up! The territorials are doing a sweep, evicting the last holdouts from the center of the city. They're shutting Christchurch down, my friends. I met our guest here in mid-crouch, as it were, as we both hid from the same patrol behind a shard of stone." Andy had gone out earlier in search of better wine, had come back empty-handed, but with a new member for their coven. He poured a glass for himself and one for the stranger. "To new friends!" he yelled. "The old ones can go to hell."

"Hear, hear!" someone else chimed in. Glasses were duly clinked.

Rafferty was studying the outline across from him. The empty space on a map. A man in want of a bowler. "New England, you say?"

The silhouette pretended not to hear.

"Where in New England, exactly? I used to have a cabin up in Maine, on the border with Vermont." Not true, any of it. He was testing the water, intrigued by the man's evasiveness. Maine and Vermont never touched. Anyone from New England would know that, and Rafferty wanted to see what the small man would say, but the small man never responded. Rafferty persisted. "The Maine-Vermont border. Ever been?"

Again, no answer.

"So tell me, Charlie," one of the journalists asked, throwing the small man a conversational life preserver—they had decided, apropos of nothing, that the newcomer's name was Charlie—"what brings you to Christchurch?"

To this, the small man did reply. "I'm with a brokerage firm. We manage assets, have investments in different countries."

"Interesting work?"

"It has its moments."

Rafferty cut in. "I feel like we've met somewhere," he said.

The silhouette turned. "I look like a lot of people. I have that type of face, I'm afraid. The curse of familiarity. Strangers on a train."

"Not a shadow of a doubt, Charlie," someone shouted. "Not a shadow of a doubt."

The conversation at the rest of the table galloped off in newer, ill-defined directions, and the small man's presence faded. He was still there, but strangely invisible—except to Rafferty. *I know you.*

"What is that, one of those new digital DSLRs?" They were asking Tamsin about her camera.

"It is." None of this smartphone crap. Tamsin shot massive RAW files, digital negatives in effect, images to be color-balanced and adjusted later. She took her camera out of its battered case. "It's the heavy-duty version. Has a real heft to it. You could bludgeon someone to death with my camera. Try that with an iPad."

It was a Canon, which immediately sparked a Canon versus Nikon debate, one as old—and implausibly impassioned—as Coke versus Pepsi, Stones versus Beatles. *Nikon handles skin tones better, but Canon makes the backgrounds richer, sharpens the subjects.* Tamsin didn't care about any of these angels-on-the-head-of-a-pin-type debates. You don't photograph subjects, you photograph light. Low in the sky or harshly rendered, twilit or in that magic-hour moment when the sun has set but its radiance has not, when the entire world seems to glow, transient light from no particular direction, a softness that leaves no shadows. Tamsin Greene was a master of the magic hour. With the halos that were always present in her peripheral vision, in many ways she *lived* in the magic hour. "You learn to read the light," she liked to say. "The camera is just a tool. I can change a tragedy into a feel-good tale, and vice versa, with a simple change of filters."

"Saw your last photo-essay," said one of the other journalists, a photographer like her. "In Harper's, I think." Like he didn't remember. "Was pretty good." Given how begrudgingly journalists admired each other's work, this was the equivalent of a declaration of fealty. "I like what you did with the foreground. Good color saturation. Strong verticals. Yeah. It was nice."

"That's what I was going for," Tamsin said with a smile so lopsided it could almost be a sneer. "When Israeli forces were firing into the crowds, and civilians were fleeing: make sure it looks *nice*." There was a reason the other journalists didn't like Tamsin.

With the camera cradled in her lap, Tamsin was changing the memory card the way a mother might change a bib. "There's a Pulitzer in here somewhere," she said. She popped the current memory card out, slid a new one into place. And then: "Smile, assholes." She fired a practice flash—and that's when it happened.

In the flash of her camera, the room became a tableau vivant, frozen in midmotion. The small man's face was lit up as though caught in a slash of lightning, less than the time it took for a heart to beat, but that was enough: gunfire and screams and flares trailing into the jungle air, tracer bullets and helicopters. Panic and pain and bare feet, running through the mud. Crowds surging forward, pushed back.

Bodies, piled like soiled laundry. Rwanda, imploding. The Congo boiling over. *He was there. In the camps.* Rafferty felt his chest constrict, trapped in a freeze-frame moment of his own.

Darkness returned.

"An interesting piece of equipment," said the silhouette. "May I?"

"Sure." Tamsin passed it across the table and the small man turned it over in his hands, admired the camera from every angle. "Remarkable," he said. He then passed it to the journalist next to him, who performed a similar tea ceremony maneuver. "Not bad. This is Canon's newest line, right? Not as good as Nikon, but still . . . Well made." And so it was that Tamsin's equipment moved slowly around the table, each person admiring it in turn. Some asked about specs, others about low-light conditions and tripod stability, autobracketing and whether it was as waterproof as the older versions. When the camera finally got back to her, Tamsin was about to tuck it into its case when she stopped, looked closer, then up at them. "Okay, which one of you assholes took out the memory card?"

"What?"

"The memory card. The one I just put in, where is it?"

This was followed by accusations and alibis, charge and counter-charge. "What are you accusing us of?" "We may be reprobates, but we are not common thieves, m'lady!" (That was Andy.) "Why the fuck would we want your memory? We've got plenty of our own." "Quit dicking around, you jerks. Those cards cost fifty bucks a pop. Freebie?" "I didn't take your fucking card." "Well, who did?" "It sure as fuck wasn't me." "Ha ha. Joke's over, assholes. Whoever has it, give it back."

Rafferty stared across the table, amazed at what he saw—or rather, what he didn't. The small man was gone. He hadn't left, exactly; it was more like he'd dissolved. As the acrimony grew and the allegations escalated, Rafferty got up, whispered to Tamsin, "I'll be right back."

Outside, the night lay heavy on the city. Rafferty walked down the street, looking for the small man and Tamsin's memory card. In the distance, an army patrol had fanned out, was moving toward the bar. Rafferty slipped away, even as he heard a muffled "Stop!" from the soldiers. He kept moving. When those soldiers reached the bar, they would have their hands full rounding up the reporters who were malingering inside. Rwanda. The Presidential Guard under attack. The Congo. A rapid exchange of gunfire. Bare feet fleeing through the mud. The wet smell of woodsmoke and open latrines, screams that would linger for hours, for days, for years, forever. Screams that echoed even now, as Rafferty crossed the tumbledown square with the fallen cross. *I know who you are, you prick.*

But where was he? This man with the mercenaries. This man with the reptilian eyes.

In the rubble-strewn square, the cathedral steeple was draped across the cobblestones like a downed dirigible. Empty windows everywhere. No sign of the small man. Rafferty turned around, disorientated. Felt lost, then realized why. The wall that had been thumbtacked in the middle of the ruins was missing. The slab of wall that had been standing upright was gone. He'd used that as a reference point, was confounded by its absence, stumbling across the wasteland, trying to figure out where he was in relation to where it should have been.

He finally spotted it, toppled in the rubble, the wall having fallen, and as he drew closer, he saw, clawlike, a hand reaching out from underneath. A body was under the wall.

From across the square, an army patrol was yelling at Rafferty. "Mate! No one's allowed in here!"

Rafferty crossed a loose scree of bricks, accidentally kicking up a metallic snake as he went. He stopped, and from the rain-slicked mud, retrieved a medallion. Saint Christopher, if he wasn't mistaken. The chain had been snapped as though yanked from a neck. *Patron saint of travelers, protector of the wayfaring soul.* Rafferty knew Saint Christopher well. Had prayed to him, drunkenly, ironically, stupidly over the years, had yet to get a reply. Finding the medal there, amid the jumble, was surreal, like running into an old acquaintance at a rummage sale—an old acquaintance who never returns your calls, lying on the surface of the mud. *It had to have come from the dead man.* Rafferty shoved it into his pocket with vague thoughts that it might help identify the body later. As it turned out, this wasn't Saint Christopher, and far from bringing Rafferty protection in his travels, the medallion would prove more a bane than a blessing.

Rafferty tried to lift the fallen slab, but couldn't. This section of wall had been standing when Rafferty left his room. The small man had slipped away, the wall had fallen, and the small man was now gone. It didn't take a detective; Rafferty knew exactly who was under that slab. Hand, like a claw. Reaching out. Rafferty had half expected to spot Tamsin's memory card clutched inside it. He could see where the wall had split on a cavity-pocked segment of mortar. One good shove would have brought it down; that could as easily have been Rafferty under that wall as the small man, and it hit him in a wave of nausea, the instability of it all: the wall, the city, the churches, all those cathedrals and certainties we build up only to watch fall.

Rafferty reeled, shouted, voice thick, as the soldiers moved toward him. "There's someone under here!"

The image remained, though, of a face. Unremarkable. But not the eyes. And it might have been an illusion, might have been the flash bouncing off the retinas, reddish pink and pinkish red, those strange feline dots that appear in the eyeballs of poorly taken snapshots, but even in that single freeze-frame moment, Rafferty had recognized a certain rage, a rage that was buried now beneath that slab of wall.

"There's someone under here!" he cried. "Hurry!"

On the other side of the world, on a small island on the edge of a very large sea, Police Inspector Shimada, senior officer, Hateruma Substation, was waking up from a troubling dream about a man whose face had been erased.

PART FOUR
THE DESERVING POOR

THE CITY WAS SMOLDERING, SHE COULD see it from here: the columns of smoke, the angel hair of haze, the constant chuttering of helicopters.

A girl in her awkward years—thirteen, maybe more, it was hard to say—was making her way homeward along a narrow path high above the plains. A loose assortment of elbows and knees and poorly cut bangs (she did those herself in the mirror). A girl in her awkward years, dressed in the drab tartan of Saint Michael's, hugging textbooks to her chest, the winds tugging at her from all sides—and honestly, who thought brown and mustard made for a flattering school uniform? A girl in her awkward years, caught between landscapes: tumbledown seascapes on one side, the broad Canterbury Plains on the other, spreading out like coarse canvas and creased cotton, the hedgerows and fallow fields, and in the middle, like so much broken masonry: Christchurch in ruins. The rains had lifted, but the city still smoldered. She could see it from here.

"There won't *be* any school, not after that," she said, pleading her case. But it was no use. Fayther, as she had dubbed him, insisted.

"All the more reason to go down, gather your schoolwork. Educational pursuits do not wait on natural discourse. Off you go, Catherine. And take care for any falling rocks."

How exactly?

When the earthquake hit, the cliffs above Saint Michael's had given way, sending large boulders tumbling down to within striking distance of the school. The playing field was now pocked with rubble, and the students had fled, but Catherine had been sent back anyway, to collect her homework.

"Won't *be* any homework." But Fayther was Fayther and once a notion had taken hold of him, he was impervious to pleas. The vats of water. The numerological calculations. The infiltration of bolder sheep. Visions only he was privy to.

So she'd trudged across the fields and down the steep and twisty trail to the schoolyard at the edge of the village, where the rocks had stopped just short of freeing her from the ongoing ordeal that was Saint Mike's. In the silence of the school, she'd gathered her chem and biology textbooks, was now making the windy walk homeward. On the checkerboard plains below: the faint bleat of sirens, still. *I warned them. Would they listen?* Fayther, awake in the Land of Nod. *Entire city, sleepwalking towards catastrophe. I tried to warn them. Would they listen?* Letters to the editor and town hall dustups, and still the city had fallen.

The path climbed through ferny grasses, ran along a high tumbled edge. Directly below was a cove, a scooped-out hollow that dropped directly, dramatically, into the sea. The swell of waves below was like the slow rise and fall of a bullwhip, lifting up—hanging in place a moment—then crashing down, onto a pebbled shore. Beyond the cove lay an endless immensity of ocean. The boat was gone.

It had been there for two days, a nondescript vessel anchored off-shore, waiting—for what? Catherine had spotted it earlier, but it was no longer present. Had she imagined it? Ships never came into the cove; the currents were too unstable, with no pier to land on. Perhaps it had been a rescue ship sent in to spirit survivors to safety, and with no more survivors being pulled from the wreckage of the city, the

ship had simply departed for other coves, other crises. Tragedies were
so easily forgotten. It was like the weather, how clouds sweeping in
from the Atlantic would pummel their home, sending their sheep into
a near-narcoleptic fear, but as soon as it lifted, all you could remember
were blue skies and summer winds.

A separate path ran down, precariously, to water's edge, zigzagging its way to the very bottom of the cove. Catherine pushed on,
over tussocks of grass, past wind-stunted bracken, to the last house
on the last hill, the only house on the hill: a farm on the edge of the
sea, a bungalow balancing act high above the plains, master of all it
surveyed, and not a single tree to slow the wind. You never got used
to the wind, not really.

Next to their house, larger and cleaner and better kept, were the
corrugated walls of their barn (or "laboratorial venue," as Fayther
dubbed it), and as she drew closer, the path twisted one last time,
a long *S* that wove its way between rocky outcrops and clumps of
grass. Suddenly—on the far ridge, she saw something that made her
catch her breath, a single involuntary intake, not a gasp but an inhalation. Poised on the ridge was an ewe, alone and backlit against the
open sky, gazing out to sea with an ovine majesty. Had it started?
Catherine's heart was tugged like a fish on the line. She looked closer,
eyes bright with the beginnings of a smile, but the ewe was not alone.
Alas. Another sheep popped up—and another and another, and her
heart sank. *Not one of ours.* They *baa*'ed and turned, loping along the
edge of the field, flowing past and disappearing one by one. She could
see their cropped tails from here. Fayther's sheep were uncropped,
tails swinging like fatty pendulums; these sheep belonged to the next
farm over. She recognized the herd instinct, alive and well, as each
followed the next along the ridge and out of sight, and sure enough,

the ramshackle figure of a farmhand appeared, ambling behind them, crooked staff resting in one hand, smartphone in the other, thumb-scrolling through messages as he nudged the flock forward.

The path grew muddier. A final familiar turn brought her into the yard, their bungalow looking more paint-peeling and woeful the closer she got. Someone once calculated the ideal distance to view a sheep, a unit of measurement that describes just how close you could get to one before they went from looking fluffy and adorable to soggy and matted: seven-eighths of a mile. That was the ideal distance, when a sheep changed from cotton ball to soiled livestock, from picturesque to pungent. She wasn't sure what that was in kilometers, though.

Fayther was nowhere in view. His stucco bungalow was surrounded by open vats of water, strategically situated along invisible energy lines, as calculated with compass and almanac. They looked like children's wading pools created by using cross sections of a large metal culvert. *The water absorbs essential vibrations.* Fayther had explained this at length to the local Chamber of Commerce during a disaster readiness meeting. *Redirects geothermic tremors, sends them harmlessly up into the air.* He'd produced charts and diagrams, had been actively ignored, if such a thing were possible. She hated attending these meetings, hated the barely suppressed smirks and sly sidelong glances, hated the fact that Fayther was so oblivious. "They're laughing at you," she would complain on the long walk home, and he would blink. "Who?" "Everyone."

They weren't laughing now, though. Fayther's water-encircled bungalow had ridden out the earthquake with nary a crack in the stucco. The barn had rattled and swayed, too, but had withstood the worst of it. "Ha!" he'd cried. "Could've saved the entire city! If they'd just opened their ears." Not their eyes, their ears. "Hearing and listening are two different things," he would remind her.

She found her father inside their home, perched over his graph papers at the dining table. The interior of their home always seemed lit as though through wax paper.

"Katie!" he said. "You made it back just in time. Tea? We're out of Bell's, I'm afraid. Dandelions will have to do. Will you grab a few, next you're out? We have a lot of work to do. The alignments are off, only a decimal or two, but it's enough to throw the entire system out of whack. I'll have to recalculate everything." His voice, like everything about him, was fleshy and folded. He spoke in rounded syllables, as though chewing on something moist, a rag, perhaps, or a reputation. "You'll see!" he said, answering a challenge that no one had issued. "I'd stake my career on it!" Career-to-be, that is. With her father, the accolades always lay ahead in a distant, barely glimpsed but brilliant future. It was, she suspected, a way of doggedly avoiding the past.

The girls of Saint Mike's had been mocking her at the very moment the earthquake hit, swishing their brown-and-mustard skirts, giggling innocently behind serrated smiles. *My dad says your dad is completely off his nut.*

Catherine was always astonished by how, on American TV, school uniforms spoke of private institutions and moneyed privilege. Not so in New Zealand. Everyone wore school uniforms down here. It was egalitarian, is what they said, much like New Zealand society supposedly was. Where Australia had been a penal colony, settled by criminals and cutthroats, New Zealand had been selected for a more genteel clientele, the "deserving poor," as they were known, given free passage to the antipodes. That was the version of history that was told here, anyway. A poverty softened by flowers, with jacaranda and hyacinth, which, having escaped the gardens, now grew wild in glorious disarray. This was the myth of their islands. But she knew better. It wasn't poverty, it was middle-class poverty, the worst kind because it pretended to be something it wasn't. It was a dishonest poverty. Out here, on the heights, or down below on the Canterbury Plains, school uniforms—blouses and blazers, and the inevitable tartan—were as common as sheep.

When the florescent tubes had begun to burst, popping like Christmas crackers, showering glass, the girls of Saint Mike's had squealed, partly in fear, partly delight, had scattered like little birds. If only those boulders had taken out her school. If only they'd rolled clean through the classrooms, the desks, the girls' changing rooms. But like everything else she longed for, it stopped just short.

"Katie?"

He'd asked her a question. "Yes?" she said, stepping out of the kitchen with its wax paper light.

"The school," he said, repeating his question. "Still standing?"

She nodded. "Still standing." *Unfortunately*. "Saw a boat," she added. "In the cove. It was there this morning. Gone when I came back." But Fayther wasn't listening.

He waved her over. "Come on, luv. Let's have a look."

With a sigh, she handed over her textbooks and he put on a pair of round reading glasses, dainty in their way and at odds with his fleshy features and that wild, flyaway frizz of reddish hair that encircled his bald pate like an afterglow. "Let's see." He flipped through the pages, shaking his head. "Pass me my marker, luv. The big one, in the tin." Slowly, methodically, he went through her books, crossing out entire sections, providing mumbled commentary as he went, more to himself than for Catherine's benefit. "Hearsay . . . never proven . . . mere conjecture . . . dubious . . . never validated . . . *highly* unlikely."

She looked down at her long limbs and knobby knees. Where had these come from? An inheritance from her mother, no doubt, laid to rest under a shrub overlooking the sea. A manuka tree. Honey producing. *Your mother would have liked it.* There was very little of her father in her, though in certain lights, her hair caught faint streaks of auburn, like an echo of her dad somewhere inside her. His entire inheritance.

Fayther handed back the textbooks, now annotated and "improved," as he put it. "Make sure you explain these to your teacher so they can contact the publisher to make the necessary corrections. They'll appreciate the help."

But of course they wouldn't. Whenever Fayther did something like this, Catherine would simply wait till end of term and then tell the school office that she'd lost her textbooks. "Again? Really, Catherine! If your head wasn't screwed on . . ." and Catherine would pay the forty-dollar fine, which she would have to sell one of their lambs to help pay for, dragging it tethered and bleating across the paddocks while her father was away, dragging it to the next farm, where her neighbors paid with an insincere smile and a feigned look of concern. "Your father, he's all right then?"

Fayther never knew how much money they had or where it went. It fell to Catherine to keep this entire creaky enterprise going. The worst part was not the pity or feigned concern or the folded bills she hid in her tampon box (there were limits to her father's scientific areas of interest), it was the stupid glee he showed whenever he next counted the flock and found another one gone. Always a celebratory moment. "Katie! It's starting!"

Sheep in the heights versus sheep in the plains. Two very different breeds. Hardscrabble, up here. The freelance shearers would arrive, seasonally employed, jaunty and carefree (part of the job description, it would seem). These boys could shear a midsize ewe in seconds, turning them over, under, around, leaving mounds of twiggy wool behind, which her father would then sell at cost to the co-op. This wasn't a working farm, after all, it was a scientific endeavor. Profits didn't enter into it, with Fayther counting his flock, mixing his nutrients, charting "acts of independence" in his ledgers. There were times she hated him so much it turned to love.

"I added a potassium derivative," he said. "It alters the vascular regions of the brain, helps oxygenate the hippocampus. That's where I suspect we'll find it. Free will." This was an obsession, one of many, him trying to pinpoint where exactly *mind* resided in the brain, where in the firing of chemical neurons free will dwelled. "Added a touch of magnesium, a bit of calcium"—he spoke as though it were a recipe rather than the alchemy it was. "Plus, a trace amount of soil." *Soil?* Better not to ask.

She was trying not to listen, but her father's voice was so loud, so insistent. He always spoke as though addressing an auditorium, as if his latest vitamin-and-mineral concoction, fed to indifferent sheep on an island at the edge of the world, mattered in the least. News flash, Dad, it didn't. If their entire farm had fallen into the sea, the world would scarcely have noticed. *Why couldn't those boulders have taken out Saint Mike's?* She wouldn't have minded, even if she'd been inside at the time, could imagine her herself, broken and dying with a final fading smile, knowing that the arena of her torment was going with her. The other girls, eyes flitting downward to her frayed gym shoes. The cruel moue that played across their lips as their gaze flitted back up to her face, her bangs. "I like your haircut. Where do you get it done?" "Um, I cut it myself." "Oh my! You should open your own salon." Were they being nice? Of course not. The head-high pivot, the rolling-hipped gait, the sudden gales of laughter as they walked away.

She envied boys.

You could walk off a punch; malicious laughter stayed with you forever. The bully boys left the targets of their attention bruised, but bruises wore off. Girls could gut you with a glance. She remembered one gerbil-faced boy she'd found cowering behind the bins, simpering and tear-streaked, who was constantly being targeted by the upper grades. Catherine would have happily swapped places with him, would have taken a bloody nose over the whispered asides of other girls as they floated past. *"No one even likes her."*

After the earthquake, the girls of Saint Michael's had been in their glory, even though none of them had even had the decency to die. They were young and in their splendor, the girls of Saint Michael's, photogenic and beauteously histrionic, "traumatized" as they liked to pronounce, arms held to their chests like actresses in a play. The earthquake and its aftermath were all about their feelings. In their world, everything was about feelings. Never mind the sewage backups and how that might affect groundwater contaminants, the earthquake was really about *them*, and they hugged each other and they wept and they practiced their lines before stepping in front of their appreciative audiences. It was the best thing that had ever happened to them. One was even interviewed by the local news station. Oh, the emotional toll!

If only those boulders had rolled a little farther.

"Zinc, chondroitin sulfate, vitamin D. I cut back on the

glucosamine, it was making them sick. Would you, luv?" He nod-ded to the front door, where a plastic wheelie bin was filled with this month's pellets.

Out in the yard, wooden hurdles, low enough for the sheep to leap across, were they so inclined, formed a miniature corral. All the sheep had to do was make that leap, navigate a simple maze, and they would be free. Such a simple choice. But none ever had. They owned forty-two ewes, a scattering of lambs, and two barrel-chested rams for breeding purposes, their hollow foreheads partially caved in from ritualistic butting sessions, dull thuds, and snorts. The rams were held in a pen outside, away from the hormonal waft of ovine ovulation that drove them mad; rams were crazy over hormones, apparently. Cath-erine was afraid of the rams, hated going near them. A younger ram had broken out once, had indeed escaped, but instead of running free across the lands had chased Catherine into her house, only to turn, with a strut, and go back to the very pen it had just escaped from.

She pushed the wheelie bin through the barn doors, left open, as always and intentionally so, inviting escape. Inside, the musty smell of root vegetables, freshly wrested from the earth, was leavened with that of silage, sweet and tart in equal parts. Stacked bales. Damp straw. A dimly lit pen crowded with sheep . . .

Something was wrong.

The sheep were wedged into the far corner as though in a rugby huddle, as Catherine rolled the plastic rattle-thump bin along the troughs, shoveling scoops of pellets into the auto-feeder—one of her father's inventions, involving an elaborate series of tubes and chutes. *What would a ship be doing way out here?* Catherine watched the pellets tumble, separating themselves as they went. Not fishing. Too small for a pleasure cruise. She checked off the date and time on the clipboard that hung beside the feeder—a ballpoint pen was sellotaped to a string for that very purpose—and was about to leave when she turned around. Something strange was going on. The sheep were definitely afraid of something. They'd forced themselves into a single, massive soggy mop, compressed into the side of the far corner of the pen, were refusing to move, even for their feed. What was it that had frightened them? In another country, one might worry about wolves or foxes, or even snakes, but not here in New Zealand. This was a land without snakes, without predators—man excluded, of course. Had some ancient irrational fear been resurrected? Catherine had seen footage of zoo-raised chimps freaking out over photos of a snake, even though they themselves had never encountered one. Certain archetypes lay imprinted in the DNA. She knew this, because it was these very imprimaturs that her father was trying to reprogram. Had some buried instinct been triggered within the flock? Or had the earthquake simply spooked them?

She climbed over the gate in her gumboots, looked around the urine-pooled and straw-bestrewn pen. There was nothing there, but the sheep were still wedged into that far corner. "What's wrong?" she asked, half-expecting an answer.

Across from this scrum of sheep, outside the pen, Catherine saw something. Just a mound of hay, but one that had been freshly turned. Still green, piled hastily. So she slopped across, her gumboots rubbing a ringed rash into her calves. Made it hard to walk, harder still to run.

She climbed over the splattered metal fence to see what was nestled in this freshly turned straw, half-expecting, half-hoping to discover an act of ovine derring-do, a stealth ewe who'd managed to scale the fence, build a home, and hide on the other side. But no. Not an act of free will. A pair of shoes. Men's dress shoes, with legs attached. The straw moved again, heaving slightly, and she realized with a start that someone was underneath it. A man. A small man, breathing raggedly, hand on stomach, sticky with blood.

With a gasp, Catherine stumbled backward, choking on fear, too scared to scream, turned, tripped, tripped again, tried to waddle-run in her unwieldy gumboots, when a voice behind her croaked, "Don't. They'll kill you. They'll kill your entire family."

There were worse things than tremors and boulders and overly dramatic girls in tartan skirts.

INTER-ISLANDER

THOMAS RAFFERTY WAS MOMENTARILY LOST at sea. An overcast sky had vanquished the coastline behind the ferry, even as a fog of rain had dissolved the one ahead of them. They had entered the tumult of Cook Strait, a fraught channel—chasm really—that separated the South Island from the North. This was a notoriously moody stretch of water, one marked by competing currents and embryonic whirlpools, and the *Inter-Islander* fought its way through, indomitable, plowing headlong into each incoming crest.

Onboard, rising and falling on waves of nausea, Rafferty stood on the deck, trying to fix his gaze on the horizon as a means of battling seasickness, a trick that worked only when there was a horizon to fix on. And still the dead man's hand was reaching out for him from under the fallen wall. A strange end, and apt, perhaps, considering the havoc that same small man had wielded in Africa all those years ago.

Rafferty was crossing over himself, after a fashion, going from the South Island to the North. These were the two main pieces of New Zealand's map, the world's easiest jigsaw. Most of New Zealand's Maori lived on the warmer North Island, and the artifacts at the Christchurch Gallery had been on loan from—he had noted the name of the town—Hell's Gate in Rotorua. If she was still in New Zealand, that was where she would probably be. *She has something of mine.* They wouldn't give out a number or a contact, but they didn't need to. He already had his destination: Hell's Gate.

A horizon, disappearing. A sea, berating itself. The *Inter-Islander* lifted up, dropped down, with Rafferty alone on deck, rolling with the motion, trying not to get swept off. *Here lies Thomas Rafferty, born: Winterset, Iowa. Died at sea, lost between islands, body never to be recovered.* He was at the age where you begin to consider the end of your obituary and how it might read.

The sea surged, washed across the deck, soaking his boots, and, with the last line of his obituary imminent, he retreated through heavy sliding doors. The interior was sickly green and rocking drunkenly; it reminded Rafferty of a hospital ship in World War I, after the defeat at Gallipoli, perhaps. The sliding doors rolled back and forth. A sour smell, stomachs churning, the sound of retching from the toilets.

On the cafeteria TV, compulsive images of the earthquake were playing, sound off and all the more horrific for it. Endless loops of falling buildings, masked rescuers. Smoke rising above the city. Lost at sea, yet tethered still by satellite signals, Rafferty opened his laptop not expecting to find a lifeline, was pleasantly surprised when he did. The usual backlog of messages were waiting: the angry emails of editors, irate and imploring. "Are you still in Christchurch?" "Where ARE you?"

He scrolled through his list of editorial contacts. Travel Ho! magazine, "a forum for smart, successful, retired people!" (also known as "advertising bait"), had various themed issues lined up six months in advance. March was the spa issue, June was cruises, September was islands, December was hotel getaways. *Islands, maybe?* New Zealand was an island nation, after all, but Travel Ho! was probably thinking of boutique accommodations with palmy beaches and peach-skinned women sporting diaphanous scarves hip-wrapped around bikini bottoms, not a real island where people actually worked and lived and farted and fucked. Not this "sleepy cul-de-sac of Empire," as such places had been dubbed. *To be a colonial is to be born into exile.* And it seemed to Rafferty that although some might choose exile, most were born into it. Perhaps, when you fall off the edge of the world, New Zealand is where you land.

But that would make for a very elegiac travel piece.

If the ferry could ever break out of this limbo of fog, they would reach Wellington Harbour at the bottom of the North Island. That was the destination. Cruise ships must dock in Wellington, he thought. Maybe a quick, front-of-the book 150-word piece—*Stopover: Wellington!*—with its contrasts and cozy cafés. (He didn't think he'd ever been to Wellington, wasn't sure, but he assumed they had cafés and that they were known for being cozy. In the world of travel writing, cafés were always cozy, as surely as secrets were always best kept.) A front-of-the-book piece like that, at $1.20 a word would fetch him—he did the math in his head—$180. No wonder he was going slowly broke.

Nonetheless, Rafferty sent off a query, ignored the avalanche of emails that had piled up even as he typed, searched instead for the 186th victim. The official tally for Christchurch sat at 185, with the city posting names as they were confirmed, alongside the dates and, when possible, time of death, but Rafferty found no one listed for the day the small man died, and he was about to shut down his computer when he decided to run an image search on "Saint Christopher's medal" instead. Maybe the medallion and chain were worth something? It wouldn't do the dead man any good, might as well see if he could get a couple of bucks for it. But when he pulled the medal and its clotted chain out of his jacket pocket, and compared it with the images that appeared, it became clear this was something else. Another saint, perhaps. Not Christopher. He typed in "other saints," but that got him nowhere.

Rafferty held it in his palm. It was light, with no real weight to it. Just a trinket, really. A keepsake. The unknown saint brought to mind memories of another necklace, another ferry: a pewter locket in the shape of a heart purchased on board a Japanese passenger gift shop as an ironic gift for an unironic woman. What he had meant as playful became a conciliatory offering instead after yet another fight, Rebecca putting the heart around her neck and then disappearing with it a few days later. It was, as it turned out, a goodbye gift.

Rafferty examined the dead man's medallion more closely. Tiny letters were engraved on the back: TLT. So he searched that, as well, found nothing of note. Just a company that sold temperature limitation thermostats. A diner that specialized in turkey, lettuce, and tomato sandwiches. An Amtrak station code. A reference to a biblical passage. An Indonesian airline operating out of Australia that had gone bankrupt years before. Nothing to give Rafferty an inkling of what he was holding, its value, or lack thereof.

What Thomas Rafferty didn't realize was that these unsecured searches he was sending into the ether on an open connection amid the yaw and roll of a vessel lost between shores were leaving a trail of silver behind, the kind a garden slug might leave across a pane of glass, faint but unmistakable. It was a trail that would eventually lead right back to Rafferty.

The dead man wasn't done with him yet.

EREWHON

SHE PUSHED COTTON BATTING INTO THE puncture wound, but the blood immediately soaked through. It was like trying to sop up a flooded bathtub with a paper towel. More cotton and cloth bandages, quickly sodden. She couldn't stop the flow; the blood wouldn't stop. The dying man moaned, held a folded compress to his wound. "Here," he said. "Press down. Harder."

She'd run to get the first aid kit, the one hanging by the barn's front door, a metal box with a red cross prominently displayed, as required for sheepshearing stations and livestock workers. Her father had packed the kit himself, so Catherine had no idea what to expect when she sprung the clasp: moon rocks or a novelty snake or even an IOU written in a florid penmanship: "I owe you one First Aid Kit." But fortunately, at least this one time, her father hadn't succumbed to inscrutable whims and the random firing of neurons; there were, indeed, medical supplies inside. But her hands shook so badly she had trouble twisting off the lid to the hydrogen peroxide. With the bloodied shirt pulled open, she'd poured the peroxide directly in, and for a moment the wound emerged as cleanly as a hole punched through paper, then quickly filled again with blood. The peroxide seemed to make it worse. She heard him gurgle in pain. His entire body winced, she poured in more, unraveled another bandage, grabbed a wad of batting.

"Press," he gasped. "Harder. Tape it."

"Is it— Is it still inside? The bullet?" She didn't want to reach into anybody, didn't want to fish anything out of any wound.

"Passed through," he said, eyes clenched, voice weak. "You'll have to . . . have to tape the back as well."

When she finished the front, she rolled him over, loose straw sticky on his back, and pulled up his stained shirt, saw a second puncture, worse than the first.

"Sulfa," he said.

She searched the kit, powdered the wound with chalk, blood seeping through, creating a paste, but the flow slowed and she taped it up, best she could.

He rolled back, face wet with sweat. "The blood. Was it dark?"

She nodded.

"Blackened?"

"I don't know. I think so."

"It's the liver, then. I'm done for." He closed his eyes. *So, this is dying.* Eyes still shut, he asked, "Where am I?" He wanted to know where the road had finally ended.

"Erewhon Farm."

"I don't know what that means."

"It's like 'nowhere,' backwards, but spelt wrong." Another of her father's missteps. Lives lived at the end of the world.

His eyes fluttered open. Through his pain, he considered the awkward girl crouching over him. She smiled, almost shyly. "You're nowhere," she said. "Nowhere at all. This is where the birds turn around and come back."

Even in his pain, he knew that tone. It was the loneliness of a radio operator late at night, speaking into the static.

"Your name," he whispered.

"You need to go to a hospital."

"It's too late for that."

"I'll get my dad. He'll know what to do."

"No." A dry swallow. Throat swollen. "They'll kill you. And then they'll kill your family."

Who were "they"? There was no *they*. "They" was everyone and no one. "They" was a dead man pinned under a wall.

She said, "I don't have a family. Only my dad."

"It's not the dying, child. It's what comes before. They will do terrible things to your father. They will assume we were in this together, when really we're just . . . strangers. Strangers on a train."

This confused her. "No trains up here. Only some farms and the ocean."

"How close?"

"The other farms?"

"The ocean."

"The ocean? Just the end of the yard. There's a cove. Really steep. It doesn't really have a name. Fayther calls it 'Chapel Cove,' as a bit of a lark, because there's a more famous one on the other side of New Zealand called Cathedral Cove. Ours is smaller, so he says it's only a chapel. But I just call it 'the cove.' You can see the ocean from there."

He started to laugh, felt it collapse somewhere in his rib cage. "So, I almost made it. There was a boat waiting, yes?"

"There was! I saw it. Do you know why it was there?"

"It was waiting. For me. The airports were being monitored."

He began to drift away.

"You have to go to a hospital."

He tried to speak, couldn't. Enfeebled by bloodletting and hunger, by thirst most of all. "Water," he whispered.

There was no reaction from Catherine's father when she came back. She wanted to tell him, to give him some sort of covert signal, but her courage faltered and she walked into the kitchen instead without saying anything. She'd discarded the heavy barn apron she'd been wearing, now smeared with blood, had bunched it up in the laundry hamper. But her hands were still stained, and she washed them quickly in the sink. The water ran red, then pink, then clear, swirling down the drain. Catherine then filled a plastic jug with tap water, kept her back to her father the entire time, not that she needed to; he barely noticed she was there. She would always be more a theoretical construct than an actual daughter.

"Fayther . . ." she began.

Lost again in his schemes, softly chortling to himself, he sat at the table, filling in graphs according to formulae that existed, so far as she could tell, only in his head. She could have stood on a chair and announced, "There is a man dying in our barn. I'm going to bring him water," and Fayther would have said, "That's nice, dear. Have fun."

Catherine lugged the plastic jug out to the barn, determined to get answers even if she had to withhold the water to do so. When the wounded man saw her, he tried to sit up, reached for the jug, but Catherine held it back.

"First, tell me who you are."

"Not important."

"If you're not important, why is someone hunting you? Are you a spy?"

Another laugh, lost in the rattle of his chest. "A spy? No."

"A fugitive?"

"Not a fugitive, no."

"A murderer?"

"The water . . . please."

"Not till you answer my question. Who's chasing you, and why?"

"The why is not important. My line of work comes with certain risks."

"You *are* a spy."

She held the plastic jug to his lips, water sloshing down the front of his shirt. He drank deeply, let his head fall when he was done.

"Not a spy, no." Memories of Falls Road. "I grew up on the other side of the wall." Prods on one side, Catholics on the other. "Protestants carry the weight of their sins to the grave, but we pass ours off. It's bred in the bone." Secrets and sins, both need sharing. And confessions begin in childhood, as most things do. A rictus home that smelled of mice where the doilies hid stains in the fabric. "I have always had a knack for finding things . . ."

He lapsed, first into incoherence and then darkness, woke to find the light had shifted and the girl, perched over her schoolbooks, using a bale of straw as a desk. Other bales had been pulled down, hiding him from view.

He gestured weakly for the jug and she poured more down the front of his shirt. Some of it even got in his mouth.

"Thank you," he gasped. He looked to her books. "Homework?"

She nodded. "Social science. I'm trying to catch up, so that when classes start up again, I won't be lost in the weeds."

"The weeds?"

"It's what my dad says. 'Don't get lost in the weeds!'" She closed the book. "I didn't do very well on the last quiz." They had been asked to fill in the prompt: *What the world needs is . . .* and she remembered the mean girls, smiling sweetly, standing in turn to read their answers to the class, Mr. Duncan beaming. *What the world needs is to be more inclusive. What the world needs is more empathy. Better allies.* These were the answers the other girls had given. *The world needs more awareness.* They'd all of them mastered the required vocabulary, were singing from the same hymnbook.

"And what did you say?"

"I said: 'What the world needs is more earthworms.'"

"Earthworms?"

"Earthworms mix the soil with other organic material, helps lower the acidity levels. That's a big problem down here. But everyone just stared at me like I was wool blind."

"Wool blind?"

"Oh, that's what we say. It's when wool gets too long, grows over a sheep's eyes, and it runs around bumping into things. We also say it when someone is clumsy or stupid."

Nice shoes, Catherine. They go well with your haircut.

The gaze of the other girls lingering on her canvas sneakers, sniggers that pretended to be smiles. She only had the one pair. Canvas sneakers and self-cut bangs. One of the girls had scribbled in Catherine's notebook: *What the world needs is better hairstyles.* "The correct answer was something like 'kindness' or 'love.'"

213

He shifted, winced. "For what it's worth, I like your answer better. Your answer exists in the real world."

"Mr. Duncan didn't think so."

"Well, Mr. Duncan is an ass. The world needs earthworms, not catchphrases."

The sheep in the pen, still jumpy, were slowly getting used to the wounded man's presence. The bales of hay that Catherine had built a wall with, blocking him from the sheep's sight, helped. The bleat and cry. The smell of wet straw, fermenting in urine. Homey, in its way.

"Romneys?" he asked. "Or Perth?"

"Perendales. You know about sheep?"

"I do. Sort of." Ulster was full of sheep once you got out of Belfast.

Romney sheep were on the plains, Merino crossbreeds in the hills. "People around here mostly keep Corriedales, though. Good for meat and for wool, both. One of our neighbors, he has English Leicesters. They're really cute. Real shaggy, look like sheepdogs. My dad, he's breeding Perendales, mainly because they're hardier. They run around like mountain goats. Really good moms, too. Are you okay? You're crying blood."

He wiped with his hands, checked his fingers. Lay back, exhausted, feverish. "The capillaries have burst. Won't be much longer now. *Sunt lachrymae rerum.*" He repeated this several times, even as his eyes clouded over and unconsciousness claimed him.

She would later look up these words. They were from a Roman poet writing in a long-dead language. "The world is full of weeping." She knew that sometimes sorrow comes out as a sob, sometimes a scream. And it seemed to her that the rest of the world would always be on the other side of the door.

Dry-throated rattles. Closed eyes. Blood tears. She watched him sleep, a face full of fever and twitches. "Get better," she whispered. *I need someone to talk to.*

And just when she thought he was gone, he fought his way back. Eyes bleary with blood. "The satchel," he said.

She had laid a damp bandage over his forehead, and it was now warm, almost steaming. "You should go to a hospital."

"The satchel," he repeated. "Leather straps. I flung it into the loft when I first got here. Is it— Is it still there?"

Catherine climbed the ladder, found it among the loose hay: a heavy satchel, canvas, with leather straps and heavy buckles. When she brought it down, he said, "It's yours. Take it. After I'm gone, take it."

"Don't say that. I don't like it when you say that."

"Keep it hidden. Somewhere safe."

"What is it?"

"It's just something I found. A game of hide-and-seek gone wrong. It's yours, in thanks for what you've done." With that came silence.

"This isn't really a barn," she said, prodding him back with her voice, thin and desperate. "It isn't, not really. It's an 'experimental venue.'"

"Experimental? To what end?"

"Bolder sheep." She was trying to keep him awake with conversation. "My dad is sort of a scientist. Self-taught. All the best scientists are, did you know that? It's true. Newton and Pasteur, they didn't need university degrees. It would've only gotten in their way. It's why we raise Perendales. They don't need a lot of shepherding and they forage really well. The wool is good, a little coarse, but my dad, he didn't choose them for the wool."

215

"He didn't?"

"He chose them for their personalities."

"Sheep have personalities?"

"Sure. Just like people. LK-107, she's really curious. And BH-232 is kind of mean. Our sheep can leave anytime they like. Really. They're not prisoners. We leave the door open all the time, they just have to overcome their nature, strike out on their own. Fayther says we are breeding them back to what they were, and when it reaches critical mass, they'll just . . . go. One day, we'll come out and they will all be gone. It's why we chose Perendales. My dad has this checklist—are they the first ones over a fence and the last ones back? Do they avoid eye contact? that sort of thing—and when one of them shows enough bolder traits, we separate them, breed them with rams of similar temperament. That's what my dad says, 'Rams of similar temperament.' We're trying to undo thousands of years of meddling. Humans have been breeding sheep for thousands and thousands of years, maybe millions, have been breeding out their true character, training them to be docile—that means shy—so they would be easier to control. Fayther says everything that is wrong with the world can be found in sheep. He says, it's the same with people. New Zealand was like this experimental venue of its own. We've been bred into docility." Her father's words, not hers.

"And once you breed these bolder sheep?"

"Well, hopefully, they escape on their own. That way our sheep will slip in with others, breed with them secretly. It will change the gene pool, that's where the DNA is, in the pool. The idea is to undo what's been done, so that it will make sheepherding impossible because the sheep won't listen or do what they're told, so the paddocks and fields will grow back, and New Zealand will return to the wild, like how it was, not pastures, but forests. That's what my dad says, anyway. I don't know if it'll work. Most of his ideas don't."

"Be careful," the wounded man whispered. "Lest you unleash uncertainties into this world." He was quoting a philosopher long forgotten, or maybe a poet, he couldn't remember. "Bolder sheep, once released? Who knows where it will end?"

HELL'S GATE

SOFT, THE WORLD EXHALING STEAM. A shifting landscape, the smell of gunpowder, of brimstone. The hiss of heat escaping.

He had driven through tunnels of green to get here, past lakes wet with mist. The filigreed patterns of ferns. A road winding through like a loosely folded rope. Fish bone clouds, thin and delicate. A terrain that was leaking smoke, and a parking lot with tour buses. WELCOME TO HELL'S GATE.

Hell has a souvenir shop? Rafferty laughed. *Of course Hell has a souvenir shop.*

Unbeknownst to the Maori, and the Europeans who followed them in, Aotearoa, as these islands were known, straddled a line between massive tectonic plates. The underworld often bubbled up, unbidden. The name was apt: Hell's Gate. It was a biblical realm filled with purgatorial pools named Inferno, and Sodom & Gomorrah, and the Devil's Cauldron.

Rafferty had come to this smelly, sulfuric domain—the Land of

Ruamoko, God of Earthquakes and Volcanoes—to sink himself into its warmth.

"Medicinal," the lady with the towels assured him as he lowered his body into the steaming mud baths of Hell's Gate. *"Ka pai?"*

He nodded. *"Ka pai."* It was a Maori turn of phrase that seemed to have entered the language as a whole. *All good! Ka pai!* It reminded him of the Japanese "bottoms up": *kanpai.*

He wasn't sure what he expected. Grit, perhaps. A scalding defoliate, maybe. In fact, the mud of the Maori gods was silken and smooth, like potter's clay, and he emerged feeling, if not younger, at the very least, less old. But it was all a ruse. Rafferty was there under false pretenses.

"That didn't take long," said the lady as he rinsed off the mud. It ran in rivulets along the gutters of the outdoor shower.

Rafferty was passing himself off as a travel writer, which, although technically true, wasn't entirely honest either. Hell had happily waived its fees and arranged for a tour guide to show him around.

"Who are you with then?" the guide asked when Rafferty came in, still towel-drying the caked mud from his hair. A typical sun-creased Kiwi, lean to the point of sinewy, affable but oddly taciturn.

"Me?" Raffety waved his hand in the general direction of Toledo. "I'm with the Free Press," he said. A lie, but not a complete lie. He had indeed pitched the Toledo Free Press a possible travel feature on New Zealand's spas; it was the Schrödinger's cat of assignments. Until he opened his email that evening, he was both on and not on assignment.

Ash-dead trees among the green. Scorch marks on the stones revealed flash points of spontaneous ignition. Deep stomach rumblings from below. A hungry landscape. Rafferty and his guide skirted the edge of a sputtering ink pot of water, the fumaroles and steam vents identified and explained as Rafferty nodded, pretended to listen.

This was where tourism in New Zealand began, in the mist-shrouded airs of this unstable, otherworldly landscape. "Europeans have been coming to Rotorua 'for the waters' since the 1880s. Ladies with parasols and men with muttonchops and top hats." They came here to float in the blood-warm waters amid a Calvinistic landscape of grim hells and scowling heights, of broken peaks and sunless valleys now rife with souvenir shops and greenstone emporiums.

Next to Hell was the Garden of Eden, a temperate rainforest with trees that glowed—literally glowed—with an effervescent fur on their bark that grew specifically in this moist, medicinal atmosphere.

"Naturally heated waterfall pool just up ahead. Maori warriors returning from battle would wash away the *tapu* of death there."

"This was Maori land?"

"Still is."

The spiced earth of a damp forest in summer, tiger-striped with light. If you listened carefully, you could hear the trees exhaling. They came out of the forest and back into purgatory. It was a place Raff knew well. Calcified minerals remained where the water had boiled off.

"Entire place looks like the inside of an electric kettle," he noted.

The guide agreed, pointing out the meaning of the colors they passed: "The yellow, that's sulfur. Gray is silica. Orange and brown are copper and iron, pink is cinnabar." He stopped. Looked at Rafferty. "Don't you need to write that down?"

"Oh. Right." Rafferty patted his multi-pocketed jacket, came up with a notepad and the nub of a pencil, scribbled down something meant to resemble shorthand.

"You mentioned the Maori," Rafferty said. "Wanted to ask you about that." He dug around in a different pocket, produced a crumpled sheet of paper, checked his notes. "Te Arawa, that's the name of a tribe, right?"

"The name of an *iwi*, yes."

"An iwi?"

"One of the seven tribes."

"So, is Te Arawa the same thing as"—Rafferty consulted the paper, couldn't pronounce it, pointed instead.

The other man leaned in, read it off the page. "Ngati Wahiao? That's a subtribe."

"A subtribe?"

"A *hapū* of Te Arawa."

Rafferty was getting closer, he could feel it. He'd jotted this info down from the exhibit display in Christchurch: *Maori war club (patu). Te Arawa-Ngati Wahiao. North Island. Rebecca Hodges, M.Sc (ethnology) curator.*

"Thing is, I'm looking for someone. An American. Her name is Rebecca, goes by Becks, sometimes. I think she's been gathering stories around the artifacts of this particular region."

"Ah. For that, you'll want to go to Whakarewarewa."

Rafferty looked blankly at the other man. Maori spellings, together with the speed with which New Zealanders spoke, had stumped him. "Say again?"

"They shorten the name to Whaka, if that helps."

A grin. "It does."

"It's a village. Not far from here. Their iwi is made up of two subtribes, the Tuhourangi and the Ngati Wahiao. If she's still around, chances are you'll find her in Whaka. They got a meeting house, treasure stores. Lot of traditions there. Good café, too. Makes a decent *hangi* pie. Meat and root vegetables, smoked in the earth. Massive portions. You know what they say, the problem with hangi is that a week or two later, you're hungry again."

Rafferty didn't give a damn about hangi. "Where did you say that village was?"

THE TAO OF BRYNNE

IT WAS LIKE WAKING INTO A nightmare, upward out of the darkness, into that land of wounded livers and blackened blood. A body, wracked. The feverish cold.

"You were talking in your sleep," she said.

Fragmented memories. A three-legged toad. The many walls of Belfast. His mother's laughter.

"It changes," she said. "When you're sleeping. Your voice, how you speak. You're not from America, are you?"

"No," he whispered.

The wind was playing the barn as though it were a musical instrument: the *tap-tap-tap* of a loose slat, the breathy aria of the open door, a whistle in high C through a thin gap in the loft, even an occasional voice-like wail.

"I said a prayer," she whispered. "More of a wish really, that you wouldn't die."

"Prayer and wishful thinking. Same thing," he said, though he knew this wasn't so. Wishes were real. A prayer was something else entirely. It was despair in the form of hope.

"So," she straightened her skirt. "You find things?"

"Is that what I said?"

"Yup. You said, 'I am the king of forgotten things.'"

"Did I?" A half laugh, a crooked smile. A waver of strength returning. "Forgotten, lost, stolen, or misplaced. And not a king. A knight errant, at best."

"You find treasures? Is that what you do?" She'd never met a treasure hunter before, didn't even know that was a possibility.

"No. Mainly just . . . things. Objects that are valuable mainly because they were lost." He could see she didn't understand. "Let me . . . Let me put it this way. Have you heard of *The Maltese Falcon?*"

She shook her head.

"No? I suppose not. Why would you? It was a movie that was made a long, long time ago, back before there were colors." A black-and-white tale of a detective on the hunt for that rarest of objects. *Such stuff as dreams are made of.* The statuette of a falcon, dating back to the Knights Templar, a treasure priceless for which to kill. "But of course, there was no Maltese Falcon. The one that appears in the film is just a prop." He knew it well. Inventory WB-90067. "When the filming was over, it was shoved in a box in a studio lot and promptly forgotten. It cost, at most, forty dollars to make. But, when the movie became iconic, the search for the lost movie prop began. It took years, but when the Maltese Falcon was finally uncovered, it sold for more than four million dollars. All for a cheap prop in a make-believe tale. Alfred Hitchcock called such objects 'MacGuffins.'"

"MacGuffin?"

"A word he made up. The MacGuffin itself didn't really matter.

Not to Hitchcock. It could be anything. A secret code or a diamond tiara. Wasn't important. Was only the means to an end, a way to justify the story. But"—he shifted, fought his way through the pain—"I always thought, 'What if Hitchcock was wrong?'"

"Wrong?"

"What if the MacGuffin *is* the story? What if that's what really matters, in movies, in life. The MacGuffins. The things we find along the way, not the machinations that surround them, but the objects themselves. Not the Commandments, but the golden calf." His blood was poisoned. He could feel the fire radiating outward from his side, throbbing, probing, snaking its way into his flesh. "In my own small way"— he made an attempt at laughter—"I am the Patron Saint of MacGuffins."

"How can something be valuable just because it got lost? I lose things all the time, and they aren't worth anything, except to me."

He tried to shift his weight again, fueling another sear of pain in his side. "If I offered you a slice of cake, you'd be happy, yes?"

"What kind of cake? I don't like raisin."

"Whatever kind of cake you wish for."

"White chocolate?"

"Certainly. Let's make it white chocolate. Now, imagine a slice of that cake has been sitting in a closet for sixty-seven years. Hard as a rock. Icing that has turned into cement. Completely inedible. Would you still want it?"

She shook her head.

"And what if I told you that slice of cake was worth thousands of pounds. Thousands more in New Zealand dollars."

"Why would someone pay that much for an old piece of cake you can't even eat?"

"Because it was lost, and now is found. That slice of cake was from the wedding of Queen Elizabeth II on November 20, 1947. It was saved as a memento by one C. H. Spackman, a guard of honor at the wedding. He tucked it away in a box in his closet, forgot about it, and eventually he passed away. That petrified piece of cake was discovered, put up for auction at Christie's, and it sold for thousands of pounds."

"Were you the one who found it?"

But the pain and fever had risen again like an ocean swell, and his head lolled back into the straw. *If this is where it ends, where did it begin?* In a doily-laden flat on Falls Road. Ceramic figurines with rictus grins, holiday snapshots in ill-fitting frames. *This is Portrush. This is Blackpool. Here we are in happier times.* "I come from Belfast," he said, surfacing again. He felt the fever ebb, but knew another wave was gathering strength for a fresh assault. *I come from Belfast.* It was the one true thing he knew about himself.

"Is it nice there?"

"Belfast? No, not really. A city of churches. Churches and chapels and endless, endless walls. A city of religion. No faith, but lots of religion."

He'd only ever told his life's story once before, and then only as a form of misdirection, a narrative sleight of hand. *Hide in plain sight.* To discover a fellow Ulsterman like Billy Moore, to separate him from the herd, a feckin' Prod no less, he'd only had to change a few details, shift his childhood a few blocks, from a flat on Falls Road to one on the Shankill, salt in some anachronistic references, a smattering of Americanisms and false leads, and he had shaken his banshee loose. But one mustn't die with an unconfessed soul. It was impolite. And the desire rose in him to tell his story, just this once, to not let it die with him. It's what we all boil down to, in the end: a story. *"The only thing we can say for certain is that he is NOT Irish, is NOT from Belfast, wasn't raised by a sad-eyed mother, has probably never been to Belfast."* He'd made a full confession to Agent Rhodes, but she would never know it; he might as well have shouted it into the wind. *And when I die, this story dies with me, untold, unmarked.* It was the worst form of confession: one without absolution. The dying man could feel his strength drain away again. "Your name?" he asked, hollow chested, barely audible. "You never told me."

"Catherine."

He smiled. "Catherine the Great."

"I don't know about that."

"Well, you found me, Catherine. And that's something."

"Were you lost?"

"I suppose, in a manner of speaking." His back was prickly with straw. For a moment it seemed as though he were looking down on the scene as if from above; a parody of the Nativity. The lambs, afraid. Wise men nowhere to be found. "This world is better served through cunning than kindness," he said. "I used to believe that. Now I'm not so sure." He looked at her. So young, so lacking in guile. "I'm dying, Catherine."

"You're not, look. See?" She unwrapped a cheesecloth. "I made you some snacks. In case you're hungry. Anzac biscuits. I made them myself. It's easy, just rolled oats and golden syrup. My mom used to make them with walnuts. Those were really tasty. These ones aren't so much. I'm not very good at baking. I'm not very good at most things." Field hockey and haircuts and navigating the cruelty of classrooms.

"Most people aren't very good at most things." It was one of the kindest things anyone had ever said to her, and she gave him one of the biscuits and he ate it and it was good, and he drank the water and swallowed hard and that, too, was good.

"Have you been to a lot of countries?" she asked.

"I have."

"What's it like, the world?"

"Bigger than you imagine. Smaller than you'd think."

"This one time," she said, "I put messages in a bottle, sent them out into the world. I was ten or eleven, maybe. I wrote: *Hello. My name is Catherine. I live in New Zealand with my dad and we grow sheep. If you want to be friends, you can write me a letter and I promise I will write back no matter what.* I gave my address at the bottom, and I rolled up these messages in twelve different bottles that I had saved, and then I flung them out, as far as I could. I was thinking about where they might end up, in Asia or Africa or even Australia, maybe Japan. I imagined a little boy or a girl in Hawaii or Iceland opening one of the bottles and reading my message and sending me a postcard or a letter. And then we would be friends." She wrapped up the last of the biscuits in a tissue, would save it for later.

"What happened?"

"The bottles? They washed back in, every one of them. When I went out the next morning, the bottles were in the cove below our house, all twelve, bobbing on the waves. I had to go down the path and fish them out, one by one." She was quiet for a moment. "That wasn't a very good day."

"But you tried."

"It didn't matter. They rolled back in, every single bottle, every message I wrote. There were no little boys or girls in Iceland or Mexico who would ever find them. There was just me." Then: "I can't wait to be a grown-up." She could see a hypothetical time when she would move through life, unopposed and unafraid, shedding former selves as she went.

He raised himself onto one elbow. "Can I tell you a secret?"

She nodded, eager to hear. No one ever confided in her, and she, in turn, had no one to confide in.

"All of us adults? Seem so confident? We're faking it. We're no more certain of things than you are, we just hide it better. There is no future you, Catherine. There's just you, patched together, stumbling forward. It's something they never tell you when you're young."

A secret shared demands a confidence, in kind. "Can I tell you something, too?" she said. "I've never told anyone." She faltered. It was the self-conscious smile of someone trying to please the school photographer.

"Of course, you may," he said. "I'm very good at keeping secrets."

"My dad has these numbers I'm supposed to keep track of for him: number of food units, response time. There's a clipboard with forms I'm to fill in. But sometimes, I just"—she smiled in spite of herself—"I just make them up."

"Good! Let him fill in his own damn numbers, right?"

"He's nice, though," she said, quickly, fearing she'd betrayed her father somehow. "My dad, he's a dab hand at anything he puts his mind to. He says, 'I can fix near about anything with just a bit of pluck and some number eight wire.' It's true. He can. He's probably a genius. The girls at my school, they make fun of us, which is okay, honest, I'm used to it, it doesn't bother me so much anymore, it really doesn't, but when they go on and on and make fun of us, of me and my dad, the teachers don't say anything, they kind of smile, too, like they secretly agree, and that's the part I don't like." She was trying not to cry, knuckled the tears back into her eyes. "I miss my mom." *Why couldn't those rocks have rolled right through the school? Why did they have to stop short like that?* "I never go anywhere," she sobbed. "Just from the farm to the school and back again." She closed her eyes, pressed her fingers into the corners, stanching the sadness the way pressure stops the bleeding, but her eyes remained raw and red. She cleared her throat, did her best not to sniffle. "Do you want the last biscuit?"

"Maybe later. Can I tell you a story, Catherine?"

She sniffed, nodded.

"I have a brother," he said. "A brother in Montreal, a niece as well. Her name is Brynne, and once upon a time, when she was very young, Brynne took me on a tour of her neighborhood. She must have been, oh, I don't know, five or six at the time. The entire walking tour was from her eye level, and it was marvelous. We marched right past a statue of a general on a horse and a fountain with Latin inscribed in stone; she didn't notice. These didn't exist in the World of Brynne. Instead, she showed me the swing in the park where her dad pushed her, the shop on the corner where they put out water for pets and how she had seen a dog messily lapping up water once and how funny it was, and a restaurant where the owner was Greek and very loud and friendly, and how the Jell-O there was very good, especially the green Jell-O, and a fence where someone had put up a lost mitten this one time and how it looked like it was saying hi every time she passed. It was the best tour I've ever had. The entire world is in your backyard, Catherine. The walk you make from your home to your school? I imagine you could write an entire tome on the way the path turns, on the plants and the grasses along the way, the manner in which the light plays across the hills, your neighbors with their woolly sheep. When

I was tromping around that neighborhood in Montreal with Brynne, she said something that has stayed with me ever since. We were walking along, her chattering away, when she stumbled on an uneven bit of pavement. She stumbled . . . and then, suddenly, ran. 'When you trip, the best thing to do is to run through it,' she explained later. I called it the Tao of Brynne." He shifted in the straw, struggled to sit up, couldn't. The weakness was spreading. His limbs felt numb and cold. "Catherine, when you start to trip, run through it."

"She seems really nice, your niece."

"She reminds me of you," he said, though that wasn't strictly true. It was something she needed to hear. Nor was it entirely a lie, either. "You're both very kind, you see."

"I don't know about that."

"I recognize kindness when I see it, because it is so very rare. The world is full of unkind people."

"Was that who hurt you, one of those people?"

"Indeed. A dishonest man, so he was. We had an agreement, y'unnerstand? And he tried to renegotiate the terms of our arrangement, after it was settled. Thought he could threaten me, you see. Thought he had me cornered."

"What happened?"

"I left him pinned under a wall."

She passed him the last of the Anzac biscuits. The pain had grown diffuse, was surrounding his body like a dull halo. A silence passed between them.

"Do you have a wife?"

"There was a wife, yes. But I didn't have her. I entertained her for a while. Had a child as well, before you ask. Lost him in the war."

"Which war?"

He brushed his hand in front of him as though waving aside one of the many blowflies that were now buzzing about, sheep feces and human blood proving a heady mix. "Does it matter?" he said. "It's all the same war. Young men die. Children suffer." Fire and fever and the awful knowledge that when some things are lost, they are lost forever. "This world of ours is full of cyphers and symbols, Catherine. You just need to know where to look—and how to look." The darkness began to close in.

Cyphers and symbols.

Catherine would write that in her journal and later, when she suddenly came face-to-face with the rage behind his eyes and the terror contained within, she would remember these words as well: *The world is full of unkind people.* She didn't realize that he counted himself among them.

When next he emerged from unconsciousness, Catherine was lying beside him, holding a cloth to his forehead. The light was different. A day may have passed, maybe more. He was growing weaker, feeling dehydrated, unable to hold his head up, and he stared at his young confessor. Her hair was in ribbons now, and curled. A smudge of pink on her lips.

This puzzled him, even in his delirium. "Are you—are you wearing . . ." But he stopped himself. She had put on lipstick and mascara, clumsily; her eyes looked permanently surprised. It would be cruel, drawing attention to it. "A new dress?" he asked.

"This? No, it's what I wear—what I used to wear—when we go to church. Before we stopped going, before they told us to stop going." *Fayther bringing up mathematical improbabilities in the scriptures.* "So now we mostly stay home, practice our prayers alone." She moved closer, lay her head on his shoulder.

"Catherine," he said. "You should go now. You don't need to stay for this." He could smell the perfume of an absentee mother; she had doused herself in lilac. When she placed her hand, tentatively, on his chest, she felt his body tighten. He took her wrist, as gently as he could, moved it away. "You should go," he whispered. Such a sad attempt at seduction. Sad and hesitant and heartfelt. It's a terrible thing to be young.

"But don't you think it means something?" she said. "The two of us meeting?"

Cyphers and symbols.

"We live on a globe, Catherine. Draw any two lines and they will eventually intersect. It's not a miracle, just basic geometry."

"You like boys instead?" Even in rural New Zealand, she had heard of such things.

"I prefer women. You are a child."

And with that he fell backward into the darkness for what he believed was the third and final time. *So, this is where it ends. In a barn on a farm just short of the sea.* And now, not only his strength, but the very core of who he was, circled down the drain. He could feel it, the greater darkness, the darkness that was always there, at the edge of all things, was almost looking forward to it.

"You don't have to stay for this," he said. "I can do this next part on my own."

She held his hand, clammy and hot, and waited for him to die. "Will you see God?" she asked.

"If he'll take me."

"God will be waiting for you," she said. "I know He will."

"And if he isn't?"

God was a theoretical construct as surely as Catherine was to her

231

dad, but she remained stubborn on the matter. "I know God exists," she said, "because I can feel His shadow." This was from a hymn in her childhood, half-remembered. They were the last words he would hear as the darkness closed in.

But then the worst possible thing happened: he got better. And he lived.

I COULD DIE OF LOVE FOR YOU

TONGUE EXTENDED, WITH EYES WIDE AND rolling back, bulging in their glares. The coiled energy and heavy, panting breaths, the elaborate facial tattoos. The cries that emanated from somewhere deeper than the throat. The stomp and drop, down on one knee and up again. Defiance, defiance. *Ka mate, ka mate! Ka ora, ka ora!* Here is death, here is death. Here is life, here is life. Palms slapping against bare chests, leaving red marks and fire in their wake.

Rafferty had never seen the haka war dance—or "challenge dance," more accurately—performed at such close range before: on a stage in a village under rising steam and falling rain. It was not the drama of it or the passion. No. It was the sheer *commitment.* That was what made his heart race. The only way to perform a haka is to go full in, boots and all, as the Kiwis say. Had Rafferty ever felt such commitment to anything? Ever? He must have, at some point, maybe back when he was young, but he couldn't think of when that would be. *Ka mate, ka mate! Ka ora, ka ora!*

He hadn't found her. Not in the humid streets of Whaka village—the very buildings seeming to sag under the weight of steam—not at the school or in the local café. They knew her name, though, knew who she was—"The American. The one who never smiles."—and he knew he was getting closer. As he tramped about the narrow lanes of Whaka, Rafferty rehearsed what he would say. It was very simple. Three short words: "Give it back."

"You should talk to Kauri," they'd said, a telling exchange of glances between the women in the village office. "Kauri Morrison. He'll know." A knowing look, a barely contained smile. One of the women, to the other, "Ya reckon?"

Rafferty walked over to the village baths, where the alkaline waters had been redirected into open pools. Communal bathers, but she wasn't there, either, and he watched as a Maori woman submerged a tinfoil-wrapped tray of meats and root vegetables into a nearby pond in the sputtering rain. Off-limits to bathers, this one. "Can cook an adult pig in two hours," she said, with a certain misplaced pride. There was the "grumpy old man" hot spring, bubbling in angry fits and starts, and a strange "champagne pool" with bubbles boiling up, effervescent but scalding. And finally, a haka performed in the village square, the women taking the stage first to spin the mesmerizing pom-poms of the poi, followed by a duet between one of the women and one of the men. "Pokarekare Ana," a Maori love song, the story of a woman captivated by the flute of a young man on a distant island. She swims across the lake to reach him, suspended by gourds. *Ka mate ahau, I te aroha e* . . . I could die of love for you. It was a song in a language he didn't understand, and he was crying again, wiping it away, angry at himself. Candles and churches and prayers and poi, and Tom Rafferty rubbing the heel of his hand into his clenched eyes.

Love and war and feats acrobatic.

The events in Christchurch had cast a pall on the proceedings, making the celebrations more subdued than usual. Tins had been set up like the asking of alms in a medieval procession. *Help the victims of the earthquake. Rise up, Christchurch!* And the spectators, to their credit, were more circumspect as well. Tourists on crepe-soled vacations watching the wild theater of the haka. *Ka mate! Ka mate!*

"Kauri? Kauri Morrison?"

Rafferty had slipped backstage after the performance. A cluttered room. A kettle simmering on a hot plate. Mr. Morrison was an impressive torso of a man, shoulders knotting into neck. Long hair, set in a kinked topknot, he was bent over a basin, washing the tattoo off his face. The other performers had left, but he had lingered as though expecting someone. Rafferty recognized him from the haka: the eyes rolling back, the tongue extended, the red slap marks on his chest. Kauri began rubbing his face into a towel, saw Rafferty in the mirror, turned with a broad grin—and is there any grin broader than a Maori grin?

"You're that travel writer, the one they told me about. Come on in. Cuppa tea? I'll get you a cuppa tea."

Kiwis and their fuckin' tea.

"Sure."

"Biscuit? Oh, wait. They're all gone." He produced coffee mugs instead of teacups, turned the kettle up to boil, and they sat at a card table, the memory of mugs past having formed an Olympic flag of rings on the table's surface. As they waited for the tea to steep, they discussed the never-ending rain that was New Zealand, mandatory in such situations. "It's not always this wet," said Kauri. "Mind you, it's never entirely dry either."

"So," said Rafferty, taking a cautious sip. "You grew up here?"

"Did indeed. Just up the hill. My nana's house. It's still there."

The eggy airs and warm vapors. "Is it healthy?" Rafferty asked. "Living here?"

"Healthier than most. Good for asthma. The waters in Whaka are known for their—how do y'say it?—healing properties, everything from arthritis to lumbago. Plonk yourself in it, y'emerge a new man."

"Like living in a spa," Rafferty offered.

"Exactly."

Rafferty swirled his tea. "I was in Christchurch—"

"Terrible business, that."

Rafferty nodded. "The art gallery had a display of Maori weapons. They were from Whaka, many of them."

"Yeah, my uncle's *patu*, I think. Stuff like that."

"I was wondering how they ended up down there, in Christchurch. On loan, were they?"

And with that, Rafferty saw the man's expression harden. Something had shifted, just under the surface, like a vein under the skin.

"Thought you were interested in the haka, is what they said."

"I am, I am. But . . . one quick question. The woman who arranged that exhibit in Christchurch, an American." Rafferty looked around him, as though she might be there and he hadn't noticed. "Is she still here?"

There was a chill unrelated to the weather. Angry emails. *I don't have it. Stop asking.* And now this: a very large man in a very small room, eyes filled with undisguised hostility.

"You're not here to write a story, are ya? You're the reason she left. She said you might show up. She wants nothing to do with you, bro."

"I just need to know where she is."

"Not here. Gone."

"Gone where?"

"Didn't say." And then this: Leaning across the table, staring into Rafferty's pale eyes, inches from his face, holding his gaze, unblinking. A challenge undeniable. "You know what a *patu* is? Polished greenstone. Blade like an ax. Close contact, isn't it? In Maori culture, you kill a man face-to-face. You look in his eyes. Arrows and muskets, those were considered cowardly."

Emotions, barely contained. Partly despair, partly anger—mostly despair. And Rafferty realized, this man had been her lover, too.

Rafferty ran a hand across the tabletop, clearing it of imaginary crumbs. "She's something else, isn't she? Our Rebecca." He looked up. "We could swap stories, if you like," Rafferty offered. "Tales of Rebecca."

"Not for the faint of heart," said Kauri. The anger had subsided, not the despair.

"No sir," said Rafferty. "Not for the faint of heart." *The feint of hearts.*

"My mother," said Kauri. "She taught me the haka. She was a giant. Me? Not so much."

"Te Arawa?" Rafferty asked.

He nodded. "That was the name of the canoe. Each iwi traces itself back to a specific canoe. There were seven that landed. The Great Fleet. Canoes across open seas, can you imagine such a thing? Te Arawa. That one was ours."

"The legend," said Rafferty.

"The history."

The rainy-day dampness had taken hold. Rafferty's sweater hung like drooping chainmail. Traces of a tattoo on the corners of Kauri's eyes. Cold tea in the mug.

"So, what happened?" Rafferty asked. "Between the two of you."

Kauri shrugged. "Not much. Pretty simple, really. She took my stories. And then she left."

A single tea steam was floating in Rafferty's cup.

Kauri's eyes were in his tea as well. "You know the Ngati Tumata-kokiri?" he said. "What happened to them? Were once the lords of the South Island, fierce, true Maori. Were the first ones to meet Europe-ans. That was before Captain Cook. A Dutch ship anchored offshore, a big battle. Held 'em back, the strangers never landed. But we only have the Dutch side of that story, because the Ngati Tumatakokiri are gone. All of 'em, and their stories too. Their descendants were absorbed into other iwi, other tribes, and the stories were lost. And without stories, we don't really exist, do we?"

"Maybe that's what she's trying to do, preserve these things be-fore they are lost forever."

Kauri laughed. "Not preserve, *purloin*. That's the word, isn't it? To claim something that isn't yours."

"I think so."

"And she purloined you too, did she?"

Rafferty nodded. *Hearts that we broke long ago, have long been breaking others.*

Time to go. The rain had stopped, and Rafferty got up. Pushed his chair back in, thanked him for the tea. But then, as he was about to leave—

"Said somethin' about Alice."

Rafferty turned. "Alice?"

"That's right."

"Did she give a last name?"

"It's not a person, bro. It's a place."

ENTER DR. ROWLEY

WHEN NEXT HE SURFACED, HE WAS not alone, and neither was she. Someone had joined Catherine at her straw-side vigil, a face blurry, a voice the same.

"I've employed a range of antibiotics . . . he may be weak for some time . . . fever should eventually come down . . ."

A reverse drain, pulling him up, toward the surface. He could feel a fresh sear of pain in his side. Not as widespread as before. A more precise pain, as though gathering in on a single spot: the bullet wound, front and back, entry and exit.

"I've stitched him up, best I could, both sides . . . will need lots of rest . . . liquids . . . Katie, we really should contact the police."

Catherine's voice, through the fog. "It's too dangerous. You won't say to anyone, right? Bad men are looking for him. He has a satchel. I had to hide it for him. My dad doesn't even know he's here. You won't say anything? Promise?"

"I promise."

Eyelids fluttering open.

"Ah. The patient awakens."

Catherine, leaning in. "How are you feeling?"

A choked response, trying to say "water." She thought he said, "well," and she beamed. Catherine Butler had saved a life.

"This is Dr. Rowley," she said.

A modest objection. "Not a doctor, child."

"An animal doctor."

"Well, yes, I suppose."

"A doctor. You make things better." She looked to the dying man, eyes imploring. "I know you said not to tell anyone, I know I promised, but I didn't want you to die, and he came right away, he only lives two farms over, but don't worry, he won't say anything to anyone, I made him cross his heart."

Catherine, running across the fields. Catherine, in near panic, down hedgerow lanes to Dr. Rowley's bungalow. Hammering on the door, in tears, breathless and scared and afraid of losing him. She had gone to rouse her father first, but he lay there sleeping. Might as well have been away. Ran instead in stumbling gumboots to the only other adult she could think of who could help, had brought him back here to Erewhon.

"You needed a doctor, you really did, and Mr. Rowley—Dr. Rowley—he's our vet, he inoculates our lambs. He's the only doctor I know, and he parked and walked across the paddocks, so no one saw him, not even my dad."

A dry swallow. "You shouldn't have done that." *First, do no harm.* Did the Hippocratic Oath apply to veterinarians?

He tried to move, felt the pain shoot through him anew. Standing behind Catherine, Dr. Rowley came slowly into focus as though in an optometrist's office, lenses clicking into place. His hair was combed across in a barcode pattern. Eyes protuberant. He spoke with that peculiar Kiwi twang, voice rising at the end of each sentence, asking a question even when he wasn't. A strange island, this, where everything was uncertain, even the intonations.

"Katie said y'wished to avoid hospitals." *Hesspituls.* "I reckon it's a police report you're wanting to dodge, rather than proper medical care." And then: "She said something about a satchel."

Rumors abound in the aftermath of any disaster. Of safety deposit

239

boxes springing open like the graves at Christ's death, of looters and mountebanks, of voluminous amounts of cash gone missing in the chaos. He was not a criminal by inclination, our Dr. Rowley. But there was an overdue bank loan and a Volvo with a faltering transmission. There was a failing practice and wife whose frown lines seemed to grow deeper by the day. She was always tired, his wife. Tired of the wind, of the lambs, the smell of silage. It seemed never to abate, the daily defeats and small setbacks. Forever gaining summits, then losing them. But here, falling practically into his lap, was an act of providence: a fugitive with a satchel, furtive and trapped. All those prayer-like wishes, answered. Dr. Rowley leaned in closer. "We need to talk, you and I. We need to discuss my fee."

The wounded man stared back. These were the conventional threats of a conventional man. "You may want to reconsider what you are about to do, *doctor*."

The veterinarian did his best not to smirk. "You don't seem to be in much of a position to negotiate." There was glee in the doctor's eyes, a man whittled down by life. Up until this very moment, his existence had been a series of diminished returns, of colicky calves and soup-stained sweaters, a wife eroded by the wind. (He was wearing one such sweater now, a charcoal cardigan with mismatched buttons.) It haunted men, some men, this sense—not of having fallen, but having never made it up the hill to start with, not a has-been but a never-was.

Catherine was confused. "If it's a fee, I can pay it. My dad has some money in a jar."

The finder rolled his head to one side, considered this young woman who, by any rights, would eventually have to be killed. It was the only way to ensure silence. Something unfamiliar was tapping on the window. Tenderness? Mercy? Or was it just Irish sentimentality? Whatever it was, it flickered and died, a ghost of a breath on the glass. "Catherine," he said, voice barely audible. "You should go."

"But I can pay. I don't mind."

Dr. Rowley chuckled in his best avuncular manner; it was the practiced condescension of the professional class. "That won't be necessary, Katie." He handed his patient a pen and pad. "If you fill in your bank information, I can arrange a transfer." At the back of his mind, like a muffled alarm duly ignored, Dr. Rowley understood—from his own experiences—that it was probably best not to prod a cornered animal, but when he felt his uneasiness begin to rise, he thought of his wife, of the lines in her face, and this quelled any doubts he might have had. "What price discretion?" he asked. "I propose a one-time payment."

The wounded man continued to stare at the doctor. Stared with lidless eyes. This doctor, so-called, was a fidgety man with a facial twitch and a sniff which never quite lined up, never quite fell into sync, the way a bus driver's wipers never do, set at different tempos, clearing the rain at two different speeds. Annoying and compelling, such syncopations, whether in buses or in faces. *When they do line up, his tic and his sniff, I shall plunge this pen into his neck, stab a hole in his carotid artery, watch his arrogance bleed out into the straw.* But no. Not that. Too messy. "All this paperwork," he said, voice weak but gathering strength. "So unnecessary. Why don't I just pay in cash instead?"

A smile.

The finder knew that smile. It was a smile saturated in greed. He had seen it over the years, had seen it in Okinawa, on the Russian steppes, in the humid heat of the Congo. Greed is a terminal condition, and such men die with a disconcerting regularity. To Catherine, again, forcefully, he said, "You need to go. I wish to speak with this gentleman, alone."

Dr. Rowley concurred. "He's right, Katie. Run along. We have business to discuss."

"But—"

"Run along."

She wasn't wanted. Catherine knew this feeling well, and she gathered her things and she left.

Inside the barn, the sheep were restless. Anxious, with fearful bleats. The darkness was stirring, taking shape.

"Well, then," said Dr. Rowley. "Here we are, the two of us. A doctor and his patient, discussing fees." The veterinarian waited for a response.

The other man looked down at the blood-encrusted shirt he was wearing, then at the doctor's own cardigan, tilted his head. "We're about the same size, wouldn't you say?"

THE GOD OF UGLY THINGS

DAWN.

Darkness, shedding itself in layers, giving way to the dull gray light of morning. On the beach, waves were folding over, collapsing, rolling, sliding up along the shore, leaving wet contour lines on the sand. Seabirds weeping like professional mourners. They always seemed so unnecessarily histrionic to Rafferty. *You can fly, what more do you want?*

The sea on one side, art deco facades of hotels lined up on the other. It was the Great Gatsby made manifest, a glittering Jazz Age promenade.

New Zealand is a land of contrasts, and nowhere is this more evident than in its magnificent North Island, which boasts rich forests and secluded coastlines, attractive villages and eclectic cities. Consider Napier on the eastern coast, an architectural treasure house of 1920s aesthetics.

Thomas Rafferty, still at it.

He'd come all this way to the end of New Zealand because of a single text. A single word, really. It was from Tamsin. Just a place-name and a preposition: *In Napier.* And he had driven across the North Island in his rent-a-car, from the purgatory pools of Hell's Gate, through towns small and unprepossessing. This improbable nation, this Kingdom of Bungalows.

He thought about the way light alters a place: the tie-dyed sunsets of tropical climes, the splintered ice of Scandinavian skies, the Sunday glow of concrete in an urban industrial park, blushing pink for no one. In Napier, it was a palette of pastels, of greens and blues, of goldenrod and cinnamon. A city slumbering by the sea. Napier's creamy marble facades—painted, not real—were stippled in the sort of light that makes Impressionists look like plagiarists. In Napier, the seasons were turned upside down. The end of February, and the parks were flooded with flowers still.

Tamsin had sent him an address: a grand hotel located in a former Masonic lodge on Tennyson Street, an architectural art deco sampler with vintage cars parked out front. One of them was a 1937 Pontiac

Indian Chief, if he wasn't mistaken, polished red, like lacquer. But even here, amid these elegant streets, the scent of the sea permeated. There was no escaping the sea in New Zealand, not for long. It was always near at hand, even here.

Inside the Masonic Hotel, a matronly hostess was pouring tea for the guests, spout bowing in turn. Wisps of steam, and women in sun hats. Men in fedoras, rakishly angled. Rafferty stood for a moment on parquet floors under tortoiseshell light, and a clerk approached from the side, like an adder. "Just missed her," he whisper-hissed.

"Who?"

"Your lady friend." It was a term only ever used sarcastically. "A tall woman. American, I believe."

Tall? Tamsin was short, squat even.

"You are Mr. Rafferty, *yeass*?"

"How did you—"

"She told me. She said, 'Watch for a large man who looks permanently out of place. Let me know when he arrives.' Her words, not mine."

Messages from Tamsin were always vague. He sat in the lobby, feeling self-conscious after Tamsin's gratuitous "permanently out of place" comment, and anyway, wasn't that the job description of a travel writer, to be permanently out of place? Across from him, a husband and his wife on some dismal leg of a journey were fast reaching a stalemate, the husband attempting to convince his wife that they were, in fact, having a Good Time, and the wife refusing to acknowledge such a possibility. Rafferty felt for him. There is no company more dreary than that of a woman who is determined—absolutely determined—not to have a good time. Rebecca in Okinawa, complaining about the sand. "Well, we are on a fuckin' beach," he'd snapped, and that had been the beginning of the end, though of course no collapse is ever caused by a single pelt of rain, no avalanche by a single flake of cold; avalanches and heartbreaks are always cumulative.

Harried by memories, he retreated to the bar, and it was there that Tamsin found him. She arrived, full of grins. "Figured I'd find you here. You'd be an easy man to assassinate, Tom Rafferty." The thin scar down the side of her face made every smile sardonic.

"Am I really that predictable?"

"It was either here or the nearest used bookstore."

They ate dinner, Tamsin's treat. She always had more money than he did, not a major feat, granted, but something he'd long since come to accept. They ordered the seafood bisque, layers of flavor and heat, followed by goat cheese tartlet and braised lamb, with crème brûlée and raspberry chocolate at the end. Wine as dry as a mouthful of crackers. So dry, you became thirsty even as you drank it.

"I've been here before," he said. He had just realized. "This town. This city. A magazine feature on New Zealand wines, ten years ago, maybe? They sent me here on a wine tour. Bon Appétit, I think."

"What the hell do you know about wine?"

"Not much." Rafferty tended to treat wine tasting like a liquid buffet, which didn't always endear him to the more refined vintners. "Mainly chardonnays and pinot gris out here, I think. But I remember—I remember this one late-harvest viognier, it was described as 'mist infused.' That's stayed with me ever since. 'Mist infused.'" It might well have applied to New Zealand as a whole.

"Wine is weather," said Tamsin. "It's what they always say." She finished hers in one extended gulp. "I like it here," she replied, as though it were a verdict everyone had been waiting for. "Entire city is like a theme park. Very photogenic when the light hits the facades. It has a Miami Beach sort of vibe." When every place reminds you of someplace else.

"It was an earthquake that did it," he said. "Back in the thirties, leveled the town. They had to rebuild the entire community quickly. They did it in the same architectural style, one recently popular, but not overly complicated. Largest collection of art deco buildings in the world, I think, outside of Miami Beach."

But any mention of earthquakes only drew the cloud of Christchurch over them. It had been two weeks and still the taste of plaster was in their mouths. Tamsin was waiting for the coroner's inquest to begin. "Some anguish shots, families crying, collapsing into each other's arms. That sort of thing. Could be a while, though. They're still cleaning things up down there. It's a mess." But not a *photogenic* mess. No one wanted images of a cleanup. "Libya is boiling over, and I'm stuck down here."

"You're like the Devil's paparazzi."

"Get fucked," she said, her voice too loud for their surroundings. *You can take the girl out of Wisconsin . . .* Other patrons were looking at them, but Tamsin didn't care. "Lissen, lissen"—they were both a little drunk—"a single image from me, one fuckin' frame, conveys more pain and reality than a thousand words from you."

"That is the going rate."

She snorted, that braying laugh of hers that he always found so annoying. And then, under her breath as the candle on their table guttered and died, "I don't shoot death." *Kali with a light meter*, he'd once called her, and it had stung, though she never quite knew why until in India she saw a sculpture of Kali, multi-armed and dancing merrily on the skulls of the dead. "I shoot *life*," she said. "Life, reasserting itself even in the darkest moments. If I just wanted dead bodies, I would hang around traffic accidents and lower-tier amusement parks."

Onward they went, cartwheeling through another round of drinks, immune to the tutted stares of disapproval they received from the other tables. They must have looked like those souls whose very wanderings are a form of punishment, Dantean figures whose torments suited their sins. Or had Rafferty only imagined that, the looks, the Greek chorus of opprobrium that greeted them?

He staggered onto his feet. "Show's over!" he declared; to whom exactly wasn't clear. And then, mangling the Italian, *"La comedio il finite."*

He'd taken a room at the Beach Front Motel on Marine Parade, where the curved balconies would catch first light perfectly, and even though her own hotel was paid for, Tamsin joined him there. He always had a knack for finding a view. When she woke, it was still dark. She was being pulled from a vehicle. In her dreams, she was always being pulled from a vehicle, and she woke up, not in Beirut or Baghdad, but back in Napier, where the most exciting thing to happen was a single earthquake eighty years ago.

Rafferty was already up, had pulled a chair to the open balcony, curtains moving like the aurora australis, on a wind more seen than felt. He'd lit a cigarette, was carefully blowing the smoke outside. Not that it made a difference; the smoke was blowing right back in. It had infiltrated her dreams; it was the smell of smoke that had stirred her from her sleep.

Drunken questions from Rafferty as she put him to bed the night before. "Why the army base?" he'd asked. "Why'd I meet you coming out'a that army base that one time?" He was referring to Seoul.

"Are you still going on about that?" She swung one of his deadened legs onto the bed. It was like trying to move an uncooperative mattress. "The base had a bar, is all," she said. "I'm not with the CIA. C'mon, your other leg too. There y'go. I'm not with anyone."

"You're not who you say you are, that's for sure."

"No one is. If they were, the world would be filled with saints and poets."

"You speak Farsi," he said. "Who the hell speaks Farsi?"

"Farsi? Hardly." She pulled the blanket over him. The agreement was that the least drunk of the two of them would put the other one to bed. More and more, that was Raff. "I only know the basics," she said. "'Sniper!' 'Don't shoot. I'm unarmed.' 'Don't shoot! I'm a journalist.' 'The world is watching.'" That last one was a lie. The world may have been watching, but it didn't care.

"You speak Russian, too. I've heard you. Who th' hell speaks Russian? Other than Russians, I mean."

"Again. I speak Russian—badly. I also speak Swahili—badly. And a bit of Arabic. It makes me semi-multilingual. I speak languages the way a bear dances. No one is impressed that the bear dances *well*, just that he dances at all."

By this point, Rafferty was half-gone, eyes closed. "Who *are* you?" he asked, though it wasn't clear who the question was addressed to.

She knew he would always resent the kindness that he'd been shown. There were times Tamsin felt sorry for men. They were always so weak, at the core, where it counts.

And now, here he was, awake again and filling the room with secondhand smoke, lost in a view. She joined him at the balcony, shared a drag off his cigarette. Three floors up and still they could hear the sea.

"I was having trouble sleeping," he said.

"Back?"

"Ribs. All around, like someone squeezing an accordion—badly."

"Is there any other way to squeeze an accordion?"

Outside, early dawn, with waves folding in. A boulevard lined with palm trees. A curve of sand. The roll and sigh, all night but still not soothing.

"You should see someone about that," she said.

"I'm just showing my age. There's no treatment for that."

This profoundly imperfect man with a penchant for woe and a predilection toward self-pity. How on earth had she ended up with him?

Tamsin pulled on one of Rafferty's oversize shirts, went for an early-morning skinny-dip. He watched her as she crossed the empty boulevard below, legs flashing purposefully. There is so much beauty in this world, he thought. It breaks your heart. The sea, as familiar and strange as always, like staring at your face in a mirror. Sand as soft as talcum powder. Restless whitecaps rolling in. Salt water and soft winds, like a breath on the skin. Tamsin shed the shirt, waded in, felt the current reach out for her.

Memories of Mosul, of Bosnia and Sierra Leone, of Darfur and bloody Basra. The fall of Tikrit, a point of pride. She had been the first journalist—the first photojournalist—on the ground, and she remembered the exhilaration of that moment, the unalloyed joy of it. *Saddam has fallen! The tyrant is gone!* But tyrants are interchangeable and no sooner does one fall than another rises. It's what kept her in business. They were looting the palaces, and Tamsin, shoulders bare, had sat in one of Saddam's opulent tubs, mimicking Lee Miller's iconic photo in Hitler's bath, boots heavy with the dirt of Dachau, in the frame and intentionally so.

Tamsin Greene in Baghdad, looking for low light and long shadows. Tamsin Greene, amid the chaos and ruin of yet another failed state, crossing into southern Sudan, clothes still smelling of Persia and woodsmoke from the last assignment. Afghanistan and its fields of poppies. Sweat-sheened men with varnished skin and Kalashnikovs, loose necklaces of ammunition—the warlord equivalent of Mardi Gras beads.

Tamsin Greene, beneath a burka, photographing women held captive under Taliban rule. Mortar fire. An interpreter who died in her arms. A Kentucky pilot laughing through the earphones just before they were hit. "If they bombed Kandahar, how would you ever know?" Tamsin Greene, running for cover. Lens raised, under fire. A life lived as a defiant *fuck you* to fear.

The undercurrent curled around her legs, tried to draw her farther out, dark and deep, pulling at her, but she slipped free and waded back to shore, slid into Rafferty's shirt again, damp now with sand.

He watched her return just as purposefully, her wet footprints, slightly pigeon-toed, plopping across the paved road. He could feel it stir like an atrophied muscle attempting to move: the urge to love. But then, in she came, tromping through his room, toweling off her hair, saying, "You lazy fuck, why didn't you join me?" and the moment passed. She would always be easier to love from a distance.

He had noticed the leather-cord, surfer-style necklace on the side table. An insect of some sort was suspended in amber. Where had she picked that up?

"A weta beetle," she said when she saw him looking at it. "Cool, right?" She was shoving a pan of hotel coffee into the tray. "*Deinacrida mahoenui*. The Maori God of Ugly Things. Reminded me of you." It was all shell and swollen joints, this weta, as though made out of spare parts, and he had to admit, he could see the resemblance. "A lucky talisman," she said, rescuing it from his grasp. She tied it around her neck. "Found this one in a shop. It's on the small side, some weta beetles are regular giants, size of your fist."

Tamsin waited for the coffee to drip through. The sun had broken above the horizon and the palm trees were limned in gold.

"There's driftwood down there," Rafferty said. "All along the shore. Did you notice? I was trying to figure out where it came from. It's just open sea from here, right?"

"Chile? Easter Island, maybe?"

"No trees on Easter Island. I've been."

"That's because it all washed up here. It's driftwood, Raff. That's what it does. Could've come from Oregon, for all we know. The ocean is one giant vortex. Send something out and eventually it comes back."

"I suppose." The wind through the open window. "Ever have the feeling that we've been living in the Golden Age of Travel, and don't realize it? That we never fully appreciated it, never really took advantage of it—not in any meaningful way. Just selfies and postcards. That we squandered it all? Ever think about that?"

She handed him his coffee. "Here. It's awful."

"Thanks. I think."

The curtains billowed and Tamsin asked, "Why do you do what you do?"

"I heard you were easy."

"Fuck off, you know what I mean."

"The richly remunerative life of a freelance writer? What else can I do? I could hardly give up the glamour of it, the allure."

"You were there," she said. "We both were. In Rwanda, on the front lines. Why didn't you parlay that into a career as a journalist?"

Panic and mud and eyes looking up, pleading for help, and Rafferty as scared as they were. I can't. I can't. I'm caught up in this too—but was that true? A million dead, and he couldn't have rescued one? Not even one? "I can't," he had pleaded. "I'm not— I'm not anybody. I'm trapped as well." But was he? Was he really?

Why hadn't he parlayed Rwanda into a career?

"Because I'm not," he said. "A journalist, that is. Didn't even want to write, really. I just wanted to travel, wanted to keep moving. Robert Bateman, the wildlife painter? I interviewed him once. Asked him the secret of his long career, and he said, 'Y'know how we all like to draw animals when we're little? Well, I never stopped.' Likewise. You remember those backpackers of our youth, the ones who hitchhiked, stayed in hostels? The ones who eventually grew up, stopped traveling? I never did."

Joggers and dogwalkers. The first of the day's cars. A Napier interlude coming to an end.

"Raff," she said. "Why don't we just keep going? We can take your car, keep driving. There's a small bay, beyond the next headland. It's where the sun first rises on the world. We're so close to the end, Raff. Let's keep going."

"I'm sated on scenery, glutted on it."

"Out there, at the end of the world, stingrays nuzzle up against you at low tide. We'll find some hip waders, slosh out, into the shallows, and they will come to us. They're curious. They move like liquid shiitakes. Sleek and elegant, but with these comically squished faces when you lift them up and look underneath." The glide of the stingray, the slow turn of sharks. A world full of undertows. "There are these little blue penguins, as well, that come ashore every night in procession, like windup dolls, like commuters coming home. You almost expect them to be carrying little briefcases." But she was confusing that with somewhere else. "Mahia," she said. "That's the name of the bay. It's Maori, for 'home.'"

But she was wrong about that as well; it didn't mean "home." It meant "a sound from a distance." Like an echo returning.

"This bay, you've been?"

"Years ago. There was this dolphin that loved humans, it wouldn't leave, kept turning up, swimming with the locals. Frolicking, really. National Geographic sent me in. I don't only shoot wars, you know. When I was there, I meant this Japanese girl, Tomoka. She worked as a chef in a French restaurant in Gisborne, spent the rest of her day surfing. She swam with the dolphin and I photographed it. Won an award, the silhouetted images I captured of Tomoka from below, her body mirroring the dolphin's." Tamsin's best work was always with silhouettes—or extreme close-ups of crying faces. "We could go there, to Mahia, find Tomoka, crash on her couch. Last time I was there, she cooked me steamed mussels in white wine. It was excellent. You'd like her, Raff. A Japanese girl, surfing alone at the end of the world. There might be a story in that. You traffic in stories, right?"

"Not anymore. Nowadays, I just live word count to word count."

"Let's find her."

"If she's still there."

If.

That's how it always went in their line of work. Intense memories, but when you returned—if you returned—the buildings would still be standing, but the people you knew were gone. It was like navigating the fallout of a neutron bomb. The past was a neutron bomb.

He put out his cigarette. "What happened to her? The dolphin, I mean."

"Died. Why, was a mystery. Washed up in a different bay, not long after I left."

"Things tend to die after you take their picture. Ever noticed that?"

He was thinking of the small man with the reptilian eyes, caught in a camera flash only to be crushed moments later under a loose-tooth slab of wall. But Rafferty should have been thinking of himself, of his own image, captured by Tamsin as he dug through the rubble in the falling rain, rescuing no one.

He hadn't told her about the dead man, wasn't sure if it really happened. Perhaps he had only dreamed it.

"You realize that Tomoka is probably gone by now," he said. "Back to Japan, or Norway or wherever." Memories of Okinawa pushing in. "Have you ever been?" he asked. "To Japan, the southern area?"

"Nagasaki, does that count?"

"Farther south. Islands at the very end."

They had camped on the beach by the ferry dock, staking their claim on the sand, Rebecca complaining and Rafferty fuming. It was the muscle-twitch spasm of a dying *something*. Rafferty, staying up all night to write down his feelings, page after page, as the wind pulled at the paper. Or was that in Hanoi? The memories were beginning to blur. Rafferty had placed a pewter locket next to her sleeping bag, a heart-shaped pendant meant to be funny, but taken as romantic, and her hugging him, holding him with her tears, whispering in his ear, "I don't want this to be over." But it was. It was, it was and no pewter heart could change that.

"We should go to Okinawa," he said. "Someday. Those islands. That beach."

"We? Since when am I included in your plans? I thought our entire rapport was based on happenstance." That, and fucking.

Was he trying to slide Rebecca's photo out of the frame, slip Tamsin's in instead? Overwrite a memory? Even he wasn't sure.

"And anyway," she said. "There's still another offer on the table. Mahia, remember?"

"Can't," he said. "I'm heading out."

He had considered slipping away while Tamsin lay sleeping, leaving a line of text as farewell, the modern equivalent of a pen-and-ink note laid gently across a pillow by a paramour departing. *"My dearest Tamsin, there has been a change of plans. I leave in the morrow for Australia."* His Gone to Patagonia moment.

"I have an assignment," he said, and she knew he was lying. He was usually lying, so that was generally a safe bet, but in this case, he couldn't bring himself to look her in the eye when he said it. A hell of a tell. *Should've played poker with the fucker. I would have cleaned up.*

"An assignment?" said Tamsin. "Where?"

"Alice Springs. There's a train that runs across the Outback. Might be a story in it."

"Might? So, you *don't* have an assignment?"

"Not yet," he said, not realizing he'd been caught out, or perhaps not caring.

She laughed, and her laughter contained traces of tears. "She's there, isn't she?"

And now Rafferty did look her in the eye. "No." And that part was true. She wasn't in Alice Springs, she was elsewhere, out in the field but still nearby. He didn't know where exactly, not yet. "I'm sorry," he said. "I have to."

"Who cares?" said Tamsin. "We are ugly, but we have the music."

"Tammy—"

"It's that stupid necklace, isn't it? That cheap little heart you bought her. Airport gift shop, am I right? A cheap little heart made of tin. Big spender." She had seen the pendant. Brittle Becky had been wearing it the one time they'd met, had shown it to Tamsin with a breezy laugh. "That's what we call her," said Tamsin. "You know that, right? We call her Brittle Becky."

"No one calls her that. And it wasn't tin. It was pewter. And it wasn't an airport gift shop, it was on a ferry." Like it mattered.

"But that is what you're trying to get? Right?"

"No," he said. "Not that."

THE DARKNESS ITSELF

FAYTHER WAS SNORING. A SCIENTIFIC TREATISE lay open on his belly, rising and falling with every wheeze, every seagull snork, his hair uncombed and reading glasses askew.

They were taking forever. It had been ages since they'd asked her to leave so that they could sort out the details of the fee, and still Dr. Rowley hadn't reappeared. Catherine was in the kitchen, looking out. *I will wait another three-and-a-half minutes*—that was the length of the song that was playing on the radio—*and then I'll go out. I'll ask them if they want some biscuits. That'll be my excuse.*

And then she saw him, on his feet, striding across the yard, and Dr. Rowley nowhere in sight. He had passed her dad's hand-painted sign, EREWHON FARMS, S. BUTLER ESQ., and was making a beeline for the house. She hurried out to stop him.

"Wait," she said, running across the yard. "My dad's inside. He's sleeping."

But the small man didn't stop. Glared. "You failed to keep your side of the bargain," he said.

He moved with a predatory gait, more prison guard than panther, and she hurried alongside him, struggling to keep up. "Don't," she pleaded. "If Fayther sees you, I'll get in so much trouble." At that age, it was the worst you could imagine: getting in so much trouble.

The striding man stopped short, stared at the modest stucco of their family bungalow. It could have been a house on Falls Road. Small lives, a doily-laden world. "Asleep, you say?"

"Don't wake him up, please don't, please. He doesn't know you were ever in our barn." And then: "Is that Dr. Rowley's sweater you're wearing?"

The small man snapped his gaze onto her. "Bring me the satchel. You don't deserve it anymore."

There was a blind rage behind his eyes; any trace of kindness gone. This wasn't the same man she'd nursed back to life. This was someone else entirely.

"Dr. Rowley lent you his sweater?"

"My satchel. Now."

"But—"

"*Now.*"

She scrambled to get it.

Dr. Rowley's body would surface three days later in the same cove from which Catherine had sent out her messages in a bottle when she was young. Like her bottles, Dr. Rowley had washed back in. The current down there turned everything in on itself, and the sweaterless body was floating facedown, limbs splayed, turning on a slow eddy, out of reach of poles, so they had to send a tinny out, battling under- tows all the way. Catherine watched the entire operation from above, the aluminum boat nudging closer as her father stood at her side, clucking about safety measures and village ordinances. Dr. Row- ley had fallen, broken his neck, apparently, on the way down—the coroner's report would find no water in his lungs—but Catherine knew otherwise, and she was left with a tremor of fear, of terror, and with it, the feeling of having brushed up against something cold in the dark. Perhaps the darkness itself.

OUR LADY OF THE CUBICLES

GADDY RHODES, HUNGRY AND UNHAPPY.

She'd forgotten to eat, was going through a stack of binders that had arrived that morning. As the agency slowly transferred its backlog of cases over to electronic files, encrypted and cross-referenced, she found herself tied more and more to her desk. Which is why, when a notice to renew her handgun certification popped up in her inbox she almost laughed—or whatever the Gaddy Rhodes equivalent of laughter was. She hadn't been to a gun range in ages, not since Okinawa, and what would be the point of it now? She hated the sanitized abstract nature of it, the earphones and muffled recoil, the outlined target pully-rolling in for her to inspect after each session. *Center mass. Two to the core, one to the head.* Easier said than done. She was never a great shot, tended to go wide, and anyway, it wasn't like she would ever be threatened by an outline. Nor did she anticipate getting attacked by a silhouette, not anytime soon, not when there were files to consolidate, memos to attend to. Gaddy Rhodes, license to collate! Our Lady of the Cubicles.

She had the news streaming on her monitor while she worked:

BBC World, because the American networks were too parochial. Working with Interpol, even here on the periphery, meant keeping your gaze turned ever outward. It had been fifteen days since the earthquake in New Zealand and already the story was being shuffled to the back of the pile, fading from view, replaced by newer disasters, fresher headlines. A tropical storm was throwing a wrecking ball through the Amazon. Chinese roadworkers had uncovered the remains of a seven-hundred-year-old mummy by accident. The sea-encrusted cannon from a ship that had once belonged to the privateer Henry Morgan had been recovered off the coast of Panama. Gaddy kept her eye on that last item, but so far nothing strange or suspicious. The recovery had been going on for years, the salvage company was well known and the project was fully documented, but still . . . She tagged it just in case.

When it did appear, she almost missed it: a news item on her muted screen. *Lost Hitchcock reel discovered*. Gaddy shoved the plinth of binders to one side, turned up the volume, but she'd missed it. On to the next story. A two-minute vigil of silence was being held in New Zealand, so she switched to print instead, pulled up the item online:

LOST HITCHCOCK REEL

MGM studio head and famed film aficionado Cameron Berg today announced that the lost reel of Alfred Hitchcock's debut 1923 movie, *The White Shadow*, long thought lost forever, has been recovered. A story of twin sisters, one evil, one good, *The White Shadow* was written and directed by Hitchcock as a young unknown, before he was famous, and although a single copy of the film has been preserved, the final reel itself has been missing for nearly ninety years. "This is a great day for cinema!" said Mr. Berg, who paid an undisclosed sum for the reel. "I'm thrilled!" The studio plans a remastered rerelease in the New Year.

A wealthy buyer, an anonymous provider with provenance unclear and value undisclosed, but clearly in the millions by the rumors that were already flying about. It had all the hallmarks. But the deeper she dug, the murkier it got. Vague tales, contradictory versions of events, a Hollywood mogul hogging the limelight while the origins of the lost reel itself remained shadowy and unclear. How would one even know where to look for such a film? She began to search "lost movies," came upon the story of an even larger cache that had been unearthed in Alaska years earlier, a wealth of old black-and-white films: a newsreel of the 1919 Black Sox, some early Chaplin, Mack Sennett.

How had they ended up in Alaska, of all places? The answer: Alaska was the end of the line. Movies back then were expensive to ship and dangerous to transport. The nitrates that were used to produce the film stock were incredibly flammable. Instead, the movie reels were passed, baton-like, along a circuit of cinemas until, eventually, they reached the final stop, after which they were simply disposed of. It might take a year or two for that to happen, and no studio bothered to pay for their return, so they were discarded. The cinema in Fairbanks was one such final post, where, over the years, reels of film had piled up in the basement. The building changed hands several times, became a butcher's, a hardware store, a storeroom, and was eventually marked for demolition. That was when the cache was discovered.

Had this lost Hitchcock reel surfaced in Alaska as well? Was he now plying his trade along the edge of the Arctic Circle?

Down the rabbit hole she went, pulling up more articles, more leads, tracing the northern routes of these old films, each ending in some dismal location: Vladivostok, northern Finland, Reykjavík, Dawson City. It was a wide net. Too wide. But then—archived in a film history site—mention was made of an obvious fact: if there were northern termini, there were also southern. The article read: "Films from the Golden Age of Hollywood were shipped as far north as the Yukon, and as far south as Christchurch, New Zealand." Her heart stuttered, a single skipped beat; low blood sugar and an overinjection of caffeine at play, perhaps, but something more as well. She began clicking with renewed purpose, bringing up images and historic sites: blueprints of Christchurch, an overlay of city planning spanning the years, and soon came upon references to the Empire Cinema, the southernmost movie theater in the world at one time, now only an outline traced on an architectural map, just one layer in a palimpsest that had been drawn over, rebuilt, and erased many times. The earthquake had stripped this away, had revealed the underlying strata, had left a gaping basement where the Empire once stood.

Gaddy Rhodes sat back. *You were there. In Christchurch.* Not Alaska, not the Arctic Circle, the Southern Cross.

Quickly now, she began scrolling through reports of the earthquake. Images of rain and rescue workers backlit heroically against the ruins. An eyewitness report, posted on a travel blog:

Update: It's just Erin now. Ewan is no longer part of this. He left. The other writers have left, as well. Only Thomas Rafferty stayed on, tried to help.

That name, why was it so familiar?

And now he's gone, too. It must have brought back too many memories of Rwanda for him.

And now the percussion grew faster, cymbals and a jag-time beat. *Rwanda.*

Her old boss and former friend Andrea Addario had often complained about Gaddy's habit of forcing the evidence to fit her theories, but how could that be a coincidence? *Hitchcock—Christchurch—Rwanda.* They lined up like an arrow pointing to a single name: Thomas Rafferty.

Why did she know that name?

Gaddy pulled up everything she could find on him, and instantly the connections began jumping out at her: Nagasaki, Buenos Aires, Vatican City. He was in eastern Congo when the Kalinga drum was taken. She scrolled through, faster and faster, until one name came to the forefront as though embossed: Okinawa.

That's where I know him from!

She moved a stack of files, pulled down a thick folder, the one labelled HATERUMA, rifled through, found the glossy travel magazine, flipped to the article: "Okinawa: A Land of Contrasts," Island Views magazine, Jan/Feb 2004. *Drowned mountains, coral reefs, a dragon ascending . . .* Author: T. Rafferty.

Gaddy went back online, brought up his author photo, heavy faced and grim. Not like the single confirmed description she had of her suspect: a small, well-dressed but forgettable figure haunting the refugee camps after the fall of the Rwandan regime. So she tweaked her theory: the small man may have been a confederate, an employee even. She'd been asking herself how he had been able to slip so easily across borders. Well, here was the answer staring out at her with sullen eyes. A travel writer. She had been asking *who* he was, she should have been asking *what* he was.

With everything falling into place, Gaddy opened a new window on her desktop. Brought up The Map with its confusion of lines and far-flung connections. A travel writer. Of course.

She fired off a message to Erin, asked her to text back.

Big fan of your work, Erin! Also, of Mr. Rafferty's.
Did you actually meet him?

The answer pinged back a few moments later.

Unfortunately, yes.

What was he like?

Broken.

Gaddy took a moment to gather her thoughts before launching another sally. She considered asking: *Did he throw money around? Seem wealthy? When he arrived, did he fly first-class? Have his own plane?* But she knew that if Mr. Rafferty's cover was indeed that of a working writer, he would need to be as unobtrusive and unremarkable as possible. Instead, she asked:

Broken? How?

Let me put it this way. When I first met him, I thought he was a misogynist. But now I realize, it's not just women. He hates everyone.

263

A misanthrope?

Exactly. He didn't seem interested in writing about the earthquake. Spent his entire time digging through the rubble.

A pause, and then: Didn't save anyone, though.

Of course not. He wasn't looking for people.

Gaddy thanked Erin, asked her if she had any idea where he might have gone, but she didn't know. Fortunately for Gaddy Rhodes, Mr. Rafferty had left a trail in the form of travel articles, written in such a perfunctory manner they could only reinforce her opinion that his writing was, at best, a cover. It was too trite to be otherwise. His words couldn't draw attention to himself, after all; they were merely meant to be an alibi. The feeling in her chest was growing, heart racing, face flushed, that dizzy dancing feeling. *I'm coming for you.* The noose, gone slack, was tightening again.

It was while she was searching flights and figuring out the unused medical leave owed her, that Erin sent a final message to Gaddy:

If you see him, can you tell him I said hi?

The author photo was still up on her screen, and perhaps it was a trick of perception, but his eyes didn't look as sullen anymore; they looked scared. *Oh, I'll do more than say hello.* And now she really was laughing, or trying to: a dry sound deep in her throat struggling to be free.

PART FIVE
STRANGE MONSTERS

THEY WERE THROWING ROCKS AT CARS again. Aboriginal kids in plastic flip-flops that slapped back as they rushed forward, venting their tedium on the vehicles that crawled past, slow-rolling tourists, come to see the agate mines, induced by company promos, driving through town as though on a human safari.

Visit Devil's Spite Creek in the heart of the Australian Outback! Experience Aboriginal lifestyles firsthand! Marvel at the region's rich agate mines!

Rental companies charged an extra premium if you were taking the vehicle out of Alice Springs. When pressed, they would explain it was because of the rocks, and visitors would assume they meant rocks on the roads, not airborne.

When one of the rented sedans slowed down so that the people inside could gawk, a barrage of rocks would pummel the hood. Eventually a police officer would be called—for a town of scarcely four hundred, it had a full contingent of constabulary on call—and the kids would scatter, only to regroup later when the officer left. As the evening wore on, they would graduate to throwing bottles. No one had thought to stuff them with rags and gasoline, not yet.

Rafferty had been pulled off buses in Ecuador and detained by Bangladeshi border guards; he wasn't overly concerned about the Aboriginal youth in a dusty town in the kiln-baked heart of a continent.

And anyway, he didn't have a car; he'd taken the train in, a straining, bronchial beast that always seemed to be rolling uphill even when the landscape was hammered flat. At one point, the train had pulled onto a siding to let the luxury express Ghan hurtle past, the passengers in dining cars flitting by like frames in a filmstrip. Then, with a groan, his own train rolled out, back onto the tracks, heading inward.

It clattered through sun-bleached outposts—Oodnadatta, Kulgera, Dalhousie—crumbling ghost towns, defeated by distance, failed oases. Date palms grew amid the ruins of Dalhousie Springs Station; the trees had been planted a century ago by Afghan cameleers who were brought in to herd freight-car camel trains across the desert.

Two days on the train and they'd only moved a few inches on the map.

The world outside was an overexposed Polaroid, and as the terrain grew flatter and flatter still, the horizon line began to waver and eventually dissolve into pooled mirages. Lakes without water. If thirst had a shape, it was the Australian Outback.

The other passengers were strangely subdued, like soldiers being transported to the eastern front, the excitement of the departure two days earlier having long since faded into the usual hypnotic lethargy of long journeys. As the days crawled onward, miniature bottles of gin and scotch, the type usually associated with stewardesses in powder-blue pillbox hats and the airplanes of yesteryear, were lined up on his tray like chess pieces. Bishops maybe, or pawns. The trolley girl who swiped his card looked surprisingly refreshed considering the nature of her job, back and forth across the same tracks, the same plains, the same terra-cotta emptiness.

"Gittin' off at Alice are ya?"

"Before then," he said. "After Titjikala." He had no idea if he was pronouncing that correctly. "I'm staying in Devil's Spite Creek," and the smile fell from her face.

"You be careful. Havin' issues up there, with rowdy boys and the like."

He knew what "rowdy boys" was code for.

Her voice became a whisper. "Vandalism. Petrol sniffing and such. If it was me? I wouldn't go there. Was me, I'd stay on till Alice."

He nodded, and she trolleyed off.

Miles and miles of miles and miles. That two-dimensional world. Train tracks converging on the infinite, into that endless forever. Magic hours and a porous moon, its surface like a weather-scarred cinder block. The moon always seemed so much closer in places like the Outback. When he had been in the Gobi Desert, the moon had seemed to rest just above the sand dunes. In the Alberta Badlands, it practically touched the earth.

"Devil's Spite Creek! Next stop!" the conductor cried, and Rafferty closed his laptop, gathered his things. But when he tried to stand, his back had locked up. This was happening more and more frequently, it seemed, his vertebrae like a zipper that had rusted shut, and in the end, he had to twist himself out of the seat in a corkscrew maneuver.

The town of Devil's Spite Creek lay in the shadow of a stone pillar, a natural column, eaten away, the top stained red with sandstone. A jagged tooth, a broken finger, a tombstone. Devil's Spite was a boomtown gone bust, the local agate mine and its proximity to Alice Springs being the only attractions. A tired-looking camel was resting on its knees beside the train station, waiting for tourists to climb on and take their picture, should any tourists show up.

Rafferty lugged his rucksack onto the platform in the falling dark, looked around with the calm elation that always comes with arrival. A dog of indeterminable breed loped by, slipping in and out of shadows.

The night was full of voices. The usual loitering louts. Teenagers performing prodigious feats of boredom watched him as he walked past with an active indifference. But Rafferty had been pulled off buses in Ecuador and detained by border guards in Bangladesh. If anything, he wanted to go over, tell his moody onlookers the one fact he knew to be indisputably true: *You can always leave.* A taxi puttered by, propelled by farts.

Australia is for lovers! Come to Devil's Spite Creek in the heart of the majestic Outback!

Streetlamps, with their attendant hovering of moths. Mix-and-match cars parked at odd angles. The entire town looked like a dresser drawer that had been upturned and picked over, a garage sale at the end of the day when all the good bits are gone.

The Fairview was less a hotel than an ongoing project, with various appendages added arbitrarily. It had a faded, antebellum feel. Paint so pale it was hardly there. Two creaky floors, rooms facing the street and the railways beyond, an open veranda running down the length of the upper floor, trying in vain to catch a breeze. It reminded him of Pusan, of Loja, of Lombok, of Louisville. *Same same but different*, as they say in Vietnam.

A threadbare man was waiting for him at the front desk. "You'll be Mr. Rafferty."

"The train was late."

"No worries, mate, train's always late. If it was ever on time, it would be early. Let's get you checked in." Thus began the Ceremony of the Guestbook, a call and reply, with credit card imprints and the all-important Explanation of the Keys.

"What brings y'ta Devil's Spite?" The way he pronounced it, it sounded like "devil spit."

"The scenery."

"Scenery?" The clerk balked—and then laughed. "Oh, there's a view, all right, but you have to look for it. Stick a pin in the middle of the map, you won't be far gone." The town was pretty much the geographic center of Australia. "This is as far in as you can go. After that, you're coming back."

Rafferty tucked his walleted credit card back into his pocket. "A group of researchers were staying here, from Sydney I believe. They were with the university. Collecting folktales and artifacts. Are any of them still around?"

"From the uni? Left last week. Which reminds me"—he shuffled through some items in the drawer. "You're Mr. Rafferty, right? One of 'em left a letter for you. A lady."

But when Rafferty opened the envelope, all that was inside was the message: *Stop following me. I don't have it.* He recognized that sharp up-and-down way of hers, like an EKG, and he turned the page over as though there might be something written on the back as well, but that was it. Just those two sentences. She hadn't even bothered to sign her name. Didn't need to.

"Where did they go?" he asked. "The group from the university?"

"Not sure. Some Abo community farther out, I imagine." He'd forgotten to censor himself. "Aborigine, I mean to say. They were out in the field, the real woop-woop. Ewaninga, last I heard. The rock carvings and so on. The petroglyphs."

"Far?"

"Over an hour, up and around. But they're not there anymore. My nephew runs the town taxi, he ferried them about, here and there."

"If not Ewaninga, where?"

"Could be anywhere. Not sure if you noticed, but this is a big country. Easy to get lost in."

Rafferty nodded. "The woman who gave you this"—he was referring to the envelope—"did she leave anything else behind? For safekeeping, maybe? In the hotel safe, say?"

Eyes narrowed. "We don't have a *safe*, we have a cupboard that we lock. But they took it all with them, everything they had."

Rafferty slid a fold of bills across the table. "Are you sure?"

This had worked in Italy, but he wasn't in Italy.

The clerk pushed the bills back. *Feckin' Yanks. Living their lives like they're in a movie.* "As I was sayin', they took everything with them. Everything." He assumed Rafferty was a debt collector of sorts. He didn't like debt collectors.

"Know when they'll be back?"

"No idea, mate. Could be weeks, could be never."

So he waited.

MOURNING DOVES

AN ALLEYWAY IN ALICE SPRINGS. A leering larrikin with dry lips and a cracked grin.

"Highly illegal, you'se unnerstand? *Highly*."

She held the gun in her hand, felt the weight of it in her palm.

"Beretta M9," he said.

Semi-automatic, slide load, short recoil, nine-millimeter rounds, fifteen to a magazine, an official range of fifty meters, but really only effective at short range. But short range was all she needed. She wasn't about to go up against the darkness unprotected.

THE DAYS PASSED, EACH THE SAME as the next, and before he knew it, Thomas Rafferty had spent a week in Devil's Spite Creek, under a punishing sky.

He thought of the cool moisture and escaping steam of New Zealand, of the underworld ponds and boiling muds, the wet air that furred the forests, and it seemed to Rafferty that he had clawed his way out of Hell's Gate only to land here, in this empty purgatory. Memories of Sunday catechisms, of lessons learned and warnings that went unheeded. Even as a boy, Rafferty knew that purgatory was a worse place to end up in than Hell. At least with Hell, you knew where you were, knew the trip was over, that you'd reached your destination, could finally unpack. Purgatory was an endless holding pattern; the torment of that—the not knowing when it would end—would have been much worse.

Devil's Spite Creek, Rafferty came to realize, was just a proliferation of bars set back off the highway, an inhabited ruin, propped up, barely standing. Only the mine kept going, wheezing and diminished. The railcars rumbled into town empty, left full. Rumbled in full and left empty. It was just about the only motion there was. That, and rock-throwing youths. *The day the ore runs out is the day this town closes down.*

On a raised wooden sidewalk, an old man, flyblown and frayed, said, "Drought is a withered woman, jealous of life." One of his eyes was cloudy, the other a polished marble, not unlike agate. Air as dry as wine. A rib cage that creaked like a hinge. Sweat that evaporated on the skin. Rafferty was having trouble breathing at times. Out here, the sun didn't just scald you, it harassed and hectored, it chased you inside, into the shaded depths of taverns where the glasses were pebbled with condensation.

A cigarette eating itself. A full ashtray and an empty glass. Loud voices at the other tables. Rafferty wasn't the only patron escaping the heat. "I told him. I said, y'have to shake your boots every time you pull 'em on, didn't I tell'm? I told'm, didn't I? Everything that crawls, flies, or swims in this godforsaken country wants to kill you and eat you, and not necessarily in that order." Squalor and ale (two parts squalor, one part ale). Rafferty was in his element. He lifted his empty glass in their direction. They lifted theirs in turn, went back to their recursive conversations. "I told him, didn't I? Y'have to shake your boots every time. I told him, didn't I tell him?" "You told him."

Rafferty ordered a glass of murky Australian stout, watched the television above the bar as the latest headlines uncurled. Christchurch had already been pushed from the lead. They were on to Hollywood now, where a producer—Rafferty didn't catch his name; it had already scrolled past—had unveiled the lost reel of Alfred Hitchcock's debut film. Rafferty seemed to recall the dead man saying something about strangers on a train and realized that this had been a reference to Hitchcock. What a strange coincidence. But then, coincidences are always strange. They are strange almost by definition. Rafferty didn't think anything of it, and Hitchcock's reel slipped away.

One of the boys at the next table was bragging in an ill-shaven baritone about these uni twats that he'd taken out, how they'd overpaid him and that was the problem with these uni types, suckling on the public teat, not *their* money they're blowing, is it? and did you not offer to refund them? fuck no, took my share, and laughter round the table.

Uni twats? Rafferty wanted to stumble over, ask "Where exactly? Where did you take 'em? Can you draw a map or drive me there?" But the other table parted ways soon after, and Rafferty wandered back to his hotel alone. He fired up his laptop. The university didn't list the specific sites they would be visiting, only that they would be empowering Aboriginal communities by gathering their stories. Songlines and gods taking the form of pythons, of spiders. That sort of thing. Not godforsaken, god *saturated*. The entire Outback echoed with these dreamtime tales.

Rafferty might well have made it through the rest of the day, almost sober, but for the hotel's library, really just a shelf of books with greasy-thumbed paperbacks and out-of-date guidebooks on offer. James Patterson and Lee Child. *The Rough Guide to the Australian Outback* (revised). Lonely Planet, even a Frommer's. And wedged in among them, that familiar green spine: *Casablanca to Timbuktu*. He pulled it free. "For Elizabeth on her birthday. Love always and forever, Micky." *Crappy present, Micky.* The inscription on the first page was dated ten years earlier, and Rafferty wondered how it had come to be separated from Liz. Lost? Thrown aside? Left behind? How many hands had it passed through since then, and were Elizabeth and Micky still together? Odds, not.

Slouched on the couch in the hotel lobby, Thomas Rafferty flipped through to the book's celebrated opening line, one that often cropped up in travel anthologies and dictionaries of quotations (a level of fame only slightly higher than that of anecdote): "What quantity of lager it took to come up with this, I do not know, but the notion, having seized our beer-addled brains, refused to let go: we would travel the bulge of Africa, unaided." A lie, of course. The trip had been conceived as a book right from the start, but it was more entertaining to present it as a wager or a wild-hearted, crazy impulse. *Have gone to Patagonia! Have made a wacky bet with my wacky mates to cross Ireland in a rain barrel. Provence softly beckoned! As I walked out, early one morning . . .* Just once, Rafferty wanted to open a travel memoir and read, "I decided to walk the El Camino because my agent got me a book deal and, having already blown the advance, I had no choice but to go."

He skimmed a few passages from this early, much admired, little-read work of his. It was like reading the diary of a distant relative or sifting through photographs of forgotten forbears, who bear a slight resemblance to you, rendered now in sepia. Here was a memory from Senegal, but it might well have been Ecuador, or Indonesia:

Our bus leaned perilously on each corner, passengers scrambling, hanging from the opposite side, trying to prevent the vehicle from toppling over the edge. Afterwards, we exchanged grins. The same grin, every time. It said, "We have cheated death, not forever, possibly not even for long—but we have cheated it here, have cheated it now, in this valley, on this bus." It was the grin of life.

He could hardly remember those words or the person who had written them. Where had he gone, that younger man, so cheerfully convinced of his own immortality? Whatever happened to him? Thomas Rafferty's unpublished autobiography still sat on a hard drive somewhere, he couldn't recall where, but it was titled *In Medias Res*, and contained only the one line: "I found myself lost in the middle of a lonely nowhere." He had scribbled that down in the Gobi Desert, beyond Ulaanbaatar, could just as easily have written it in a mall or a suburb or any number of hotel rooms.

He stared at the front door of the hotel, the glare of heat outside staring back at him. He was sweating alcohol; he could feel it. Bangkok and Bali. Mumbai and Malacatos. Sordid transactions in the dark. Love affairs that were hardly either. And with a lurch, the world moves backward like a train leaving the platform, picking up speed. Tibetan prayer wheels and his father dying in a bed at the Madison County Memorial Hospital in Winterset, three blocks from the house he was born in, such a small trajectory. Walking alone under the African moon. All those truths that can be understood but not explained. God, perhaps. Or love. When you are tethered at the center, all journeys become a circle.

A ceiling fan was stirring the heat.

The gray tide of Christchurch. Lombok in the rain. The anvil of the Outback, reverberating from the heat. He peeled himself off the sofa—his back had locked again—left the book behind, and made his way to the hotel bar. It was empty, and the threadbare clerk followed him in to take his order. Just a gin and tonic, and still he wrote it down. Came back a few minutes later. "Tonic, right?"

Nicotine walls. A spiral of sticky paper speckled with flies. The slow singe of gin. Rafferty's thoughts turned with the predictability of a compass to the girl from Des Moines who stole stories. That was what she did for a living. "It's what she does," he said to the empty room. Call it folklore archivist or ethnologist or whatever you liked; she trafficked in stories. And he wanted to bring it to a close, the Story of Becky and Tom. That's all he wanted.

It had ended in Okinawa, though they didn't realize it at the time.

Had staggered on, stomach shot, till they reached Hanoi. Her leaving, and him not even realizing she had left. Not at first.

Thomas Rafferty had thrown himself into marriage like a drunk down a flight of stairs. Doomed from the start, one supposes, as all love affairs are. *The one Almighty Fact about love affairs is that they end.* He'd read that somewhere, couldn't remember where; his memories were blurring more and more as he got older. He thought he could hear the sound of birds. Mourning doves, maybe. Or was it morning? He was never quite sure.

A sky full of stars and a tent on a beach by the side of the sea. And maybe life is supposed to break your heart, maybe that was the whole entire point of it. The girl with the rose madder lips, what was her name again? Erin. Tear-streaked but strong. *They had to amputate their legs to save them.* Erin, in the world. Had he ever been that young? Had he always been so—What was the word he was fumbling for? So *chary*. A good word, that: careful + wary = chary. *Should write that down.* He looked around for a scrap of paper, smoothed out his napkin instead, and when the waiter next checked in on him, Rafferty asked to borrow his pen.

Reluctant, he handed it over. (How would he be able to remember the order without it?) "Any tuck?" he asked.

"What do you have?"

"Can do a nice chiko roll."

A contradiction in terms, that: nice and chiko roll. Cabbage, barley, and beef tallow deep-fried in dough. "Sure. One of those."

The chiko roll arrived, along with another gin.

He was still there in the empty bar, hours later, mumbling to himself about items lost and lexiconic, when the woman with the gun sat down across from him.

EXIT VERONICA LAKE

IF IT ENDED IN OKINAWA, WHERE did it begin? That was an easier question to answer: in Sydney, at the dawn of a new millennium, six years after Rwanda, at a champagne-fluted reception on a richly lathered, moon-illuminated night on Lavender Bay.

Tom Rafferty, younger then, had taken the ferry across Sydney Harbour to a modernist café-cum-art-gallery at MacMahon's Point, a thin wedge of glass, right on the water. The gallery's café—Sails, it was called—faced Sydney's iconic bridge with the city's opera house perfectly framed below. The view from Sails also included Luna Park, with its giant harlequin's mask and neon Ferris wheel turning slowly atop its own wave-mottled reflection, wet and bright in the night. But it was the opera house that everyone's eyes were drawn to, lit up like cockle shells on the shore.

"More like nuns in a rugby huddle," someone said with typical Aussie aplomb.

The clink of glass, the tinkle of a piano, the constant hum of murmured gossip. Canapés and the connect-the-dots outline of the Harbour Bridge. This was where Rafferty's life went askew.

"The guest of honor!"

A hand on Rafferty's elbow steered him away from the view. This was Rafferty's first time in Sydney and he'd been mesmerized by it.

"Come, come, Mr. Rafferty. *So much* to talk about."

Cornered at a cocktail party, trying to escape from the conversational headlock the curator had put him in, Rafferty kept searching about for a pretext to worm free, but found none. All he could do was nod in a vaguely noncommittal way. "Art is no different than a bowel movement, when all is said and done," proclaimed the curator. "Inevitable, you see." Sure. Why not? Another nod, another swallowed yawn. "One *consumes*," said the curator. "One consumes, and one purges." No argument there.

Rafferty's hearing gelled over soon after that. The room was both boring and bizarre, like a zoo on a Sunday afternoon—and what a collection it was! Bon vivants and dilettantes, debutantes and dahlings. Arched eyebrows and piquant opinions, all charmingly provocative, and a gallery owner whose mind moved with the alacrity of a cash register.

A bumptious art critic, loudly assertive, was holding court in the far corner. (Here was a man who had clearly dressed in the grips of delirium: clashing plaids, with lime greens and yellows so radioactively bright as to be combustible. That he critiqued art for a living amused Rafferty to no end.) And everyone ignoring the actual canvases, bombastic works replete with Aboriginal motifs and ghost-like faces superimposed on each. It was the artist's own face, Rafferty later learned. "A comment on the nature of art," the curator assured him. "The Ego Has Landed," the critic would later write.

The Artist Himself had yet to make an appearance, and many of the guests stood around like awkward statuary, awaiting His Arrival. How had Rafferty come to be invited to such a soiree? He wasn't sure himself. One moment he was in a marketplace in Indonesia, and the next moment he was answering a frantic phone call from his agent (long since fired; Rafferty went through agents the way diabetics went through needles), who, breathless and buoyant, wanted to get him to Australia for an "Author and Artist event." Or maybe Artist and Author. Better than a launch! he assured Rafferty. This was technically true, because there were very few things on this earth worse than a book launch. Poetry readings, perhaps. Interpretive dance, certainly. But little else.

Rafferty was supposed to be networking, though to what end wasn't clear. His agent was still stateside, so Rafferty had no informants to whisper details in his ear about who mattered and who did not. (Slowly, he realized that he himself was among the latter.) It had indeed been advertised as Artist & Author, painter and wordsmith, but no one gave a damn about the writer in the room. Why should they? Anything interesting about a writer is left on the page, and who has time to read these days, anyway? Painters worked in splashes of color; writers sat alone in a room, pecking away at their keyboard, inventing imaginary conversations between make-believe people who didn't exist—and yes, that included travel writers. A good deal of *Casablanca to Timbuktu* was "reconstructed" after the event, including entire swathes of conversation. Painters were crazy—crazy, exciting. Authors were crazy, too, but not crazy *enough*—and what is an author but the empty shell that follows its book around? Rafferty knew where he stood: he had all the appeal of a bottom-shelf celebrity. Had a daytime TV star showed up, she would have instantly trumped the artist, just as a B-list film actor would trump daytime TV. There was a pecking order to such things.

"And you are the author?"

"That's what they tell me."

Rafferty among the dowager class. He wanted nothing more than to not be here, in this gallery, with these people. He wanted to be back on the red earth of West Africa, the scalloped paddies of Bali and Lombok, even the backstreets of Belfast. Anything was better than this. But that was before he met Rebecca.

The man who had taken Rafferty's elbow hostage now guided him through the room, sidestepping donors and the verbal incontinence of po-faced patrons, until they reached at last an overstuffed sofa, where an equally overstuffed man waited with papal indulgence. "Ah, there you are."

He didn't rise, but rather placed his hands on either side and propelled himself upward, like a hippo rearing onto hind legs. A bulbous face. Even his eyelids were fat. It was one of the reasons Rafferty would still remember him, years later. "Welcome, welcome, Mr. Rafferty." The man's voice gurgled like a tap with too much air in the pipes. His name was Melvyn—with a *y* the curator quickly added—and he had the leathery scent of wealth about him, *old* wealth, the kind that doesn't rot, but decomposes like so much warm autumn mulch.

"Amongst the effete elites, eh Mr. Rafferty? Preening fools, strutting about with the cock-a-hoop pride of peacocks. Not men of action, like you or I."

What the hell was he on about?

The fat man held his gaze a beat too long. "The Kalinga drum? Ring a bell?"

How a drum would ring a bell wasn't clear. "A drum?"

"I am a broker, Mr. Rafferty. I arrange, shall I say, certain services." He stared again into Rafferty's eyes as though expecting a certain response. "Ah, I see. I was, perhaps, misinformed about your role in the matter. Forget I even mentioned it. Water under the proverbial bridge. I served with a travel writer, in the war. Jan Morris, though of course I knew her as James."

"Sure. Jan Morris. One of the best." He was already getting tired of the fat man.

"And Bill Bryson? You've met him, as well? He wrote a book about Australia, you know."

"Sure. Bill and I go way back. Let's see, last I saw Bill he was snorting crack off a hooker's ass. That would'a been at a brothel in Vietnam, or maybe an opium den. I can't recall. Anyway, we'd outrun the military police, a misunderstanding really, could have happened to anyone, but you know Bill, with that temper of his. We almost got in a knife fight with our rickshaw driver over a Hanoi handshake. Classic Bill, with his switchblade and glass eye. Did he show you his neck tattoo? Gang tats, I think is the correct term."

Eyes agog. "Really? *Honey!* Come here, you have to listen to this." The fat man toddled off to find his dowager wife, never returned.

Hell with this.

Rafferty was just about to leave when the Artist finally arrived, sweeping in with a dash of hauteur, the physical equivalent of a scarf flung over a shoulder, an almost weightless presence eeling through the crowds, from clutch to cluster, preening and purring, making small talk to no one in particular, leaving half smiles and sighs as he passed. He was followed by the usual coterie of admirers. And how easily a coterie becomes a cabal. There was something sinister about the man, though it may have been the cliques and claques that surrounded him, caught up in their echo-chambered chorus. Never did a face need punching more, yet no one stepped up to the task. Instead, everyone seemed to be very much impressed with him. Not everyone, though, as Rafferty was about to discover.

"You paint with words, my friend," said the Artist, hand extended graciously in Rafferty's direction. "You, too, are an artist—in your way." Artists always think the highest compliment you can pay other people is to say they are an artist. "We are both artists."

"And you're like a writer," said Rafferty. "But with paint."

Not so much a conversation as a competition. When the Artist smiled, he showed all his teeth. He dropped hints of Very Important Meetings, spoke of his mission, his mandate, his passion.

"I've always been inclined toward the Sad Clown school of painting myself," said Rafferty. "That, and young Elvis on velvet."

The Artist paid no heed. Turned instead to his apostles. "Now, this one," he said, a sweeping reference to a vast canvas; the artist's face superimposed over Aboriginal motifs. "Came to me in a dream."

At which point there was a tap on Rafferty's shoulder and a breathy tickle on his neck. "Insufferable, isn't he?"

Rafferty turned and was immediately pulled into the gravity well of her presence. She reminded him of—who exactly? Veronica Lake. Sultry to the point of lethargic. But she wasn't Veronica Lake, she wasn't even American. She was British, the consular general's wife, and with her appearance a parallel narrative opened up, not a promise, but a *possibility*. Rafferty had always enjoyed other men's wives, ambassadorial especially. There was a boudoir boredom that he found alluring, and over the years, the woman at this party would become emblematic of missed chances.

She was wealthy, or at the very least had access to wealth: her husband's. Every artist needs a patron, perhaps she could be his. The consular general's wife might well have transformed Thomas Rafferty, still reasonably young and reasonably vibrant, into a kept man, might have sponsored his flights, fanciful and otherwise, might have cast him in a cinematic adventure of her own making. Either way, had Thomas Rafferty pursued the consular general's wife that night, no matter how it played out, he would not have found himself here in a dead-end town south of Alice, in this bar, on this day.

It made him think of a story that had confused him as a child, the tale of a prisoner and his clandestine lover, the queen. Condemned to choose between two doors, one of which held a ravenous tiger, the other a beautiful maiden, the prisoner had hesitated. This was a dangerous choice, to be sure. Rafferty had skipped ahead to the last line, where the story threw back its challenge to the reader: *Which door did the prisoner choose?* What a strange question, Rafferty thought. The one with the girl, of course.

That night, at a glass gallery on Lavender Bay, a similar choice had opened up, though he didn't realize it at the time. It was a choice that led straight to a failed marriage, a nylon tent and a heated argument, obsessive regrets, a message waiting in a faded hotel: *Stop following me. I don't have it.* Looking back, he could see portents of those last moments in the first: her temper, the self-stoking anger, even the waver in her voice; it was all there in front of him that first night, and still he had chosen the wrong door.

It was the accent, not the argument, that first caught his attention. He turned, saw a fiercely determined woman going nose-to-nose with the guest of honor. She was so clearly angry, so clearly upset, and was so clearly trying not to let her voice betray her, and still it did; a tremor ran through everything she said. It was the waver that did it.

"As an artist, what right do you have to use Aboriginal images?"

Rafferty knew that accent. Corn fed, Middle America. Sweet jams and pickled carrots. A daughter of the drylands. His people. And thus, with a vague wave of his hand, Rafferty lost all interest in the consular general's wife. Veronica sank back into the lake from whence she came and Rafferty pushed in closer to the confrontation.

"An artist doesn't choose his material, dahling. The material chooses him."

"Those images belong to the Aborigines."

"And you speak on behalf of Aborigines, do you, dahling? Of course, you don't. You're not even Australian. Aboriginal art is in the public sphere. It's part of our shared world. It's their *stories* that are sacred. Many of their traditional stories can only be told by designated storytellers, and, even then, there are some that are protected among Aborigines themselves, stories that one needs to be properly initiated even to *hear*. Have you been properly initiated? I didn't think so. I admire their *art*. But you? You plunder their souls." A bit melodramatic, but point taken.

This immediately led to an acrimonious debate about the differences between science and art. Any argument, pushed far enough, eventually comes down to semantics, and this one was no different; it was an argument that ran in increasingly smaller circles, in imminent danger of disappearing up its own arse. At which point, Rafferty cut in. "Des Moines?"

This threw her back a bit. "Do we know each other?"

"I'm from Winterset, we're practically neighbors." And from this would come the affectionate term and, later, bitter designation of Rebecca as "the girl next door."

She had readied herself for the party, she who was more at home in the field, in the sun. She had put on lipstick, had paid for a perm, too tightly coiled, with foundation and eyeliner applied in an attempt to bolster self-confidence, only to make her feel more self-conscious. Rafferty could see the makeup line along her jaw where it went suddenly from powder-pale to a neck that was still reddish and real. She wasn't very good at makeup, but she had tried, and he had no choice but to fall in love with her after that.

Here was the strange thing, though: For all the Artist's pomposity, he was right. The swirls and colors and patterns used in Aboriginal art were indeed out there in the world, to be shared, to be appreciated and adapted. These patterns were part of the public sphere; it was the Aboriginal stories that were held close and kept secret. One doesn't plunder light, one plunders stories—stories and the objects attached to them. For all Rebecca's certainties, she was wrong about the artist, wrong perhaps about the nature of her own work as well. It was a lesson Rafferty would learn—too late, unfortunately: that being absolutely certain about something doesn't make your views any more accurate for it, that being righteous is not a synonym for being right.

He tried to extradite her from the melee, but she couldn't let it go, had a dingo-like grip, wanted to crack the bone, reach the marrow, a trait that would cause Rafferty no end of anguish over the years, though, of course, he didn't know it at the time. The Artist had become bored with her by this point, had turned back to his cabal—and how quickly a cabal becomes a coven.

"Let's get a drink," said Rafferty. Always a stopgap solution. "They're serving a nice shiraz," he said. He was from Iowa. Back then, he didn't know the difference between a shiraz and a sauvignon. Fortunately, neither did she, and he managed to disentangle her from further escalations.

He handed her a drink. "Tom Rafferty," he said, and he waited for a reaction.

But she had no idea who he was. So much for the authorial fantasy of women swooning into your arms. (When asked what the best thing about being an author was, Rafferty invariably answered, "The hordes of love-starved women who are constantly throwing themselves at you." The worst part? "The fact that said women are wholly imaginary.") He repeated his name on the off chance she'd missed it.

"Who?" she asked.

"The author. *Casablanca to Timbuktu?* Y'know"—he gestured to the banner hanging in plain sight. "The Author and the Artist. He's the artist, I'm the author."

"He's an asshole, is what he is."

"Aren't we all."

She didn't bother with a handshake. "Rebecca Hodges. And you are?"

"I just told you."

"Oh. Right. I'm still a little addled." She swallowed her drink, took a steadying sigh. Short hair, green eyes that rarely blinked. (She had an unnerving habit of maintaining eye contact for longer than necessary, or socially acceptable. It was an intensity that would both attract and repel him over the coming years.) Eventually, her anger subsided and the waver in her voice faded. But it would be back. Oh, it would be back.

Rebecca and Thomas, a.k.a. "Becky and Tom," a.k.a. "Becks and Tom-Tom" in their more cloying moments: it had all started at a soiree in Sydney with a panorama of the opera house lit up in front of them. They talked about art and music and politics—he didn't give a damn about art and music and politics—and by the end of the night he had completely fallen for her. It would take her a little longer. If ever.

When she told him she was a graduate student, studying ethnology at the uni (she'd already picked up the local slang), Rafferty had asked her, "Have you heard about this drum? The Kalinga, I think it's called." He didn't realize then that it wasn't an Australian artifact that the fat man had been alluding to, but Rwandan. It was just as well. Even after these many years, Rafferty was still dealing with the fallout of that African genocide, had no wish to revisit it.

"The Kalinga?" she asked.

"I think so."

She hadn't heard of it. "My area is more folklore, stories, that sort of thing. Not artifacts, unless they're attached to a specific story. Why?"

"No reason, it's just—I had this odd conversation." He looked around, but couldn't see him. "Anyway. He mentioned that drum like it was a secret that we shared. I thought, maybe, with your background— Never mind."

She shrugged it off and so did he, and with that, they returned to items trivial and semi-truthful. He never mentioned Rwanda; she never pretended to have read his books. One always falls in love over trivial matters. It's why love so rarely lasts.

ULURU

TAMSIN AT SEVENTEEN.

They were waiting for her after school, at the bottom of the stairs beside the flagpole, the stars-and-bars rolling on a loose Milwaukee wind. It was the last bell of the last day of the last semester of high school, and Tamsin wouldn't be sticking around for the prom, so this was it. She jogged down the steps, not bothering to look back, and a flock of Ashleys were waiting. (She never bothered to learn their names, assumed they were all called Ashley.) Feathered bangs and honey hair, these were the girls who organized school dances, the girls who took notes during field trips. Tamsin, meanwhile, was the one with her feet up in the school cafeteria, headphones on, a Ramones riff blaring. Short, solid hipped ("childbearing," as her grandma said, trying to make it a compliment), with black hair spiked in a failed attempt at a Joan Jett hairstyle, Tamsin was a mob of one: Tamsin Unlimited. She was the one who slowly removed her headphones and slowly looked up when Mr. Pritchard, the vice principal, shoved her boots, told her to get her feet off the table. She was the girl who *slooowly* took her feet down, first one, then the other, and then put them back up as soon as Mr. Pritchard was gone.

The feathered Ashleys wore shoulder-padded jackets at right-angle extremes. Big hair and square shoulders: this season's look for Popular Girls, apparently. (Though truth be told, Tamsin didn't know if they were popular or not; she was barely aware of their existence, let alone where they ranked in the social strata.) If the linebacker look was in, Tamsin hadn't gotten the memo. She had on her ratty but beloved Siouxsie and the Banshees T-shirt, a jean jacket, studded with safety pins, and homemade clamdiggers—she'd cut her jeans off, midshin—and instead of her usual Doc Martens, high-top sneakers. Semi-formal, in other words. At first, she thought, hoped, that the Ashleys were waiting for someone else, one of the Brads maybe (the male equivalent of an Ashley), but no. They were waiting for her.

The main girl separated herself from the flock. The flicker of a smile, testing the waters. "Sign your yearbook?"

"Um . . . yeah, sure." Tamsin shoveled around in her backpack, pulled out her Class of '86 yearbook. Handed it over while the other girl readied her pen. This would be the only high school signature Tamsin would collect that year.

The other girl signed carefully, closed the book quickly and handed it back. If she was expecting Tamsin to return the gesture, she was sorely mistaken. Instead, Tamsin shoved her yearbook into her backpack and went home. Only later did she check to see what the head Ashley had written, assuming something mean or mocking or, at the very least, patronizing in that passive-aggressive Ashley manner, was surprised instead by what she read. It was written in curly blue cursive, with circles dotting the *i*'s: "Tamsin Greene is a cool machine." It set her back then, still did now.

All these years, and Tamsin wondered if everything she'd ever done had only been an attempt at living up to that inscription. Wondered if maybe that wasn't true of everyone, that maybe we are all of us trying to repudiate—or validate—the verdict we received in high school.

Tamsin Greene in the arid heart of a lost continent. Bone dry, with a fly net draped like a pesticide-imbued onion bag over her face. Tamsin Greene deep in the Australian Outback, wondering whether the many varied roads that had led her here had started with a signature in a high school yearbook. Strange that her thoughts would turn to Hamilton High, *Home of the Wildcats!* when she was so far from anywhere resembling home.

But home, of course, was only a notion. Uluru was here, was real.

She'd hung around the art deco diorama of Napier for a day or two after Rafferty had left, and had then traveled north to the very end of New Zealand, searching for a Japanese girl she once knew, the girl who swam with the dolphins. But Tomoka too had departed for points unknown—"I think she's in Oslo, of all places," her former landlord had said—and the compass needle had swung slowly back to that asshole Rafferty. *Well. I guess I'm going to Australia.*

She sent a one-word message to her editors in New York: *Away.* They could let the wire services cover the coroner's inquest; how hard is it to photograph weeping families? The images that she captured of Christchurch had already had their impact, so she loaded up her gear, cashed in her frequent-flyer points, jumped on the next plane to Sydney. From there, another three-hour flight took her inland to the hotel village at Uluru National Park, where she rented a Land Rover—with requisite roo bar, should any kangas leap suicidally in front of her hood—and had driven it in from the Uluru airport, across the thornbush plains.

The silvery blue of eucalyptus. The golden rings of spinifex grass, prickly and ubiquitous. Tufted grass and Dr. Seuss trees, and the same four or five elements endlessly repeated, and now—rising up in the middle—the monolithic singularity of Uluru. Red, now orange, now mauve: it changed color with the angle of the sun.

A wind was moving across the curves and caves of Uluru, whispering ululations, but Tamsin had to turn her head to catch it. An IED in Taliban territory had once lifted a jeep up from beneath her, had burst her eardrum as surely as bubble wrap, leaving her deaf on one side and recasting her world instantly from stereophonic to mono, something she stubbornly refused to acknowledge. But she hadn't come all this way for sounds. She was here to capture the light.

Uluru up close is very different from Uluru in long shot. What appeared monolithic from a distance became striated and variegated the closer you came: fleshy folds, curtains of stone, which hung like fabric; she swore she could see it move at times, as though rippling on the wind. But as she drew closer, it changed again. The surface became mottled with a metallic skin of iron and silica, scaled in chemical decay.

Every few years someone died on Uluru. The constant flow of climbers had worn away a thousand years of patina as they hauled themselves up, single file along a chain, conquering this minor

Everest, *minga*, as the local Anangu called them: ants. The trail they left behind was known as the Scar of Uluru. The climbers that day included a bachelor party of hungover celebrants from a nearby resort and at least one team of Elvis impersonators, congratulating themselves on having mastered the sacred. It was the casual suppositions of the ill-informed traveler: Rafferty's truck and trade. Where was he anyway, that prick? She'd called every hotel in Alice Springs, five hours away, had left message after message, to no avail. He seemed to have vanished. It was one of his more enduring habits.

The insect file of tourists plodded onward. A silvery trail. Scars, near at hand and far away. An Afghan chieftain. The dark chuckle of tannin-stained teeth. A straight razor drawn like a painter's brush down the side of her face, almost a caress—but not quite. Instantly opening, a clean slice, not the jagged tear wrought by a blunt machete, but almost surgical—but not quite. A slice of pain, burning to the bone. Crude stitches on a medic's gurney. Endless rounds of reconstructive surgery when she got home, severed nerves trying to reengage and mostly failing, a numbness on the face and a lopsided tilt when she smiled. Rafferty said it gave her a certain charm. He was the only one who did.

She changed her lens. Compensated for glare. Told herself to stay focused in the here and now. *Forget the past, Tammy. Forget it.* But the past was always present; as soon as you pressed the shutter, you've captured the past. Every photograph is an historic document, after all, and it seemed to Tamsin that there were only two types of memory, neither new. It was either Polaroids or flashguns, a slow emerging or the sudden magnesium explosion of old-timey photographers, hooded like an execution.

Tamsin Greene watched the sun play along the sides of Uluru, was forced to keep the fly net draped over her face even while she was framing the shot. *We see Uluru as through a veil.* And it struck her, somehow, that this was perhaps appropriate.

She had charted a walk around the base, starting at the scar. *The dryness will fool you,* she'd been warned. *It is very easy to become dehydrated when you aren't sweating.* Out here, perspiration evaporated before it appeared, leaving crusts of salt on shirt collars and stubbled armpits. A desert without dew. In North Africa, the moisture-depleted harmattan winds from distant seas still managed to leave traces of their passing in droplets of dew. But not here, not in the Outback. One liter of water for every hour, so she was lugging five liters in her already crowded daypack. Granola bars, polarizing filters, a collapsible tripod, and a floppy hat draped in a fly net. She began shooting through the netting, a softened, pixilated effect, as a possible photo-essay took shape: *Uluru in a new light.*

A sudden *kii* and Tamsin looked up.

Birds of prey were riding the updrafts, watching for rodents, tracing lazy lethal circles in the sky. *They must roost in the cliff face.* She considered changing lenses, firing off a salvo, trying to catch them in midflight, but the moment quickly passed and the birds were soon lost to the sun.

Women's caves and men's: the first relating to childbirth, the second to hunting. Inside the caves, the art was a thousand years old, tawny ochres and charcoal that had been mixed with animal fats, tree sap and honey kneaded with rusted iron oxides. Dots and lines, swirls and spirals, and lower down, the red-eyed image of the Devil Dingo Dog, used to frighten children for generations into behaving properly. *"Don't sneak out at night, or the Devil Dingo will get you!"* A thousand years of human history were overlain in the art of Uluru.

Tamsin pulled out her tripod, set a long exposure to coax the colors from the stone.

Past these caves, a sandy path led eastward, into the worst of the sun, with Tamsin clinging to shade wherever she could find it. She was standing beneath the spectral protection of a ghost gum, photographing a strange rock formation, when someone spoke. She turned, saw a uniform. The immediate identification and evaluation of uniforms was a crucial skill in Tamsin's line of work. Government forces (sympathetic?) or government forces (hostile)? Regular army? Police? A border patrol? Or the always dreaded Presidential Guard?

It was none of the above. A heavyset Aboriginal man in the khaki green of an Uluru park ranger was walking toward her, and he didn't look happy. Eyes deeply set, unperturbed by the flies that flustered about, a face that was muscular, a stare the same. He was glaring, not at Tamsin, but at her camera.

"Off-limits, innit?" he said, his voice softer than his bearing would suggest. There were all kinds of authority at play here. Tamsin, abashedly, hadn't seen the NO PHOTOGRAPHY sign, and even if she had . . .

"C'mon you." He waved for her to bring the camera over, and they scrolled through the images together. "Delete that." She did. "And that. That, as well." When they got to the photographs of the cave art, with pigments richly rendered, he couldn't help himself. "Nice." Then: "Flash?"

"Tripod."

"That's okay then." On it went, life in reverse, Tamsin reeling in the walkabout that was her life until, unexpectedly—smoke and rubble and a cross appeared. "Is that Christchurch?" he said.

"It is."

He handed her camera back. "Journalist of some sort?"

"Sort of. But without words. And you? You're from around here, right? Aborigine?"

"Anangu," he said. "That would be the correct term, in this area. Aborigine, that's just something you Whitefellas came up with."

He walked with her to the next ceiling of stone, black with soot. "Old man's cave," he said. "They would sit and tell stories."

"Can I?" She gestured to her camera.

"Sure. It's just certain spots, ones too scared for photographs. This is more like a learning cave, where the old fellas would teach the young. In Anangu culture, we're raised by our grandparents."

"Me too!" she said.

"Were you?"

"I was! In a faraway mythical land known as Wisconsin, in a magical city known as Milwaukee."

"Maybe you're Anangu too. Your grandparents, kind were they?"

"Grandmother, and yes."

They followed the trail past prickly bushes ringing with birdsong. "Grandparents," he said. "They're really important," and Tamsin agreed. "They raise the kids," he said. "The parents had to focus on hunting, surviving, so they gave the children to the grandparents, who knew more stuff, were more patient. Sad for the parents, maybe. But when they got older, it was their turn."

Slabs of stone, like warm clay. Dark stains ran down the flanks of Uluru, and when she asked about these, he said, "Waterfalls. When it rains, Uluru streams with water. It's something to see, it really is. There's these plants, 'everlastings' they're called, can lie dormant in the earth for years waiting for the right moment. It rains, and they bloom. Pink petals opening up. Very beautiful. And there's these plants, resurrection ferns. Looks dead and dry in the soil, under rocks, hiding in crevices, notches in the stone. Looks dead. But when it rains, comes back to life."

"Like Lazarus," she said.

"I guess. And there's these trees, on the plains, we call them bloodwood. Their roots can wring moisture from the driest soil, and the sap is really thick and red. You cut them and they bleed." They walked awhile in silence, and then he said, almost shyly: "My name is Malya, by the way."

"Tamsin," she said.

"Nice name."

"Thank you. Yours as well."

The heat and flies were getting worse. She stopped to take some water under her veil.

"Uluru," she asked, after she'd realigned her fly net. "What does it mean?"

"The name? It means 'meeting place.' Lot of songlines converge here."

"Is that part of the Dreamtime?" She had heard of the Dreamtime.

"We don't like that word. There is nothing dream about it. We call it *Tjukurpa*. It's the basis for everything we do. Everything that's real, everything that's right, everything you can see, everything you can't. Stories and lessons, all of it. It's ongoing—like creation. Hard to explain. The Anangu, our way of being, it's thirty thousand years old." It was the oldest existing culture on earth, protected by the United Nations. "Those pyramids in Egypt that everyone keeps going on about? What are they, three thousand years old?"

"Something like that."

"A blink of the eye to the Anangu. I studied at a Catholic mission. The crucifixion? That was like yesterday to us. Anangu believe every ripple, every groove, every hole, contains a story. Most of these stories are off-limits, can't be shared. C'mon," he said. "I'll show you where Kuniya the python woman fought Liru the poisonous snake man. That's a children's story, so it's okay to share. Good photos, I reckon."

It was the story of a mighty battle, still embedded in the surface of Uluru. Kuniya, protective of her eggs, had attacked Liru. Pointing to the surface above one of the water holes, Malya showed Tamsin the shape of Kuniya rippling down to strike at Liru. He later pointed out the wounds that Kuniya had inflicted as well, pocked in the stone.

"Can even see the stain left by the blood from one of Liru's wounds, over there. Do you see it?"

She did.

The Australian sun was higher and harsher now. Flies in a hectic flurry. Pythons in the rocks. She couldn't think of any place like this place; it reminded her of nowhere else but here.

"This entire park," he said, "everything around it, is Aboriginal freehold. Too arid for grazing."

"That's right. I didn't see any sheep," she said.

"Cattle," he said, "and that's farther out. Pastoral lands, they call it. Massive stretches along the train route. There are cattle stations out there the size of Belgium. That's what they tell me. Ranches, I think you'd call them."

They had followed the path past Kuniya Piti to the eastern tip of Uluru.

"This is where I leave you," he said. "You can keep walking, I have to turn back. Kuniya Piti is man's business. But around that next corner is Taputji. That's women's business."

It was a fundamental divide, one that Tamsin might have rankled with, but she also recognized that when the oldest existing culture on earth tells you something, it was, perhaps, something worth heeding. She thanked Malya for his time, asked for a photograph—she had long since outsourced her memory; if it wasn't on a memory card, it didn't really exist. She promised to send it to him, but of course she wouldn't, and was about to push on alone to the stone island of Taputji and the women's business beyond, when he asked, "Why do you go about photographing fallen-down buildings like that?" He was referring to Christchurch.

"Well, someone has to, I suppose."

"But does it have to be you?"

"No," she said. *It doesn't.*

THERE ARE TREES THAT REQUIRE FIRE. The extreme heat cracks open their seeds, and though the tree itself dies, the seeds burst, falling into the ash-rich soils. Acacia and eucalyptus are two such trees, spreading with every wildfire, living torches known to explode at high temperatures. The scorched earth and charred wood, the skeletal branches of burned shrubs reaching out. Lightning strikes that ignite the landscape, the flames that both consume life and create it. Kali, dancing on her mound of skulls.

Tamsin had been warned to watch for dragons on the road, but this was not the season for dragons, and there were no lizards sunning themselves on the blacktop. As the heat of day bled away, Uluru become redder still. She wanted to capture this moment. Driving out to one of the park's designated "sunset viewing points," she parked the Land Rover, pulled out her gear, walked up the bristly ridge, and let her tripod fall open. Crickets in the dunes. The landscape was singing.

Tour buses began to arrive, pulling up in convoys, their uniformed staff hurrying off ahead of the guests, producing champagne and canapés with a flourish of tablecloths and linen napkins. These were sunset tours, and the guests held up their drinks, took photographs of Uluru through the lens of the champagne glass, upside down in the reflection.

The moon appeared.

Uluru became a silhouette, and in the sky above, the Southern Cross slowly took shape. Fragments of the past. Stars so bright they cast shadows. Voices that remained long after the faces were gone.

Anangu women had appeared. They quietly spread out their canvases for sale, sat on the ground behind their artwork, waited silently. The art was exuberant. Colors and contours, curves and myriad dots, wild wavy lines and ripple-like patterns that seemed to emanate with vibrations, never static, always in motion. It was the oldest existing art tradition in the world: the shimmering, pointillistic world of Anangu women. A few sales, not many. And when the tour buses pulled away again behind their cones of light, the Anangu melted into the Outback. They lived nearby in villages not marked on maps, and Tamsin watched them disappear. The entire scene seemed sad and surreal, from the canapés to the idle chatter to the artwork and the equally idling coaches.

She locked in her camera on top of her tripod, set a long exposure time, and recorded the stars carving perfect arcs across the sky, like the grooves in a record. She was alone now. She packed up her gear under the chill of the night, tromped back to her Land Rover, the only vehicle in the parking lot, and then drove out, into the night. Down here, the stars were upside-down, constellations gone topsy-turvy, and her headlights were full of moths. At the main road, Tamsin slowed to a stop. Left would take her back to the hotel and the campsites, with their satellite relays and email pleas. *Syria is on fire. Where are you??* Right would take her farther into the Outback. Most of her gear was already in the vehicle. What would she be abandoning, really? A toothbrush, some laundry powder, a couple of cotton T-shirts, a pair of cheap sandals. Items more often lost than found. (How many toothbrushes had she left behind over the years? Strange to feel wistful over lost toothbrushes.) Those songlines we follow, and those we lose. And slowly the compass needle spins back around.

She put the Land Rover into gear, cranked the wheel to the right, signaling even though there was no one there to see her, out of habit, one supposes; longing, one suspects. An empty highway, mice bounding across the road in front of her were caught in her headlights, the same headlights that were pulling her forward, through the darkness, across the interior of a continent that was, if not entirely lost, at the very least mislaid.

Here, then, was the end of many things.

She couldn't do it, couldn't go back to the world, couldn't face the plunge into another fray where ignorant armies clashed by night. Her cell phone was blinking, but Tamsin Greene was out of range, beyond the brute force of news cycles, and the only voice was the one she hummed to keep herself company, a rhythm of her own making as the gap in the stars that was Uluru receded in the mirror behind her. And ahead of her, only night.

ENTER THE BANSHEE

IT SEEMS SO LONG AGO.

A pewter locket, a nylon tent gritty with sand, a storm-tossed beach in southern Japan. And now here he was in Devil's Spite Creek, nursing a drink in the dry heat of a faded hotel tavern, with a half-eaten chiko roll in front of him, a severe-looking woman across.

She was balancing a cup and saucer in front of her, strikingly out of place, both the woman and the teacup. She smiled, but not with her eyes. Dunked the tea bag like she was drowning a mouse. "You're taller than I expected," she said. "Heavier, too."

Thin, blond, anemic. He could see the bones under her face. Pale as a bride behind a veil, eyes of Prussian blue. She was wearing a blazer—in this heat. Age: undetermined, but on the far side of thirty, certainly. She wore the years well. More than he could say for himself.

Rafferty smiled back, eyes and all. "Thanks. I think." *Taller than she expected. Heavier too.* The first was possibly a compliment, the second a little off-putting. But what the hell, he was lonely and half-cut, and she seemed to be interested in him. Lips, narrow, almost non-existent, a mouth bracketed by deep lines, parentheses of worry. He tried to imagine kissing those lips, couldn't. Some were leg men, some were ass men; he always started with the lips. His smile was returned, unopened.

Taller than I expected.

"Is this what passes for a pickup line?" Rafferty asked.

The woman placed her cup and saucer to one side, stared at him. She seemed to be studying everything he did, as though gathering evidence—and perhaps she was. Rafferty, unshaven. A face like wet cement. "How's the food?" she asked.

"I've had worse," he said, though he couldn't imagine when.

"Given the parlous state of today's publishing, I would think you should be out hustling stories, instead of sitting ensconced in a bar in a dead-end town in what I believe is the geographic middle of nowhere."

Ah. A fan.

"You've read my book," he said. It should have been plural, but he'd only ever written the one memoir of note. The others had dropped, unheralded, like pebbles down a well.

"I skimmed parts of it, yes."

Okay, not a particularly *committed* fan, but still.

"I can't help but wonder," she said. "What brings you all the way out here? Searching for dinosaur bones, a lost treasure, perhaps?"

"You could say that."

"One other question," she said. "And understand, this is purely curiosity on my part, but indulge me if you will. Can you whistle?"

"Can I . . . ?"

"Whistle. You aren't from Belfast, are you?"

This question confused him even more than the last one. "Why would I be from Belfast?"

"Didn't think so. If not Belfast, where then—exactly?"

"Me? Nowhere really. Just a place. Winterset. It's in Iowa."

"Yes, I know. But where are you *actually* from?"

"I just told you."

"You've been to Okinawa, Mr. Rafferty."

Conversation by non sequitur. "I have, yes."

"Hateruma Island?"

303

"Which one is that?"

"The last one."

"Probably." What was the name of the last island? The one where Rebecca had interviewed the priestesses?

"Not probably, you have, several years ago. I read your article. You spent a lot of time in the southern islands, Mr. Rafferty. Hateruma included."

"If you knew, why'd you ask?" Jesus. Was any lay worth this rigmarole?

She had stirred up memories as well as tea . . .

Rafferty had been to Okinawa. Twice. Had gone there with Becky; it was their first trip together. "We'll camp on the beach," he'd said. "We'll sleep by the sea, and make love like sex-crazed rabbits." Becky was a child of the Midwest and unacquainted with the sea, and she paced out a spot for them on a clean sweep of sand, below the grungy boa of flotsam and seaweed above, and he'd had to explain to her that the reason the sand was so clean was because it was *below* the tide line. Had they pitched their tent, when the sea came in during the night they might well have floated away. At the very least, it would have made for a soggy sleep. "Have you tried to wring out a sleeping bag? It's not a lot of fun." Instead, they slept on a diving platform that was stranded at low tide, had woken to find themselves afloat after all, wading back to shore past confused tourists, backpacks on their heads like characters in a jungle expedition, laughing and in love (probably). Was that the last time he had been truly happy? In Okinawa, that first trip?

It was in Okinawa that she first heard about the world of the noro priestesses, had applied for a grant to return, and he had come along with her in a doomed attempt at re-creating that moment, but now she only complained—about the sand, the wind, how he breathed, how he chewed. The noro women had refused to cooperate, smiling all the while, parrying every query, and somehow this was Raff's fault. He had purchased a gift, a pewter heart, hoping. False hope, as it turned out. But then, most hope is.

He blinked.

The thin woman was staring at him.

"Have you been?" he asked. "To Okinawa?"

"I have indeed. Just last year, in fact."

"Remarkable, isn't it? Fruit so lush, so heavy, so *laden* with ripeness they look like lanterns lit from within. It's like an untended bonsai garden. Hateruma? Is that the one with the secret society? The priestesses? Noro, I think they're called."

Moving on. "You were in the Peace Corps, Mr. Rafferty. Back in 1991. Ecuador, I believe."

She seemed intent on going over his entire CV. Was this a job interview of some sort? The prelude to a romp? Was he required to prove himself worthy of her loins? "I joined the corps, yeah. When I was young. I wanted to go out into the world, find people less fortunate than I, and do good to them, whether they wanted me to or not." It was a line that usually got a laugh. Not this time.

They had now come to the crux of the conversation, if this could be called a conversation. It was beginning to resemble more of an interrogation than a chat. She leaned in, watched his face carefully when she spoke the next word—"Rwanda"—saw him react as if to a blow. The breezy smile vanished, the eyes narrowed.

"Congratulations," he said. "You've read my wiki bio."

"Oh, I've read more than that. You were in Rwanda to write a travel article about the gorillas, but that's not entirely true, is it? You were, in fact, a guest of the country's minister of the interior with ties to President Habyarimana's genocidal regime. I've seen the paperwork."

"The minister oversaw Rwanda's national parks, so, yeah. I had to go through his office. I didn't have a choice. Listen, that letter kept me alive."

"I'm sure it did. You were in the camps as well, in eastern Congo after the government of Rwanda fell."

The conversation had entered darker depths, but he didn't know what this meant. First Belfast, then Okinawa, now Rwanda. And still the shovel hadn't hit stone.

"You were in Rwanda, you were in the Congo, and," she said, "most recently in Christchurch, New Zealand, right after the earthquake."

"During."

"You've had quite the life, Mr. Rafferty."

"If you can call it that." He held out his arms like the Christ over Rio. "Guilty as charged! The rumors are prodigious and insidious, but they are true I'm afraid. They cannot be shaken nor ignored." He dropped his hands onto the tabletop, palms down. "A full confession is in order. I am indeed monstrously endowed and phenomenally informed in bed. But why take my word for it?"

She didn't smile. Not even a flicker. "You think I'm interested in you? I'm not interested in you. I find you about as appetizing as hobo's breath." She reached inside her jacket, flashed her badge. "Interpol," she said, slipping it back into her pocket.

"Oh no," he replied, voice flat. "The jig is up." He threw back the rest of his drink, shoved the half-eaten roll to one side. "Listen, Miss . . . ?"

"Rhodes. Agent Rhodes."

"Whoever the fuck you are. As far as——"

"I'm with the ICA, the International Crimes Agency, it's a division of Interpol. And yes, Mr. Rafferty, the jig is most certainly up." She finished her tea, savoring the moment, leaned back, considered her quarry. "A travel writer. *Of course*. Why hadn't I thought of that? A perfect alibi, able to slip in and out of countries on a visitor's visa, leaving only a trail of poorly written articles in your wake——"

Hey!

"——and no one the wiser. For a long while, I wasn't even sure if you existed. But now that we've met?" Her voice became grim. "I find myself decidedly underwhelmed. You have blood on your hands, Mr. Rafferty."

"I'm American, so yes."

"Does the name Billy Moore mean anything to you?"

A blank look.

"Billy Moore. The man without a face. No? How about Alonso Ricconi?"

"Doesn't ring a bell."

"An antiquities dealer in Vatican City. You cut out his tongue to send us a message." This was called "throwing chum." You toss a few chunks of raw fish into the water, see if you can draw the shark closer.

"Did I? You'd think that would be the type of thing I'd remember." It was like a dialogue with Alice, if Alice were high on mushrooms. *Curiouser and curiouser. Men without faces and tongues removed.* "Okinawa. Rwanda. Vatican City. What are you on about?"

"I have a dossier on you, Mr. Rafferty."

"I'm sure you do. Listen . . . Agent Rhodes, is it? Can I give you some advice? Maybe eat a sandwich now and again. You look like a fuckin' stick insect. Your ribs probably rattle when you get fucked."

She smiled. "I'm afraid only one of us is getting fucked today, and it isn't going to be me."

To besmirch a man's reputation is no small thing—and no easy feat. He pushed his empty glass to one side. "Badge or not, I'd be careful who you repeat those allegations to, Miss Rhodes."

She was twisting her empty ring finger, and Rafferty watched as her eyes flitted over the room. *Christ. She's checking the exits.* And was that a . . . ? It was. Tucked inside her jacket, a holster. A fucking gun. She wasn't just a lunatic; she was an armed lunatic. How the hell does one manage to bring a handgun into Australia, even if you are—supposedly—employed with Interpol? Must have purchased it when she got here, in Alice Springs probably, black market, or maybe it's just a replica and she's just bluffing, or crazy, or a combination of both.

Agent Rhodes's eyes locked onto his. Any pretense of pleasantness was gone. "*'Life being what it is, one dreams of revenge.'* That's from Gauguin, from his diaries. The clock has run out, Mr. Rafferty. I win."

You just missed her. Your lady friend.

"Good god. You've been tracking me since Napier." But one doesn't get old and cynical without learning a thing or two along the way. "Before you haul me in, Miss Rhodes, can I see that badge of yours one more time? You can't expect me to surrender to the first loopy lady who shows up. I do have my standards. They're very low, admittedly—a sort of Mariana's Trench of standards—but still. May I?"

"Of course."

She handed it over and Rafferty examined it like an Antwerp diamond dealer. "It says 'administrative supervisor.'"

She hesitated, and in her hesitation told him everything.

"You're not actually law enforcement, are you?"

"I told you. I'm with the ICA, a division of Interpol."

"You're with admin. You're basically a bureaucrat. You can't arrest me, you can't even detain me."

She met his gaze. "I can contact the Australian police easily enough."

"Oh, yes, I'm sure the local billabong constabulary will snap to it if you show up barking orders. *'Yes, ma'am! Just let us finish rescuing this koala from a kookaburra and we will get right on it.'* You have no more authority than any random nutjob on the streets of Devil's Spite Creek. Less so, in fact, what with you being a foreigner and all."

Thomas Rafferty had been pulled off of buses in Ecuador and threatened by armed guards in Bangladesh. This was nothing.

"Here's what's going to happen, *Agent* Rhodes. I'm going to get up and walk out that door over there, probably raising my middle finger as I go—I haven't decided yet; might be overkill, no? And you are going to shoot me in the back, if you like, that's honestly fine with me, but think of the paperwork. Plus, your own inevitable arrest and trial and incarceration. You'll lose that badge of yours as well, the one you seem to think gives you supernatural powers. You might as well go about flashing your library card at people, it would have about the same amount of authority. So, you can shoot me, if you feel so inclined. Or, and this is the more likely scenario, I will walk out of here, finger raised, un-shot, and you will fuck off back to whatever sad little bureaucratic hole you crawled out of."

He stood, slowly, deliberately, turned his back to her—and she did consider it. *Center mass, two to the core, one to the head, as trained.* But on what charge, and to what end? And what if she was *wrong*? When she'd said the name "Billy Moore," it had meant nothing to him. She could see that. Not a glimmer of recognition. Her doubts grew.

From his table to the exit was only nine steps, but they were a long nine steps. Hand on the door, about to leave—Rafferty could already feel the dog's breath of heat outside—he stopped, turned around, faced his banshee.

"Rwanda. Why did you say Rwanda?"

She was still at the table, hadn't drawn her weapon or tried to stop him. She looked, if not defeated, at least deterred. The laser-like focus she'd shown earlier was gone from her eyes, and—was that doubt he saw?

Rafferty came back, stood above her. "Why Rwanda?"

"Because you were there. You left bodies behind when you left."

"There were bodies aplenty in Rwanda. They didn't need any help from me. I was just trying to get out."

"With the Kalinga drum, in tow."

That stopped him cold.

"The what?"

"The Kalinga drum," she said. "Royal emblem of the Tutsi kings. Buddy Holly's glasses. Muhammad Ali's medal. The egg—the Fabergé egg. The urinals and the chess piece. I can't connect you to all of those, not yet, but I will. You were there when that drum was taken. You hired mercenaries to do your dirty work."

Jesus Christ, she really is crazy.

But then—

Memories of Sydney. An art gallery soiree and a fat man with a leering look. *"Not men of action, like you or I."* Rafferty sat down. "That's the weirdest thing. Someone else asked me about that drum, years ago."

"Who?"

"I don't know, he was rotund, ex-military, Australian, maybe

English. You would need someone like that, wouldn't you? To know how to arrange for mercenaries. Like you, he thought I was involved in the operation. He said as much."

"When was this?"

"Ten years ago, maybe more."

"Where?"

"A gallery, in Sydney, you could see the opera house, it was across the harbor from the bridge."

"So . . . a man you don't know, whose name you can't recall, who may or may not have been Australian, or possibly English, asked you about the Kalinga drum at a cocktail party somewhere in Sydney, ten years ago, or more, you're not sure."

When she said it like *that* . . .

"Better get crackin'," he said. "Before the trail gets cold."

"Know what I think, Mr. Rafferty? I think you are trying to gaslight me. I think this is a clumsy attempt at misdirection, something a second-rate magician might employ at a child's birthday party. I think you're trying to cover your tracks." She leaned closer, eyes burning. "I know you were in Rwanda when the government fell, I know you were in the Congo afterwards. I know about your associate as well, a small man, does your dirty work. We have witnesses that place him in the Congo too, when the drum was taken."

"A small man?"

She nodded.

"Well dressed? Sort of nondescript?"

Another nod.

Rafferty felt his chest constrict. "I know exactly who you're talking about."

With that, the world froze, just for a moment—less than a moment, a heartbeat really. Gaddy could feel the tectonic plates beneath shift and fall into place. "The small man?" she said. "You know him? You admit it?"

"Fuck yeah."

"Does he work for you?"

"What? No."

"Do you work for him?"

"Fuck no. But our paths have crossed—more than once. I saw him years ago, in Africa, in the camps like you said, and again, just recently, in Christchurch. I saw him in the sudden flash of a camera. Who is he?"

"A collector."

"Art?"

"Things. Objects."

"Is that why he was in Christchurch?"

"He saw a window of opportunity, yes. He thrives on chaos. To him, earthquakes and civil wars are simply acts of misdirection played out on a larger scale, allowing one to slip through doorways undetected. When he saw the buildings fall in Christchurch, he made his move."

"Why Christchurch?"

"New Zealand's South Island is the end of the line. The old black-and-white movies that Hollywood used to ship. Massive film reels, soaked in nitrates. When they reached the end of the circuit they were simply thrown out or shoved into storage and forgotten, often in the basement of the last cinema that played them. A few years ago, a treasure cache of lost Chaplin films was discovered in a cellar in Dawson

City, Yukon. When the Christchurch earthquake wiped out the architectural overlay of that city, the same thing happened."

Rafferty rummaged around in his shirt pocket, produced his passport, slid it across the table. "Check the date. The entry stamp." New Zealand was in the process of switching over to a wholly automated passport reading system, but not yet, not when he'd arrived on a media visa. "Look," he urged, but she already knew. When she hesitated, he flipped the pages for her.

"I arrived in New Zealand the day *before* the earthquake. Do you see? Here, where they stamped it. I would need some finely tuned psychic abilities to predict an earthquake, don't you think?"

"You could've bribed someone, could've forged that stamp." But she didn't sound convincing, least of all to herself.

Rafferty could see the certainties drain from her face. He almost felt bad for her. "How long have you been looking for him, this man of yours?"

"Since before I was born, it seems."

A heart desiccated, dry as any page-pressed flower. "Well," he said. "I have some bad news, or good, depending on your state of mind. This man you're looking for, he's dead."

If he was expecting a reaction, a gasp or a jolt, a clutching of pearls or a fainting couch swan dive, he received none. She'd been down this lane before. "No. He's not," she said.

"But—"

"He's not dead."

"He is."

"Let me guess. Overcome with guilt, he killed himself, left a heartfelt confession behind."

"A wall fell on him."

"How convenient."

"I saw the body." Not the body, not exactly: a hand, clawlike and reaching out. Rafferty felt a faint tremble of doubt in his own chest, but he pushed it back down. "I saw him. He's dead. He'll be in the official tally by now. They have records, a list of the deceased. I can give you the exact time and date he died. There will be a coroner's report, I'm sure."

"You spoke with him?"

"I did, and I can tell you one thing, he's not from New England."

"Is that what he's claiming now?"

"He's dead, Ms. Rhodes."

She felt her doubts flicker and grow. That's how it begins—faith, science, self-sabotage—with a single flicker of doubt, like a candle in melted wax. The long flight and carefully contained excitement. The noose tightening. An Aussie yob with dry lips, an alleyway in Alice Springs, money changing hands. *Semi-automatic, slide load, short recoil.* Gaddy Rhodes, armed and ready, all for naught.

She looked at Rafferty, trying not to plead, not with her voice, certainly not with her eyes. "You're sure about this, about the body?"

Rafferty considered the Saint Whatsit medallion tucked away in the desk drawer of his hotel room. "Yes, I'm sure. Hundred and ten percent, as my coach used to say."

Growing up in the Midwest, Rafferty had played baseball as a boy. Not well, of course. Most people aren't very good at most things. But he remembered his coach and he remembered the exhortations. Unfortunately for him, and for Agent Rhodes, 110 percent is not a real number. And the finder was not dead. He was waiting. Was closer than they realized.

TAMSIN VERSUS THE LARRIKINS

IT RAINED DURING THE NIGHT.

Rained, but not in her dreams. She was trapped again on the Afghan steppes, pulled from a vehicle, was crouching behind the rusted shell of a Soviet tank as the shriek of Taliban bullets needled past above her head, an AP stringer by her side, a young man, a boy really, pink-faced and wide of eye, who would die anticlimactically a year later in an auto accident in Delhi, and the two of them, caught in a crossfire and Tamsin laughing—laughing till her heart hurt, laughing at the craziness of it all, the emptiness, the sheer absurdity of what she was doing, laughing until she cried, and then, during a lull in the shooting, her stringer running out, adrenaline the drug of choice, zigzagging across debris fields, returning with a canteen wildly swinging, caked in sand—both the canteen and the boy—and now he was laughing too, and how could you not? You had to laugh, you had to, and then, rising like soft applause in the background, the sound of rain and she woke with a spasm.

She was sleeping in the Land Rover, had pulled off the highway, and had woken to the drumming of a metal roof, restless fingers in the night. She lay awhile, listening to the rain. Uluru would be streaming with water right now. *Malya must be smiling.* The rain ended and dawn arrived.

She climbed out, cotton-mouthed and groggy, watched the first shimmer of sunlight break above the horizon. Fields of flowers had appeared, a haze of yellow on the grass-covered dunes. It created a halo effect of its own, unrelated to the lingering aftereffects of

315

Tamsin's eye surgery. She slung her camera bag over her shoulder, climbed a tussock hill. Uluru was gone, lost in the distance, and on the other side a drift of camels was moving across the plains, slowly, almost gliding. These were the descendants of animals brought in from Afghanistan to act as pre-rail freight trains, now feral and unfettered. Beasts of burden, freed of their burden. The camels slipped away, and Tamsin considered pursuit, a telephoto lens maybe, a high depth of field to flatten the distance, but there were miracles closer at hand.

Strewn bouquets, beaded with rain, had appeared while the world was sleeping, softly pink and veined with red, ornamental flowers that had long since escaped from backyard gardens and now grew wild. Everything has a habit of escape.

Drought-evading plants that flowered only after a rainfall had been lying dormant, waiting—waiting for precisely this moment to make their presence known. Burned-leaf cassias and the lilac-tinted teardrops of the mulla, the succulent herbs and ephemeral fan-flowers, desert myrtle in the swales, clinging to the dunes, green and glorious. And daisies! (one always needed to add an exclamation mark to that word, Tamsin felt), bright white with buttery hearts, these romantically denuded she-loves-me-she-loves-me-not flowers in the Mind of God. When children draw flowers, they draw daisies. Even the thornbush acacias had bloomed.

Mad dabs from a highlighter. Pom-poms and poached eggs. And suddenly, Tamsin could see the colors and patterns behind everything. They had been there in the art of Anangu women, in tufted clumps of grass endlessly repeated as dots, in the interlocking circles of spinifex, in the serpentine trails in the sand; it was all there, the songlines and stories sculpted into the earth, a direct glimpse into the Dreamtime that wasn't a dream. Tamsin felt elated, euphoric, unsteady. Heat and dehydration at play, perhaps, but maybe not and no less real for it.

Flowers exuberant, and birds exultant. Babblers and budgies and many-colored parrots. Cockatoos, uncaged and elegantly crested, gold-flecked and regal, chattering away royally as they rooted about for seeds. Finches flitting in and out of the tussock grass and shrubs, drinking in the dawn. It was the first day of creation, when the world was sung into existence, when that first inhalation had yet to exhale, a breath suspended in amazement and joy. The light behind the darkness.

Tamsin in the magic hour, walking out into an overflowing emptiness.

Animals, hidden, and creatures unseen. Honey ants, swollen with a musty sweetness, burrowing beetles and scorpions incognito, nocturnal hunters dangerous when disturbed. All invisible, revealed in the early morning by the tracks they leave, cyphers crisscrossing the sand, the curlicue trails that were left behind. Legless lizards. False snakes, as they were known, these gentle twisting creatures. Bird track hieroglyphics and the ditto-dash of hopping mice: a frenzy of footprints pogo-jumping among bushes.

She walked on, farther and farther from her vehicle, discovered the wavy ripples of a surface-swimming sand mole, blind and gold-tinged, out for a romp after the rain. *Rafferty was wrong. It wasn't a redundancy. There are non-subterranean moles.* Cryptic mammals—she loved that name—were very good at hiding and seldom seen. Cryptic reptiles as well, creatures that disappeared as quickly as they appeared, slipping under spindly thorns or into the sand itself, wiggling their way into the earth.

And still she walked.

The most poisonous snakes in the world live in Australia, but the average snake can strike only about a third of its body length. Tamsin had heard that somewhere and had decided to take it as the gospel truth, swinging wide when she saw one, a thin-faced whip-snake, loosely coiled in the shade. Her heavy leather, high-ankled boots would (should) thwart any serpent strikes or scorpion stings.

Dragons and lizards. And demons too.

Moloch horridus, as they were more correctly known, named after the Canaanite deity Moloch, chief among Satan's angels. A "horrid king, besmirched in blood," according to *Paradise Lost*. Tamsin had been looking for one such thorny devil, and she found it as it gobbled down a line of ants, toad-like and wart-armored. *The gods of ugly things. Weta beetles and thorny devils.* Tamsin lay down on her belly, quietly brought the creature into focus, froze it in time. Still on her belly, she spotted a procession of white caterpillars that was snaking across the sand in front, joining end to end to form one extended feathery bullwhip.

The coolness of the morning had provided respite from the flies, but the growing heat brought them out again, maddening and persistent, crawling across her viewfinder, tickling their way into her ears, tracing patterns on exposed skin, congregating at her tear ducts and the wet corners of her mouth. Tamsin had left her fly net back in her vehicle, too far to run back for now, and she swatted uselessly instead, succeeded only in stirring them momentarily as she worked. So fixated was she on these ghostly caterpillars, and so distracted by this annoyance of flies, that she didn't hear the ATV approach or the footfalls coming nearer. And anyway, the wind was against her and they had approached from her deaf side.

"*Oi!*"

Startled, Tamsin rolled over, brought her arms in, cradling her camera, protecting her head, an instinct born of war zones.

"Wouldn't git any closer, luv."

He stood above her, back to the sun. Quickly, Tamsin rolled onto her feet, brushed aside the dust, and circled around—another habit born of war zones—put the sun behind her instead. *Let him squint.*

Sun-bleached stubble, a face so tanned his lips looked white. Aussie shorts and heavy boots. Khaki for the most part, even his hair.

Behind him, in the heat-distorted distance, she saw an all-terrain vehicle parked on the side of a hillock. Leaning against the ATV was another lanky man, similarly attired. Beyond that, hazy in the heat, her own vehicle looked far away indeed.

"Gotta watch out for those ones," he said with a jawed gesture to the caterpillars that Tamsin had been photographing. They were moving elegantly across the sand, a ghostly procession, wispy and pale.

"The hairs on them ones can cause blisters. Worse'n nettles, irritates the skin, burns like a farker. Those ones there? Going home, back to their nest. Night prowlers, generally. Rain brought 'em out. Caterpillars, very active after a rain." He grinned. A mouth full of broken crockery. "They're so stupid, sometimes they'll circle a tree by mistake, accidently link up with the last one in line, form a ring, will keep turning and turning till they exhaust themselves. You can see their nests hanging off branches, easily mistaken for bird nests, so be careful. Toxic."

She put her camera away. "Thanks for the tip." But he wasn't done.

"Those wildflowers, over there, little purple ones the caterpillars were curling around? The cattle eat those. Chomp 'em up. Roos, too. Good bush tuck, that. The Abos will tell you—sorry, I mean Blackfellas. This whole region, it's like a supermarket for them ones. My

319

name's Frank. Where's my manners? Frank Hann, that's my name. My mate over there, that's Jack Watson."

"You live out here?" Hard to imagine.

"Lost Creek cattle station. It's up Luritja Road a ways."

"Well, it was nice meeting you." Tamsin tried to step past but he blocked her way, stepped in, uncomfortably close.

"Don't get a lot'a Sheilas out here. Not many anyways." He stepped closer still, studied her. She could feel his breath on her. "Got'a bit of Chinese in you, do ya? And what's with the scar?"

"A knife fight."

"Yer joking."

"Should see the other guy." She looked to her Land Rover, impossibly far away. A torment of flies and heat. Tamsin felt light-headed, brushed at the midges that were clotting her eyes and nostrils. She was already past the Curtin Springs Roadhouse. Next gas station was two hours away. Her hat and netting were in the car, along with her water, and her cell phone. She couldn't dial 911, and was it even 911 out here? She seemed to think it was triple zero. Or maybe 112? And how long would it take for anyone to reach her, even if she could get to her phone, throw a distress signal into space, a cry wanting an echo?

"Haf'ta git used to them, the flies. Youse need to learn the Aussie salute." He waved his hand in front of him, scattering them, midair. "Problem is, y'kill one of the buggers, six more come to the funeral." Another grin, more broken crockery. "They like the eyes, lips, where the tears and saliva gathers. Any wet spots, really. They love wet spots. You have any of those? Wet spots I should know about?"

The glare. The flies. The empty stomach and the parched throat. The growing headache of the heat. *He told me his name. I know where he lives. He told me their names. They can't let me go after they're done.*

They would drive her vehicle into the Outback, would have to burn it probably. After that, a shallow grave, but any resourceful dingo would find her soon enough. Tamsin had photographed enough shallow graves in her day to know that the dead never stayed hidden for long, and she realized, with a certain sadness, that no one on earth knew where she was at that very moment, not even Raff. The weight in her chest turned to a sigh.

"This isn't going to end well, is it?" she said.

"That depends, luv, on how much resistance you put up."

"Oh," she said. "I didn't mean for *me*."

THE ATV, HITTING EVERY GODDAMN ROCK, bouncing wildly, Frank shrieking, voice hoarse, hands wedged deep into his crotch, and his mate Jack yelling, "Hang on, Frank! Hang on!" He would be airlifted to Alice Springs, where the doctors would spend three hours retracting his left testicle from its pelvic cavity, pumping him full of opiates and performing an emergency intubation, inserting an inflated tube down his windpipe to prevent his throat from closing due to the secondary trauma of his windpipe, the doctors asking his friend afterward, "How did this happen? How?"

"Jest fell, like."

"Fell?"

"On a fencepost. Repeatedly."

And Tamsin on her own, freewheeling down a highway, her Land Rover all but taking flight, the fun-loving larrikin lad grappling with the front of her shirt, not realizing that this wasn't an ambush but a dance, a tango in the sands with Tamsin taking the lead, stepping forward, then sweeping her leg inside, a countermove followed by a simple wrist lock that took him down, then a boot to the balls, once, twice, followed by a straight-legged stomp to the throat, with buddy there spurting up mucous and bile, a spastic reflex, eyes rolling back into his head, nary a whimper escaping as Tamsin stepped back, blew away the hair that had fallen across her face, and then teeing up again, delivering another, final, heavy-toed boot, full force between the legs, and now a whimper did escape, "No more. Please." Tamsin, leaning in on a whispered snarl, "I was in Beirut, motherfucker. You think I'm scared of you?" She would have spit on him as well, but her mouth was dry and he wasn't worth the wasting of water. Instead, she left him there, writhing on the red sands of the Outback like a see-no-evil monkey poorly aligned, hands cupping his crushed manhood, and Tamsin striding directly toward his friend now, angry at having lost the light, and the other chawbacon yokel gape-mouthed and agog as she approached, saying nothing, and Tamsin, as she passed. "I think your friend could use a little help."

And now, here she was, skimming across a landscape like a flat stone on a still lake, the windows down, one hand out, riding the updraft, and the other on the wheel, fingers tapping out a rhythm of her own design. *Tamsin Greene is a cool machine.*

THE CURATOR OF LOST SOULS

A TRAIN ENGINE WAS BEING SHUNTED onto a sidetrack in the railyard. Moths and listless louts, both of them hovering under streetlights. Dusk, falling. The day, ending.

He'd left her with her tea, cold in the cup, and his chiko roll, half-eaten, had walked back up to his second-floor room, had the usual drunkard's difficulty in getting the key into the door, getting the handle to turn, the light to stay on. In the dimly pooled light—and hotel rooms are always caught in the twilight—Thomas Rafferty stopped to consider his domain: a bed so lumpy it could have hidden a corpse and no one would have been the wiser, an open veranda facing the train yards, curtains billowing like slow sails on the faintest of winds. Life was a series of indifferently decorated hotel rooms.

Had he left the veranda open like that? He couldn't remember.

In some far room, a radio was muttering to itself, and in the tavern below, the music was thumping. Could feel it in the floor. A party of cattle station ranch hands had arrived just as Rafferty was leaving, had found a jukebox he didn't even know was there. AC/DC and Banjo Peterson, alternating. Wild bush horses and highways to hell. No need for a reason, no need for a rhyme. Jaysus.

Gaddy Rhodes and the dead man, under his slab of wall, and Rafferty wondered if any of it was real. Maybe they'd dreamed him into existence, Rhodes and Rafferty together.

He reeled back, steadied himself. Stepped onto the veranda. Entire balcony seemed to be leaning one side, though that might have been the gin. In the railyards, the heave and lurch of another train departing, like an old man woken, who grumbles himself back to sleep. The air was surprisingly cool, almost cold, raised gooseflesh across his forearms. Was she ever coming back? *She has something of mine. Not lost, stolen.* Not stolen, never returned.

When Rafferty stepped back into the room, the dead man was waiting for him. Sitting in a chair, calmly, and very much alive. Hard to kill, this guy.

"There is a ship," the small man said, as though in midconversation, "that surfaces from the sands in southern Australia every, oh, thirty or forty years. No one knows where it came from or what its name is, but it was first spotted off a distant shoal in 1836. A mahogany ship, variously described as either the ruins of a Spanish galleon or a Dutch man-o'-war, or even a Portuguese vessel that had disappeared during an unknown earlier mission. It sounds like a ghost story, but I assure you it is quite real. Imagine finding such a vessel! The value, the excitement, and yet, the ship itself is little more than a jumble of dry-rot timber by this point. No treasure has ever been reported on-board the mahogany ship or, if there ever was any, it is long gone. No rubies or relics. It is a wreck, plain and simple, valuable only *because* it was lost. Like a missing piece of a jigsaw puzzle, it is the *absence* that provides its worth. Kidnappers, crude though they may be, operate on much the same principle. It is a desire for return, for equilibrium as it were, that imbues such objects, such people, with value. What do I do for a living? I find mahogany ships, Mr. Rafferty. This is what I do." He gestured to the seat across from him as though it were his room, and Rafferty the guest. "Please, sit down. You look as though you've seen a ghost yourself. But I assure you, like a ship that surfaces from the sand, I am quite real." He smiled. "A rear window. A torn curtain. The smallest glimpse can reveal so much. Don't you agree?"

Figures on a landscape, far away but near at hand. Rwanda. The Congo. The eroded shoreline between memory and myth. Rafferty swallowed, throat dry. "You're looking well," he said.

"Thank you." The small man was receding into the shadows as the day slowly died, was gradually becoming a silhouette again.

Rafferty took the seat across from him. "Friend, I don't know who you are, but I know exactly what you do."

"And what do I do *exactly*, Mr. Rafferty?"

"Like you said, you find things." *You kill people and find things.*

A glimmer of teeth in what might have been a smile, catching the last of the light. "It's the strangest thing," said the small man. "On the way over here, as I was crossing the street, I heard a rooster crowing, like a dusty cough. It's not true, of course, that they only crow at dawn. I was once hired to find the missing page of a paperback novel, long thought lost forever, *The Rooster Crows at Midnight*. Based on a misunderstanding, you see. A clue that wasn't there. Roosters crow whenever they wish. A man died for that. Hard to imagine, isn't it? Dying for a single page from a dime-store novel."

"People die for all sorts of reasons."

"The sound of a rooster crowing, I hadn't heard that in years, and with it, I was hurtled back in time to South America, other towns, other roads. You were in Ecuador, Mr. Rafferty, you will know of what I am speaking. The sound of a rooster. And I thought to myself, what we need is a Museum of Lost Sounds, ones that need to be preserved before they are lost forever. The clickety-clack of a rotary dial. The *oof* of a maid-assisted corset being tightened. A passenger pigeon's evening coo—wouldn't you love to hear that? The phosphorous flash of an old camera. The swish-tide of an X-ray being developed in a chemical bath, the smell of the same. Perhaps we need a Catalog of Lost Scents, as well. Did you know that the moon smells of gunpowder? It's true. Or so I am told. I once retrieved an exorbitantly rare sample of lunar rock for a wealthy client. The samples were sealed, so I wasn't able to confirm it firsthand, but I am told that the moon smells of gunpowder and blood. The rarest smell on earth, I would imagine, the smell of the moon. Would take prime spot in my catalog. Hard to capture, though, isn't it? Sounds and scents and the like. They lack a certain . . . tangibility."

There was nothing to stop Rafferty from getting up and walking out, nothing to keep him there except for a soft voice and a thickening silhouette. Nothing at all, but he was pinned in place nonetheless. "Listen," he said. "I'm bushed. I appreciate you dropping by, it's been swell. But I gotta say, I've had a *very* long day." His back was beginning to throb.

"What did you tell her?"

"Tell who?"

The smile disappeared. "You know full well who. I ask you again: What did you tell her?"

What *could* he tell her? That the person she'd been chasing down corridors all these years, a man of indeterminate age, lost somewhere between semen-marche and senility, unnervingly nondescript, was right here? What was there to tell? "I told her you were dead."

"But she didn't believe you, did she?"

"Not sure. She seemed to know more about you than I did, trying to glean what I knew, impressions, that sort of thing. I didn't have much to give. I said, I don't think people interest him, only things."

The smallest sliver of a smile reappeared. "Not *things*. Artifacts."

"She seems to think you're the anti-Christ."

And for a moment he almost seemed hurt. "I'm not anti-anything," he said. "You must understand, Mr. Rafferty, that I come from slender means. I have always lived by my wits."

"Is there any other way?"

"Most other ways, in fact. You'd be surprised how few people do employ their wits, relying instead on luck, inheritance, a plodding routine. The world is full of sheep, Mr. Rafferty. But we are not sheep, are we? Chance has brought us together, here in the deadest of ends, the backest of waters. So little rain out here. A shame. I like the rain, it so nicely covers up one's tracks, though I imagine the wind does the same thing out here, erases footprints—buries evidence. Deuteronomy 33:2. *The Lord came out of the desert.* Our mistake is to assume He is still there. The silence is deafening, isn't it? One can hardly think due to His echoing absence."

Rafferty shifted in his seat. His back was knotting up again. Fight or flee? He could hardly move, tried to keep the pain out of his voice, but the pain gave him away. It always does. "The emptiness you describe may be more a self-diagnosis than anything," he said.

"Perhaps." The small man stared at the sky outside. The day was almost done, the setting of the sun cast a glow, and in these final moments, the silhouette became a man again. "Tell me something, Mr. Rafferty. Have you ever heard about the legend of the three-legged toad? An emblem of the unattainable." A world reduced to a curio cabinet. "I collect them, in a manner of speaking."

Three-legged toads and mahogany ships.

A silly knickknack from a holiday shop in Portrush. Ceramic, and Chinese, which is very far indeed. *"Don't lose it. This lucky figurine will bring you good fortune."* But, of course, he had lost it. He was only a child, after all. Children lose things all the time, knickknacks and lottery tickets, parents. And later, when he set off from home for the first time, another warning. *"It's a too-big world, so you take care."* A church-bought medallion to protect travelers from woe. *"Don't lose this one, like you lost the last."* Saint Christopher, she said. But it wasn't Saint Christopher.

"You have something that belongs to me, Mr. Rafferty. A

medallion, lost in a tussle. I will give you until darkness to return it to me."

Don't look. Don't. Do not look, not even a glance in the direction of the desk, not even the hint of glance. Rafferty took a slow breath. *He probably thinks it's in a hotel safe somewhere, but there is no safe, only a desk, only a drawer. Do not look. If you look, he will kill you, and he will take it anyway. Do. Not. Look.*

"Valuable, is it?" asked Rafferty.

"To me, yes. To anyone else, no." He leaned in, face lit in orange. "I won't ask again. My medallion. Where is it?"

"Have you checked your sphincter?"

A sigh. The small man leaned back. "Ah yes, the homespun wit of the humble rube. Winterset, am I right?"

A chill.

First Ecuador, now this. "Congratulations, you've read my wiki bio." But Rafferty knew there was more to it than that. *I outweigh him by at least twenty pounds. I'm taller by a foot.* But still he knew he would lose. *Don't look. Keep your eyes locked on his. Don't look. Once he has that medallion, there is no reason for him to let you live.* The afterglow of orange began to seep away and the finder slipped back into silhouette. Darkness had arrived and Thomas Rafferty understood now what he was finally facing, as terrifying and banal as he always expected it would be.

If I can get to the door . . .

Rafferty leapt to his feet, or tried to, but his back had locked, and he couldn't get up, was knotted with pain.

When the finder spoke, there was a certain tenderness in his voice, there—just for a moment—and then gone. "Rapid-onset ankylosing spondylitis," the small man said. "An autoimmune disorder, begins in the pelvis, works its way up the spine, one vertebra at a time. They fuse like bamboo, become rigid. Eventually reaches the rib cage, until you're trapped inside yourself, unable to move. There is no cure. True, there are biologic treatments that might slow it down, but only if one hasn't been exposed to TB or any variant of hepatitis, and I imagine in your field of endeavor, you have encountered both, more than once. Which would make such treatment all but impossible. A philosophical question, Mr. Rafferty: If someone defines himself by motion, and is no longer able to move, does he still exist?"

Rafferty felt his chest constrict, his voice become scratchy. "How?"

"Oh, it's not that complicated. Whisper into the void, and eventually the void whispers back. Medical records, readily available online, protected only by the flimsiest of firewalls. It's all there, the blood tests and grim prognoses. So on and so forth. One needs to be familiar with one's foe, after all."

"Is that what I am? A foe?"

"We shall see. It will depend on how the next few moments play out. Consider it a pre-emptive move, this sifting through of medical records. I like to know everything about the people with whom I do business: marital status, family, psychological reports, even visits to one's therapist. You'd be amazed what can be tapped into. Truly, we are living in days of miracles and wonder. But you've never seen a therapist, have you, Mr. Rafferty? Not as far as I could tell, anyway. Which leads me to believe that you are either perfectly sane or so hopelessly confused as to be beyond help."

"The latter."

"The sands have run out, the day has died. The time has come for you to hand over that which is mine."

"And what do I get in return?"

The small man was surprised by the question. "Why, your life of course."

"Not enough."

"I beg your pardon?"

"What makes you think I value my life so highly?"

The sun was gone and night was at hand. Only a distant streetlamp, barely there, gave any light, any contours to the room. Two shadows, alone in the dark.

Memories of Winterset.

"My father," said Rafferty, "was thirty years dying. Thirty years. First, it was his heart—he was convinced it was going to go at any moment—then he was sure he had a tumor, then an impending aneurysm, then something that he was convinced was beriberi, which was funny considering he'd never left Iowa. Always fretting and pacing and fixating on symptoms of impeding ruin, obsessing on something, which, when it came, came in his sleep like a guest overdue. He was dying for thirty years, my father."

There was once a time that Thomas Rafferty had seen himself as a self-anointed exile, searching for a country to be alienated from, a modern-day Count Cagliostro, wounded but still wandering. Now? Now he was only tired. When he was young, he had dreamed of moving through life, hoarding memories like postcards, falling into love violently and just as violently out again. Instead, he had stumbled on like the rest of us, making it up as he went along, bruised and abetted by the ones we purportedly love.

"You've traveled too much," said the small man. "Perhaps it's time to rest."

"Six," said Rafferty. "That's how far I got. That's how close I came. Never made it to Antarctica." He had promised himself as a child, his family's *Book of Knowledge* splayed open to exotic places like Timbuktu and Akron, that he would visit all seven continents by the time he reached the inconceivably distant age of forty. But forty came and forty went, and the seventh continent remained undiscovered. The promise lingered, however. To live a larger life. To be something more. And a promise is a promise, even if it's only to one's younger self—especially if it is to one's younger self. "So, I ask you again. What makes you think I value my life so highly?"

"Fair enough. If not you, someone else, perhaps? Someone who relies on you? Might we not bargain with other people's lives, instead?"

"No one relies on me. Not even me. It's the one good thing I have done."

"Then perhaps there is someone *you* rely on."

Thoughts of Tamsin. "None—and again, not even me."

The mind cries out. Mud and panic, and a stampede of bare feet and voices screaming and children crying and Rafferty numb and bedumbed. *Here lies Thomas Rafferty, he never saved anyone.* The threat of extinction was no longer a threat, it was almost an enticement.

Something passed between them, if not an understanding, an impasse.

"Mr. Rafferty, when first I saw you, I thought to myself, here is the type of man who is always drawn to the far side of the hill, to the shadow side of the valley, where the sun so rarely reaches. Restless, perhaps, but not foolhardy. Never for a moment did I think of you as foolhardy."

A smile from Rafferty, Cheshire catlike in the dark. "One does one's best to live up to one's reputation. And when was that, exactly? When we first met?"

"Why, in Christchurch, of course. Though you seem to have been under the impression that our paths had crossed somewhere before. I have that type of face," said the faceless man.

He's bluffing. If he knows everything about me, he knows about Rwanda, he knows I was in the Congo. He is laying a wager that I haven't been able to place him in any of those camps, among the dead.

"Listen, Mr. . . . ?"

"Moore. But please, call me William."

Does the name Billy Moore mean anything to you?

"I may be foolhardy—I've been called worse—but you're right, I'm not a fool. You may think this is a hostage taking, Mr. Moore, but it's not. This is a negotiation."

"Tread carefully, Mr. Rafferty. When you train a falcon, you train him by hunger."

It was an exercise in archeology, speaking with this man: words with more words packed inside, the meanings one within the other. It reminded Rafferty of the Interpol agent, how she too spoke in ellipses and asides. Had she already left for Alice Springs? Did she have any idea just how close her quarry was?

Rafferty felt the throb in his back subside. "She's getting closer, you know that, right?"

"Who?"

"You know very well who. You don't have much time, Mr. Moore. If you want your Saint Christopher's medal—"

"It's not Saint Christopher. And it's not yours to bargain with. There is no monetary value attached to it, only value. It is Saint Anthony, Patron Saint of Lost Objects. Given in error. My mother thought it was Saint Christopher as well, but I checked. She had her saints confused. She often did." *Constantly walking in and out of rooms like a character in a play who has forgotten her lines, endlessly baffled by the turns her life has taken. Folding her son's hand around the medal. "For you, son, to be safe." Forgetting she had ever given it to him.* There were worse diagnoses than a fused spine. "It belongs to me, and I would like you to return it."

"That medal was lost," Rafferty reminded him. "I found it, remember? This would infer a certain amount of ownership, no? I mean, that's how this works, right? Finders, keepers. Listen. I will return Saint Anthony to you, but I want something in kind, something that requires your area of expertise."

"Which is?"

"I want you to find someone for me."

The small man wasn't sure he'd heard correctly. He waited, but there was nothing more. "That's what you're asking? But why? It's the easiest thing in the world to find someone. A cursory search, social media, address books, online CVs, location-coded Instagram images, LinkedIn accounts. It requires very little expertise on your part. A woman, I suppose?"

"Correct."

"Where?"

"Here. Nearby. Her name is Rebecca, she's with the university, they're in the Outback somewhere, an Aboriginal community, collecting data."

"Data?"

"Stories."

"Again, you hardly require my assistance, Mr. Rafferty. A simple search of university sites should reveal the information you require. You hardly need my help."

"So, you can't—"

"Won't. The word you're looking for is won't." Memories of Belfast crowding in, cross-walled rendezvouses, small sighs in the dark. What was her name? His first touch, his first kiss? Grace? Gracie? Mary? He'd forgotten. Names were starting to slip away; they were always the first to go. "Love, was it, Mr. Rafferty? Or something approximating it?"

"It was." Is.

The finder could hear it in Rafferty's voice, both the weakness and the glory. What a sad and farcical thing it is to stagger through life with a self-inflicted wound. "And what is it about this particular person that beguiles you so?"

"I saw in her a willingness to be deceived." Stubborn and strong, but also incredibly naïf, in her way.

"An attractive quality, I'll grant you that. But I am not in the lonely-hearts services, Mr. Rafferty."

"I told her I had something great to say, if I could only find the words." A smile. "That was my deepest secret, you see. I didn't." He still carried the presence of her, like the smell of smoke in a scarf. Her hair had the scent of summer, of warm rain or wet leaves, of sliced apples.

"Apples, Mr. Rafferty?"

He had said that last part out loud. "Find her for me."

"The medallion, Mr. Rafferty. I have indulged this forlorn nonsense long enough." He waited but nothing happened.

Confessions always occur in the dark. "She has something of mine. I want it back."

"Ah. So, it's not the girl, but what she *has*. Now, that is much more interesting. Not a someone, but a something. Tell me, what would this particular three-legged creature you're searching for be?"

"A letter."

"A rare letter, I imagine."

"You could say that."

"And what does this letter of yours contain?"

"I don't know."

"I see. You don't know what is in this letter, but you want me to find it for you and bring it back. Interesting. And who wrote this letter?"

"I did."

A heavy silence, awaiting answers. When none came, the figure lay a soft accusation at Rafferty's feet. "You are speaking in riddles. You say you are the author of this letter, but you do not know what it contains. Perhaps you were in a trance when you wrote it, channeling angels—or incubi more likely?" This was meant to be derisive, but was closer to the truth than he realized.

"You're not a drinker, are you Mr. Moore? I didn't think so. Well, I am, and I stayed up an entire night to write that letter, wrote it in a frenzy, back when everything was falling apart. I was drunk. It wasn't a love letter. At least, I don't think it was. Wrote it in a hotel in Hanoi, in the grips of a fever. Gin induced, I'm sure, but it may also have been an attack of calenture, a delirium brought on by the tropical heat."

"I know what calenture is, Mr. Rafferty."

"Whatever the cause, I scribbled it down, everything that was in me, page after page, everything that I'd done wrong, everything she had done likewise. Everything I was and everything I wasn't, everything I could offer her, and what I never would. It was raw and open and relentless, and I don't remember a goddamn thing I wrote. But I know she has it, and I want it back."

"Why?"

"Because," he said, "it's the only honest thing I've ever written."

It wasn't about Rebecca. It had never been about Rebecca. It had been Tom Rafferty, groping his way home again in the dark, trying to figure out where he was, and who.

"I see. And how do you know she even has this letter anymore? She must have thrown it out years ago. I'm not a magician, Mr. Rafferty. I can't retrieve something that has been destroyed. That which no longer exists is beyond my purview, I'm afraid. I can't conjure objects out of smoke and wishful thinking. So, before I accept what might well be a fool's errand, how do I know this letter exists? You say she still has it. How do you know?"

"Because I know her. She collects stories, it's what she does. She'd no sooner throw that letter out than you would discard a lost artifact. I gave her a locket, as well, a pewter heart I purchased on a whim in a ferry gift shop. I don't give a damn about that. Only the letter. I want it back. Three years she's had it. Three years."

Hanoi was tapping at the window. A drunken walk down an alleyway stenched in piss. The sour smell of the monsoon season. Rafferty at the post office, fumbling through his Vietnamese phrasebook, the hazy image of a letter being stamped and sent. He didn't know then that this was a moment he would return to, one that would follow him like a stray dog as the years went by. Had he even scrawled the correct address? He had phoned her, weeks later, and after letting it ring and ring and ring, she had finally answered. Yes, she had the letter. "And, ah, what did you— What did you think of it?" A long pause. "What am I supposed to think?"

"Look, I don't remember what I wrote, okay? Not exactly. I had been drinking. But whatever it was, it was from the heart."

Another ice-riven pause. "You were drunk? I assumed as much. Huh. So you really don't know what is in that letter?"

"No. Can you tell me?"

"No."

"Can you return it to me then?"

"No. You don't get to decide when this story ends, Tom. Not this time."

Here then was the punishment for the drinking and the distances, both real and imagined, for the infidelities and the mumbled remorse that followed, for the nights when he never came home and for those when he did.

Three years. And now, suddenly, an opportunity presented itself in a tatterdemalion hotel room in a tatterdemalion town, with a small man in need of a saint and the chance to close this chapter, to bring the narrative to its rightful end.

"She's in the Outback," said Rafferty. "Somewhere, gathering stories. Find her, get that letter, bring it back to me, and I'll return your medallion."

"And if something happens?"

"Nothing is going to happen."

The small man smiled, sadly it seemed. "Ah, but something always happens, doesn't it? In the end."

Rafferty ignored this. "So, we have an understanding?" he asked.

"We do. A lost medallion for a lost letter." He held out his palm.

Shake hands with the devil, baby. Cold to the touch, and a grip so light it was barely there. It was not unlike the silhouette across from him, an inkblot given human form.

LOST ALONG THE WAY

HEADING EAST ON THE LASSETER HIGHWAY, then north along the Stuart, down gun-barrel roads of black asphalt and wild skies. Tamsin, alone at the wheel, a cooler full of beer and gas-station sandwiches beside her, transport trucks cannonballing past. Tamsin Greene, crossing the red heart of a continent, pulling the storm behind her like an angel of the avenging kind. She could see the black clouds in her rearview mirror, piling up.

Rafferty was wrong. Of course he was wrong. He was always wrong. She wasn't with the CIA. (Why on earth would she be with the CIA? Those snakes.) No. It had been the US Defense Intelligence Agency that had first provided her with a cover, that of photojournalist. She'd shown aptitude in this area, had been trained accordingly. The CIA overthrew governments; the DIA sought to minimize casualties.

And that's what Tamsin's photography was—at first: a means to an end, a cover for collecting data, assessing troop movements and possible ambush points, potential adversaries, prospective allies, dangerous bottlenecks. On the ground and in the field, but then she won her first journalism award and all that changed. Turned out, her cover was who she really was, who she was meant to be. And so, without as much as a backward glance, she'd finished up her defense contracts, had signed off on all the requisite nondisclosure agreements, and had then simply . . . walked away. Away from the DIA, but not from the war zones. That would prove a harder habit to kick. And here she was, on a highway in the desert after the rain. Tamsin Greene, lost between shores.

Feral beasts and pariah dogs. Cattle, kicking up amber clouds in a dusty field. Road signs counting down the kilometers, and the radio picking up voices through the static. All these many and varied songlines that define us, the echoes we trail behind as we move through life, all the possibilities and plans we made, lost along the way.

Tamsin Greene is a cool machine.

PEWTER HEARTS

NOT A PERSON, BUT AN APPARITION, a trick of the light. The wavering heat created worms of convection above the sands. One could almost see through him. Lyle watched the man approach. But from where? It was as though he'd walked out of the desert—and in a suit, no less.

A suburb of tents, half a dozen or so, had laid their academic claims to the Outback, semi-permanent structures on raised platforms, canvas sides. Lyle, a scarecrow of a kid, had gone out to meet the mirage that was even now striding toward him, a small man that coalesced as Lyle drew near, separating himself from the wavering landscape behind.

"Can I help you?"

The day was shrill with heat, and Lyle, in short sleeves, with a name tag lanyard loosely noosed around his neck, felt light of head, queasy even. The nausea of distance.

The mirage stopped in front of him. "I wish to speak with Miss Rebecca Hodges."

"Where's your lanyard? You don't have a lanyard."

"I believe she goes by the name 'Becky.' Perhaps 'Becks,' in her more carefree moments."

"Everyone has to have a lanyard. If you don't have a lanyard, you need to leave."

Why would he need a name tag in the middle of a desert? The small man tilted his head, studied Lyle's own lanyard. "Lyle, is it? May I?" He extracted one of the pens from Lyle's shirt, unscrewed the top, and removed the thin tube of blue ink inside. He tucked those into his pocket (one mustn't litter), blew through the hollow cylinder, then raised it to his eye, peered in, satisfied. He held up this tube as though it were evidence in a crime as yet uncommitted. He was staring, not into Lyle's eyes but at his throat. "Lyle, you have two options. Two, and only two. So consider them carefully. You can tell me exactly where she is—or—I can perform an emergency tracheotomy on you, right here, right now, and you can whistle the information to me instead. The choice is entirely yours."

It would haunt Lyle, his not doing anything to stop this, would haunt him how the other man had been able to reach into his chest so easily, grip his arrhythmic heart in his fist and squeeze it so cruelly, so efficiently, so . . . elegantly.

IN THE DAYS OF CREATION, KUNIYA the python had battled Liru, a venomous snake, a crushing embrace pitted against insidious poison. Rebecca made a note: *Do these represent the two main ways to die? Catastrophe from the outside or something from within. A drought or a rockfall, for example, versus disease or madness. The external versus the internal?* The answer, of course, was neither. It represented python and snake.

Once were giants: the wagtail woman and the blue-tongued lizard man, wayward travelers transformed into stone pillars, smoke that became lichen, lichen that was turned into fire, a world that was constantly forming and re-forming.

The sides of Rebecca's tent were now moving in and out, inhaling and exhaling as she sat hunched over the small ad hoc desk, a crate turned on end with a folding chair pulled up. She had dry-broomed the tent clear of sand, had laid out the latest objects and photographs to be cataloged and considered, had her notebook opened to an empty page. Inhaling and exhaling.

Hidden narratives were entwined in the artifacts: a shale pendant on a rope made of braided hair; a necklace of animal teeth, wallaby mainly; quartz knives sand-polished to a fine and lethal sheen. Disparate, yet clearly connected. How to fit these together? The pieces didn't interlock, but overlapped.

She was struggling with this when the flap of her tent was thrown open and the winds of the Outback blew in a Liru of another kind.

Rebecca, instantly indignant. "What is this! You're letting in sand."

The small man pulled up one of the other canvas chairs, placed what looked like the shell of a Bic pen on the desk in front of her as though it were some sort of peace offering. But no, not a peace offering. A promise. *"Who,"* he said. "The word you're looking for is 'who,' not 'what.' '*Who* is this?'" He folded his handkerchief, once, twice, dabbed his forehead four times, put his handkerchief away. Smiled.

She knew that smile. It was a conjuror's smile. A faint twitch of the lips, the county fair carney who knows he has already won, who knows that the switch has already been made before you even started, and all that remains is to go through the motions, to let it play out. As she stared into his eyes, Rebecca saw a familiar darkness as well. The demons of the Nirai Kanai in southern Japan, legends of the Wendigo, the cast-out angels of the Old Testament, the Devil Dingo Dog of the Anangu.

"Who are you?"

"A friend of a friend, shall we say?" He looked at the pewter heart that was even now hanging around her neck, her open collar, and she knew, with a sinking certainty in her stomach, it was Tom. Somehow, he was behind this. How she knew wasn't clear, but she knew.

Rebecca of Des Moines, defiant. "I don't have it."

"I think you do." He considered the plastic tube of the pen in front of him. "Sometimes the simplest solutions are best." He looked up, locked his eyes onto hers. "The letter."

"It's mine."

"Let him read it. Just once."

"No."

"Let me read it."

"No."

"Does it even exist?"

"No."

"Are you telling the truth?"

A pause. "No."

Love always ends, not in tragedy, but in farce. What a paltry tale. The small man said, "I can see from here that your hair doesn't smell of sliced apples."

She stared back at him. Glacial contempt. "You can see smells, can you?"

He nodded. "I can taste colors, too. I can hear numbers. And I can see certain scents. Here's something: Did you know that there is another version of you, out there, turning circles in the mind of a burnt-out, second-rate travel writer? A more interesting version of you, I must say. But isn't that always the case?"

"You need to leave." These were the same words Lyle had used. *You need to leave.*

"Not without the letter." The anger behind these words was distant, but clear. The silent howl of an ice storm outside an airplane window.

"I don't have it," she said, but her eyes betrayed her, a flick to the stack of cardboard boxes in the corner of the tent.

With that, his anger relaxed. "I'll take that pendant, as well. It's pewter. No inherent value, only sentimental. But, of course, the sentimental is always worth more than the inherent."

"I carry my nitroglycerin in it."

He stopped. "Do you?"

"A faulty heart."

Was she lying? Probably just a story. But he was immune to such stories. "You'll have to find someplace else for them."

And that is where it should have ended, with Rebecca pulling out the folder, handing the thick envelope over, slipping off the pewter heart, but Lyle had roused himself in the interim, had alerted another member of the team about their visitation from the desert, and now a burly boy had burst in, all biceps and brow, young and bold and brimming with bravado, not yet aware of his own tenuous mortality. A fatefully perilous age, that. When one's cockiness has not yet been reeled in. Such men die with a disconcerting regularity.

"What's this then?"

A sigh. The small man, weary. "This doesn't concern you. Go."

"If it involves Becks, it sure as heck involves me." Heck, not hell. The young man threw a yearning look in Rebecca's direction, and the penny dropped as pennies do. With a rattle and a clink. Her lover. Or, more accurately, a would-be lover. The worst kind. So much to prove.

"How old are you, son?"

"Old enough."

A child. And the Aussie accent made him only seem younger still. "I have what I came for," said the small man. "I will be leaving now. I would recommend that you do the same." The locket was wrapped in his fist like a rosary, the letter was stuffed into his jacket. He smiled, a smile that was wan and dying like a flickering VACANCY on a highway at night, the kind that repels more than it entices. "Step aside. Please. That would be best for everyone."

Somewhere in the young man's inner cerebellum, deep in its reptilian core, he could sense danger—camouflaged, perhaps, but danger still.

He stepped aside.

Rebecca, churning with anger, thinking the tide had turned (it hadn't), shouting, "Don't let him go!"

The burly boy hesitated.

Rebecca, a grating voice, demanding the boy do *something*, and the boy in love and not knowing what this entailed.

"He's a thief," she yelled. "Stop him!"

And with that the boy was lost. He had no choice, you see. He had no choice; love demanded it. He couldn't step aside, had to insert himself back into the scene.

He died in front of her, silently, with only a youthful gurgle and a look of confusion. His features were soft and unformed—life hadn't drawn its decisive lines on his face yet—and to have died like that, not fully shaped, seemed to the finder a worse tragedy than the death itself. *I never even learned his name.*

The tent was quiet, the canvas sides were breathing in and breathing out. There was always a strange vacuum, the finder noted, whenever someone died, as though their soul had been sucked out of the room. He turned his gaze to Rebecca. Wiped the blood from his hands with a handkerchief.

Rebecca's throat was raw, constricted. "And now?" she asked.

"Now? Now something bad happens."

WHEN HE WAS CLEAR OF THE university camp, he pulled over onto the side of the highway, slowing to a stop beside a thicket of thornbushes.

Termite mounds and a lizard disappearing into the dirt. Grassy swales in the deep red earth. The wind was picking up, and in the distance a dark line was forming along the horizon; a storm was taking shape, was moving in from the southwest. The sands were beginning to stir.

He opened the creased envelope, thick with pages, folded tightly, and he thought, as he often did in such moments, *Someone died for this.* A violin. A set of dog tags taken from an Okinawan tomb. A one-cent magenta stamp. *Someone died for this.* He had stood over her in the heat, had hissed, *"You did this. You killed him. And what will you tell them when they ask?"*

She'd repeated what he told her, voice wavering, about how the boy had begun to choke, how she had tried to save him, had failed, and so distraught was she that no one questioned her story—except for Lyle, who had confronted the figure when it first coalesced, had let it pass, mutely pointing out which tent was Rebecca's. But Lyle would say nothing. He would keep the glass stopper firmly in place, and, years later, when he began to unravel, he would recognize that this was the moment when it all started.

In the desert, parked beside some thornbushes, the small man unfolded the pages in the epistle of Thomas Rafferty. "To Becks" was scrawled across the top in drunken letters. The writing was cramped and undisciplined, scratched madly onto the paper as though with a quill that was running out of ink rather than with a ballpoint pen.

> *I lie awake & wonder if you are lying awake in pain or feeling alone, going through the years in my mind, the gallery in Sydney, should've known, shit, and maybe its true, with everything that's happened, its still the most beautiful marvel—music that LACKS ONLY YOU—like some sort of sword in my flesh because in all this jabber and babble are so many in my confusion once you finish the work WE will be together once and forever because you <u>influence</u> me and you are the number one reason.*

The small man shuffled through the pages, amazed. Read on.

> *my heart is full of you yet when I seek to say to you something words fail me even in bed <s>espetially</s> and my thoughts go out to <u>you</u> today and yesterday, tearful LONGINGS—my farewell tour, in bed with bad ideas and I can only wander about for SO LONG, at <u>home</u>, but can that even exist under our circumstances? to be calm but still angry and*

Whatever he might have been expecting, he hadn't been expecting this: disjointed, full of arbitrarily capitalized words and forcefully underlined terms.

but never—NEVER—doubt the faithfullest heart that has made me selfish because I cannot and I am <u>forgetful</u> of every thing, I would be martyr'd for you in the face of mid-night that time I walked on those telephone wires to LOOK DOWN and see you coming, every haze & mist, I couldn't see or hear or feel or think, and maybe our lives are going to let us have another other ~~night~~ that's like BEGGING for mercy for fuck sake, this is what you are, and what fuckin words can I write anyway when I don't know how to tell you how, such agitation, a life ~~for the~~ outline and the tint

Sound and fury, signifying nothing.

is why I can't be <u>clever</u> and stand-offish with you, and I don't really resent it, but I am REDUCED to a <u>thing</u> and I wanted to compose a beautiful letter to you in the sleepless nightmare hours of the night but it's all gone, fuck it, the un-dumb letters, and I would never write so elementary a phrase as that; with me it is quite stark

He flipped through to the last page, the writing becoming more frantic as it reached the irrational climax.

fuckin LOVED the dynamo of it with your chameleon's soul, no matter WHAT storm! or home wherever we <u>are</u> in the morning, TOGETHER and the stresses of so many terrible years, we were

*always cheerful and jokers together but really it was like I had to
beg to know EXPRESSLY your intention, I suppose most of us
are, but cure is the discovery of our need—now that I know just as
unendurable, so NEVER never imagine there is to it, as I did, like a
prayer I can't keep, so fuck it anyway! whatever you can dole out—I
wish I could write about it but I can't EVEN IF and I need you to
understand when I*

And there it ended, in midsentence. Not even a full stop at the end. Starting and ending on "I."

The small man sat back. Considered who was waiting for him at Devil's Spite Creek, a man who had valued his own life so cheaply, but yearned so strongly *for this*, was willing to risk dying *for this*. Fretful and stir-crazy, no doubt, waiting in a dismal room *for this*, desperate to discover who he really was—and maybe this *was* his true self, Thomas Rafferty at the core: absurd, drunken, disjointed, a figure more to pity than to ridicule. *It's the only honest thing I've ever written.*

Some things are better left unfound.

Letter in hand, the small man walked out into the desert, found a hollow in the sand, lit the pages on fire, cradling the flames with his palms, watched them burn, curling inward like a wasp's nest, flakes floating free, butterflying away. He then opened the pewter pendant, gathered some of the ashes, and walked back to his car. He had promised he would return the letter to the travel writer, and the small man always kept his promises. But he hadn't said in what form he would return the letter. It was the kindest thing he had ever done.

CENTER MASS

"ALICE, IS IT?"

She still wasn't used to how they referred to the town by its first name, as though it were a person rather than an outpost in the desert.

"Yes," she sighed. "Alice Springs. The airport."

Gaddy Rhodes had a flight to catch, but the wind was picking up, distressing the streets of Devil's Spite Creek, raising spirals in the dust, swinging the signs on rusted hinge.

The taxi driver had come around to open the door for her, an incongruous act of chivalry, like a pickpocket tipping his hat to a passing lady.

"Won't be any flights out today, I'm afraid," he said, climbing in up front. He angled the mirror. "You with the uni?"

She had no idea what he was talking about. "If not the airport, my hotel then." She gave him the name of the Travelers Inn in Alice. "On Khalick Street." She would have to book another night, leave when the flights resumed. She'd have to get rid of the gun as well, maybe bury it in the sand. Gaddy felt hollow and alone, her defeat complete and unabashed, was only going through the motions now in a simulacrum of care.

The wind was beginning to shriek, driving a suffocation of dust before it, the way an army might, and the taxi crawled through it, headlights on and wipers flailing. They reached the highway and picked up speed as the world outside slowly disintegrated.

They passed the airport on their way into Alice Springs and in a gust between clouds of dust, she saw it: an aircraft tied down on the runway. A Learjet, streamlined and clean, its rear stabilizer curving up like a scorpion's tail, ready to strike, tethered against the onslaught.

"You said there were no flights," Gaddy yelled from the rear.

"Nothing came in. Nothing went out. Not t'die anyway. Thet'll be a private plane. Grounded, too, from the looks of it."

"But it's on the runway."

"Waitin' on someone, I reckon." He chuckled. "But TLT won't be flyin' today, can tell you that much."

A jolt—and she was awake. "What did you say? Just now. What did you say?"

"I said, they won't be—"

"The company. The name."

"Thet? Oh, right. Should'a said 'Aerojet.' Changed their name a few years back. But I'm old enough t'remember. They were Tri-Lake Transport, before they became Aerojet. Operated out of Asia, I think. Maybe Indonesia? Who knows, not like I'm taking a private jet anytime soon, right?"

He looked in the mirror but she didn't smile back. She was thinking of three-legged toads and all the various TLTs that had been scrubbed clean. But not forgotten.

He's here. "Turn the car around."

"Whet?"

"You heard me."

They were going back to Devil's Spite Creek. She would find Tom Rafferty, would shove the barrel of her Beretta down that fucker's throat if she had to, pull the trigger if she must. She would make him talk. *He's here. I know it.*

•   •   •

THE FAIRVIEW HOTEL WAS UNDER SIEGE from every side. The windows were rattling in their panes, amid wails and whispers, creaks and moans and arthritic pops.

The dust storm that had pulled a curtain over the town had reduced the daylight to dusk, and they sat, as they had before, facing each other as another day slowly died.

Rafferty turned the locket over in his hand. A pewter heart, filled with ash.

The small man said, "She wore it close to her heart. The letter was burnt. Those are the ashes." Not a word of a lie in any of those statements, and Rafferty never thought to ask *when* the letter was burned, or by whom.

"And Rebecca?" he asked. "How is she? Is she . . . Is she doing okay?"

"She was fine when I left her."

"Did she understand why I was doing this?"

"Eventually."

And now? Rafferty supposed he should have been devastated, or at least disappointed, at never getting the words he'd written returned to him, but he wasn't. Not exactly. He felt empty, but free. Free of that letter, free from the smell of sliced apples, free of it all—and yet. In a strange way, he already missed it, the hold she'd had on him. It was like watching a balloon slip free. Tamsin. He needed Tamsin. Tamsin and her annoying laugh and loud gestures, her crude love. *Probably in Syria, by now. Or Libya. Or Purgatory itself.*

"There is still the matter of the medallion. I have kept *my* promise, Mr. Rafferty."

"Right. The Saint Christopher's medal—"

"Saint Anthony."

"Right. The Patron Saint of Lost Things. It's in the desk drawer, over there." Wrapped in a cloth like a holy relic.

And so it was, they kept their bargain, each of them: an exchange of jewelry, as it were, neither of the pieces worth very much—the items or the men. A lost medallion for a heart-shaped locket filled with ash, and it struck Rafferty how damaged and incomplete the two of them were, clinging to objects of little value and lesser use.

The small man stood, straightened his jacket, which needed no straightening, tipped his head in farewell.

"Where will you go now?" Rafferty asked. *Don't leave. Stay.* "I have some brandy if you'd like."

Please stay. I'm lost and lonely and I don't know where to go.

"Where? Back to the world, I suppose." The small man looked at the darkness and dust flying by outside, the empty streets below. "I'll wait this out, leave in the morning. I don't imagine you will ever see me again." Although a man like Rafferty might come in handy sometime. Rafferty didn't realize it, but a pact had been made.

In the street below: a solitary lamp, swept with wind. A single figure, standing beneath it. Oddly familiar, but then—silhouettes always were. With that, the small man walked out into the storm, down the stairs and along the hallway, through the lobby and into a white noise of wind.

She was crossing toward him, and they stopped in the middle of the street, each taken aback by the sudden appearance of the other. She stared, uncertain. At first. But then he smiled.

What he had wanted to say was: *"You did it. You found me. You're amazing.*" Instead, he simply smiled. It was a smile of recognition, of friendship even. And with the smile, she knew.

Gaddy Rhodes drew her gun, fumbling for the safety, eyes stinging as the sand raked across the street. "Don't move!"

"Agent Rhodes. How very wonderful to see you."

"Fuck you! On the ground, *now*. Hands behind your head."

"Oh, but we both know that's not going to happen."

Even as he spoke, the wind and the sand were erasing him, a disappearing act unfolding right in front of her. The wind from all directions.

"Now! On the ground!" He had almost vanished by this point, his smile the last to go, was now only an outline, and barely that. *Center mass, two to the core, one to the head.*

She fired twice, rapid succession, felt the gun kick back like a thunderclap, the sound of it quickly swallowed by the storm. Sand scouring the air. Eyes watering, she moved forward, one step carefully in front of the other, arms locked, gun raised. But she was lost, and he was gone.

In the hotel room above the street, Thomas Rafferty thought he heard something, probably just a screen door or an unsecured shutter thumping, nothing more.

Just 100 years ago today, the Aborigines of this part of the world must have seen—to them—a novel and awe-inspiring sight: the approach of two strange monsters, one from the west and another from the east. The arrival of the first ships. What marvels would follow!

—From a Report on the Proceedings of the Royal
Geographical Society of Australia, 1890

• • •

TAMSIN GREENE, DRAPED IN A LAZY BED in an art deco room in New Zealand, was watching him pack. "Even if you get to the Outback, even if you track her down, even if she gives you what you want, what then?"

Raff thought about this. "I suppose then I would be done."

"Done? Till when?"

"Till forever."

"Forever's a long time."

The dust storm had enveloped her Land Rover now, the blacktop barely visible in front of her, high beams on to no avail, when—past the turnoff and careening into view—a figure appeared on the road, buffeted by the wind. Tamsin swerved, braked hard, slid to a stop on the side of the highway, rolled back to wave him over.

He climbed inside, a small man in a suit. He looked shaken and disoriented.

"Thank you," he rasped.

"Are you lost?" she asked.

"I am. I was."

"Well," she said brightly. "I found you!" She put the Land Rover into gear, pulled back onto the sand-swept surface. "You okay?"

He checked the front of his chest, up and down, smiled. "I am." He seemed genuinely surprised. "I am indeed."

Tamsin passed him a bottle of water. "You look familiar," she said. "Have we met?"

"The wrong man, I'm afraid. I have that kind of face, you see." It was a face that was hardly there. A silhouette that seemed familiar, but silhouettes always do. It would have taken a flash of Tamsin's camera for her to recognize him.

He looked at the highway hurtling toward them. "Can I ask where are you going?"

"Alice Springs," she said.

"In the middle of a storm?"

"I'm looking for a friend. I just wanted to let him know where I am."

"He's in Alice?"

"Last I heard. That's where he was heading, anyway. And you? Where would you like me to drop you off?"

"The airport would be nice."

"Won't be any flights in this."

"I don't mind. I can wait."

He had a small medal of some sort tightly wrapped around his fist.

"Saint Christopher?" she asked.

"Not quite. But close enough."

PART SIX

BOLDER SHEEP: LEGEND OF THE THREE-LEGGED TOAD

FAYTHER WAS ASLEEP IN HIS THREADBARE chair again, the graph papers and hand-drawn diagrams open on his lap, mouth agape, eyes shuttered and dreaming. Sun hardly up, and already snoring. A cardigan, tight across his belly and haphazardly buttoned.

His funeral suit hung on the doorway. Poor Dr. Rowley—that was his Christian name now, after the tragic accident—fished out of the drink. Tragic, that. Poor Rowley had been given a proper burial with all farms present, both the Corriedales and the Perendales, past schisms put aside momentarily. His widowed wife, oddly subdued, and Fayther afterward, walking the edge of the escarpment where the veterinarian had plunged to his death. Fayther, pacing it out as he plotted new safety measures to prevent future tragedies of this sort, which the local council would reject based on cost and the fact that "there's only the two of you alone up there, anyway," and what was Dr. Rowley doing tramping about on the edge of a cliff to begin with? Should have known better. Perhaps a sheep had startled him, a rogue sheep, a bolder sheep, and Fayther feeling vaguely guilty, but also a little thrilled because maybe it was starting, maybe the sheep were on the move, and now Catherine was pulling on her gumboots, her jolly, jolly gumboots, stepping through the screen door while her father dozed.

Catherine, with a plastic bucket in each hand, sorting out the proper scientific blend of feed pellets, feeling bad for fudging the numbers (again), promising herself that she would do better, would enter the data properly this time, and still the sheep had not escaped as they were supposed to, were happy enough just being sheep.

On the plains below: Christchurch, still wounded.

She'd gone down to the city, had walked among the rusted girders and crumbling brick facades, where the buildings were cordoned off, engineers and architects in hard hats standing under empty skies, projecting blueprints of their own onto the city, carving out a new Christchurch in their minds. The front of the cathedral had completely fallen away. Birds in the rafters. Holes in the roof. Christchurch had become a city of scaffolding. Container cars had been brought in as temporary shops, gap fillers as they were known. A city of gaps. And still the Avon flowed through, a braided river where currents crossed like fingers in prayer.

The city barely seemed real. The haze of smoke that had once hung above had been replaced by the dust of reconstruction and demolition. Walls falling, intentionally this time. Distant thuds, scarcely audible.

At Erewhon Farm, a strong wind was blowing. She struggled with her poorly balanced buckets, stopping several times to put them down. A constant avalanche of waves was breaking, unseen in the cove below, and out there, beyond the sea: Somewhere Else. On the far side of nowhere, Catherine Anne Butler was feeding her father's sheep.

She picked up the buckets one final time, awkward-walked them across the yard. And when she entered the musty interior—barn doors open, as always, like an invitation declined—she sensed right away that something was wrong. The other day, a lamb had gamboled off and Catherine had tracked it across the moor-like heights, even as her father shouted, "Katie, no! It has escaped. Let it run free!" But it hadn't "escaped"; it was lost, mewling pitiably on a precarious nook of land, missing its mom, and Catherine having to inch out to lob a rope around it and bring it back. The rest of the flock had been both agitated and relieved when the lamb was returned, but today—today was different. The sheep, deathly quiet, had wedged themselves into the far end of the pen, and she knew. She knew.

Softly, Catherine put the buckets down on the straw-strewn cement. Urine and wet bales. Darkness in the corner.

"Hello?" she hazarded.

The darkness answered. "Hello, Catherine."

As her eyes adjusted, he emerged, first as a silhouette, then as something resembling a man.

"You're back!" she cried, and for a moment, she forgot to be afraid. *This must be what it's like when a friend returns.* She had always wondered. But, of course, he wasn't a friend. Not exactly.

"I am, indeed. Back from the dead, as it were. Thanks to you, Catherine."

"Did you kill Dr. Rowley?"

He crossed over to her, voice calm, eyes unblinking.

"Catherine . . ."

"Did you?"

He sighed. "Dr. Rowley brought about his own demise."

"But—was it you who . . . ?"

"He made his choice. That's all life is, Catherine, a series of choices."

She swallowed. "Why are you here? Why did you come back?" She wanted him to say something like "I missed you," but that wasn't what the cards held.

"Unfinished business, Catherine. A ledger that needs reconciling." There was sorrow in his smile, and he said, "You would think, as one gets older, that one's sense of the sentimental would have set-tled, that you'd finally see the bottom of the pond—but no. In a single moment, the silt is stirred up again, turbid and murky and sad."

"Are you going to hurt me?"

"Catherine, you know who I am."

"I don't—I really don't. I don't know anything. You can ask my teachers. I'm always forgetting stuff. I would forget my head if it wasn't screwed on. It's true, it's what they say, 'Catherine, you would forget your head if it wasn't screwed on,' so even if you told me your name, I probably forgot it, honestly."

"You know that I'm from Belfast. You know I have a brother in Montreal, a niece named Brynne, a son who died in the war."

"But I don't even know which war. Really, I won't tell anyone, I promise. I couldn't, even if I wanted to. I don't have any friends to tell, just my dad, and he doesn't listen."

He could see her perfectly, the young girl walking beside the road, head down, hugging her books. Lives lived at the end of the world. "Come closer, Catherine."

Trying to be brave. "My dad, he would be really sad if any-thing . . ." Fayther, finding her awkward body, having to fish her out of the cove as well. "It would break his heart, his heart would be broken, it really would, and I wouldn't even be there to pat him on the back and say everything will be okay."

"Come closer. Hold out your hand."

"Please," she said. "Don't." But even as she said this, she held out her palm, trembling, eyes closed, trying to squeeze back the tears.

A voice, whispering reassurances. "Don't be afraid. Be strong."

And he placed, not death, but something else, something small and cold in her palm. When she opened her eyes, a jade figurine.

"A Chinese god, the three-legged toad," he said. "It's an emblem of the unattainable. Everything we yearn for, everything we search for but cannot find, it is all of it contained in those three letters: TLT. Such stuff as dreams are made of. Keep it with you, Catherine. It will protect you and, if you wish, you may sell it someday. I daresay it is worth more than you might imagine. There are very few good people in this world, Catherine. You are one of them."

The small man walked away and didn't look back, but stood, framed in the light of the open barn. He seemed to hesitate, just for a moment, looked one way, then the other, as though considering which direction he might take, as though, just for a moment, he too was lost.

It was only much later that she came upon it, nested in a mound of straw, in the spot where she had first nursed him back to health: a bottle with a note inside. He had written: *What the world needs is bolder sheep.*

GADDY RHODES

SHE DUG A HOLE IN THE SAND and buried the Beretta, and it was never found, but it wasn't like anyone was looking for it. After the winds had died and the dust had settled, Gaddy had searched the streets, but there was no body, only drifts in the earth and a nagging doubt, one she couldn't shake herself free of: *Had she fired to miss?* She'd had him dead to rights. *Center mass, point-blank range practically.* How could she possibly have missed? Or—and here the doubts grew septic—perhaps she hadn't missed at all. Perhaps the bullet had passed right through him, like he was made of smoke.

Perhaps.

A long flight to LAX, then on to LaGuardia, another taxi and a sparsely furnished apartment waiting when she got back. Our Lady of the Cubicles, adrift amid the file folders and the mission statements, the towers of paper leaning into each other for support. A dried tea bag in her mug. A scattering of pens and paper clips. The ghosts of memos past. No one had noticed she was gone. Tired, defeated. Stuck on a sandbar. The serpent in her liquor bottle was looking more opaque than ever, marble-eyed and murky, with jaws distended, a formaldehyde strike that never came. *Had she fired to miss?* And that was when she noticed the envelope.

It was waiting in her tray. Standard manila, 8½ by 11. No return address. A lump in the middle. Gaddy slit it open. Empty, except for . . . She tilted the envelope, dropped the contents into her hand—and froze. It was a wedding ring.

And before Gaddy looked, she knew. She knew that on the inside, hidden like a secret, would be an inscription only she would know about: GR + ML 4 VR, and now she was running, down the corridors, cubicles blurring, past the elevators to the reception, demanding, out of breath, frantic, "When? When did it arrive? How long ago? The envelope. When!" and the woman at the desk stammering, "I dunno, this morning, maybe?" Not maybe. *When?* "This morning. Definitely this morning." *Who?* "A courier. Just a— Just a regular courier. His instructions were to make sure it was on your desk before you returned, that's all. Where were you anyway?"

Behind reception, through the glass, she saw it: a gap in the skyline.

Gaddy at the window. "The cranes. They're gone."

"Cranes?"

"The Commonwealth Inn."

"Oh, they tore that down."

"But all of that machinery."

Underground tank pulled up, workers sifting through the rubble . . . A massive operation, to what end?

"You didn't hear? The company went bankrupt. Shut it down. It's just a parking lot now. Huge scandal, apparently. It was in the papers. Why?"

The voice of Syd, her fraudulent, flatulent therapist, clued out and writing it all down: "Maybe that's why you're obsessed with finding things."

"Not finding, retrieving."

"Sorry?"

"Nothing." *Tearing out the hotel's underground tanks, sifting through all of that rubble.* Dazed and elated, and no longer alone, she walked down the aisle, back to her cubicle, with her lost ring in hand.

MAYBE ZERO

WHEN CATHERINE THE GREAT CAME OUT the next morning, the sheep were gone. She almost didn't notice. Catherine in her gumboots, shoveling in the food pellets, recording the mix of nutrients, walking across to the barn, entering an unforeseen emptiness.

She stopped.

Had she forgotten to bring them in last night? Of course she hadn't. They were simply . . . gone. All of 'em. Every single one. She began to look around, then stopped, and laughed. *As if they'd be hiding in the loft or behind the barn door!* No. They were gone, they were all gone, the entire flock.

Catherine ran, stumbling in her boots back to the house, roused Fayther from his morning nap, told him the news, the news, the good news! And he hurried out after her, pulling on his jacket, eyes joyous and wide, and him laughing and her too, and Fayther turning, turning, pirouetting, crying, "Katie, we've done it, we've done it! They're out there, in the world! We've reset the clock to zero," and maybe zero was the best they could hope for, and now she was spinning too, and they were free, were free of the sheep, were free of the notions and hopes that had pinned them to this farm.

Beyond Erewhon, on a corrugated sea that was open and endless, a low flat-bottomed boat rose and fell. A barge, cramped and wet with mud bespattered, it smelled enticingly of damp wool and ovine urine. Bleats and baying, and a small man in a suit standing on the prow looking down at his ruminant cargo, thinking, *Now, then. What am I going to do with all these sheep?*

RIVER STONE

A HOSPITAL IN NAHA, AFTER THE BIOPSY. "You will need someone to drive you home." Having no wife, Detective Gushiken had called his partner and they sat now in silence, waiting for the results.

"Strange, isn't it?" said Gushiken. "The second tomb."

"The dead foreigner?"

"Mm. Why the second tomb? Nothing was disturbed." Just some dog tags gone missing.

But then the doctor stepped into the room, and Gushiken's world shifted forever and the dog tags fell over the side of the coral cliffs above the castle, fell and were forgotten.

Six months later, Kawaishi would stand, almost the only guest, as Detective Gushiken's body was interred in a turtleback tomb with rites and rituals that Kawaishi didn't understand in a language he couldn't speak and, unexpectedly, both to himself and the noro priest-esses attending, he would suddenly sob. But that was still far away, and today he sat with his partner in silence, the two of them as immo-bile and dignified as stones in a river.

DRAGONS, LOST AND FOUND

SENIOR POLICE INSPECTOR SHIMADA, Hateruma Island Substation, Okinawa Division, was rummaging around in the lost and found, looking for a bicycle key—his bicycle key—when Tamura-san from the ferry port stepped in, closing the door behind him, bobbing his head in the approximation of a bow.

"Foreigners," he said. "Down by the dock."

"And?"

"They're camping in the grass."

"So?"

"It isn't right, is it? They shouldn't be there, right? What if they step on a habu or something?"

Unstated between them was the presence of another foreigner, the one with the missing face. How many weeks had that been, and already it was slipping into the realm of a half-remembered dream?

"Just thought you should know."

Shimada nodded, reluctantly. Said nothing.

"Maybe you should investigate?"

With the noblest of bureaucratic sighs, the officer opened his police log—the one that no one read, not even him—and entered the time and date: Thursday, March 10, 2011. A quiet day in Japan. He checked his watch, added the time and where he was going, tugged his cap into place. And all the while, Tamura-san waited.

"Are you going to bike it?"

"I'll walk."

"I've got my truck—"

"I'll walk."

Shimada tucked in his shirt, turned the ON PATROL sign over, shoved his shirt back in, then stepped outside into the sun.

Narrow lanes and bamboo stands. Lion-dogs and turtleback tombs. Sugarcane fields and goats in tall grasses. He walked down the long slope toward the port, drawing the widow's guesthouse toward him as he went. Kept his eyes on the front door as he passed, hoping he might see her hefting her futons over bamboo poles to air them out—her guests slept on mattresses, but she on futons—or maybe slopping wash water into the gutter, hair pulled back under a kerchief, a single strand having slipped free, face pink, a downward glance, a small smile, but she was inside when he walked by, and try though he may to think of an excuse to knock on her door, he couldn't come up with anything, and anyway, he could hear the radio playing soft music inside, saw her shadow through the kitchen window, moving, maybe swaying, almost dancing.

Beyond the widow's guesthouse, her husband's boat was tethered still, awaiting sale, finding none—bad luck had attached itself to the vessel—as the crumbled cement of the pier reached out into a haze of sea and the curve of the earth beyond.

He wondered if she'd changed the number on the door.

She had confessed, when he'd gone back to see her, that she'd been unnerved by what had happened. "I'm not superstitious," she'd said, "but—it's like something dark passed through Hateruma." Caught in a labyrinth of coral walls, escaping out to sea.

He had assured her, as the island's senior police inspector, *only* police inspector, that he was there for her, should she ever need him, anytime, even in the middle of the night, just call and he would come. But she never did, and he never had.

The morning's ferry was now disappearing into the distance. Other islands, lost at sea.

The beach where he'd seen the sea turtle was farther along, out of reach and out of view, as were the cliffs on the other coast and the observatory that stood above them. The observatory was now closed, temporarily it was hoped, following the police investigation, but the Southern Cross itself was still visible. At night, if you stood, perched at the very edge of the world, peering over the horizon, south by southeast, you just might see it.

Hateruma's only police officer followed the tramped-down footpath through the grass, along the shore, and past the pier, stepping carefully, watching for foreigners and coiled reptiles alike. The season for fireflies had passed, but not of habu. He wondered if the visitors were aware they'd been sleeping among serpents, but he was never able to ask them, for when he arrived at the campsite, they were gone, as insubstantial as a rumor. A flattened circle marked their presence, but even that would be gone with the next monsoon.

There was a smattering of clues as to their identity, items forgotten or discarded, it was hard to say. He gathered these up and dutifully tagged each item, entering them in the ledger after he got back to the police box: one (1) lens cap; two (2) plastic tent pegs, still embedded in the earth, which he worked free and brushed clean; one (1) bottle of wine (empty), and a single pewter locket, shaped like a heart. Shimada placed these items in the lost and found, and when several months had passed and no one had come to claim them, he gave the locket to his wife.

POSTSCRIPT
LOCH LOMOND, ON THE
RAINY SIDE OF THE LAKE

POSTSCRIPT
LOCH LOMOND, ON THE RAINY SIDE OF THE LAKE

He was on his second pint when the poison began to take effect.

A rainy day in a rainy pub on the rainy shores of Loch Lomond, the weather drumming restlessly outside, the amber glow of a fireplace within. A damp country, Scotland, even with a fire to warm you. He was dimly aware that something was wrong—the early stirrings of a fever perhaps, or simply the chilblain and dark bitters taking hold—but then his body suddenly jerked. His hand lunged across, knocking his pint to one side, the foam inside sloshing.

"Easy there," said the small man sitting across from him. "You don't want to cause a fuss."

He struggled to look up, lips moving as though chewing on his words. No sound came out. He was young, in a heavy sweater and an oversize rain jacket, had been passing himself of as a local, had failed.

"The first of September and already the leaves are starting to fall," the small man said, somewhat wistfully. He raised a glass to his companion. A proper whisky for him, none of this bitter ale or Guinness. He took a long, contented draw. Single malt, peaty, with tinges of burned oak. "Shall I order you another round? No? Had enough, have you?"

The fire crackled and hissed. A knot of wood popped, and the rain continued, restlessly, relentlessly, pelting the window, sliding down the panes of glass, rendering the world outside a ruined watercolor.

"Did you know," said the small man, as he swirled his scotch, considered its hue. "Over in Brig O' Turk, not far from here, an hour's drive at most, there is a bicycle caught in a tree. I don't mean the bicycle is *on* the tree, I mean it is *in* the tree, embedded in the trunk. A bizarre sight to behold, so it is. The handlebars, the tire rims, the rusted frame, all of it swallowed by a sycamore. Story is, there was a village lad who had headed off to fight the Hun and had left his bicycle resting against a tree. The boy never returned, and over the years his abandoned bike was slowly absorbed into the wood, rising off the ground as the tree grew. I imagine his own bones may be twisting themselves into roots of their own, out there in Flanders." Memories of Okinawa, of shoes knotted into trees, spiraling upward.

The man in the knitted sweater tried again to speak, but couldn't. Something unintelligible, thick with saliva.

"That will be the paralysis kicking in," said the small man, helpfully. "Your tongue will be starting to swell, as well." He finished the last dram of his single malt. "Ah, yes. Sherry-casked and aged to perfection, carries the scent of the Highlands, of bracken and heather, of thistle and cold waters. It's like drinking a landscape. This village we're in, it's named Luss. An odd name, don't you think? It was originally Clachan Dubh, 'the Dark Village.' Something to do with a murder on its shores, but more likely because of the mountains that surround it. Come winter, very little sunlight reaches this town. Gloomy, in that Scottish sort of way. Now, Luss, this comes from a baroness, born of the village, who married a French officer and moved away, only to die—tragically, as baronesses are wont to do. Her grief-stricken husband brought her home in a casket arrayed with fleurs-de-lys, lilies that would eventually take root in these cold Scottish environs. The name *Luss* comes from the Scots pronunciation—one might say, degradation—of the word fleur-de-lys. A beautiful story, wouldn't you say? And a beautiful village, as well. Low stone cottages, slate roofs, and garden walls entwined with roses. But where are the lilies? Gone, you might suppose, but no, not gone. Hiding. French lilies now grow wild in the swampy grounds south of town. But that isn't why we are here, is it? The two us. We haven't come all this way for lilies."

Outside, the rain, restlessly falling, falling.

The small man considered his empty glass. "Shall I have another dram? Perhaps some Arran Gold instead? Have you tried it, a liqueur from the Isle of Arran? It will restore your faith in man. Smoky and sweet at the same time, like honey and hickory. On the Isle of Arran, above the distillery, a barren peak rises up. They call it the Devil's Punch Bowl, so named because once a year, when the angle of the sun is just right, the ridge along the top throws a shadow onto the hills of Cioch na h-Oighe, creates a silhouette of Old Nick. Chin and nose and horns, the very profile of Beelzebub himself. The devil appears on that one certain day, so they say, but—here's the thing." He was staring now, unblinking, into the other man's gaze. "That's not entirely true. The devil was always there, you see. He was only *revealed* on that day, but he was always there, they just couldn't see him."

The small man took out his handkerchief, said, "You're perspiring. Is something wrong? Perhaps it's the fire. Here, let me get that for you." He reached across to mop the other man's forehead. "And are those tears?" he asked. He dabbed the man's eyes as well. "There you go. All better." He folded his handkerchief in half and began, methodically, to wipe his own glass clean. "It's the church, isn't it? That's why you're here, tracing Saint Kessog's footprints, as it were. It was Kessog who first brought the Holy Word of Our Lord to these lawless lochs, did you know that? It was Kessog first raised a northern cross in the heart of this dark Druidist world. They killed him, of course.

Martyred him on the lakeshore in 530 AD. Best thing for him, really; martyrdom is always a smart career move among saints. Then came the Reformation. In a frenzy of piety, Catholic symbols were smashed and altars destroyed across this fair land. Here in Luss, the frightened parishioners hurried away two key icons of faith: a stone carving of the saint himself, a contemporary likeness, in fact—think of that! A crude stone bust a thousand years old, spirited to safety, along with the church's baptismal font. They were buried under a cairn by the crossroads, to be recovered after the madness passed, but of course it never did. Over time, the font and the saint were forgotten."

He leaned across, onto his elbows, the fire dancing in his eyes.

"Remarkable isn't it, that one could misplace a saint? Now, this may sound immodest, but I've always had a knack for finding things. A blessing, let's call it, or a curse perhaps, either way it is a talent I have sedulously fostered over the years. But even I would have been stumped by the stone head of a dead saint buried five hundred years ago under an unmarked cairn with no records to sustain the location. In such cases, it is usually happenstance that brings such objects to the surface, and so it was with Saint Kessog and his baptismal font. A corps of army engineers was widening a road, and they unearthed these relics, long thought lost. Hidden, forgotten, found. Such was the arc. They are on display at the church, even now: the baptismal font and a stone saint. A primitive rendering, I must say. Just the rough shape of a face, much like an outline waiting for the details to be filled in. You think that's why I came here, isn't it? To Luss, to the rainy shores of Loch Lomond. But you are wrong."

The other man began to pitch forward, his hands on the table, knotted in fists. The small man leaned across, gently tilted him back.

"There's no shame in being wrong. But I must say, the notion that

I would come here for the saint is mildly insulting. I am not a common thief! That stone sculpture and baptismal font have already *been* found. I haven't come all this way to engage in an act of mere thievery." A dash of anger, quickly subsiding, and then a smile, all teeth. "Did you notice the workers from earlier? The road crew, the ones in the orange vests, down by the river, behind the church? No? No one ever does. Council orders, they assume, or parish, it is never clear. You see, the Luss church is surrounded by graves. You must have noticed. You had to walk through them to get to the church when you came sniffing about, setting up your"—and here he laughed; he couldn't help it—"security cameras. As though a store-bought motion detector and wall-mounted lens would deter the likes of me! So fixated were you on that stone head that you missed the graves outside. A beautiful graveyard here in Luss, particularly beautiful in the rain. Lichens and moss, headstones leaning as if into a wind. Behind the church, among the other graves, is one particular tombstone. Very unusual. It looks like a loaf of bread with fish scales, but of course it is no such thing. It is a Viking grave, meant to imitate a longhouse with cedar shingles. What on earth is a Viking grave doing in a quiet churchyard in a small village on the shores of Loch Lomond? An invasion, of course. The last great Norse incursion. It was here, in this labyrinth of lakes and islands, that the Vikings were finally turned back. They battled their way in, but were unable to battle their way out. Had to drag their longboats over a neck of land just to get here. Such determination! But that doesn't answer the question: Why that grave, and why here? Regular Vikings would have been buried where they died, thrown into a pit, more or less, and sent on their way. The Viking burial, ship ablaze, is largely a myth. We know from the size of this stone monument that it is the grave of someone of great importance. But why at a Christian site? Near as I can tell, there are only two possibilities: either it is the grave of a Viking Christian—there were some, even then, even as they hacked their way across these British Isles—or it was an act of defiance, a way of lording it over a cowed populace, placing a pagan grave smack in the very heart of Saint Kessog's Christian mission." The small man held up his hands in mock surrender. "Who knows? The mystery remains. The only way to find out is to look. To lift up that slab and dig down, into the heart of it. Norse coins, a shield, a sword to fight your way into Valhalla, or perhaps, even more valuable, a Viking cross. Not lost, you understand, because we know where it is, but *forgotten*, because we don't know what it is." The fire cracked and popped. Wood crumbling into embers, an everyday act of transubstantiation. "It always starts with forgetting, doesn't it? With memories that fade and erode over time, dissolving, leaving only riddles and hints at what might have been."

The rain and the fire and the empty glass.

"What lies buried beneath that stone? We do not know, because we are not allowed to move it. Parish rules and such. But"—and here his face brightened—"what if one were to come in, *from the side*, from the bank of the river, say, snake a fiber-optic camera through, poke about? The next step, and understand I am speaking only hypothetically, would be to present oneself as, oh, I don't know, an historic restoration expert, I suppose, concerned about the sad state of the graveyard. Have I given you my card? No? How very rude, I apologize. It reads: 'National Trust Historic Sites Restoration Agency,' followed by a string of postgraduate letters, all bogus I'm afraid, but people are so very impressed with abbreviations. After that, one need only surround that section of the graveyard, put up a tarp, blocking the view, clean some of the tombstones, straighten a few—mainly as a courtesy—and, of course, move the Viking capstone off, burrow down, retrieve that which has been forgotten. Over and done with in a single weekend, before any questions can be asked." Another flash of anger, distant but sharp, like a lightning strike behind a hill. "At least that was the plan, and a good plan it was, but of course *you* had to show up like an uninvited guest at a wedding. You just had to muck up the works, didn't you? It was your accent that betrayed you, by the way. Trying to pass yourself off as Scots when I'd wager the closest you've been to Glasgow is a dialect seminar in London. Don't feel bad. Happens to the worst of us. I'm still trying to shake off the last bits of Ulster from my own speech."

The barmaid came over, but the small man stopped her with an embarrassed nod in the direction of his friend. "I'm afraid he's had enough." Then, staring into the other man's eyes. "Isn't that right?"

She cleared the glasses anyway, and after she'd left—with the evidence, as it were—the small man tugged on a pair of lambskin gloves, reached across, and retrieved the other man's wallet from his inside jacket pocket. Flipped through it, pulled out various pieces of ID, a driver's license, and—"What do we have here?" He studied the name card with a mockingly disappointed shake of the head. "You have been less than honest with us, haven't you? Passing yourself off as a humble security consultant from Glasgow, come to update the kirk's system, protect the saint's head and whatnot. You've taken advantage of our trust, haven't you? Catch yourself on, mate. Interpol, is it? And third-tier from the looks of it. Probably your first big case. Such a shame. I'm afraid she has pulled another unsuspecting soul into her world of fantasy. You do realize I don't exist, yes? Ask anyone." Another sigh, sadder than the first. "I would ask that you give my best to Agent Rhodes when you see her next, but I daresay that won't be possible. Perhaps, instead, you might convey a message to her on my behalf? You're drooling. Here, let me get that." He leaned across one last time, pressed his handkerchief against the sides of the other man's mouth, then took out a pen, turned one of the young man's ID cards over, wrote on the back: *You did this. All I wanted was the grave.* He tucked the card into the wallet, the wallet back into the man's jacket.

The small man then stood up, turned his collar against the cold and damp, pulled his scarf in tighter. He looked around him, and then laughed. "I've gone and lost my umbrella. Funny, don't you think? No matter. These things happen. Not lost, as my mother would say, only misplaced." And with that he bid farewell and walked out into the rain.

ON OBJECTS LOST AND FOUND

NOTES FROM THE AUTHOR

THE OBJECTS THAT GADDY RHODES IS hunting—Muhammad Ali's gold medal, the stolen Stradivarius, the Kalinga drum, the Fabergé eggs, Buddy Holly's glasses, the postmodern urinal signed "R. Mutt," and the lost reel of Hitchcock's first movie—are all real, are all still out there waiting to be found. All except one, which has indeed been recovered, though not quite in the manner described in this book. I will leave it to the reader to discover which. The story of the fifty-year-old wedding cake, the one-cent magenta stamp, and the lost Pollock are allusions to actual events as well.

The locations are real too. These are all places I have visited, from the beaches of Hateruma Island to the rockabilly joints in Okinawa City, from Uluru to Lavender Bay, from Hell's Gate and Whakarewarewa to the art deco city of Napier, from Gushikawa Castle to Cape Kyan, from the Viking grave in Luss to the Devil's Punch Bowl on the Isle of Arran. The story of the boy's shoe in the tree, the unicorn horn on Kume Island, the bicycle in Brig O'Turk: these are all real places. All except one. Devil's Spite Creek does not exist. If one were to search for this purgatorial community on the ghost line of an abandoned rail track, it would be an hour south of Alice Springs, and then east from the Stuarts Well Roadhouse along the Hugh River road, but I urge you not to try, for it is folly to do so, and if you did, you would find only sparse foliage, a kiln-baked emptiness, and ominous warnings posted on unwelcoming gates.

The Okinawan family, the Ono-Isu, does not exist either (nor could it; Japanese do not hyphenate their surnames), but rather is a combination of familial syllables. Likewise, the Kara clan is an invention and should not be confused in any way with the Shō, Okinawa's true royal family. The Kentucky Kid is real enough, though; his story is based on the war crimes of Kanao Inouye, known as the "Kamloops Kid." For crimes that went unprosecuted, see the namesakes of the two Aussie yobs Tamsin crosses paths with in the Outback: Frank Hann and Jack Watson, and the horror of Lawn Hill. Erewhon Farm, meanwhile, is a reference to a work of utopian fiction by the onetime New Zealand émigré Samuel Butler.

The character of Tamsin Greene was both inspired by, and is an homage to, such indomitable women war photographers and photojournalists as Alyssa Banta, Corinne Dufka, Susan Meiselas, Catherine Leroy, the tragic and iconic Lee Miller, Deborah Copaken Kogan (a.k.a. "Shutterbabe") and especially Lynsey Addario, whose memoir *It's What I Do* is an electrifying read, harrowing but full of heart. (Make *It's What I Do* the next book you read.) But I hasten to add that Tamsin's self-destructive tendencies, her drinking and loneliness and the many scars she carries, are not based on any one individual, living or dead, but are wholly fictional. I thank the photographer Don Denton of Victoria, BC, for first putting me on the trail of these remarkable women. Tamsin's surname is, naturally, a reference to the great Graham Greene. Her first name, the feminine version of Thomas, means "twin," which is what Tamsin and Tom Rafferty are in many ways. (Though I confess that she is really named for Tamsin Greig, an actress I have had a crush on since I first saw her in the British TV series *Black Books*.)

Thomas Rafferty, meanwhile, is named in honor of one of my all-time favorite novels, *Wandering Rafferty*, by the cowboy poet Ken

Mitchell, a book that is now criminally out of print but well worth tracking down. Anyone looking for parallels between myself and Thomas Rafferty will be richly rewarded. I, too, have worked as a travel writer for far too many years, on assignment from Rwanda to Moose Jaw, have been privy to encounters eerily similar to those described in this novel; some of the conversations among the dissolute travel writers in this book were basically transcribed word for word. I, too, have proudly written about New Zealand as a "land of contrasts," and did indeed pen a budget guidebook to Japan that sent readers into the ocean at one point. (Though I hasten to add that my reputation does not precede me in the way that Rafferty's does. I am not any sort of royalty, tarnished or otherwise.) My very first assignment was for the Daily Yomiuri newspaper in Japan, back in 1995, a travel article about the Shinto island of Kinkazan, which has since been preserved for posterity (infamy?) in an anthology of my writing titled *Canadian Pie*. But that is where the comparisons end. Mostly.

I should also like to take this opportunity to thank, and apologize to, the many travel hosts and magazine editors who have had the misfortune of working with me over the years. (I should also add, by way of clarification, that I once had drinks with Bill Bryson and, as far as I know, he doesn't have any gang tats or anger issues; nor does he carry a switchblade. As far as I know.) Given the strange depths of travel writing that this novel plumbs, and the many—all too real—conversations and characters it includes, I thought I might end on a positive note about the squalid existence of this genre by sharing some select works of travel literature at its best, works that have beguiled and inspired me over the years: Bruce Chatwin's *The Songlines*, Sara Wheeler's *Terra Incognita*, Pico Iyer's *Video Night in Kathmandu*, Alan Booth's *The Roads to Sata*, Donald Richie's *The Inland Sea*,

Bill Bryson's *The Lost Continent*, Simon Winchester's *Outposts*, Paul Theroux's *Dark Star Safari*, and the various collected travel essays of Jan Morris. (How many novels include a recommended reading list at the end? Talk about value added!)

Finally, in a story about objects hidden and waiting to be found, I thought it only fair to note that *The Finder* includes almost a dozen hidden references to the films of Alfred Hitchcock woven throughout. A treasure hunt, as it were. Strangers on a train is the most obvious, and the most apt. But vertigo is also mentioned in the very first chapter. The colonel references *Psycho*, there are thirty-nine steps to Rafferty's hotel room in Christchurch, and so on. Even the wine that Andy the Englishman scoffs at, Santa Rosa, is a reference to the California location of Hitchcock's own favorite film. There are six more of these for readers to find, including one that is actually the inversion of a famous Hitchcock title. There is even a possible red herring in the form of *The Maltese Falcon*, which is not a Hitchcock film, though is often confused for one. (If you are one of those weird people who checks the notes and acknowledgements at the end of a book before you start reading it, congratulations! You have a leg up. No need to search them out. You can simply watch for them as you read.) Oh, and you know how Hitchcock was always making a cameo in his movies? In *The Finder*, that would be Melvyn—with a y.

ACKNOWLEDGMENTS

I WOULD LIKE TO THANK THE irrepressible Nita Pronovost, VP, editorial director, at Simon & Schuster Canada, for guiding this project through to completion, and Kevin Hanson, president and publisher, who took a rather natty author photo of me as well, during a bibliographic expedition into the basement of MacLeod's Books in Vancouver.

The always insightful Barbara Pulling read through my manuscript and provided invaluable feedback and keen editorial suggestions. Copyeditor Doug Johnson did his best trying to rein in the worst of my stylistic tics and idiosyncrasies. Karen Silva provided last-minute triage. And my brother Ian Ferguson gave me a key piece of advice on the story, namely, to have Gaddy Rhodes zero in on Rafferty by mistake.

The Alberta Foundation for the Arts and the Canada Council for the Arts provided support for what turned out to be a much bigger project than I could ever have imagined, and I thank them for this.

To my son Genki Alex, my various friends and everyone at Book Warehouse in Vancouver who provided feedback on the cover and title: Thank you! Especially Dasha Yildirim, an illustrator based in Vancouver, whose advice was spot on.

During my travels in New Zealand and Australia, a great number of people conspired to help me. In Canada, Pam Cook put me in touch with her Kiwi friend Chris Cooper, who gave me a wealth of materials and tips, and in turn connected me with her sister, Lusia Johnson, in the Auckland area, and her friends Stephen Stehlin and James Turi. (Stephen also provided helpful feedback and advice on the Kiwi-isms in the manuscript, though any errors remain my own.)

Kim Izzo initially commissioned the "Maori Mornings" article for Zoomer magazine, and Vivian Vassos saw it through to completion. Michele Jarvie at Postmedia (Calgary Herald) commissioned a three-part travel series on New Zealand that took me from Christchurch to Napier. Thank you to all these long-suffering editors and freelance-writer wranglers! I sometimes suspect that I created the character of Rafferty just to show my editors how much worse it could have been.

Paul Holman at AHA Creative and Emma O'Reilly at Tourism New Zealand made the trip a reality, and the following warm souls helped me along the way. I thank you all, and if I missed anyone, apologies *ka pai*? Here they are, in order, from most interesting names down: Sara Bunny, Sally Shanks, Tiaana Anaru, Paora Tapsell, Lu Jiang, Schariona Parker-Potoi, Joy Sajamark, Lou Baddiley, Kim McVicker, Andrew Whiley, and Betty Mason-Parker. Thanks also to Anna Quin, the expat Aussie in Wellington who set up my Uluru trip with aplomb, and Tomoka-chan, the surfing chef of Gisborne, who swam with the dolphins and found me an extra bedroom to crash in when I showed up at the end of New Zealand without a clear plan in place. And a thank-you to Cliff for providing that bedroom.

My travels in Scotland—to Loch Lomond and the Isle of Arran, on assignment with Zoomer magazine—were aided and abetted by Evelina Andrews and Summer Martin, a.k.a. "Limey and the Canuck." (Evelina is the daughter of a travel writer as well, so you'd think she would know better.) John Taylor, the beadle at Saint Kessog's, let me in to the church on a rainy day in Luss and told me the story of the hidden saint within and the Viking grave outside.

Rafferty's rambling dispatch to Rebecca is a mash-up of a dozen famous love letters from couples as disparate as Johnny Cash and June Carter, Frida Kahlo and Diego Rivera, Emily Dickinson and Susan Gilbert, Hemingway and Marlene Dietrich, and Beethoven to his unnamed Beloved. The unit of measurement when a sheep becomes picturesque (one-eighth of a mile, a.k.a. "one Sheppey") was developed via vigorous scientific testing by authors Douglas Adams and John Lloyd. And the line from the Tom Phillips song is taken from "The Ballad of Miss Rose" on Tom's splendid *Spanish Fly* CD.

But my deepest and most heartfelt appreciation must go to Terumi and Yūki Alister, who had to put up with my long absences and repeated disappearances for the better part of two years. I could not have done any of this without their kindness and support.

I had always thought that the initial impetus for this novel came from an article in Mental Floss magazine, "Ten Missing Treasures You Should Really Be Looking For!" which I read in the bath, thinking, *What if* . . . What if someone tried to find, not one, but *all* of those objects? But as I worked on the manuscript, I realized that the roots of the story stretched back much further, to a children's book I wrote and illustrated for my niece Barbie, when she was just six or seven, titled *Barbara Joy and the Gorilla King*, which featured a character dubbed the King of Forgotten Things. I put this homemade book together as a broke university student when I couldn't afford to buy my niece a proper present, and now, after all these years, the story has come round, full circle. Thanks, Barbie! And thanks, as well, to my niece Brynne who, when she was little, taught me an important life lesson: "When you start to fall, just run through it."

ABOUT THE AUTHOR

© KEVIN HANSON

WILL FERGUSON worked as a travel writer for more than twenty-five years. His memoirs include *Road Trip Rwanda*, a journey into the new heart of Africa; *Beyond Belfast*, which covers a 560-mile walk he took across Northern Ireland in the rain; and *Hitching Rides with Buddha*, about an end-to-end journey across Japan by thumb. A three-time winner of the Stephen Leacock Memorial Medal for Humour, he has been nominated for both the International IMPAC Dublin Award and a Commonwealth Writers' Prize. Will Ferguson's novels include *419*, which won the Scotiabank Giller Prize and, most recently, *The Shoe on the Roof*, a darkly comedic tale of a psychological experiment gone wrong.